For Corporal Angelo F. Tudda,
an honest and simple soldier.

Barbara A. Tudda,
not only my Mother, but also a patient friend.

Kathy Tudda, a real hero.

DGAGB

Acknowledgments

I would like to thank many individuals for their assistance with this project, but first and foremost I would like to thank all the proud men and women of our Armed Forces; Army, Navy, Air Force, Marine and Coast Guard.

Bill Gwaltney of the National Park Service whose unselfish dedication is keeping the history and integrity of the Buffalo Soldier alive today. Mr. Gwaltney gave of his own free time to assist with this project; he's a class act.

Dr. Floyd Thomas, of the African-American Cultural Institute in Wilberforce, Ohio, your countless acts of generosity were well appreciated.

Mr. Anthony Powell, who graciously donated the photograph for the cover, from his own personal collection.

William "Wild Bill" Guarnere, and Donald Malarkey you are Angels from Heaven. Thanks for talking to me.

Mr. Clarence Sasser, exemplifies an American Hero. Words seem countless, to explain how wonderful you were for this project.

Brigadier General Philip Bolte (Ret.) you're classy.

Dr. Chris J. Tudda (PhD), my brother and my personal confidant.

Lucia St.-Claire Robson, I hope I made you proud.

"Once let the black men get upon his person the brass letters, 'U.S.'. Let him get an eagle on his buttons and a musket on his shoulder and bullets in his pocket, and there is no power on earth which can deny that he has earned the right to citizenship in the United States."

Frederick Douglass

"READY, FORWARD!"

The flashes of light and the booms from the gunfire grew closer to the tunnel's exit. "Listen, you boys hold them off, I got something that will really stop them soldiers." The sheriff's men crouched down behind crates and began to open fire on Moses and his men. McMaster ran down the tunnel toward the exit. Estimating fifty feet from the exit of the tunnel, he looked down for the charge. Clearing off some rock and debris, he located it. The shots were growing closer. Bullets ricocheted off the tunnel walls showering the man with rocks. "Damn," cried McMaster as a piece of rock sliced into his cheek. "The hell with them!"

The characters in this novel, are fictional and are products of the author's own creative mind. Historical accuracy is maintained as much as possible, while trying to entertain the reader.

PREFACE

Raised near an affluent area of Boston, Moses Trinidad was the son of servants to a doctor.

They granted the boy permission to join the ranks of the Bugle Corps of the Union Army. This was to be an incredible honor for himself and his family.

The black man watched as his boy ran carelessly through the pumpkin patch. "Moses," called his father. "Don't you go running to far now ya hea,' we got us a job to do. We have to pick the best pumpkin around. If we don't, Ma's Halloween is gonna be bad," hollered Obediah Trinidad. Lexington, Massachusetts in 1856 was an exceptionally lovely place to be in the month of October. Blacks were common in the north at the time, escaping to the North in large numbers due to the Underground Railroad. Becoming servants or nannies to the social elite was a blessing in most ways. A chance for an education and a better way of life for their families was the reason why most Negroes came.

"I won't Daddy," he yelled, leaping over the pumpkins. Moses Trinidad was quick for a boy of eight years. "Is Mama going to make pumpkin pie?" The boy raced around in circles playing gleefully in the afternoon sun.

"Ya betta believe it." The father laughed to himself as he watched his boy run carelessly through the patch. Moses tripped and fell over a pumpkin. Hopping right up, he continued to run never skipping a beat. "I think I found one," pointed Obediah with excitement. Moses stopped right in his tracks and smiled a pearly white grin. Turning quickly, he sprinted toward his father. Lying amongst the roots was a beautiful round pumpkin; its orange skin was tight and smooth, the sun dancing brightly off it.

"That's it, Daddy, that's the one!" The boy jumped up and down, clapping his hands with delight. The black man removed his knife from the sheath and cut the stock cleanly. Obediah lifted the pumpkin with the help of his son. They carried the orange object twenty-five yards to the wagon. Setting the pumpkin on a quilt in the wagon, they covered it gently. "We found another one for mamma." Leaping off the wagon, Moses found the perfect pumpkin lying a few yards away. Young Moses held it triumphantly above his head and ran to his father. Jumping in to his outstretched arms Obediah whirled his boy around in circles, while Moses laughed uncontrollably. "We must go now."

The ride back to the house was the same as most of their talks. This time was also spent learning from his father secrets of life and ways to become not only a man but also a well-rounded person of God. Moses was a curious boy. He believed in God but didn't understand him. "If God was round, why do people die or get fever?" Obediah tried his best to answer the questions. There were many questions, some times so many that Obediah just threw his hands up in the air. "Guess that's what the Almighty wants." The love he felt for his son made him happier than any other man alive. Obediah pulled him close and Moses hopped in to his father's lap and worked the reins all the way home. "I want you to get schooling, it's most important." They leaned back and Moses smiled, feeling safe in his father's arms.

One

The year was 1863, and the beach near the harbor of Charleston was beautiful, peaceful like it would be in a child's dream. Tufts of green plants were sprouting everywhere in the snow-white sand. The smell of salt water was bathing over everything and everyone. White seagulls hung on the wind, sailing on invisible waves of air. A blue sky, deep penetrating blue, was surrounded by clouds as white as cotton bales on a plantation drifting aimlessly.

Rows of proud black soldiers stood in ranks on the beach of South Carolina. Their blue uniforms tattered and torn, yet worn with dignity and pride. The American flag with other regimental colors snapped smartly in the wind. The 54th Massachusetts Regiment, led by Colonel Robert Gould Shaw, considered by his men a battle tested veteran, was about to undertake a costly and deadly mission for the Union.

Clouds of smoke rose in the distance as loud thunderous blasts and booms were echoing across the shores. The Union Navy was pounding on the Confederate Army dug in at Battery Wagner. This particular fort was vitally important to the Union because of its location and seizing it would be costly. The cannon balls and howitzer rounds slammed into the sand dunes, in an attempt to weaken the fort's structure. Explosions from aerial bursts sent tidal waves of sand in all directions making visibility impossible. The only way into the fort was a direct assault across a narrow strip of sand flanked by a thick marshy area and the Atlantic Ocean on the right. Potential casualties in the lead company would be heavy.

News of the black soldiers volunteering for this heroic mission quickly spread through the white units. Many of the men lined the beaches to see this spectacular scene and cheer on their fellow soldiers.

"Moses," spoke a young boy. "Moses, we goin in with'um?"

Two black boys were lying on a grassy slope near the sandy beachhead. One was staring aimlessly at the clouds above, the other staring steely eyed at the troops forming on the beach.

"Moses, boy, you dun listnin' to me, you outta be watchin' these boys fight."

"We won't be going in with them, we're too young. You don't have to watch it to know what's going to happen. Take a good look at the old 54th, that's the last time you're gonna see them in one piece."

"Ain't ever seen dead man before."

Moses Trinidad was fifteen years old and assigned to the Massachusetts Regiment as drummer boy. Along with his friend of six months, Quentin Bernard, they had wanted to get a good view of the day's events.

While taking the steamship DeMolay down from the North, he met Quentin and the two instantly became chums. A runaway slave, Quentin had not enjoyed the same advantages as Moses. Very few blacks received formal schooling. Moses' parents' task enabled him to receive an above average education. He excelled in grammar, writing and mathematics. Moses began tutoring young Quentin

Bernard, and many a night was spent teaching A, B, C's and 1,2,3's. From that point on, the two were inseparable.

"Boy, you da one who be want'n to see them attack, why ain't ya lookin?"

"Pronounce the words properly Quentin. You're never going to learn if you don't practice."

"Practice, practice, what's the use in soundin' likin' dem white folks anyhow? Shoot, aint never gonna treat us da same."

"Never give them an excuse. Ignorance or sounding ignorant gives them a reason to think less," said the boy staring into the heavens.

"Attention company!" came a booming voice from behind.

The boys jumped quickly to their feet and shook the sand from their uniforms. Their drums banged loosely against them as they quickly returned to the rear ranks of the company.

Colonel Robert Gould Shaw rode calmly with a certain air about him. Riding silently past his men, he nodded approvingly. Dressed so dapper and refined, one would think he was on the way to a military ball or social gathering. Yet, you could see the look of the unknown that appeared in his eyes. The men broke into cheers for their commanding officer.

"Three cheers for the colonel, Hip Hip Hoza, Hip Hip Hoza, Hip Hip Hoza!"

Moses had never met the Colonel but had much respect for him, the way he carried himself, the way the men rallied around him. Looking down from his horse, Shaw pointed to the young boys. "You boys, report to the rear."

The soldiers began marching toward their fate. Moses stared misty eyed at the Colonel.

5

Placing his hands on the young man's shoulders, Shaw looked him straight in the eye and spoke with a nervous tone in that Massachusetts voice. "Don't worry young man, this tale is fa from ovah. You be sure and have a hot pot of coffee waitin', ya heya?"

Drawing his sword and turning, Colonel Shaw yelled orders to his men.

"Fix bayonets,....shoulder arms..... charge bayonets!" The first row of men dropped their weapons to their midsections, and the next column did the same.

"Quick time forward march,.......double quick time march,..........charge!" With what seemed to be one loud thunderous roar, the regiment quickly moved at the double step. The soldiers were all engulfed in a black whirlwind of loud booms and chilling screams. Just like that they disappeared.

Moses stood on the dunes overlooking the battle. Then his head dropped low. Sounds that only man's evil hand for lust and greed could have the power to make roared in the distance. Bright flashes of light and clouds of thick gun smoke covered the horizon. Thoughts of the Colonel and the 54th Regiment raced in his mind. Do all good men die in battle? Was this some sick joke that only God had the answer to? Dropping to his knees, Moses wept openly.

What followed was for some a crushing defeat at the hands of the Confederate Army. The regiment had suffered staggering losses, including Shaw himself. Shaw's regiment of black soldiers had indeed breached the Confederates lines at Battery Wagner. The fruit of their efforts would be realized at a later date.

* * * * * * *

The mid-afternoon sun was setting over Fort Barre, bathing the large cavalry outpost in a fiery red blanket of light. The post was one of considerable size and was being constantly expanded by the army. The garrison in this particular fort numbered three hundred soldiers. There were many buildings inside the fort: guardhouse for those under restriction, mess hall, a supply house, headquarters of the commanding officer and a stable for the horses. Some rocky plateaus stood near the complex, along with a sizeable creek, which not only supplied the post with water but also was one of the major watering holes in the area.

Fall was creeping in, and the United States Army had five hundred plus soldiers stationed in the surrounding areas covering well over four hundred square miles. Their main goal was to bring to justice any non-reservation Indians or Mexican bandits. The railroads were extending further out west and Indian attacks on workers were growing more common.

Located half a mile from the fort was the small town of Flat Fork. It was steadily becoming one of the busiest trading posts in Texas. Its inhabitants were mostly of European descent, and several individuals from the former Confederate States. The town had taken shape quicker than most. It had a bank, hotel, blacksmith's shop, stores, and a saloon that would tempt the holiest of men to reach for a whiskey. There were ranches around; cattle rustling was always a problem. A new railroad depot was the main attraction in the town. It brought many people from back east to a new territory seeking their fortunes.

The two soldiers stared wondrously at the skyline. The mixture of red, pink, and yellow colors seemed to calm their insides. They continued in silence until the smaller man spoke.

"Just look at those colors, would ya. If you ever thought God wasn't for real, that is the proof right there."

"That it is," said the bigger man. "Bet I beat you to the fort?"

"You're on!" They raced across the plains. Their horses seemed to glide along neck and neck kicking up clouds of dust and pebbles. Experienced riders in the saddles, the two Buffalo Soldiers streaked over the sands and down toward the fort's main entrance.

"Riders approachin'!" yelled the guard on his beat. The man squinted. "Well I'll be, they's soldiers, nigga soldiers."

Coming to a slow trot, the men entered the fort. Feeling the eyes of every white soldier in the fort on them, they dismounted.

Sergeant Moses Trinidad stood 6'2 and was built solid as an oak tree. At thirty-one, he looked intimidating standing there in his dust-covered uniform. Other than a slight growth on his face from days in the saddle, he was regulation from top to bottom. At his side stood Corporal Quentin Bernard, 5'4 in height, thirty-one years in age, who like his friend was a soldier's soldier. Quentin had a deep scar on his cheek. Both weathered from their time in the Army, the year was now 1879.

"Excuse me soldier," Moses called to a young man sitting on the corral fencing. "Could you tell us where we can find the commanding officer?"

The young soldier looked up and stared at the two black soldiers. Noticing the crossed sabers on their Kepis caps and yellow chevrons on both men's blouses, the soldier snapped to attention.

"Haven't seen colored soldiers before," said Corporal Bernard smiling. "Certainly not a sergeant and corporal, I'll bet."

"Not many coloreds where I came from Sergeant," responded the young man holding out his hand. "My name is Oliver."

They shook. "Sergeant Moses Trinidad and Corporal Quentin Bernard reporting for duty."

"Heck, you're two full days early. Don't understand why anyone would report early."

The soldier shrugged his shoulders. "Well, I guess that will impress the Captain."

The young trooper pointed to a small building with a light glowing in the window. The sign over the door read "Captain H. J. Taylor", commanding officer.

They secured their horses on the hitching post and began to walk across the compound toward the office. Corporal Bernard rapped on the door.

"Come in."

The door swung open and the men walked in. The office was quite spacious. A young trooper was sitting at a small wooden desk was a company clerk. Noticing the stripes adorning their uniforms, he rose quickly to his feet.

"Trooper, we are here to see the commanding officer."

"Yes, sir, I mean, Sergeant."

Hayes walked over to the Captain's office and knocked on the door.

"Come in!"

Entering quickly, the young man informed the Captain that two black soldiers were standing in the outer area. "Show them in," said the officer.

The young captain rose from his desk, trying quickly to smooth out the small wrinkles in his uniform. First impressions were meant to be good impressions.

"Sergeant, Corporal, the Captain will see you both now."

They strode into the office and snapped to attention with a salute. "Sergeant Moses Trinidad and Corporal Quentin Bernard reporting as ordered," barked the ranking NCO.

"At ease Sergeant, Corporal," said the young officer, returning their salutes. "It's a pleasure to meet the both of you." Looking both men straight in the eyes, he extended his hand to them. This caught both soldiers a little off guard. "My name is Hennecker J. Taylor."

"Pleasure is all ours, sir."

Young, athletic and very handsome, Taylor had taken command of the post when hearing it was to be integrated. A West Point graduate, he somehow managed to squeak by in his academics. Some officers blackballed him, accusing him of consorting with enlisted men and blacks; this was frowned upon by most. It didn't concern him; all men who wore the blue uniform were equal in his mind. The current assignment of Ft. Barre was considered a low-level position. Many officers were asked to lead this command of white and Negro soldiers, but refused considering this assignment beneath them. Captain Taylor was eager to prove them all wrong.

"I understand that both of you men admired General Talbot," smiled the officer, sitting down on his chair. "I have patterned my own military career in his manner. My father and he were acquainted in the military."

"You knew the general, sir?" said Moses, smiling and looking at Bernard. General Irwin Jonas Talbot was once considered a topnotch graduate from West Point. Appointed to command one of the first Buffalo Soldier regiments in the Army, he was literally run out because of his commitment to his colored men and was considered a rabble-rouser. Unable to live with the shame and disgrace, he took his own life.

A look of sadness crossed the faces of the two enlisted men when they thought of the general's death. Yet, maybe this would be the assignment and the commanding officer that they were looking for. Hopefully, additional colored troops would soon be arriving.

"Let me cut right to the point," said the officer. "We've been having problems with Indian attacks, the Comanche. Several civilians scalped and murdered. Supply wagons pillaged and horses stolen."

"How about patrols, sir?"

"Yes, patrols every day at noon."

"There's the problem sir," Bernard said calmly.

"How's that Corporal?" answered the Captain with a peculiar look on his face.

"You have to stagger the patrols," Bernard said bluntly. Moses looked over at his friend. "Different times and different size patrols. These Indians aren't foolish, they watch, they learn, they know when you come and go."

"How stupid of me," replied Taylor placing his hand on his head. "I should have thought of that. Tomorrow we will begin the new routine".

"Begging the Captain's pardon sir, the Corporal and myself haven't had a good night's sleep, a bath or any grub in a few days," said Moses.

"Yes, of course, how rude of me. Hayes, report."

The young man darted into the office and snapped to attention.

"Yes, sir."

"Take the men over to their new barracks and get them settled in. Draw what you need from the Quarter Master's Storehouse, blankets or any other gear. Make sure all paperwork is in order. Get bedded down and first thing in the morning I'll brief both of you and show you around. Then I'd like to take a small patrol out and begin scouting for possible renegades, criminal types and such."

Snapping to attention, Moses saluted the commanding officer and quickly exited the office.

"If you follow me sergeant, corporal, I'll lead the way."

They walked across the compound and entered the barracks, which was made from wood. Striking a match, the soldier lit the candle lamps that were hanging on the crossbeams. Large in space, the quarters were in decent shape. Two wood burning stoves were situated on either side of the room with one large fireplace, in the center. There were bunks for up to ninety men. The bunks were in good condition, and the mattresses were stuffed with hay as normal. Another door led to private quarters with two racks, field trunk, and a pot bellied stove.

"Sergeant Trinidad, this will be the orderly room for the senior NCOs."

"Hayes is it?"

"Yes, Sergeant?"

"Where's the rocking chair?" The young man stood dazed and confused.

"Rocking chair Sergeant?" Moses held up his hands while chuckling.

"Just playing with you, Hayes." said Trinidad, his eyes moving back and forth across the room.

Moses grinned with delight.

"Sergeant, your quarters are at the end of the hall in the NCO barracks." Moses and Bernard looked at each other and walked down to the end of the room.

"You're moving on up," smiled Bernard, slapping Moses on the back. "Where can we get a bath?" The soldiers gazed at Hayes.

"There's a small body of water just outside the rear of the fort. Just gotta haul the water to the barrels out behind your quarters; there are bathing tubs hanging on the pegs. When winter time comes, you can just pick an area for the bathing tubs to be placed when being used."

"Corporal, take young Hayes over to the Quarter Masters Storehouse. Grab blankets, soap, and some extra ammunition."

"Yes, Sergeant."

"Oh, see if you can rustle up some tobacco for our pipes." They hurried out the door. Moses removed his grate coat and hat and hung them on a hook. He walked across the room to the rack located near the stove. Seeing the small pile of wood on the floor, he began making a fire, placing the small kindling pieces first, then putting the logs on top next. A quick flick of a match, and whoosh, it was aflame. It felt good, nothing like a nice fire to warm the old bones. Moses thought a rocking chair would be a wonderful touch; nothing like relaxing by the fire and rocking yourself off. He noticed a small mirror located on the wall, and walked over and looked at himself. The years in the army had been hard on him. Moses tried to remember that young boy on the beach. He pulled out a stool, then sat down and began removing his boots. Stretching his back, Moses released a bear like yawn. A small desk stood in the corner. Grabbing his small bag, Moses pulled out a small leather case, containing an ink pen and notebook in it.

September 23, 1879,

Arrived at Fort Barre in the late afternoon and made immediate contact with the Commanding officer. The man's name is Hennecker J. Taylor and he's an Army Academy man. Seems to be a decent officer, very young so there will be some mistakes because of lack of experience. Sensed the white men didn't care for having blacks assigned to the post. Quarters have been established and to my surprise they're not bad at all. Corporal Bernard has the assignment of drawing supplies from the Quarter Master Storehouse. The CO's adjutant took him over.

Name is Hayes from Vermont, still wet behind the ears. There is something about him that I like. He has the potential to become a good soldier. We unfortunately expect to come into contact with a few individuals that still think our color will prevent us from doing our duty. I know that this will be an assignment that could show the *whole country what we're made of. I pray that God will help us in this fight that seems to have no end. Getting a little tired now, so I think I'll call it a night. The CO wants to brief us in the morning on the new assignments that we will be undertaking.*

Moses walked over to his bunk and stretched out on it. Closing his eyes he drifted off into slumber.

* * * * * * *

"Where you from, Hayes?" The two men walked across the compound.

"Vermont, corporal."

"Verr….mont, is that here in America? I mean do your ma and pa still live there?"

Hayes stared at the man. "Yea, it's right above Massachusetts in the northern corner of the country. They live in the northern part of the state, St. Albans. Ain't nothing like this place though; green trees, big fields to run in, and the fishing, dang." The boy looked ahead.

"You don't like the army?"

"Heck no, I love the army. It's just too dry here, too much of the same scenery. Hot, hot and more hot. Not to mention the fact I haven't seen one Indian since I've been here. Where about you from, Corporal?"

"'Round Georgia. My mom and pappy were slaves on a plantation. I ran off when I was a young man and joined the Army. That's where Moses and I met."

"When's the last time you saw them?" Hayes put a piece of straw in his mouth and began chewing on it. "Your parents."

"About a year ago, out in Georgia. They're holding their own I guess, not easy though."

14

They came to the building known as the Quarters Masters' Storehouse. More than a room it was a one-story building. Inside tending to his supplies was an old sergeant. Unshaven, reeking of cheap whiskey, he was a sorry sight of an individual. The shelves were loaded with anything and everything, soup to nuts.

"Sergeant, the CO wanted me to bring the corporal here to draw some supplies for the barracks, for the new soldiers."

"Errrr," he grumbled. Sergeant Reynolds was a drunken old man. The South was lost and the slaves were freed, two things he never would accept. "Don't tell me that we're gonna be having some slaves here?"

"I don't see any slaves here," said Bernard, shaking his head in disgust. "Drunk on duty says everything about you reb."

The tension was thick in the air. It was plain to see the supply sergeant didn't feel that Negro soldiers were of any worth. He stared angrily at the Corporal. Bernard clinched his fist and bit his lip.

"Just give us what we need, and we'll be out of your hair, okay?" said Hayes. "I don't think the CO would appreciate your attitude."

The two men gathered their supplies while the sergeant stood there grumbling. He drank swiftly from a small bottle he kept hidden in a barrel.

"Thanks, Sergeant," nodded Bernard with a grin. "Don't be a stranger."

"Just get the hell out of here," said the rebel, waving his hand.

Emerging into the afternoon, Corporal Bernard and his young friend walked over to their new barracks with two armloads of packages. "He's a real piece of work, huh?" said Bernard.

Hayes smiled lightly. "He's an idiot!"

15

Bernard laughed.

The fire crackled in the stove; it warmed the whole room. Sergeant Trinidad lay in his bunk snoring. The two men walked in quietly so as not to disturb him.

"Corporal, I gotta get back to the Captain. If you need anything, you know where to find me," whispered the boy putting the packages on an empty cot. "Here, I grabbed this when the sarge wasn't looking." Hayes tossed Bernard a small bag of tobacco. "Tell Sergeant Trinidad I'll work on a rocking chair next."

"Thanks, Hayes."

Extending hands, they shook. A quick wink, and the trooper was gone. Bernard walked over to his bunk area and began to fix up his rack. There was a small closet located at the rear of the room. Grabbing the supplies, he began stacking them on shelves. Blankets, soap, and other items were tucked away neatly. Turning to look at Moses, Bernard laughed quietly to himself. Fool never took off his waist belt. Extra shirts and trousers were hung on pegs from the wall. Bernard removed his pipe and packed it with a generous portion of tobacco. Striking a match he drew it near and puffed with delight. The sound of Taps by the bugler seemed to float on the wind. Looking out the window, he saw the men retiring colors for the day. Trinidad's snoring only grew louder. Bernard grabbed a chair and walked outside. With pipe smoke circling his head, Bernard enjoyed sitting there in the crisp night air. He wondered would this be a post where a colored man could make his mark in the Army, or would it be another hard fought battle in life. Well, we're sure as hell gonna find out. Tapping his pipe on his boot, he stood up and retired for the evening.

The familiar sound of reveille in the early morning air stirred the men from their bunks. Moses was already dressed, cleaned and shaved. Corporal Bernard was finishing up with his morning chores. Straightening his bunk and stowing his gear, he strapped on his side arm.

"Let's find the Mess Hall."

They emerged from their quarters into the slightly chilly Texas morning. Walking by the flagpole, they saluted the colors.

The chow hall was big in size and very noisy. As they walked into the room it seemed like the world came to sudden halt. White soldiers who sat at long wooden tables stared at the colored men. Some continued eating, while others made rude comments under their breath. .

Striding up to the table, they stopped and introduced themselves. Several of the men rose from the table and walked off. This brought an immediate scowl to Bernard's face. Moses, seeing his friend's anger and sensing an uneasy situation developing, whispered calmly in his ear.

"Pssh, we'll establish ourselves, then they have to respect us." Bernard glanced at his friend with a questionable look and nodded, okay.

As they walked over to the chow line, they noticed the cooks snickering at them. They proceeded to a table, alone. Hayes walked over to the both of them.

"Sergeant, Corporal, may I join ya?"

"Sure Hayes, pull up a seat." The soldier placed his tray on the table and sat on the bench.

They sat together, to the dislike of some eating their food and laughing up a storm.

"This chow ain't so bad," said Bernard.

"Isn't bad. I don't want to be reminding you of grammar every time." Moses grinned. Stirring the steaming coffee he blew on it before sipping.

Bernard pointed his fork towards his friend. "The sergeant here is a regular walking school book factory, Hayes. Taught me everything that I know, which some might think is not much." Hayes laughed.

"What about you Hayes, your parents give you the proper schooling?" Bernard asked, with a mouthful of food. Grabbing a napkin he wiped his mouth.

"Well I'm pretty good at the basics, A, B, C's and my 1,2,3's. My science and history are okay. My English could use a little work. Mom sends me short story books. "

"Sounds like you have some good folks at home that love you," said Bernard.

"Yup, nothing like having good parents."

"Yes, I'm lucky," said the young man, using a knife to cut into an apple.

Hayes noticed that Moses said very little while he ate. His mannerisms were odd. But it was his eyes that made him intimidating. There was something behind them, a certain pain that the sergeant had endured. Blacks were treated rough and unfair by most. This was something that Hayes never could or ever would understand. What was the problem white folk had with the colored?

The door burst open and Captain Taylor hurried with excitement. Scanning the room the officer saw Moses and the others seated together and headed over.

"At ease Sergeant, Corporal, I have some splendid news from the War Department in Washington. There will be ninety plus colored soldiers arriving in the next few days. A total of 720 men will comprise the 9th Troop." The Captain could barely contain himself. "This unit will replace the entire white 4th Troop. One of the first United States Army posts made up entirely of black soldiers. The remaining white soldiers will be shipped out to a different post in Eastern Texas under the command of two young second lieutenants who will be arriving on the same train." Flipping the paper front and back the officer scanned the list. "They don't list their names though. Ooh, Hayes has volunteered to stay." Trinidad and Bernard looked at the boy and smiled.

"Sergeant, they will be placed directly under your and an additional arriving sergeant's supervision. All facets of this post will be handled entirely by colored soldiers: medical care, blacksmiths, supply and any other jobs." The men sitting directly behind the group began to talk loudly, uttering disrespectful words. The Captain hearing this whirled around quickly. "That will be just about enough of that talk!"

Rising from the table, the officer climbed up on the bench. The officer then motioned for all the men in the mess hall to cease their discussions and listen up.

"It has come to my attention that there are a few of you who feel a little less than happy with the arrival of our new troops. Let me just say these men are here and here to stay. They are members of the Army of the United States just as you are. Don't let me find out that any of you feel that you're better than the rest of them. Most of you will be leaving this post in the near future, quit griping!" Then Taylor jumped down from the table.

"Sergeant, I want to accompany you and the men on this morning's patrol. Our goals are to check maps and plot any areas that have water for strategic importance." Moses sat there with a look of pleasure on his face.

"Sir, you're coming on patrol?" Hayes looked around and smiled quietly.

"I'm a cavalry officer, Hayes, that's what we do."

"Yes sir, I meant no disrespect."

"None taken. Sergeant, how many men do we need for this patrol?"

"Well sir, I suggest at least ten men fully armed. That's side arms and carbines."

"Wonderful! Hayes, after you and the others finish chow, we'll muster the men for morning patrol. I'll be back."

The men rose to attention as Captain Taylor went to his quarters. Trinidad and his men headed toward the stables and then on to breakfast. A massive structure, the stables housed up to seventy horses. Building an addition to the stable was a chore that the arriving soldiers would have to undertake. Grabbing their saddles, the men quickly prepared their horses. Canteens, blanket rolls and carbines were slung on the mounts.

Captain Taylor emerged from his quarters to see an impressive sight. Lined up in a perfectly straight row was his morning patrol: Ten cavalrymen armed to the hilt, holding the guidon. Smiling with pleasure, he climbed on his mount. "Ready, forward." The soldiers galloped out of the front gate and headed into the Texas territory.

"Ain't that a sight," snickered the sentry. "A white officer leading niggers and greenhorns on a patrol."

TWO

Several hours had passed and no enemy sightings. Moses squinted in the sun, trying to keep a watchful eye out. Several large rock formations towered in the distance. Bernard wiped the sweat from his brow.

"Damn, this is some kind of boredom, huh?" said Hayes, taking a swig from his canteen.

"Sergeant, we should send a small detachment ahead some yards, to spot trouble" suggested the captain riding up next to Moses.

"Yes, sir."

Moses motioned to Corporal Bernard to take three men and ride ahead, cautioning them to stay within eyesight of the rest of the patrol. The small group galloped ahead of the pack kicking up dust in their wake.

"Keep a watchful eye out," yelled Moses with concern.

"Sergeant, how long have you and the corporal been together?" asked Taylor.

"Bernard and I have been together a long time. Since our days with the 54th."

"The Massachusetts 54th commanded by Colonel Robert Gould Shaw?" The officer darn near jumped out of his saddle.

"The one and only. Damn shame that boy died, helluva leader. There wasn't anything those men wouldn't do for Colonel Shaw. Most senior officers don't realize it is the men that move the army."

The young officer stared ahead. "I would hope that one day someone like yourself would say that about me."

"Captain, all we ask is the chance for us to show what we are made of. It's not a big mystery that we want to serve without being treated like lower class individuals. Treat us with respect and it will be returned." They were coming up to Blackbird Pass, a narrow passage between two rocky hillsides. Perfect for an ambush.

* * * * * * *

The Indians stared in amazement at the small group of riders heading in their direction. Lying on their stomachs the group of seven warriors was perfectly still. Pointing toward the lead rider, they noticed his almost black skin color. The Comanche's' bodies were tense and ready for a fight. They wore three colored stripes over the bridges of their noses: yellow, white and green, and were armed with rifles, bows and arrows.

"Buffalo Soldiers," said Red Wolf, tilting his head from side to side. The nickname was given to colored soldiers because of their wool like hair. The eldest son of the chief, Red Wolf knew when to be cautious. "They're tougher than the white soldiers." The Indian motioned for his men to take up positions in the rocks.

"Weak, they are all weak," scowled Snake That Strikes Quickly, his hands tightening around his weapon. "They can never survive the winters, and they're bad fighters. Let us

22

take these men's scalps for our lances." Spit flew from the warrior's mouth, and foam churned up in the corners of his lips. His hate for the soldiers was deep.

"Patience," said Prowling Gray Wolf. "Respect them first and then we will find their weakness."

"This is my land, they will leave when I tell them," said the warrior, grabbing a rifle. The other men tried to calm the hothead down, but he was off and running. To the horror of his peers, the warrior rose from behind his hiding spot. Taking careful aim Snake That Strikes Quickly squeezed off a shot, missing its mark. The only thing it did was give away their positions, and the Indians began searching for cover.

"Fool," yelled Prowling Gray Wolf, diving for cover. "Your actions have careless results."

"Ambush," yelled Bernard, leaping from his mount and drawing his revolver. "Take cover."

The bullets whizzed over their heads. The soldiers were ordered to dismount and take up positions behind some rocks, to return fire. Linking all the horses together, one soldier pulled the animals to the rear, while the remaining men were deployed to skirmish.

"Hayes, Hayes you okay?" yelled Bernard, squeezing off a hastily aimed shot. "Where the hell are they?" The bullets shattered the rocks, spraying the men with pebbles.

"On the cliff, behind a group of trees. Looks to be a few of them," said the young soldier with some excitement in his voice. Pebbles ricocheted off Corporal Bernard's back painfully stinging him and tossing his pistol to the ground. "Oohhh!" Regaining his wits the corporal retrieved his weapon and returned fire.

Moses and the others heard the shots. Drawing their weapons they rode feverishly into the direction of gunfire. "Set sites at 200 yards, and fire!"

Captain Taylor leaped from his mount and took cover behind a rock. Cocking the revolver, he began crawling in the direction of the shouting. A quick crack from a rifle and a soldier fell in front of him. His chest was hit, and blood began welling up through his shirt. The young man began screaming with pain.

"Sergeant, there's a man down," hollered a soldier.

Staring at the trooper covered in blood, Taylor was paralyzed with fear. "My god he's bleeding all over!"

"Stay calm, Sir. Put some pressure on the wound with your hand," shouted Moses. Captain Taylor applied pressure to the man's chest, but the blood continued flowing.

"That's right sir, good job."

Grabbing his revolver and swinging to his right the officer fired two quick shots cutting down a warrior. Captain Taylor noticed another young white soldier huddled on the ground in fear.

Moses stared into the distance noticing another Indian trying to outflank them. Grabbing his carbine and taking aim, he squeezed off a round. The warrior dropped to one knee on the ground. Again aiming carefully, Moses fired a second shot hitting the Indian in the chest and flipping the warrior on his side. Out of nowhere, a small band of Indians appeared in the distance.

"More Indians trying to flank us," yelled Hayes, rising up from his position quickly. Taking aim, he fired two shots hitting their marks as two braves fell to the ground in wrenching pain. Corporal Bernard grabbed some men and formed and "L" formation returning fire.

"We don't stand a chance!" cried a hysterical soldier.

"Stay down!" yelled the Captain. "I'll be right over, don't move."

The young man had a petrified look in his eyes. Dropping his weapon, the man fell to the ground and curled up in a ball. Moses crawled over to where the captain and the wounded man were lying. Grabbing the man's wrist, he checked for a pulse. The blood was bubbling from his lips, and he was shaking violently. The officer watched in horror as life slipped slowly from the young man's body.

"He's dying sir, leave him."

The young man's body went limp and lifeless.

"Sir, he's with the Almighty."

Clearly the shock of losing men under his command was hard for Taylor to handle. Moses saw the look of disbelief. He grabbed the officer by his blouse and pulled him close. Death happens, this was the business they chose, he needed to get his head into the game. Suddenly from nowhere, a brave leaped from behind a rock and tackled Moses. The Captain backed up in surprise. Trinidad drew his knife and with a quick strike, dug it deep into the Indian's body.

"They're trying to surround us," said Moses, wiping the blood on the dead Indian's pants. Moses looked over to the young man still curled up on the ground. "Sir, you tend to him, I'll go and check on the others." Moses grabbed his carbine and crawled off.

Corporal Bernard and his men were scaling the rocks. Climbing up into the flats, they crept silently toward the braves. Unaware of the soldiers sneaking up from behind, the Indians continued firing on the cavalrymen.

Young Rabbit, an inexperienced brave, was crouched behind a rock still trying to fasten his bow when a figure appeared in front of him.

"Well, well, well," said Bernard standing there holding his weapon. "Did you think you'd outsmart the ole corporal and the United States Army?" Bernard stared. "Sweating right through those buckskins ain't ya." Death was imminent. Trying quickly to go for their weapons, the Indians were hit with a barrage of gunfire. Smoke circles filled the air. Bernard kicked the bodies, they didn't move. Walking to the edge of the cliff, he started shouting.

"We've secured the high ground!" Moses stared up in delight and began to dart from rock to rock.

Captain Taylor had made it over to the dazed soldier. "Pull yourself together man!" yelled the officer shaking him violently. "Your comrades need you." The boy made several attempts to push the man away, but the officer was firm. Grabbing the enlisted man by his collar, Captain Taylor slapped him across the face. The boy sat frozen on the ground. "Now go and help your comrades!" The bullet slammed into the soldier's body, ripping a path through his organs. Falling forward the dead trooper rested face first in the awestruck officer's chest.

From out of nowhere, Snake That Strikes Quickly rode straight for the young officer, tomahawk in hand and screaming at the top of his lungs. Pushing the dead soldier off, Captain Taylor scrambled to his feet. He stood there frozen. The look in his eyes was one of total fear. As he fumbled, the war cry grew louder. The young officer's hands shook violently while squeezing off round after round. Closer and closer the Indian came. Bullets seemed to be bouncing off the oncoming brave, yet the officer could not take his eyes off the gleaming tomahawk. Pulling a wounded brave on his horse, Prowling Gray Wolf stared at his comrade charging towards the officer.

"Focus, concentrate!" yelled Moses. Bernard and the others stood in silence as the rider came closer. "Do it now!"

BOOM! With a thunderous roar the final bullet slammed into the chest of the warrior. The man's body hurled backwards off his mount. The beast thundered past the stunned officer and the Indian's lifeless body came to rest at his feet. Breathing a sigh of relief, Taylor dropped to his knees. Prowling Gray Wolf could only shake his head in disgust as he saw the now lifeless body of his Indian brother lying defeated on the earth's floor. Prowling Gray Wolf decided it was best to retreat into the hills with Red Wolf following behind on foot.

"Roll call, ammunition and horse count!" yelled Moses, noticing the second dead soldier. Kneeling down beside him, he whispered softly. "Never had a chance."

"All secure here Sergeant Trinidad," shouted the Corporal. "Now, let's see just what these boys have that we can use." The soldiers swarmed over the bodies like vultures. Indian articles brought decent money or could be traded in the town. Knives, tomahawks, beads and anything they liked were gathered together in a pile.

"Corporal, lookie what we dun gots here," laughed one soldier. Under a tree, a large number of horses were tied up. Buffalo skin blankets; sacks of jerky, and extra bullets were fastened to the beautiful animals. "We dun hit the jackpot."

Hayes emerged from behind his rocky barrier his expression was one of total excitement. This is what he joined the Army for. "All's clear here, Sergeant."

Walking up to the bodies of the braves, Hayes poked them both in the chest with his carbine. Bending down, he stared into their empty eyes. Beside the bodies, he found two interesting items. First, a beautiful bone handle knife that would fit smartly in his belt and second, a small toy doll. Worn out, the little doll looked as if it had been played with often. He never thought about the children that could lose a father. The young man stared silently at the hills. Now he realized for the first time that these were not animals that they had killed, but humans with families like his.

"Hayes, do you plan on joining this party!" asked Corporal Bernard. "Start going through your kill's stuff son. There's no telling what kind of items you can find."

Unseen by the others, Hayes gently tucked the doll next to the bodies.

Captain Taylor walked slowly over to the dead soldiers lying in the sand. They looked almost peaceful as if they were sleeping.

"I didn't even know your names," he whispered.

"Sir, sir, you all right?" asked Moses softly.

"I've never seen anyone killed before, guess it shows."

"Seen plenty of men die sir, it never gets any easier. Be proud of the fact that you could pull yourself together. Normally, I would recommend that we pursue them, but we lost two men and didn't pack much ammunition. Do you agree with my assessment sir?"

Nodding his approval, the young officer walked away toward his horse. He cradled the beast's head in his hands and hugged it lovingly.

Bernard raced down the mountainside toward Moses. With a big wide grin he told of the hidden treasures that they had discovered. The cavalry had the extra necessities that they would need to pursue the Indians. This brought a smile to Moses' face.

"Sir, let me take a small detachment and them down." The men waited eagerly for the officer to reply. Captain Taylor squinted as he gazed up at the sun.

"Fine, Sergeant."

Moses grabbed Bernard, Hayes and two additional men and loaded up five fresh horses. The patrol then raced off in pursuit of the Indians. Loading the dead soldier's bodies on horses, the remaining men and their leader headed back to the fort.

The first half of the patrol limped lifelessly back into the fort. "Patrol coming in!" yelled the guard on duty. "We got men wounded!" Men came running from their duties to assist their comrades. Dismounting, the dejected leader walked to his quarters and slammed the door behind him.

The soldiers removed the bodies and carried them to the dead house.

Captain Taylor lit the small lamp on his desk. Removing a bottle from the drawer he poured a generous portion in his cup. How could this happen? It was their first patrol under his command. How would he explain this to Regimental Headquarters? What would he say in the letters to the dead men's families? He gulped the whiskey and winced.

THREE

The five riders thundered across the prairie, covering an astounding fifteen miles in a few hours. Yet, they had seen not a single Indian. Nighttime was setting in and the temperatures were dropping. They found a grouping of rocks and started to make camp. Digging a small hole the soldiers lit a fire in the middle, its warmth spreading quickly. Horses were fed and watered. Two guards were posted. The other men curled up in their blankets and drifted off. Reaching into his bag, Moses removed his writing book and pen. The fire would give off just enough light. With his pistol lying at arm's length, Moses began to write.

September 24, 1879

Patrol was not all that we had hoped for; we were ambushed by a group of Comanche and we lost two men. To see the shock in the eyes of the captain was one that I could have easily lived without. He was scared, yet regained his composure quickly and even got himself an Indian. His reaction was one of sadness not of joy, not the killing sort, but he will make a good leader that I can assure anyone. The men's actions warranted the highest accolades, they reacted with professionalism and military readiness. The young soldier Hayes was a wonder with the carbine, told me that his father taught him to hunt deer in the mountains of Vermont. I've never met a kid that is so likeable and doesn't care what others think, very sure of himself. I like that. He will be a good soldier, one that will lead others. Bernard came through like always. Bernard and Hayes are laughing up a storm by the fire, it's like they've been pals their whole life. Never know that they were different colors though. Temperatures are beginning to drop some. Nights on the open prairie are nice the stars and the moon sure are beautiful. We dined on dried meat that we found in the pouches of the Indian's horses, and their buffalo hide blankets make this desert floor a helluva lot more comfortable. Best get bedded down now, morning will be here and the decision to pursue these Indians further will have to be reached then. The patrol is tired and the deaths of their fellow troopers are very evident in their faces. New recruits will be arriving on tomorrow's train and I hope to be back for their arrival. We have yet to deal with the townspeople and the thought of having so many blacks around won't sit well with them. I don't care though, they sure as hell will learn to deal or they'll pay a price that they won't forget. We won't tolerate being treated like second class citizens anymore.

Stowing his writing gear, Moses rolled over and covered up. Listening to his men chattering around the campfire he slowly drifted off into sleep.

"Boy, where in the hell did you learn to shoot like that?" asked Bernard, laughing and passing a cup of steaming coffee to Hayes. "Everything you aimed at you hit."

"I owe it all to my father, he was the one who taught me everything I know. Like I told the sergeant, shooting deer in the hills helps."

"Let's get some shuteye. Tomorrow the rest of the troop is reporting to the fort and we're going to need to be there for them." The fire gave off a dull glow.

It was morning; the smell of fresh brewed coffee permeated the air. Most of the patrol was awake and readying their horses. Moses was still sleeping. Hayes came running up to Bernard and reported unknown riders coming from the east.

"Moses, wake up we got company," Bernard called. "Hayes, go cover them." Loading his carbine, the young man positioned himself for action behind a small rock formation.

Shaking off sleep, Moses rose to his feet. He stared at the blurry formations on the horizon. "Not Indians, don't look to be Mexicans either." Moses gave a quick whistle. The soldiers formed a line of fire and pointed their weapons at the ready.

"Hold your fire," shouted a white man's voice. Three dirty looking men rode up to the small campsite. Noticing the badges on their clothes, Moses lowered his weapon. They were lawmen of some kind.

"Morning, enough coffee for three more?" smiled the man leading the group. Hayes stared over the sight of his weapon suspiciously.

"Depends, who are you?" Moses kept a watchful eye on the men. They looked to be lawless not lawmen.

"McMaster, Jonah McMaster, Texas Rangers. These boys are Collins and Armstead." Sitting on horses with rifles across their laps, the two men nodded. They were covered in dust from head to toe and the heavy growth of their whiskers indicated to Moses they had been in the saddle for some time. The only question was, doing what? An empty look glazed their eyes, almost sinister. Nodding in the direction of the two men, Moses knelt down to fill his cup.

"What are you men doing this far out, with no protection. Indians are running rampant around these parts. We were hit a day ago, lost two men. We got eight Indians and their horses." Moses pointed toward the trees where the horses were grazing. "Lost their trail though. We're heading back to Fort Barre."

The rangers climbed down from their mounts. "Don't surprise us none, they been hitting settlers all over. You can tell your men to lower their weapons we're not the enemy." Moses motioned to the men to safety their weapons.

Extending the coffee pot, Bernard filled the ranger's cups. Hayes couldn't stop staring at the men's horses.

"You got some problem with us boy," said the one named Armstead. Striking a match from his belt, he lit a cigarette. "You've been staring a me for quite a while now." He was tall and blond and with his hat tilted across his dirty face, he looked mean.

"No, just admiring your horses," commented Hayes. "They're beautiful." The boy strolled over and brushed his hands along the horse's body.

The man smiled with delight. "The young boy has a good eye." Armstead patted Hayes on the shoulder with appreciation. "Picked them up from an Indian in New Mexico. How far is the nearest town?"

"Flat Fork is about a day's ride," said Hayes, stowing his gear in his saddlebags.

"Much obliged, we have a few more stops to make before we reach the town. You say that you ran into some Indians yesterday, they put up much of a fight?"

"Enough to kill my men, sir." Pouring sand on the fire, Moses and the men began securing his gear and readying for the ride home.

"Appreciate the coffee, gentleman." The rangers mounted up and headed out east.

Bernard looked over to Moses and Hayes. "They don't sit right with me, Moses. They're not so law abiding, I feel it in my gut. I'd say that they're looking to kill anybody for anything." Moses glanced over to Hayes who stared oddly at the men.

"What's on your mind Hayes, speak up?"

"They're lying Sergeant." Bernard quickly looked at Hayes.

"How would you know, you were smitten with their horses the entire time!"

"Not so much with the horses. Did you notice the blood leaking from the saddlebags? Look at your feet." The sand contained small trickle marks of red. Kneeling down, the young man rubbed the sand between his fingers and examined the stains. "Where there is blood something was living at one point. Why don't we follow this trail, let's see where it leads?" Moses stared at the rangers as they rode off in the distance. Questions were running wild in his mind.

"Prepare to continue patrol," said Moses. "We'll ride for a few hours. If we turn up nothing, we head back for the fort." The soldiers agreed and headed out to follow the blood trail.

FOUR

Time passed quickly. Moses was sensing there was nothing to be found. The men dismounted and began walking their horses to conserve energy. Coming to a small creek bank with a large rock formation looming over it, the group decided to stop. Bernard posted guards to keep an eye out. Hayes walked over to a rocky area.

"Hayes, where in the hell are you going, son?" shouted Bernard.

"Just gotta make water." Walking around the rocky hill, he began undoing his trousers. Looking down he noticed a substantial dark stain in the sand. "Holy cow!"

The young man tripped over his feet backing up. Moses and Bernard turned quickly and vaulted in his direction, revolvers drawn.

"Good god," exclaimed Moses. Bernard looked away holding his stomach. Three Indians laying face down under some small brush. The man had been stabbed several times and scalped. The women's head had been crushed with a stone. Noticing her ripped garments, it appeared she had been assaulted. What was most disturbing was the small child shot in the head.

Sergeant Trinidad's eyes scanned the area. "They were killed over there," he said pointing to the edge of the creek bank. "Dragged under the brush. Look at the marks in the sand. Bury the bodies first, and then hunt around for additional evidence of who may have done this. Pay attention."

"The rangers did it sergeant," said Hayes uneasily.

"What leads you to believe that, son?"

"Look at those footprints, ain't no moccasin of any kind. The print goes too deep into the ground. Those weren't made by military issue boots."

"Another trait your father taught you son," Bernard winked at the young man. Hayes saw something hung up in the creek rocks. Walking over to the water, he bent down and noticed a buffalo hide water pouch. Shaking his head back and forth Hayes stared in disbelief.

"I can't believe they were killed going for water."

Grabbing a small shovel and pickaxe from the saddlebags, the soldiers began digging. The ground was hard and riddled with stone. A shallow hole was all they could muster up. Wrapping the bodies in army blankets, they placed them carefully in the hole and covered them with earth and rocks. Bernard removed a small tattered bible from his pocket and whispered some words of prayer.

"Lord, we don't know who they were. We only know they didn't deserve the death they got, bless their departed souls."

Packing up their gear, the men began to head for the fort. The afternoon train was expected in a few hours, and the new arrivals would be on it. The patrol dismounted and walked the final mile to the fort. They were tired, but had a feeling of renewed strength and pride. The sentry alerted the commanding officer that his men were returning. Captain Taylor stood on the porch of his office.

36

"Sergeant, please give me a full report." Saluting the officer, Moses motioned to Bernard to secure the detail and take care of the horses. The two men walked over to the HQ and stepped inside.

"Did you see them Sergeant; did you get them?"

"No sir, no additional sightings of hostiles. We met some interesting characters this morning though, rangers of some sort. We believe that they had contact with the Comanche."

"What leads you to believe that?"

"Hayes saw blood leaking from their saddlebags. We assume that they had scalps. We didn't ask and they didn't offer. We followed a blood trail to some grisly findings though. It was a family of three Indians butchered and scalped while going for water. They're dirty sir, and that's the truth." The young officer sat with a look of dismay as his sergeant reported his findings. His stomach turned sickly.

"We'll have to put this issue on hold for now, the train will arrive in an hour. Get yourself cleaned up and looking sharp. We'll ride out together. The funerals for the men will be held tomorrow in the graveyard on the hill. They'll be the first men killed in an Indian campaign under my command. Sergeant, I'm sorry that I froze out there. You must think me a coward, unfit to command?"

"You did what an officer and leader does. You pulled yourself together and got the job done. I'll be back sir." Moses saluted and exited the office, and headed to his quarters.

Moses walked to his quarters. Inside, Bernard was cleaning up and securing the gear.

"How's the captain doing?"

"He blames himself for the deaths. Surprised me that an officer would accept responsibility for this. Makes no difference anyway. It's not his fault. The men aren't coming back from the dead." Moses sat on the edge of his bunk and removed his boots.

"Ooohh! These dogs are tired," said Moses extending his foot out straight; the knuckles in his toes cracked.

"Well, he's young, he'll have to learn that death comes with the territory," said Bernard, removing his blouse. "Did a good job as far as I could tell, Hayes is gonna make one damn fine cavalryman. Never seen a man shoot with such accuracy; those other white boys did well too."

"If I didn't know any better I'd say that you and Hayes are becoming pretty close," smiled Moses.

"He's easy to like. The first white man that I ever was friends with."

The two soldiers washed, shaved and changed into clean uniforms. Checking themselves in the mirror everything looked perfect. The train would be arriving soon. They hurried outside to meet the CO. Captain Taylor was running a few minutes behind schedule. Moses walked over to the office. Inside Hayes was busy writing out a report on the attack. The officer emerged from his quarters neat as a pin.

"Looking sharp sir," said Moses saluting.

"Thank you Sergeant, are we ready?"

"Yes, sir."

The men emerged from the office and mounted up. The train depot was less than a half a mile from the fort. It was a quiet ride. Different thoughts were running through all the men's minds. Would this new plan of integrating these soldiers be a success, or would this only add fuel to the fire. The train's whistle blew in the distance and puffs of smoke were rising in the air.

"How are you in the saddle sir," asked Moses tightening the grip on his reins.

"Let's find out, men. Ya." The officer bolted forward, his steed's mane blowing in the wind. "Ya, ya!" The soldiers were shocked and pleasantly surprised. They pounded across the plains into the train depot and came to stop. The smile on the officer's face was glowing, just the boost to his ego that he needed.

"Damn fine riding sir," said Bernard with a grin.

"Thank you, Corporal. That was fun. Now let's find these new recruits and get them settled in. I am assuming the two young officers will be riding in the coach."

"Here comes the train now sir," pointed Trinidad. The whistle screamed, and the smoke stacks bellowed thick pockets of smoke. The massive black locomotive sailed majestically into the depot coming to a halt beside the platform. "Town of Flat Fork, all off for Flat Fork," barked the conductor.

The train depot was bustling with activity. Men, women and children were exiting and boarding the passenger cars. Several deputy sheriffs were watching, keeping the peace. Exiting the rear car were the two young officers, fresh from the Academy. Behind them a weathered looking colored sergeant emerged.

"Men, fall out on the double and form ranks!" yelled the sergeant. His name was Sergeant Powers Nouba, a veteran of eighteen years. "Move it!" Exiting the car hurriedly, the Buffalo Soldiers moved quickly and formed ranks along the station tracks. The grizzled veteran stood there with his hands on his hips rocking back and forth. "Move it!!!" The two young West Point Graduates were caught up in the confusion.

"Your places should be in front of the new arrivals, sirs," said Sergeant Nouba holding out his hand. Young women scurried to get out of the way and men gave odd looks. Surely armed black soldiers is something that most white civilians never would have imagined seeing. Captain Taylor and his two NCOs marched to the platform to greet the new men. Snapping quickly to attention the officers and sergeant crisply saluted.

"2nd Lieutenants Judson Henry McAllister and King Adrian Brandon reporting as ordered." The men stood straight. "May I present Sergeant Powers Nouba."

"Pleasure to meet you," Taylor replied, returning the salute. "May I present Sergeant Moses Trinidad and Corporal Quentin Bernard." The enlisted men exchanged handshakes while Captain Taylor and his young officers walked up and down the ranks inspecting his new men.

"Men, it is my pleasure to be commanding you." The young captain walked up the ranks. They were a stunning sight to see: brass buttons shining in the sun, deep penetrating blue uniforms, shiny black boots and those yellow handkerchiefs of the U.S. Cavalry. "Yes, yes, a fine looking group of men. I have but one order to give you right now. It's very simple; you men will be fully armed at all times." The crowd let out a collective gasp. "No excuses! Sergeant Trinidad, let's move 'em out."

Corporal Bernard handed the reins of his horse to the new sergeant. "Sergeant Nouba, take my horse and ride along with the officers and the sergeant. Your new mount is at the fort corral. You'll take possession upon arrival." Pulling the horse's head close to his, Bernard whispered in her ear. "All right girl be gentle now, ya hear."

"Mighty decent of you Corporal," said Sergeant Nouba bounding into the saddle.

"Attention! Right face, forward march." The new arrivals marched off toward their new home. A cloud of dust kicked up in their wake. "Left, right, left right." The townspeople were emerging from their stores and shops to see the black soldiers marching in formation.

Peering out from behind the curtains in his office, Sheriff Watkins shook his head back and forth and began talking to himself. "That's a helluva lot of soldiers being transferred in here all of a sudden. This could mean trouble."

"Sergeants, I've got some reports to tend to, and I would like to brief the lieutenants on the activity in the area before their departure," said Captain Taylor. "I will return in two hours to inspect the barracks. The funeral will be tomorrow. Following the ceremonies, soldiers and their supply wagons will be readied for departure. The following morning they will set out to the new post in the eastern part of the state. Sergeant Major O'Brien will be leading this patrol and upon arrival will be mustering out for retirement back East. I believe his family has already gone out and will be awaiting his arrival."

"Mighty good picking for the Indians, sir," replied Moses. "Will these men be properly equipped to handle this task?"

"The Sergeant Major is a veteran of over thirty-two years in this man's cavalry," said the officer. "If he doesn't follow all the military guidelines, retirement won't be any fun with shrapnel in his backside." The men got a quick chuckle and headed out.

Upon arrival, the new soldiers went right to work. They were immediately dispatched to retrieve any additional supplies needed. Securing their gear in proper military fashion, they were informed of the inspection that would take place later that afternoon. The men hustled quickly to turn this space into a military barracks. Carbines were stowed in the gun rack located in the center of the barracks, bunks made in proper fashion, and additional uniforms and overcoats hung neatly on hooks on the wall.

"Men!" boomed Nouba. "You'd better make damn sure that these barracks are in topnotch condition. I plan on busting your lowly asses to make sure this is the best damn cavalry unit in the United States Army. Is that understood? Don't you dare disappoint me!"

Sergeant Trinidad and Corporal Bernard stood back and watched the new men run in circles. The three NCOs walked out the barracks into the compound.

"Nouba, I think that we are going to be a good team," said Moses. "The way you jumped on these men and immediately began to assume control leads me to believe you're just the man we need."

"My objective is to mold these men into cavalrymen," replied Nouba. "They're not here to be mothered. Bullets, bandits and danger don't play favorites. I hate to lose men, so they'll learn not to be targets for the Indians."

"Speaking of targets," said Corporal Bernard. "After the inspection we will be headed to the gun range. These men will be skilled in side arms and carbines. It will become their best friend. They'll learn to eat, sleep and breathe it. We have a young white trooper named Hayes that shoots better than anyone I've seen. They will be just as skilled with the carbine after I get done with them."

"Sergeant Nouba, I don't have to tell you how difficult a task we have ahead of us. These white folks around these parts aren't used to blacks in this capacity. They see them only as slaves or people of lesser intelligence. That particular train of thought is a bunch of crap. We are the protector of these people, and they will grow to appreciate us, and that's an order," said Moses with a look of conviction.

"I agree with you, Trinidad. These white folks never cared for us because they are afraid of us. I been serving in this man's army for seventeen years, can't say that they have changed any though. It's my opinion that they only seem fit to appreciate us when their backs are against the wall. Can I live with that? Sometimes it's the only thing I can live with. My duties are to the Army, and to the President. These people merely are the excess baggage that comes along with our duties. I'd like to have a look at the town after the inspection and see what it has to offer. See just what we're protecting."

42

"It will be our first visit also. Since we have arrived, we haven't had any time to stop in and see the place." Glancing down at his pocket watch, Moses noticed the inspection was approaching. It was time to go to the captain's office to summon him and the junior officers for the inspection. Nouba retreated into the barracks to give a quick once over. The men were ready and looked sharp. Nodding with approval, he walked up and down their quarters making sure every detail was in place.

Moses walked into the outer office area where Hayes was tending to paperwork. The door to Captain's office was ajar. Hayes motioned for Moses to go in.

"Soldiers standing by for inspection, sir." The officers were seated at a small table enjoying some coffee.

"Outstanding, let's go." The men proceeded across the compound to the barracks area. As the officer entered the barracks, the soldiers jumped to attention. Nouba saluted and announced that all men were accounted for and ready to be inspected.

"Very well, Sergeant Nouba," answered the young officer. Gliding up and down the rows, he was thoroughly impressed with the new arrivals. The barracks was transformed into a military housing space in hours. "Men, this is just the kind of barracks that any commanding officer would be proud of. Fall out to receive work detail orders from, Sergeant Trinidad and Sergeant Nouba, stand fast."

"You've pleased me, gentlemen. This is a good beginning. Now, I would like both of you to accompany me into town. You would be wise to familiarize yourselves with it and the people. Have my horse readied and we'll be on our way."

"Yes sir," said Moses. "We were supposed to be taking the men over to the gun range, sir."

"Have Corporal Bernard and Hayes take them over. They are the two best shots in the company, sorry Sergeant Trinidad. Is there a problem with that?"

"No problem at all, sir. Sergeant Nouba, please give the Corporal his assignment."

Nouba walked over to Corporal Bernard and informed him of the additional tasks he would be assigned. Bernard was to get Hayes and take the new recruits to the firing range and assess their levels with their carbines. Walking out to the corral, they saddled up their mounts. They worked feverishly and had the horses ready in no time. Sergeant Nouba was a little surprised to see his commanding officer saddle up his own horse. Mounting up, the men headed out of the fort toward the town of Flatfork.

Bernard and Hayes led the detachment of men to the range. Excitement was evident in all of the men's faces. The range was located conveniently a few hundreds yards outside of the fort. Targets were placed against a dug out sand dune. There were three different distances 100, 300 and 600 yards out. Bernard was first to step up and address the men.

"Listen up!" yelled Corporal Bernard. "Everyone of you are gonna learn to shoot just like myself."

Removing his carbine, he stepped up to the makeshift line and stood at the ready. Standing still he aimed. Gently squeezing the trigger he began firing. Three perfect hits on the target which brought a cheer from the men.

"Now let's just see what we have here," said Bernard, pointing a finger at a few men. "Step up to the line and show me what you got." Five young soldiers stepped nervously to the line and began firing off rounds, none of them finding their marks. Corporal Bernard shook his head back and forth and held up his hands.

"That was some of the most pathetic shooting I've ever seen, sit your tails down." Taking a seat on the ground, they listened to the instructions. "Men, this weapon is only as good as the person that possesses it. You must learn to shoot with expert accuracy, because I guarantee that your enemy will. Everyone step up to the line". Some commotion was heard as the men rose and positioned themselves on the line. "Ready, aim, fire!" A huge volley of bullets were let loose. Some hit their marks, some strayed off to the left or right. Bernard rolled his eyes and remembered that he once was a new recruit, like them. Hayes chuckled quietly in the background. The firing slowly stopped as they turned to stare at the white boy. The laughing slowly drifted away.

"Attention, Hayes, just what are you laughing at son?" asked Bernard, walking up to the boy and standing in his face. "You think that you can do better? Well, come on soldier, let's see what you have." Wiping his hands on his trousers, he walked up to the line.

Hayes placed the carbine to his shoulder and began squeezing off round after round like a flash of lightning. All bullets hitting the target square on the mark. The soldiers stared in amazement at the white trooper. After several hours of intense lecture and additional practice, the soldiers returned to the line and began firing at the targets, this time faring better.

FIVE

The town of Flat Fork was like most small towns on the rise in the West. White men were settling constantly and pushing the Native Americans further and further out. It had all the normal amenities that other towns had: bank, hotels, barroom, blacksmiths, bathhouse, whorehouse, doctor's office, post office, telegraph station, and a sheriff's office. The main employers were the railroad, and cattle ranching. White people had homes in town and kept mostly to themselves. Mexicans, blacks, and oriental workers were kept segregated in a not so wonderful area located outside the town. Run down shacks and tents were the main structures, yet some small homes were being erected. These people were taking what they were given and trying to create a home for themselves and the scores of young children. There was a small missionary located north where monks worked and prayed. Missionaries from the church were teaching the children reading, writing and arithmetic in small makeshift schools. To these people, the Buffalo Soldiers were a sight.

Pointing out all the important sites, Captain Taylor and his men rode throughout the area. These Buffalo Soldiers were to be the new keepers of the peace; whites were a bit unsure of their abilities. They dismounted and hitched up their horses in front of the sheriff's office.

"Let's meet the sheriff, so we can figure out if he's on our side or just another jerk running the show," Taylor said. "We may need him if things get rough." Entering the office they noticed a man dressed smartly sitting behind a desk. Cells empty, there were several wanted posters peppering the walls.

"Afternoon gentlemen," said the sheriff, rising from a large wooden desk. "What can I do for you today?" Extending his hand to the men, they all shook. "Name is Thomas Watkins, sheriff of Flatfork." Tall with a medium build, the sheriff was dressed like a dandy in a three-piece suit with bolo tie and a red flower on his lapel. Silver star on his jacket, colt revolver on his hip, complexion dark with a cheesy little mustache, he looked more of a businessman than a lawman. "This is my deputy Carl Johnson." Johnson was middle aged, of slight build and rough around the edges. Sitting near the sheriff, he was cleaning out the barrels of a shotgun.

"I'm Captain Taylor, this is Sergeant Nouba and Sergeant Trinidad. We're in charge of maintaining security of the plains area. We wanted to meet you and make you aware of the new arrivals at Fort Barre."

The sheriff returned to his chair. "Yes, the blacks. I saw them at the railroad station early this morning. Please have a seat gentlemen." Pulling up three chairs the men all sat down. Watkins stared rudely at the two sergeants. He removed a cigar from his desk and slowly slid it under his nose for the aroma. "Well, most folks aren't sure about having black soldiers protecting them. They have heard rumors that they were deserting in large numbers. No disrespect, sergeants," said the man with sweet little smile. Striking a match, he puffed gently on the cigar. "With rumors like those floating around, how do you expect people to feel safe?"

Captain Taylor sat with his legs crossed, gloves and hands across his lap, rolling his eyes in disgust. "We were assigned this task and it's one we fully intend to follow through with. If people are so idiotic to think the color of a man's skin would stop him from performing his duties, they are as dumb as rocks. How many additional men are assigned to this office?" asked the Captain straightening his gloves and cap in his lap. The sergeants smiled happily at their leader.

"Myself, Mr. Johnson and three deputies. I didn't mean to upset you or offend your men. If that is way I appeared, I do apologize." Watkins extended his hand to the officer. "May I offer you a whiskey?" Removing two glasses from his cabinet, he poured the golden liquid from a crystal decanter.

"No thank you," replied the Captain Taylor. "The number of men in your office doesn't sound like enough to stop any Indian, Mexican or any other thug from doing harm."

Taking a sip, the sheriff sat back down in his chair. "I assure you, Captain Taylor, my men and I are more than capable of handling any situation that may arise. I myself am a veteran of the war between the states," he said pointing to the Confederate flag adorning the wall. "Serving with General Stonewall Jackson and seeing my share of difficult situations. Certainly able to handle any task that your coloreds could do." His tone had a distinct note of southern sarcasm. "I'm sorry to say that I haven't had much to do with colored people other than servants on my parents' plantation down south." Placing his cigar in the ashtray, the sheriff blew small rings of smoke in the air and smiled that sickening smile. Moses and Nouba stared at the man with a peculiar look on their faces. Moses's eyes became fixed on Deputy Johnson sitting near the desk. The man looked constantly over at the sheriff; this guy was no genius.

"I assure you, Sheriff Watkins, that my men and I are more than capable of handling any and all problems that arise." The officer's eyes danced around the room to look for anything out of place.

Sheriff Watkins retrieved his cigar from the ashtray. "I don't take kindly to drunken soldiers brawling and causing trouble in this town. They will be dealt with just like normal civilians. No favors will be given. We have a peaceful town here and that's the way I plan to keep it." Relighting his cigar he puffed a thin line into the air and smiled.

Captain Taylor snatched the cigar from the sheriff's mouth and placed it into the whiskey glass. It sizzled. Moses and Nouba unbuckled their holsters and stared at Deputy Johnson. Placing the empty weapon on the desk, Johnson smiled and held his hands up.

"My good sheriff, I don't have to remind you that when military personnel are arrested by civilian authorities, the post commander is to be notified at once. Sergeants, let's go." The young officer and his men rose easily from their seats. "That is the way that I plan to keep it. Good day, sir." The three soldiers exited the building slamming the door behind them.

Shocked and a bit amused, the sheriff and his deputy laughed. "Well, I can tell that these blacks and their white leader are going to be trouble for our operations." He struck a match off his revolver handle and lit a new cigar, sucking in deep breaths. The smoke rose in circles by his head, his eyes peering through the smoke. "Yes siree, big trouble."

* * * * * * *

"That man is trouble with a capital "T", and those deputies are following his lead," said Bernard, straightening himself in the saddle.

"Well, I'm glad to see that someone else picked up on that," said Moses. "Sir, he's crooked all right. I say that as long as we stay away from him, he'll stay away from us.

Right now we have bigger issues at hand. These Indians are not going away quietly, and I don't expect them to either." Captain Taylor stared back at the sheriff's office. Moses noticed this. "Don't give it another thought now sir, we'll deal with them later." The group slapped their mounts and road out of town.

Returning to the fort, the three men noticed two wooden boxes lying by the rear of a wagon. Names edged in the covers, the smell of fresh cut wood permeated the air. The winds kicked dust up from the plains and splashed it over the coffins. They looked desolate and lonely lying there in the setting sun. Was that all those men had been reduced to-two wooden boxes? Captain Taylor stood there, with a look of confusion on his face. "Make sure there is a guard posted for these men," said the officer. "They deserve full military honors."

A patrol the following morning lead by Corporal Bernard and the new soldiers would encompass a ten-mile radius for security. It was getting late so the men decided to relax for the evening. Chow was being served in the hall, and the men were famished. Nouba and Trinidad relaxed by the campfire out in back of their quarters. Enjoying a pipe, Nouba sat in his chair reading his bible.

"I do believe a rocking chair would be a wonderful idea," said Moses, reaching for his writing journal. The glow from the fire danced against the fort walls, with pretty orange colors.

September 25, 1879

Another day in the United States Army has come to a close. New recruits are better than I had anticipated. All have conformed to a military lifestyle faster than the White Soldiers. Sergeant Nouba was the ranking enlisted man that accompanied them to the fort, real army. I'll have to pay close attention to the men, make sure Corporal Bernard and I stay on top of things.

Met the sheriff in town and I have to say that he's a complete ass. A rebel from the South no less. A Confederate flag hanging from the wall, made me sick. Thought Nouba was going to whip his tail. Captain Taylor wasn't impressed with his attitude. Tomorrow afternoon we have the funeral for the two men we lost. It's been some time since I've attended a military funeral.

"Well, I guess I'll have to start this conversation out," said Nouba. "Where the hell you from Trinidad?" Moses put down his pen in his journal and closed the cover.

"Boston, Massachusetts and yourself?"

"Louisiana, born and raised just outside of New Orleans. My mother could whip up some gumbo that would make your head spin. Damn, she could cook."

"Sounds good to me," laughed Moses. "That's one of the things that I miss about my mother also. Baked ham, fried chicken, sweet potato pie and those greens, woo boy!"

"My pappy was a white fur trader from Canada," said Nouba. "Don't remember which part offhand. I think it was Quebec or Montreal. Met momma when he was down doing some trappin', says it was love at first sight. Don't doubt it though; she was pretty as a picture. Tougher than nails too, never took a lick of lip from anyone. I remember this one time when I was just a kid. Momma was working as cook in this little restaurant in New Orleans. She would take me to work, and I would play around outside. Well, one day this man comes in and starts given her lip. She gives him lip right back and he gives her a backhand. Momma goes sailing across the ground. Scared me right in my tracks. Momma gets up and whacks this man clean out with a log." Moses slapped his knees in laughter. "The other guy moved toward her and that gives me the courage to hit him with the axe handle and down he goes. She done grabs me by the hand and we run all the way back to Pappy. She showed me plenty of courage, so I thought the Army could show me more."

"Women, they do the most oddball things. My parents were great too. Father was a servant for a doctor. He was a self-educated man, made me read every book I could ever get my hands on. Mother was a genuine lady, but could put in a day's work like it was nobody's business. Pushed me to my education, the smartest thing that I ever did. Are you married Nouba?"

"Was."

"Was?" asked Moses.

"She passed on about seven years ago. We didn't have any children so that was a plus. Army life is hard on a man's family, all that moving around and such. How about you Moses, anyone special in your life?"

"They're all special," said Trinidad with a catlike grin. "No one that stands out though." The two men exchanged laughs and eased back in their chairs.

"Sergeants, good evening," came a voice. Sergeant Major O'Brien emerged from the dark. "I hope I'm not intruding?"

"Of course not, Sergeant Major," said Moses. "Pull up a chair. May I introduce Sergeant Powers Nouba?" The sergeants exchanged pleasantries and sat down.

"My apologies for not introducing myself earlier. I understand from the captain's report there was trouble on the patrol yesterday."

"Don't worry about that, and yes, trouble is exactly what we had." Trinidad described the events leading up to the patrol and the chase of the Indians. He also informed O'Brien and Nouba of the Rangers they encountered, and the bloody mess by the creek. The look of disgust was evident on their faces.

"I guess that I'm retiring just in time. One last patrol and I'm home free. I guess I'll turn in. It was a pleasure chatting with you both, good night." After exchanging handshakes, O'Brien retired to his quarters.

"Sounds like he could have been a good man to work with," exclaimed Nouba. Trinidad agreed. The ambers from the fire popped and crackled into the night.

The following morning an honor guard hoisted the coffins from the ground and loaded them into the rear of the wagon. The silence was almost deafening.

The cemetery overlooked a desolate and rocky plateau. It was filled mostly with graves of the early settlers. Tombstones were leaning on their sides, or broken in half. Two holes were dug out in the rocky prairie ground, both coffins lying next to them. The sign, which hung over the cemetery gates, creaked in the wind.

Rufus Hood, a Tennessee minister, stood at the front of the group and softly spoke words of praise for the young men.

"We mourn the losses of our dear departed brothers who gave their lives for this command and their fellow troopers. Listen to our agonizing cries God our father. Hear us as we call out for you. We cannot go along this journey without you O'lord. We pray that you will deal patiently and lovingly with us. We are blind without your words to lead our way. We pray to you. Amen! "

Captain Taylor stepped in front of the men and spoke. "They were good soldiers, never wavering in their duties and never forgetting the brotherhood of the soldier. Death in combat is something that happens frequently in this line of work. Let no one here forget why these men died, and let us all remember what lies ahead."

The Buffalo Soldiers were lined up in ranks and stood in total silence. A young soldier, a former farmer, burst into a song. "Amazing grace, how sweet the sound that saved a wretch like me. I once was lost but now am found, was blind but now I see."

"Honor guard, attention!" barked Trinidad. Three soldiers stepped forward and raised their weapons to the heavens.

BOOM! BOOM! BOOM! The noise seemed to travel a hundred miles in the distance. Three men stepped forward on either side of the coffins. With ropes, they lowered the boxes into the ground. The only sound to be heard was the lonely tune of Taps.

"Company dismissed." Heads lowered, the cavalrymen wandered back to the fort.

* * * * * * *

In preparation for departure, numerous wagons were parked by the Quarter Master Storehouse, being loaded down with supplies by white soldiers. Sergeant Reynolds, taking a slug from his little brown bottle, emerged from his shed. Noticing five colored soldiers standing near the corral, he began shouting.

"Hey, get your asses over here!" The soldiers ran over to the platform where the sergeant was standing. "You sons a bitches are just standing there, while good white boys are sweating and loading a wagon." The men loading the wagon stopped and looked over at the blacks.

One young soldier responded. "You tryin to tell me these white boys would lift one finger to help us?" The man's name was Charles Ruth of Louisiana.

"Don't you sass me boy, you won't like what you get," yelled Sergeant Reynolds. Taking a swig from the bottle, he turned to walk away staggering slightly.

"Ain't nuthin' but a rebel drunk. I smell your stankin' ass and breath from here." The soldier stood fast and didn't back down. The remaining black men formed a wall behind Ruth.

Throwing the bottle to the ground, Reynolds stepped toward the men. "I've had it with your type, I kept quiet long enough. You're gonna get the southern wuppin' that your types richly deserve just like you're back the plantation." Reynolds threw a punch and the soldier ducked.

"I wasn't raised on a plantation," said Ruth firing two quick rights. They connected on the sergeant's jaw, knocking him back.

"Why you shifty darky," yelled Reynolds, feeling his jaw. "You're a dead man!" The man dove wildly at the trooper and dragged him down to the ground.

Rolling around on the ground, Sergeant Reynolds overpowered the soldier. Sitting on Ruth's chest the drunken man smiled with delight and began beating the soldier's face. Ruth reached for some sand and hurled it into the sergeant's face momentarily blinding him. Ruth managed to slide out from underneath Reynolds and rose to his feet. Ruth's punches were cascading all over Reynolds' face and body; blood was now trickling from his nose. Dropping to his knees, it was apparent Reynolds was tiring. Some of the white soldiers were ready to jump in; noticing this, the colored men stepped forward.

"One on one, it's a fair fight," said the black soldiers, stepping forward. The other white soldiers held their hands up.

"No more," hollered Reynolds. "I can't take this anymore!" Ruth stopped and stepped back, with his fists still up in defense. Turning away to leave, Reynolds rose to his feet. The rebel removed a knife from behind his back, and lunged forward. BOOM!

The men scattered for cover. Behind the cloud of a smoking revolver, stood Captain Taylor. Moses and Bernard ran from their quarters after hearing the shot.

"No, Sergeant there are, no knives in a fist fight." Holstering his revolver, Taylor stared shamefully at the man. "You're a disgrace!" the Captain shouted lunging at the Sergeant and tackling the drunk to the ground.

"You sorry excuse for a soldier," yelled Taylor. His fists were pounding on the man's face. "What makes you think that you're so damn good anyway?" Trinidad and Bernard raced over and pulled the captain from the sergeant. Reynolds lay on his back bleeding profusely from the bridge of his nose. Sergeant Major O'Brien ran to the site of the altercation.

"What in the hell is going on here?" O'Brien starred in disbelief as he saw his commanding officer being held back. "Release that man right now. Sergeant Trinidad, what is the meaning of this?" Trinidad and Bernard held tightly to the officer's blouse.

"It's not their fault Sergeant Major, Reynolds's pathetic attitude pushed me over the edge." Captain Taylor wiped the dirt from his blouse. "Take this disgrace of the Army to the guardhouse. Let him sleep off his drunk!" Taylor pulled away from his restraints and retreated to his office. Ruth walked over to O'Brien and began to explain his actions. Upon hearing this news, O'Brien turned to Sergeant Reynolds. Disgust was the only thought that crossed his mind, as he looked the drunken man up and down.

"Corporal Bernard, escort this man to the guardhouse."

"You gonna let two niggers take me to the jail," cried Reynolds. "This man's army is going to hell." The two men grabbed their prisoner and began pulling him toward his cell. "Get your filthy hands off me." Bernard whirled the man around and looked him square in the face.

Placing his fingers on the chin of the sergeant, Bernard replied. "This is the last time I'm gonna tell you old man, you get your ass in the guardhouse now, or I'll put the shackles on you." Bernard withdrew his revolver and placed it in Reynolds' face. "The choice is all yours." Reynolds seethed in anger. The prisoner was placed in a cell and left to sleep off his whiskey. Bernard shut the door, and looked at Moses. "One down, and only God knows how many more."

SIX

The sun rose over the Texas sands, illuminating the horizon with glorious red, yellow, and orange colors. Wagons were being checked over to ensure that ammunition, water and supplies were ready for the trip east.

Sergeant Major O'Brien was up early, with a cup of steaming coffee in his hand, he watched the horizon's colors dance awake.

"Sergeant Major, excuse me," said Captain Taylor. Snapping to attention O'Brien saluted sharply.

"Good morning sir."

"At ease. I wanted to take this time to wish you good luck in your retirement. My only regret is that we don't have enough time to hold a formal ceremony."

"Army business always comes first. Transferring over personnel is never an easy task. These blacks will do fine, I can sense it, sir." Sergeant Major O'Brien sipped his brew. "Their sergeants are professionals, even an old mick like me knows that," said the man with a scratchy Irish accent.

The Captain extended a wrapped package to O'Brien. "This is a little token of gratitude from your fellow cavalrymen." Unwrapping the package, the Irishman stood in

57

stunned silence. Shining in the morning sun was sterling silver flask adorned with the cross sabers of the cavalry. The number 32 was engraved in bold numbers on the container.

"I, I don't know what to say sir, it's beautiful." Shaking it, he smiled again. "It's full."

"Irish whiskey," joked the officer. "I know English whiskey wouldn't do. The number 32 is for the number of years that you've given to the Army. The Cavalry is losing a fine leader." Taylor snapped to attention and saluted O'Brien. Returning the salute the sergeant welled up. "I'll leave you to your thoughts now." O'Brien turned toward the rising sun.

The morning moved on; there was a slight chill in the air. The sun had retreated behind the clouds, and the sky became overcast. A small detail of men escorted Sergeant Reynolds in shackles, to the rear wagon where he was secured. Sergeant Major O'Brien was at the head of column. The guidon bearer was behind him, followed by forty men and four wagons.

"Forward!" O'Brien waved his hand forward, and the troops headed out. Exiting the fort they were met with a wonderful sight. Lined up on both sides of the roads were the new occupants of Fort Barre; in formation and sporting their new colors. Mounted on horses in front of the group, were their non-commissioned officers Sergeant Nouba, Sergeant Trinidad and Corporal Bernard. The three soldiers saluted simultaneously bringing chills to the Sergeant Major. He returned the salute and the group proceeded east.

"Dismissed!" barked Nouba.

Watching from up on the hills was a small group of Comanche warriors on a scouting patrol.

A thin dark finger pointed to the line of soldiers departing the fort. Their faces were bronzed and aged by years in the sun, and pure anger blazed in their eyes. "Those men will pay for the deaths of our brothers at Black Bird Pass," whispered Red Wolf, a warrior of much importance in the tribe.

"Their crime is trespassing on our sacred land." Rides for the Wind was a young muscular brave with shining jet-black hair. "They do not decide where we live or where we hunt. Those soldiers will pay."

Red Wolf despised the fact that the white men were moving further into his people's land. "We wait until tomorrow. Before darkness comes they will be miles from the fort and no help will come for them. Then we will offer the "Great Spirit", the **blue uniforms** for the buffalo's return." Sliding backwards the band of men retreated into the hills.

The time passed quickly as additional assignments of reinforcing the fort were attended to. The men were given the task of rebuilding the corral and building additional room in the stables for the new horses. Rocks were being piled six feet high to reinforce the walls. The work was back breaking hot and boring. The men began to complain.

Peters walked over to the water barrel and began to chatter. "Damn, this detail is horrible! I'd rather be on those boring patrols with Sergeant Nouba." Scooping out a generous amount of water with the metal ladle, he doused himself. Corporal Bernard strode past the men.

"I don't want to hear any belly aching out of any of you. You would really be complaining if the horses get taken in the middle of the night by some Indian." The men made faces at the corporal.

"I saw that." The men stopped and looked, as the corporal continued walking not missing a beat.

Massive wooden beams were being hoisted into place to make the skeleton of a barn near the corral.

Moses walked up to Bernard. "I need you to pick two of the smartest men from the squad and have them meet me in the Quarter Master Storehouse. The captain wants that place squared away now. Who do you recommend?"

"You're talking about men that are good with numbers and such, right? I think that Pike and Davis would do." Marcus Pike and Nathaniel Davis were two former laborers from Georgia. Both the men had some schooling and were far and away more educated than the other men. Always assuming additional responsibilities, they found a home in the Army and did well at any task assigned to them.

"Send them over to me," said Moses. Bernard walked back to the detail at the corral. The two men walked over to the Quarter Master Storehouse where Sergeant Trinidad was waiting inside for them.

"Pike and Davis reporting as ordered, Sergeant."

Moses spoke. "It's come to my attention that both you men have skills in math, reading and writing. Is that true?"

"Yes Sergeant," said the men standing at attention. "We both have had some schooling."

"Good, this room is your responsibility now." Moses extended his hand around the room. Covered in dirt and dust and smelling of stale smoke and whiskey it was a disgrace. "This place is pathetic, almost as pathetic as the last man whose responsibility it was to keep this place up to snuff." Moses began pacing back and forth across the room. "Men, your task is to turn this pit back into an Army Regulation Quarter Master Storehouse, is that understood?" Both men nodded. "Inventory is the key. You will each be keenly aware of what is in stock. Detail records will be kept, and logs will accompany them. Hayes in the CO's office will have all the necessary items you will need to handle these duties. Make no mistake that there will be times when certain items will be unattainable, but this is the Army; we can do without. Also there will be times when we will need to purchase certain items from civilians. That is only to be done with the proper authorization from the CO, Sergeant Nouba or myself. Any questions?"

Davis spoke up. "Sergeant, we didn't join the cavalry to become store clerks. We want our chance to fight."

Moses raised his hand. "Rest assured that you will still be accompanying patrols from time to time. You both possess the skills to handle this task, which is most valuable to the unit at this time. This assignment also keeps you from more of the menial tasks. Most important, this room is to be locked at all times, no excuses. If there are no questions, get cracking." Trinidad exited the storeroom.

The men looked around in silence. Removing their caps and rolling up their sleeves, they got to work. "This won't be that bad," said Pike. "Winter is on its way. When the rest of the men are freezing their tails off, we'll be inside where it's dry. Besides, I could deal without being shot at."

"Guess you're right," said Davis. "Let's get the dust cleaned off this stuff and go from there." The men worked steadily for over six hours cleaning, arranging and counting things. They talked and laughed away the afternoon. The potbelly stove in the middle of the room looked in perfect order. Grabbing some wood from the bin, they soon had a nice fire roaring.

Moses and Bernard stood watching the Quarter Master Storehouse. "They haven't come out of there in hours Bernard, should we check on them?" The corporal shook his head.

"They know how to follow orders."

Inside Davis and Pike were shifting the bulk of supplies to one side of the room. "Let's check out these barrels next. I bet if we moved them to the other side of the room, there would be more space. Go slow though, they look heavy." Pike began to push on the side of the barrel. Anticipating a heavy weight, he was hurled forward as the empty barrel gave way. Davis doubled over with laughter.

"Very funny, very funny." Pike stood up and wiped the dirt from his uniform. He heard a hollow sound, as he stepped on a board. Something didn't sound right so Pike tapped his foot several times on the wood. "Davis, come over here." Kneeling down, the soldier pounded on the loose boards. A hollow space! The men removed the boards and noticed a hole with a wooden ladder descending into it. Grabbing a candle lantern, they shined the light in the hole. A tunnel! "We should get the sergeant and the corporal," said Davis. "Now!"

Both men exited the supply room and ran to where the sergeant was now standing. Moses ordered them to secure the area and said he would be right back, and then raced over to headquarters to brief Captain Taylor.

"What do you mean they found a tunnel," said Taylor. "We have no tunnel that know of." The men hurried from the office and gathered at the mouth of the hole. A crowd had formed near the supply room, hearing of the unusual findings. Bernard leaned over, gazing in amazement at the large hole.

"Let's get going and see what we have here," said Moses removing his revolver and seizing a lantern. The group descended down into the unknown.

The ladder led some ten feet down a crudely dug shaft. The tunnel opened up to five feet in width and seemed to stretch a long ways. Several candle lanterns were hung on nails, spaced out about fifteen feet apart. Pike and Davis led the detail.

"These are pretty clean; someone comes down here on a regular basis," said Pike. Lighting each one, the men continued down the tunnel. Going some distance, the air became thicker and mustier. Pike began to move ahead of the group.

"Hold up now Pike," yelled Davis. "Be careful, let me light this other lantern." Fumbling to light the hanging lantern, he dropped his matches. The room went completely dark.

"Dang!" Striking a match, Davis lit the lantern. The soldier was gone!

Davis pulled out his revolver. "Pike, Pike where the hell you at?" he yelled nervously.

"Down here," a voice moaned from the dark. Shining his lantern, Davis peeked over the lip of a hole. At the bottom lying on his backside was Pike.

"Damn, you all right?" cried Davis. The captain and the others caught up to the men.

"Yea, I'm fine!" hollered Pike. Setting his lantern down on the edge of the hole, Davis lowered himself over the side. A dugout shelving system had been set up. Supplies were stacked from top to bottom; blankets, guns, government cartridges and other items. "We got ourselves a heap a weapons down here." The men stared in disbelief.

SEVEN

"More Indians coming from the right flank!" Bullets were whining and smashing all around. Wood from the wagons shattered into bits and pieces, raining down on the men.

"Key, I need a damn key!" yelled a voice from inside the wagon. Bullets ripped through the wagons' cloth canopies. Indians were swooping down from out of nowhere. Soldiers were dying on the prairie floor, while wounded men were crying out in pain. The patrol was only a day's ride out of Fort Barre and their worst fears were coming true. Ambush!

"Sergeant Major, we're surrounded. We need help!" shouted a young soldier. The words seemed to echo for a second, as a bullet slammed into his chest and another into his head sending the man tumbling down in the tall grass.

"Son of a bitch, watch the flanks. Get ready for anythin'." O'Brien cocked back the hammer on his revolver and let a volley of bullets fly at his enemies. The U.S. Army's finest were fighting tooth and nail. The sea of Indians seemed endless. Yelling and screaming the warriors swarmed over the men. Flaming arrows pierced the wagons, setting them ablaze. Flaming bodies flew from the wreckage, while their comrades tried in vain to extinguish them with blankets.

"Get the ammunition off those wagons, now!" Men raced nervously to pull whatever boxes they could off the wagons; it was utter chaos. The Indians had breached the lines and were inside the perimeter. In the midst of the commotion, two soldiers held on to each other in fear. A young cavalryman named Thomas P. Little, held his eldest brother Henry dying in his arms. A large portion of his head had been shot away, blood and brain matter dripped from the wound. Eyes still flickering, his body trembled uncontrollably. Thomas wept quietly, amongst the raging battle.

"Mother's comin' Henry. She'll fix everything like she always done," cried Thomas gently brushing his brother's blood soaked hair. "This ain't how it's supposed to be. You're supposed to take care of me, not the other way around." Henry's lips moved but, only bloody bubbles appeared. "Don't worry none, Mother's comin', it's gunna...CRACK!!" A single shot pierced Henry's body and slammed into Thomas's chest; the blood spewed from his lips. The soldier collapsed backwards on the ground, cradling his brother's dead body. They lay in the middle of the circle, two more casualties of the battlefield. Sullivan lay frozen on the ground, his eyes fixed on the two brothers.

Monstrous booms and bangs from ammunition boxes on fire exploded in every direction. Men dove for cover behind whatever they could find. Rudolph Hines from Ohio was hit in the throat. Helplessly rolling on the ground, he held his hands around his neck as blood cascaded from the wound. Seeing the man wrenching in pain, another soldier lost it mentally.

"We're gonna have to make a break for it, ain't got no other choice!" hollered a scared soldier. The man continued firing his weapon in a fevered attempt to hit anything. Bullets were flying everywhere but where they should have, at the Indians. "It's the only way we can salvage anyone. This will be a total massacre otherwise, just like Custer." The young man bolted out of the circle and ran.

"Get back here!" screamed O'Brien. Shooting erratically the young man pedaled around in circles firing in all directions. Click! Click! Click! The carbine was out of bullets. The man dropped the weapon and ran. Noticing the deranged soldier, a warrior on horseback headed straight for the man. Instead of gunning him down, he lassoed him. The soldier tried desperately to free himself from the rope. Letting loose a war cry, the warrior slapped his horse, and the beast took off. The corporal's body smashed over the rocks and through the brush, his nightmarish cries echoing through the air.

"Son of a bitch." O'Brien looked dazed for a moment. Visions of his wife and children raced through his mind. They were waiting back east for him. Their plans of a nice home for the children seemed now to be out of reach. Settling down was the one thing that he was looking forward to most. The children shouldn't be without a father. He could see his wife, Claire's face, so sweet and innocent, recalling the time when they first met. The big tough soldier was so afraid to approach her it was comical. Making the promise that he would always take care of her was the one thought that kept him sane. O'Brien quickly regained his composure; and began to reload his sidearm.

"Sergeant Major, Sergeant Major do you hear." BANG! "Unngh!" The bullet knocked the soldier flat on his back.

"Rally by company!" yelled O'Brien. "We make a stand now, or as God is my witness we'll all be seeing the Almighty sooner than we'd like."

The men formed a hollow square and quickly began to gain some momentum. Slowing down their fire, the soldiers began to hit more targets. Sensing the tide was turning, the Indians broke off the attack and retreated into the hills.

"Alrighty lads make every shot count. Aim low!" The lapse in the fighting gave the soldiers time to regroup. Crouching low to the ground, O'Brien moved from man to man checking their conditions, passing several of his men dead in the sand.

Red Wolf and his Comanche party retreated into a raised section of rocks and began to regroup. Clacking along on the rocks, they dismounted and took cover in the cliffs. The Indians formed up and began to discuss plans for the next attacks.

"Why did we stop?" asked Red Wolf with an angered tone, clenching his fist. "We had them right where we want them, we're wasting time." Reloading the weapon with cartridges from his vest the warrior looked around at the others.

"Patience, my brother," said Rides for the Wind, raising his hand. "We have all we need right here to finish them off. Let's take our time and think things through." The Indians began preparing for the second assault. "We ride in, make several passes and break into the circle. The key is to break through their lines. Prepare to mount!" This war party wanted no soldiers to leave the plains alive!

Behind the shattered barriers the men readied themselves for another group of Indians. The only question was where would they come from?

"Buck up lads, we're not finished by a long shot. Look alive, watch for them Injuns," shouted the Sergeant Major. The men began feverishly digging shallow holes to take cover in, moving the broken wagons into makeshift barriers. Barrels that hadn't been destroyed were also used for their protection. "Pull those wounded men behind cover. They will be sure as hellfire coming in for a pass." O'Brien stared at the wounded lying in the grass. They were in terrible shape. The soldiers held their ground gallantly, but now time and the elements were wearing against them.

Winston Oliver was the closest thing to a doctor that they had. Grabbing a bundle of bandages, he began darting from one soldier to another to offer his help. Staring out, all he saw were men dying in the sun, with the smell blood on the air. One young soldier looked up with such helpless eyes. Leaning over him, Oliver pressed down on the man's chest and tried to slow the bleeding. The boy's eyes rolled over white and he died. "You'll be the first of many," whispered Oliver.

"We're gonna be all right ain't we Sergeant Major?" asked a young trooper frantically reloading his carbine. "I mean we are gonna get out of here right?" The men stared with concern at their leader.

"Aye, boyo, the good Lord would never take a fine Irish Catholic like me in me prime. Reload and get ready to defend this ground at all cost. J.D. get over here now, son." J.D. Sullivan, a Texas farmer, crawled over to O'Brien. "Can you ride bareback?

"Yes, no problem." The boy's hands shook. "Don't mind ma hands none. That just means I'm excited."

O'Brien looked into the young man's eyes. "We need a horse for this one, and all of ours have bolted. The first warrior we shoot, yer gonna grab his horse and head fer the fort. We'll swing every gun on your position; give you as much cover fire as possible. Nighttime will be settin in so there's no tellen what lies ahead, but we do know what will happen here unless we get help. Ride until yu can't ride, then ride some more. When the time comes, rest. You'll be no good to us dead."

"I dun seen the Little brothers both get shot. They were laying in each other's arms." The young man looked around in all directions.

"Don't ya wurry abut that laddy, just pay close attention and remember where ya headed and whut ya doin'. Grab some extra rounds for yur revolver. The rest of you men distribute the remaining ammunition and choose yur shots wisely." Nodding his approval, the young man readied himself for the task.

"Look alive!" The Indians came riding down the slopes hollering at fevered pitch. Arrows followed by bullets seemed to shower the soldiers. "Aim,low, ready!" O'Brien rose from behind his barrier and let loose with a series of positioned shots. The Indians were hit flush and dropped off their mounts. "J.D., get ready." An Indian came pounding toward the men; his cries grew louder and louder. Time slowed down, and the warrior seemed to be moving in slow motion. O'Brien holstered his side arm and withdrew his sword. It gleamed brightly as the soldier cut into the Indian. The red blood splashed over the bronze skin, as the body the ground hit with a thud. In that instant Sullivan leaped up, grabbed the animal and hopped on. Throwing a quick salute the man flew off into the desert on his mount, with three braves in pursuit.

"Right oblique, aim, fire!" yelled O'Brien. Soldiers popped up and fired, hitting several Indians and clearing an escape lane for the young man. "God bless ya son." The soldier headed off into the setting sun, in hopes of finding help.

Sullivan raced across the plains, his heart pounding as fast as the hooves on his horse. By his estimate they were at least a full day's ride from the fort. Would there be a patrol out? How many men would there be? The young Texan slowed down to notice that the Indians were nowhere in sight "We gotta keep going," he said stroking his horse's mane. "Giddy up now." The soldier continued riding until the glow of twilight. Sensing the horse was beginning to tire, Sullivan dismounted and began walking. Was he headed in the right direction? The trooper and the horse had covered a large distance in a short period of time. Opening his canteen he took a small swig, then he poured the water into the horse's mouth. The beast's tongue lapped up the water with passion. Sullivan cradled the animal's head. "Don't worry, we're gonna get through this, we ain't gonna be no buzzard bait." The young man stopped dead in his tracks. Voices! Indian voices! His heart began racing and his insides began to tremble.

Sullivan crept slowly around the rocky area, which overlooked a creek bank. Peering over the edge he saw an interesting sight. Leaning in the water below quenching their thirst, were two warriors. Their horses, a few hundred yards off were, drinking endlessly. Something shiny suddenly caught his eye. Against a large boulder gleaming in the late day sun were two U.S. Army carbines. The Indians wore Army blouses and headgear but he couldn't see a regiment or company number. "Thievin' sons-a-bitches." Checking the chamber of his weapon, he had only two bullets remaining. Sullivan quietly closed the chamber and cocked the hammer. Displaying stealth movement, Sullivan crept down the slope. Placing his foot on each rock and giving them a slight push to make sure they would hold his weight, the boy edged on patiently.

"Evening." The Indians whirled around quickly. The Texan stared angrily into their eyes. How did the soldier do that to us was the only thought that crossed their minds? That and the two bullets he placed precisely between their eyes. The bodies splashed almost softly into the waters and rocks. Sullivan stood over them and said nothing. He wasn't quite sure how he felt; thoughts of his dead comrades in the sand streaked through his brain. The Little brothers cradled in death was a sight he'd never forget. As he stared into the crystal creek, the waters fogged over red. Hesitating, he pulled the Indians from the water and laid them in the sand. Sullivan started stripping the bodies of all tools or weapons he could use: Water canteen, gun belt with pistol and cartridges, knives, pouches with dry meat and those two carbines. Strapping on a gun belt, he grabbed a fresh horse. Darkness was setting in, along with fatigue. "No time for sleep now," said the soldier climbing on a fresh horse. "We got men who need help."

There seemed to be no end to the stream of Indians. Like locusts they quickly engulfed the patrol, penetrating the lines. Men began fighting hand to hand.

Sergeant Major O'Brien stood tall, his sword in one hand and the revolver in the other. Fighting with a newfound sense of survival, the soldiers began overwhelming the Comanche. The Indians again retreated over the bluffs.

"Sergeant Major, why are they pulling back?" The young soldier was frantically reloading his weapon. Noticing a dead comrade lying next to him, he quickly removed the man's gun belt and grabbed the ammunition.

"They're toying with us lads. Hit and run is their tactic. Watch your ammunition. We relax a little, and then they swoop down, hit us, and head for cover. Sneaky little..... ," said O'Brien. Several other soldiers were removing ammunition and other useful items from the dead men. Extra canteens were being distributed. Wounded men first and able-bodied men second. Oliver was attempting to patch up as many men as possible. Many of the wounded were a lost cause. These Indians were good shots.

"Oliver, what is the situation?" barked O'Brien.

"I need some more bandages." The men hunted around for any clean strips of cloth that they could find, including cloth from the wagon canopies that hadn't burnt. Darkness soon began setting upon the desert. Perfect time for an ambush. The only sounds that penetrated the night air were the gentle moans of the dying and wounded. Sullivan had been gone for some six hours. Corporal Paul Crawford from Maine crawled over to the sergeant major's position.

"Sergeant Major, if we get in total darkness, we've had it. Those Comanche will come sneaking in to the position and slit our throats," exclaimed the corporal opening his side arm and reloading it.

"My thoughts, exactly boyo," barked the gritty Irishman. "What about lighting two fires on the northern part of the square? We'll be able to see clearly. My guess is that they haven't gotten behind us either. We haven't caught anything in the back." Crawford stared out into the abyss and nodded in approval.

"It's either that or we pray for a full moon and by the looks of those clouds that doesn't look to be happening. There should be enough wood from the fallen trees, brush and the wagons. Is there any coal oil around?" Crawford crawled away in search of some. O'Brien instructed the men to begin digging two holes in the sand that would hold the fires. The sounds of shovels and pickaxes permeated the air, as the men worked feverishly filling both holes with any wood or brush they could find, the men doused them with the coal oil.

"Light 'em up lads!"

Lighting the torch, the corporal ignited the brush. WHOOSH! The bright orange flames rose from the ground and began crackling in the evening breeze. Crawford scanned the area for warriors.

The temperature in the desert was beginning to drop, so keeping the wounded men warm was a chore. The dead bodies were placed face down in the sand. A gangrene stench hung on the air. One sober faced soldier was given the task of removing items from the bodies. Piles of holsters, carbines and other items were mounting up by the makeshift hospital.

"How we holding up, Doc?" asked O'Brien. "Can you save them?" Oliver glanced up from his work and gave a skeptical look to the man. His hands were soaked with blood from applying pressure to a chest wound. Placing his hands around the man's neck he felt for a pulse, nothing.

"We need to keep them warm through the night, or there is no telling how many more we could lose." Oliver stood up and walked over to another casualty lying in the sand. Dropping to his knees, he rolled the man over. Wincing, he quickly turned away. The man was dead, his mouth open and his eyes staring wildly. Oliver looked around with a lost expression and began weeping. "I, I can't save them all Sergeant Major." O'Brien grabbed the man by the shoulders.

"Take it easy now lad, sit down." The soldier muttered to himself. O'Brien felt in his blouse and removed the flask. "Here lad, have a drab". Chugging from the container, Oliver shivered. O'Brien patted him on the head gently. "We're gonna make it, boyo. You're doing a damn fine job." Taking hold of the flask himself, the gentle Irishman winked at the soldier. "Here's to swumming with bow legged women," smiled the Sergeant Major taking a big swig. The clouds that had once covered the evening sky, drifted away. Moonlight illuminated the area and stars peppered the sky. Someone up there was looking out for them.

"Thank you, God," whispered O'Brien. "You'd never let a good Irish Catholic lad like me die at the hands of Injuns." The men crouched low to the ground and prepared for the attack, but none came. They did their best to try and stay awake, but the soldiers were physically and mentally wiped out.

Daylight was beginning to peek out over the horizon. Tired, hungry, and worn out faces blackened from gunpowder and sulfur burns peered from behind makeshift barriers. Heads dropping from fatigue quickly popped up at the snap of a twig. The men chewed on dry meat and fruit from the supplies that survived. Where was Sullivan? O'Brien lay flat on his stomach, there was nothing. "Where are ya injuns at?"

"Woooooo!" Emerging from the tall grass a large party brandishing an array of weapons headed straight toward the tattered group of soldiers.

EIGHT

Trotter and Pullman were lead scouts on the morning patrol, and were some distance ahead. Stopping to glance over the territory, they peered out from behind a rocky barrier and watched the horizon. So far the morning ride had been less than eventful. "Getting colder every morning isn't it," said Pullman, pulling his collar up closer. "Bones are achin."

"Looks quiet," said Trotter, shifting to get himself comfortable on his rocky perch. "Wonder how them white boys is doin? That territory theys in is full of Injuns. Hope they don't get a whippin'. How mad do you think they'd be if we helped them out?" Since things were going smoothly Pullman decided to have a morning smoke. Packing his pipe generously, he struck a match and puffed softly on the pipe. The two soldiers joked as they scanned the territory.

A half a mile back the remaining men from the patrol sat around the fire sipping coffee and eating hard bread. Waking up on the prairie was one aspect of cavalry life that was appealing in a way. Most the men shared the same sentiment. Nouba was staring out at the horizon, as his men were finishing their morning routine and getting ready to depart.

Scouts had been out for some time and no news of unwanted individuals had been reported.

Shooter Rogers from Medford, Massachusetts appeared.

"Morning Sergeant. Where are we headed today?"

"Further into the east, Rogers," said Nouba. "Got word that some Indian warriors have been causing problem. Damn fools, if they'd just conform to the regulations that the government wants, there's no problems. They could survive longer as a people."

"We've robbed them of their lands and freedom," exclaimed Rogers. "How do you expect them to conform to these rules, when they have been here all this time." The two men stared at each other in amazement. "We should admire the fact that they're willing to risk the welfare of everything they hold near and dear to defend their way of life."

"Bull," barked Nouba. "We don't have to admire one damn thing about it. Let me tell you something young man, these people's foolish pride will be the downfall of them you mark my words. Hell, I ain't no professor or nothing, but I do know what happens when you go against the grain." Nouba got right into the soldier's face. "Custer and those white boys were just small pieces in a big puzzle. The whites have got more guns and they got men that are itching to get an Indian scalp. The simple fact is that right now these white folks run the world and when they don't want someone around, they'll be gone."

"How can you say that Sergeant? Look at us, do you think we will ever get a fair shake in the white man's army?" Rogers tossed his còffee out on the ground. "We end up doing the white man's dirty work. These Indians haven't really been doing anything that you yourself wouldn't do if they hurt your family. They're using the black man to rid the world of the red man for the white man." Nouba's jaw began to tighten up and his fists twitched.

"What the hell did you join for?"

"What else could I have done? Farming, laborer or be a servant. At least here I can have a gun on my hip. I want to do some good."

"So quick to knock the Army," smiled Nouba, turning toward the vocal man. "You need its help." Nouba pulled out his pipe and began packing it with tobacco. "This Army provides a way for people like **us** to have something that most other people never get, the choice. The choice to do right from wrong, it's very simple. My entire career in the Army I was never asked to kill a person for the hell of it." Lighting his pipe, he puffed until the smoke steadily streamed out. "The color of our skin simply scares people." The smoke from the pipe couldn't hide the tired look in his eyes. "Go collect your equipment soldier!"

* * * * * * *

As the afternoon wore on, the shattered patrol was readying for another assault. The stench of dead horses filled the air. Several men were overcome and began throwing up. Winds began kicking up and showered the wagons with sand, snuffing out the flames. Cries of the wounded filtered through the winds. "Motherrr… mommma…God please!" Flies and insects buzzed over gaping wounds on the bodies. This was war in all its glory.

"Damn wind!" hollered O'Brien. "The one time I need smoke in the sky, it gets blown out. Are you testing me, God?" he cried, raising his fist in the air. Corporal Cyril Riggs crawled over to O'Brien.

"How you doing Sergeant Major?" inquired Riggs his eyes crisscrossing the terrain.

"Fine boy'o. Bet ya ain't seen a fight like this in ya posh New Yak settings." O'Brien laughed loudly. Corporal Riggs was a rich kid from New York who had joined up to escape his overbearing folks; he was a surprisingly good soldier and listener.

"I can't see them anywhere," said Riggs quietly. "I smell their sweat in the wind. My guess is that they're lying behind those rocks, there." He pointed to a small grouping near the high brush a few yards off in the distance. "They have to cross that large patch of no man's land; that's to our advantage." O'Brien tightened his grip on his revolver.

A small group of Comanche warriors crawling low to the ground jumped up and headed straight toward the soldiers. Their cries chilled the insides of even the most battle-hardened soldier. Grabbing Corporal Riggs by the blouse O'Brien pulled him down to the ground. Firing two shots, the veteran soldier dropped them to the ground with a thud.

"Action front!"

Whooping and hollering more Indians returned for another strike. Biting their lips O'Brien and Riggs cocked the hammers back on their revolvers. One young soldier, who was fishing through the wreckage, came across a wonderful discovery. "Whoa, dynamite!" Sergeant Major O'Brien's eyes lit up.

"Get over here now. You other boys cover him," cried O'Brien. "Volley fire. Ready, aim, fire!" The soldiers let loose a serious volley of gunfire. The young man crawled over to O'Brien. "Corporal, take these sticks and cover the right flank. We'll cover this side. Get moving and keep your heads down. If we throw these every so often, we will save bullets." O'Brien struck a match and lit the fuse. That joyous crackling sound was like music to the men's ears. Hurling the stick towards his enemies, it made a thunderous roar. BOOM! The Indians seemed to be lifted off the ground before his eyes. The bodies or what was left of them hit the ground with a thud. Cheers rang out from the soldiers.

"Hooray! Hooray! Thatta boy Sergeant Major." Seizing a dynamite stick in one hand, Corporal Riggins and another soldier lit the fuse. Getting a running start, they aimed it for the next group of attacking Indians. BOOM! The dynamite exploded prematurely. They were blown apart in the blink of an eye, as debris from the soldiers' bodies sprayed all over. O'Brien's jaw dropped as he stared in disbelief. There was a small crater where the men once stood. The remaining Indians froze on the battlefield.

"Hills, go back to the hills," cried Rides for the Wind. Leaping on to his mount, the warrior began directing his men. "Go back! Go back!" The Indians grabbed their wounded and scampered quickly into the hills. Prowling Gray Wolf and Red Wolf reared their horses to the right and began fleeing towards the hills.

"We've got them on the run boys," yelled O'Brien. "Open fire on em!" A small grouping of soldiers began to fire at Red Wolf's position. A hail of bullets hit one of the horse's legs, sending it crashing to the earth, pinning its rider. Red Wolf sat up from his position behind the dead animal's body and continued firing on the soldiers.

"He's pinned down by the horse boys, he ain't going nowhere," shouted O'Brien running towards his position. "Cover me lads." Coming slowly up to the dead animal, he peered over its body. Waiting on the side was Red Wolf and his gun. CLICK! "Miss fire!" Staring straight into the Indian's eyes, O'Brien waited, and then slowly pulled back the trigger. The Indian clinched his teeth. BANG! Wasting no time, the burly Irishman returned to his position.

* * * * * * *

The scouts trotted along quietly in the morning sun. The point rider stared out across the sands. Someone or something was headed their way and kicking up a cloud of dust.

"We gots company," said Trotter motioning to Pullman. Grabbing the weapon from his bag, he climbed down from his horse. "Can't make out who they is. I'm gonna fetch the sergeant, cover me." The soldier galloped back towards the patrol to report the findings. Trotter leaned against the tree and set his sights on the rider. "Who the hell is ya friend?" The image rode closer and closer. Seeing the black riding boots, pale blue trousers and regulation blouse it had to be a soldier. One rider, that has to mean trouble.

Sullivan's eyes burned from the sand and the salt from his sweat. He noticed a wonderful sight ahead, Buffalo Soldiers.

"Yooooo. Over here," hollered Trotter, waving his hat. "Over here!" The rest of the patrol had caught up to the scout.

"What's the commotion," asked Nouba. "Is there trouble?" Trotter pointed to the lone rider coming their way.

"He's white, Sergeant. Could be from the patrol that left a day ago." The man rode toward the soldiers; unable to stay in the saddle the exhausted man fell from his mount. The horse was extremely tired and was foaming at the mouth. The soldiers rushed to the soldier's aid.

His fellow soldiers knelt down beside him. "Sullivan, 4th Troop." His throat was burning.

"Canteen, now," said Nouba. The man drank in gulps. "Slow down son, tell us what's happening." One of the colored soldiers removed his hat. Filling it with water he placed it under the horse's mouth. The beast lapped the water passionately.

"Patrol was ambushed, several hours ride from here one hundred or more from a war party. The Sergeant Major had me ride for help. They're kicking our tails, heavy casualties."

"Are you strong enough to ride? Do you remember where they are?"

"Yes, Sergeant they shouldn't be hard to find," coughed the young soldier. "The wagons were on fire and the smoke should give us a perfect marker. I've been riding steady for hours." One soldier handed the boy a biscuit, which he devoured instantly.

"Patrol, prepare to mount," barked Nouba. The soldiers helped the young man up onto his horse. Sullivan swayed back and forth in the saddle. "There are soldiers who need help. Ready forward!" The men began a time sensitive ride toward their comrades. Would they be in time? Would the ghosts of General Custer's men haunt another patrol? These questions plagued the entire group, as they rode hard to their brothers and the hours passed on.

Gunshots and loud explosions echoed over the prairie. Screams of the dying pierced the air. Pounding hoof beats shook the earth as the first scout slowed down at the top of the hill. From his perch on the hill, Nouba could see Indians had the patrol completely surrounded, and it looked almost over. Clouds of dust were being kicked up in all directions engulfing both soldiers and savages.

Nouba withdrew his sword. "Char-r-r-rge!" The bugle sounded the command, and the patrol swept forward over the lip of the hill. It sounded like the earth was coming apart at the seams. What it must have looked like, some could have only imagined. Their uniforms like blue streaks sailing over the plains with gleaming metal rattling at their sides. The amount of time between crossing no man's land and being in the thick of the battle seemed like seconds. Leaping from their mounts, the soldiers attacked the Indians. The fight that some had waited all their lives for was on. Carbine butts collided with chins. Broken teeth flew from Indian lips as black skin crossed bronze skin. Kicking up dust, one couldn't tell friend from foe, white or black from red. Men wrestled in hand-to-hand combat. .

Elmer Danzig was wrestling with a much larger warrior. Gaining the upper hand the Indian removed a tomahawk from his belt and swung at the man. Danzig swung his carbine in front of his chest and the stock and barrel of the gun took the brunt of the first blow. It sent an odd feeling rippling through his arms. The second blow tagged Danzig on the jaw and knock him out cold. The warrior leaped on his chest and grabbing a handful of Danzig's hair began yelling.

Nelly Dobbs, a preacher's son from Mississippi, tackled the Indian to the ground. Dobbs slid the shining blade of his knife slowly across the bronze neck, discarding the body in disgust. Grabbing Danzig by the shoulders, Dobbs pulled the man under the wreckage of a wagon. Then he picked up his revolver and wasted no time returning to the battle.

Sergeant Nouba rode into the pack masterfully working the reigns on his horse; he moved the beast's head back and forth as his sword slashed through the fight. It was if he was untouchable, every Indian that came near was cut down in an instant.

"Thank yu lordy," said O'Brien rising from behind his barrier. Shaking his fists in the air he began to yell. "Ya bastards you'd never take me...THUNK!" The force from the arrow's impact sent the big Irishman crashing into a barrel and to the ground. Prowling Gray Wolf pulled his horse's head to the left and headed toward the man. Another warrior leaped on top of the Irishman. A quick blast from his pistol and the first Indian tumbled off O'Brien's chest. Prowling Gray Wolf leaped from his mount onto the sergeant major's chest and began twisting the arrow.

"Iiiieeerreggh!" Letting out a bear-like roar, the sergeant major swung wildly at the Indian, striking him down with his revolver. O'Brien rolled on to the ground in complete agony. Twitching from any muscles sent ripples of agonizing pain through his body. Prowling Gray Wolf picked up a broken branch from a tree and swung at O'Brien. The sergeant major tried desperately to lift his arm to avoid the next blow but the pain was too much. He could only wince and brace himself for the impact; it hit him square in the chest. It felt as if someone had taken the breath from his body; gasping for air he dropped down. Removing his tomahawk the Indian turned toward the wounded man. He placed his knee on O'Brien's chest and reached down for a handful of hair.

Pullman steadied himself in the saddle and fired a perfect shot with his weapon. The Indian's arm fell to his side and dropped to his knees. The second shot ripped a large hole through the savage's back dropping him face down in the dust. Spurring his horse, the Buffalo Soldier immediately rode to the left flank to secure the area.

Rides for the Wind watched his friend die and stared in disgust. From a distance away two bullets pierced the Indian's shoulder, throwing him from his mount. Rides for the Wind hung on for dear life as the horse bucked once and darted off into the foothills, dragging its wounded master.

"The Sergeant Major is down," yelled Pullman, waving his hands. "Get some help over here now." Two white soldiers tried to lift the heavy man and were cut down instantly by Indian rifle fire.

A warrior on horseback started straight for O'Brien. Crouching low to the ground Pullman waited as the Indian came near. Using his gun at close range the soldier smashed the butt of the weapon into the warrior's chest. The Indian was hurled backwards and crashed into the brush. The young soldier stood over his man with the gun pointed squarely in his chest. The Indian began mumbling something as the blood trickled slowly from his mouth. "Too late for you now Injun." BANG! BANG! The young man popped two quick shots as the warrior's body jerked on the ground. The boy stood there in silence as all hell raged around him. Looking for his next target, the trooper dove back into the fight. The Buffalo Soldiers fought with military precision and with fevered ambition. Realizing that the sure victory was slipping from their hands, the Indians decided to retreat back into the foothills.

"Hooray! Hooray!" came the cheerful cries from the soldiers as they waved their hats over their heads.

"Attack the retreating Indians!" shouted Sergeant Nouba, placing his sword back in its sheath. Removing his pistol, he began firing off round after round. "Corporal, don't let them get away." The Buffalo Soldiers mounted up and gave chase into the hills after the Indians. Seeing that their horses had bolted, some of the Indians tried to escape on foot. Soldiers had surrounded the fleeing Indians in a circle formation with guns aimed at the ready.

"What do we do with em'?" asked Cooke on horseback swaying nervously back and forth with his carbine pointed at them. Foster and Pullman galloped to the head of the pack joining Corporal Crawford. The Indians pointed their weapons in a defensive position and stood silently as more soldiers arrived.

"Don't be foolish," said Corporal Crawford with his weapon pointed straight between the eyes of a Comanche brave. The Indians stood tensely, knowing full well what awaited them. They would never choose the white man's jails. One brave made the fatal error of cocking back the hammer of his rifle.

"Fire! Fire! Fire!" The angered soldiers let loose a huge barrage of gunfire on the outnumbered Indians and dropped them in the grass and rocks.

"Cease fire!" yelled Corporal Crawford. Climbing off his mount, he removed his pistol. "Search the bodies and keep what you want." The men swarmed over the Indians, removing everything, leaving the bodies in a pile.

Sergeant Major O'Brien lay peacefully against a broken wagon wheel. The arrow that was imbedded deep in his chest was covered in blood. Oliver was vainly applying pressure to the wound. Nouba bent down beside the big Irishman and noticed his shattered arm.

"Damn Comanche," coughed O'Brien. "Ruined me bloody retirement." The man coughed violently. "The boy, Sullivan, he should receive a letter of commendation. Good

Irish lad." Staring into the sky, he muttered. "I'm comin' to ya Lordy."

"Lay still now, O'Brien," smiled Nouba uneasily. "You're gonna be all right. Besides you're too ugly to die." The men chuckled quietly together. Nouba gently patted the Irishman's leg. O'Brien removed the silver flask from his blouse.

"Join me in a drink mate," hacked O'Brien. Putting the flask to his lips he drank, the whiskey burning his cut lip. He extended the flask to Nouba; the sergeant took it and drank. O'Brien's hands began to shake. Dropping the flask Nouba, grabbed the hand of the Irishman as he coughed violently. "CCClairrre", hack.. "CCCClairre." Hack, "tell her I lo-ove herrrrr...." The life drained quietly from the massive Irishman as he lay in the arms of the Buffalo Soldier. Nouba placed his hand on O'Brien's face and gently pulled his eyelids down. The man everyone had come to respect was now gone. The little silver flask lying unnoticed in the grass.

Rides for the Wind had lost a lot of blood, but his horse had managed to flee through the foothills and head west. Barely alive, he rode into the hidden village several hours later. The warrior fell from his mount into the tall grass. The women in the village tended to his wounds.

The smoke and the dust subsided with time leaving behind only scorched earth and shattered remains. The soldiers walked amidst the remains of the patrol looking for survivors. Hands of the wounded would reach out for comfort and reassurance. Bodies of the dead Indians were laid out rows. Wounded soldiers were carried to the makeshift hospital area. Oliver and others worked desperately to control the bleeding. Some men were beyond help; they were simply waiting to die. Sifting through the remains of the supply wagons was quite a task. Two of the four wagons were still intact; these would be used to transport the dead and wounded.

The soldiers began gathering around the back of a burned out wagon. A body hung over it. Rogers poked at the body with his weapon. Nouba watched as a brown bottle slide from the corpse and shattered on the ground. It was Sergeant Reynold's remains. "Guess he ended up **black,** in the end," smiled Rogers.

Indian casualties numbered ninety plus killed, none taken prisoner. The white soldiers losses numbered thirty dead, two seriously injured and one missing. The patrol was a failure. Buzzards began circling the sky above. The soldiers placed the bodies of the Indians into a massive shallow grave, covering them with dirt and rock. Horses that had been killed were dragged to the ravine and pushed over. Several others were discovered grazing and were retrieved.

Corporal Crawford took a small detachment of men a mile or so out into the desert, in hopes of finding the missing corporal alive. Their attempt, though noble, produced only a cap and some tattered garments. The man was never seen nor heard from again.

Nouba gathered his men around. "Men, may I be the first to say your actions today were of the highest caliber. Yet, there is much left to do. The big question is, do we bury the bodies here or take them with us?" The men looked around at the area. Custer's troops were buried at the spot of their massacre.

"This ain't no place to bury a soja," said one man standing at the rear of the pack. "They need to be with others like' em, back at the cemetery on da hill." They all nodded with approval and began the ugly task of loading the dead soldiers on the wagons. This along with numerous other jobs would take them into dusk.

"Sergeant Nouba, Rogers has something he wants to show you," said Corporal Crawford. Nouba walked over to where Rogers and several men stood over a pile of weapons.

"What's the problem, here, Rogers," asked Nouba with a curious look. "Make sure we have the flanks covered effectively, men!"

"Well sarge these da weapons we dun rounded up so far," said the soldier holding up a gun. "Brand spanking new."

"What the hell is so odd about that, Rogers?"

"Sir, these ain't our guns, deys from da Injuns." The men stared down at the pile of weapons in the grass. Nouba stood with a look of confusion on his face.

The men began to secure the area and set fires for the night. Guards were posted in every corner of the makeshift camp. "We have a sufficient enough force to repel anything they could throw at us now," said Nouba. Men began to water and feed the horses. Plans were made to hitch four per wagon; there was a lot of dead weight to pull.

Winston Oliver had done all he could for his men; he sat in the grass emotionally and physically spent. The blood of his comrades was thick and dry between his fingers.

"C'mon boy, let's get you cleaned up," said a deep Negro voice. Cleetus Ray a former Georgia servant held out his hand. "C'mon now." He gently picked up the young man and led him over to the fire. The big man hummed to himself as he slowly began washing the trooper's hands. The cloth turned a cranberry color because of all the blood. Cleetus Ray smiled pleasantly while he wrung out the cloth. Oliver said nothing, just stared into the fire. After he dried his hands Oliver was led to the area where the white troopers were sleeping. As soon as his head hit the ground, Oliver was out.

Corporal Crawford had made a makeshift tent out of some ripped cloth from the wagons; he propped them up with pieces of wood staked in the ground. Removing his ammunition belt and boots he dropped to his knees and clasped both hands together in prayer. "Lord, I don't know why you saved me but thanks. I'm sure I don't deserve it." Crawling beneath the tent he pulled his blanket up close to his chest, and lay motionless. From a hole in the cloth he stared out at the star covered sky. How peaceful he thought. Does anyone know that they fought a battle here today? Crawford gazed at the stars, when only ten feet away lay his fallen comrades. Exhaustion crept over the man like a fog and slumber set in. A peaceful breeze blew across the plains. Nouba checked and double-checked all the sentry posts before he lay down. The men sat by the fires enjoying hot coffee, a good pipe and stories of their first major victory.

"C'mon boy, time to go," said a deep voice. Oliver squinted as he woke and covered his face with his hands. The sun had come up. The weathered face of Lucas Ray was smiling a toothy grin. "Time to head back to the fort."

"Yes sir," said Oliver, sitting up quickly. Wiping the sleep from his eyes, he took a slug from his canteen. Looking around, he noticed the rest of the patrol was preparing to mount up.

"Here, take this horse if you like," said Corporal Crawford pulling a brown horse by the reins. "I didn't think you would want to ride with those guys." Crawford pointed to the wagons containing the bodies of dead men. Flies made annoying buzzing sounds as they landed on the bloody corpses.

"I think riding will be all right, thanks." Oliver patted the horse on the head. "A whiskey would also be all right".

Crawford grinned with delight. "When we get home, it's a promise."

Nouba rode to the head of the patrol, turning back quickly to glance at the site of the attack. Bloodstained grass and burnt wagon remains littered the ground, along with empty shell casings. "Ready forward!" The remaining men of the shattered patrol and the Buffalo Soldiers headed home. Lying in tall prairie grass gleaming in the sunlight was the little silver flask.

NINE

Captain Taylor climbed down into the dug out area to check out his man. "You all right, Pike?" asked Taylor. The young man was holding his head.

"Damn," cried Pike. Taylor gazed at the wound.

"Davis," said the officer. "Run back up there and grab some men to help fetch Pike." The Captain stared in disbelief at the ammunition and weapons. "Sergeant Trinidad, get down here and look a this." Moses and Bernard hopped down to look at the stash. They stared in amazement.

"There is no way in hell that drunk, sonava bitch moved all this without any help," said Bernard. Moses was crouched down looking for any markings on the crates.

"This, this is just insane. Sergeant Reynolds is a thieving piece of dirt," barked Taylor. "My god, there's enough weapons and ammunition to invade Mexico." Bernard opened the crates. Eight brand new carbines shone in the lantern light.

"These are new, ain't been used." Bernard pulled one from the case. "Whoee, this sure is sweet."

"Haven't been used," said Moses with a grin. "These were meant for other outfits. Look!" Moses pointed toward the markings of the 5th and 8th Infantry Regiments. "I don't

88

remember any shipments coming in since we've arrived, and why would they be marked for different units?"

"You wouldn't remember Sergeant, that was a little before your time," said Taylor. "The day of my arrival to this post there was a shipment of guns meant for those two particular units that was robbed." The officer glided his hands over the dust-covered cases. "That was over nine months ago. The units have since moved on, and the guns were considered a loss. Headquarters will be quite happy with the discovery I'm sure." Moses climbed up from the hole. Additional men arrived to assist with removing Pike.

Moses began to wander a little further down the tunnel until he noticed something a bit odd. "Hayes, come over here and stay on your right side." The young man walked side step cautiously over to where Moses stood. "Take a look on the ground over there, tell me what you see."

Bending down on one knee, Hayes noticed **footprints**! "Well, I'll be." The soldier walked up beside the prints and glided his hand over them. "Two sets. One U.S. Army regulation boots, the other is a moccasin."

Hearing this news, the captain rolled his eyes back and gasped. "My god!"

"Someone took a lot of time and effort to do all this, so it's a good bet that they'll probably be back for these weapons soon," said Moses. "My guess is if we set a trap, someone or something will fall right in it."

"One thing we should do is find out just how far and to where this tunnel leads," said Bernard. The group proceeded about another hundred yards down. A few boards covered up the exit. Slowly removing the wood, they were able to get a view of their surroundings. The base of the tunnel was down by the shallow creek bank that ran along the fort's northern side. Covered by clumps of large brush, it was almost undetectable by the human eye, and with the water running it muffled all sounds.

"Well, my guess is that we post a guard in the Quarter Master Storehouse until further notice. Nighttime would be the most logical time for them to attempt to steal the weapons," said Taylor. "If any one finds these men, we do the best we can to try and take them alive. Also, we are going to remove half of the guns and secure them in our powder room. If something was to go wrong, at least we have some of the rifles retrieved. Leave the empty cases."

"Good idea sir." The soldiers lined up one after another and began handing the weapons off to each other.

"Sergeant, the magazine is to be locked and guarded, with no exceptions." The captain climbed out of the hole, then leaned over and extended his hand to Moses. "Let's start working on a plan. This is uh…going to take some time," said the officer, while hoisting the man up. The two soldiers retreated to the office. Darkness would soon be setting in.

* * * * * * *

The ride back was made in silence. Nouba and the others leered blankly ahead. The lonely wagons bouncing and jerking across the dry earth was the only sound. Faces were drawn and told of the horror that they had endured. They had avoided a total massacre so they were lucky. It was beginning to get dark and the men were growing weary. Off in the distance they could make out the silhouette of the fort's buildings against a blood red sky.

A lone sentry paced in the twilight. "Patrol returning!" That's odd when they left yesterday they had no wagons. Sergeant Nouba signaled to Hayes who had just emerged from the chowhall.

"What's going on, Sergeant?"

"We found what was left of the departing patrol; they were ambushed. Go get the captain," said Nouba, climbing down from his horse. Hayes ran to the office. "All right everyone listen up, we got wounded here, let's go!"

Captain Taylor and Sergeant Trinidad had been working at the desk, when the door burst open. "Sir, we got more trouble. Sergeant Nouba just returned with what he said is the remains of 4th Troop, San Antonio Patrol. Comanche hit them. It looks bad." The men raced from the office into the compound.

You probably could hear the officer's stomach hit the ground. The color drained from his face as he walked slowly to the wagons like a frightened child. He pulled back a ripped section of canvas, which revealed its horrific sight. Bodies were stacked like bags of grain. Uniforms tattered and blood stained, holding together only shattered remains. The officer stared with a blank look on his face. Nothing, he felt nothing inside this time. The minutes slowly passed.

"Sir, sir we should get the men off loaded and inside," said Sergeant Trinidad, wiping his mouth on his sleeve. Captain Taylor stood frozen. "Sir?"

"Yes, of course," he replied in a somber tone. Corporal Bernard went over to the chow hall, and opened the front door.

"Patrol ambushed, let's look alive and help out," he shouted. Clanging and banging of dishes and crockery was heard, as men leaped from the tables and hurried outside. Captain Taylor stared straight ahead. "Sergeant Nouba, your report, if you will," said the young man in a sobering tone.

"Well, sir, early this morning our scouts came across Sullivan. The young man was exhausted from riding for several hours straight. He informed us that the patrol had been ambushed and were taking casualties at an alarming rate. It would only be a matter of time before they would get overrun. We mounted up quickly and double-timed it to the area. Upon our arrival on the bluffs overlooking the site, we noticed a large number of hostiles engaging the patrol. I gave the order to charge. We hit them with everything we had and beat them back. We secured the area and gave chase to the fleeing hostiles. Numerous soldiers were dead by this time. We offered assistance to the wounded. More men died overnight; some of their wounds were just too serious. The Sergeant Major was alive when we got there. He had an arrow stuck in his chest; there wasn't much that I could do, sir. Oliver, Dobbs and Sullivan along with Corporal Crawford should be commended. They performed their duties in the highest tradition of the United States Cavalry."

"Fine report," said the officer. "Very precise and detailed. I wish to commend you and your men for an exceptional job on the field of battle. If you hadn't come along, there surely would have been a total massacre. There will be certificates of merit and possibly more." He extended his hand to Nouba.

"Begging the Captain's pardon, but there was one thing that struck me as odd. Those Indians had as much weapons as any military patrol. We retrieved over eighty guns from their dead."

"I'll bet I know," said Moses. "We've had a pretty interesting discovery since your departure yesterday, Sergeant Nouba. First, let's get these men tended to and have the rifles secured."

Moses and Nouba watched in sorrow as the remains of the white soldiers were removed from the wagons. They were to be placed in a storage barn for the evening. Some corpses stared madly at the heavens, while others seemed peaceful in their slumber. Doc Ames was gently tending to the wounds and wrapping the bodies in sheets. A young soldier was removing the tattered garments.

"That was supposed to be me," said a voice. Moses turned around. Hayes was standing in the doorway of the barn. "I was supposed to be with them, if it hadn't been for you, Sergeant Trinidad. I owe you." The boy moved without emotion among the bodies.

Nouba stood back and spoke quietly. "Haven't seen this many dead white boys since New Market Heights."

The piles of ripped garments, boots, belts and other items were growing higher. The guidon lay among the blood stained uniforms, Moses bent down to pick it up. He stood there holding the flag and staring out the window. Outside Captain Taylor looked lost, while staring silently in the night. The sergeants both exited the structure.

Taylor noticed the men coming towards him. "This is going to drive the brass back in Washington out of their minds when they hear about this one," said Captain Taylor, playing with some pebbles in his hand. "We'll have every bounty hunter and Indian killer in the West coming in to settle the score. Not to mention the fact that the San Antonio fort will not be receiving their replacements." He threw the rocks as far and as hard as he could. "This job is going to age me several years before I'm through with it."

"Unfortunately sir, that is exactly what will be occurring. That's why I think we need to use a little surprise ourselves." Moses walked up to the broken wagons. "We gotta find out where they're hiding and hit the Indians with a quick shot," he said with a determined look. "What do you think Nouba?"

"I'm trying to understand how they could have had all those guns?" Moses snapped his fingers quickly.

"My apologies Nouba for not remembering to fill you in on our little discovery. Please follow the captain and myself." The men walked over to the supply depot, where two armed guards were standing watch. Removing a key from his blouse, Moses unlocked the door and proceeded inside. Striking a match, he lit several lanterns. The glow from the flickering lights danced against the wooden walls. "It seems we have some rather large mice that have been scurrying about," he said, pulling back the wooden board to reveal the opening. Nouba's eyes lit up with astonishment.

"The tunnel runs a distance down to a dug out storage area, where a large cache of weapons was discovered. We believe these to be the missing weapons from late last year. We do know that Sergeant Reynolds was a major player in these thefts. He didn't by chance survive?" asked the captain.

Nouba rolled his eyes in frustration. "No sir, burned alive, still in the shackles."

"Well revenge is a dish best served cold. His was apparently a little warmer than most," chuckled the captain. "Sergeant Trinidad has come up with a recommendation on how to give the Indians a taste of their own medicine. The plans are back in my office. First, I think a letter needs to be drafted to Regimental Headquarters about this incident with the San Antonio patrol. I plan to refrain from informing them about our little discovery seeing as how we've recovered the guns. You men get your rest and we'll get cracking on this in the morning." The group covered up the hole and left the building.

Most of the excitement had died down. The wounded were being tended to, and all the bodies had been removed. The two wagons from the ambush were left in the middle of the compound. The tattered and blood stained cloth flapped in the breeze. Captain Taylor walked slowly up to the wreckage and placed his hands upon the wooden rails.

"Corporal Bernard," called the officer in a disgusted tone.

"Yes sir," snapped the soldier.

"Take these two wagons out behind the fort and burn them! Is that understood?" The man leaped to action. Bernard grabbed some men and they quickly hitched up the wagons and hauled them to the rear section of the fort. The broken down wagon carcasses were pushed into a sandy ditch, doused with kerosene and set on fire. The flames seemed to climb straight to the heavens. The fire crackled and popped as the men watched in silence. Captain Taylor retreated quietly to his office.

Hayes had lit a fire, warming the room and bathing Taylor in an orange light. Grabbing the poker, he played with the glowing embers in the fireplace. He poured a whiskey from his hidden bottle and sat down in his chair feeling like he'd aged a hundred years. Rolling the crystal glass between his fingers the captain drank in gulps. It was time to write to Washington.

September 29th, 1879
Commanding Officer
9th U.S. Cavalry
Department of War United States Army
Washington, D.C.

Report on status of patrol dispatched from Fort Barre over two days ago. Patrol ambushed. Help arrived from the 9th Cavalry avoid total loss of life.

Cavalry losses number thirty confirmed dead, seven wounded and one soldier missing in the action. Two officers killed and non-commissioned officer also killed. Names of the three individuals are listed below:

2nd Lieutenant Judson Henry McAllister of Hartford, CT.
2nd Lieutenant King Adrian Brandon of Manchester, NH.
Sergeant Major Shamus Flynn O'Brien of Boston, Ma.

Recommendation for Commendations for the following men for "Conspicuous Gallantry Above and beyond the call of duty".

James D. Sullivan 4th Cavalry
Winston Oliver 4th Cavalry
Paul Crawford 4th Cavalry
Lucious Potter 9th Cavalry
Edwin Pullman 9th Cavalry

Will await word. Until then, patrols will be dispatched as normal.

The young officer was exhausted, mentally wiped out. Letting the pen drop to the pad, he silently drifted off into slumber. The embers crackled and popped in the stone fireplace.

Moses lit a fire behind the barracks, his usual nightly routine. His body sunk like a stone into a chair. Jotting down a few notes in his journal, he put down his pen and stared deep into the flames. Flashes of the dead men's faces were dancing amongst the blaze.

"Helluva night." Bernard appeared from the dark and pulled up a chair. Moses could only look over and nod his head in agreement. They didn't speak again.

Morning came, flames from the smoldering wagons were slowly dwindling. A thick stale air drifted about. A patrol would be saddling up for a twenty-mile ride. Corporal Bernard was placed in charge, with a force of ten men. "Do we stay out overnight, or do we patrol and come back by dusk?"

"Do what you think needs to be done," replied Moses. "We shouldn't alter the plans too much, then they think that they have us where they want us. Make sure that everyone has their eyes and ears open. The last thing that we need is more casualties. Don't try to be a hero." Trinidad gave his man a pat on the shoulder. "Now get going."

"All right men, make sure your weapons are loaded and are at the ready," barked Bernard. "These bastards are still out there and it's only gonna be a matter of time before they slip up. Ready forward!" The ten-man patrol galloped out of the fort entrance and into the territory.

Bernard was as skilled a soldier as there was. The men were well aware of what had happened to their comrades; they would not be caught in the same trap. Scouts were sent the normal distance ahead, yet keeping the main body of the patrol in constant sight. The day passed on without much excitement; no hostile sightings at all.

Word of the Indian attack on the white soldiers was already spreading through the town. Most people were furious at the thought of the white soldiers being sent out on such dangerous patrols. Under their breath people even thought that the more dangerous or life threatening patrols should be given to the blacks, for they were of less worth.

The sounds of pick axes and shovels cracking into the hard dry earth could be heard almost all day. The men stood back and stared at an almost surreal sight: thirty open hollow graves dug out of the Texas earth.

The patrol had covered twenty miles on horseback that day. Temperatures were beginning to drop, and dusk was setting in. Hopefully the Indians would be in shelters for the night. Corporal Bernard's group had decided to stop at the watering hole near an old church. It was a decent area to bed down for the night. The building was once home to a small group of missionaries that had come some years ago in hopes of educating the Indians. The monks had built the structure and were teaching there when they were attacked one evening by a group of renegade outlaws. They were beaten and murdered. The church, after being robbed, was set ablaze. All that remained, was the steeple and a burnt out courtyard area with some poorly thatched structures.

"All right, let's do a quick sweep of the area for hostiles," said Bernard, withdrawing his sidearm. Dismounting, the men split up into small groups of threes and began looking into every crevice of the structures.

"Damn, looky likin the churches back home where I from," said one soldier. "Burnt!" The group stared in awe. Stepping into the burnt out rubble, they looked up through the roofless structure. The steeple looked impressive against the dark and star covered night. "Still pretty though."

"Area secure, let's begin setting up camp for the night," barked Bernard, removing the saddle from his horse. Saddles were near and dear to each man in a different way. They say that choosing the right saddle is like choosing the right woman. You need the perfect one. Each cavalryman kept his saddle, along with his carbine, within arm's reach. The men began to set up there camp for the night. Small fires were lit in the structures for warmth; coffee pots appeared ready for brewing. Hardtack was the entrée for the evening. The horses were secured, and guards were put in place. Men wrapped themselves up in blankets and drifted off into slumber. Seated by a cozy little fire in the corner of the courtyard, sat Corporal Bernard with a young soldier.

"You been in this army long time, Corporal?" asked the curious youngster, sipping on a cup of coffee. The boy was startled as an animal cried in the night. "What the hell was that?'

"Just a wolf, and yes it has been a long time since '63, the campaigns with young Colonel Shaw." Bernard picked his teeth with a blade of grass. "Bravest group of men that I've ever seen. I still can see them running down the beach." By the light of the fire you could see his eyes welling up and a single tear run down his face. Removing a cloth from his trousers, Bernard wiped his eyes. Embers crackled and popped in the air. The young man stared through the flames.

"How'd you get dat scar on yur face? I don't thinkn' shaven dun give you that cut," said the young man, standing to stretch his back. Bending down he refilled his cup.

"Got that from a confederate, years back." The young man's eyes lit up in excitement.

"Johnny Reb gave you dat? Tell me how it happened Corporal." The kid sat up and looked straight into Bernard's eyes.

Reaching down to pour himself a cup of coffee, Bernard began to speak. "It was right after the Confederates had surrendered. There were many bands of rogue rebels running loose causing all sorts of problems, looting and pillaging the civilian population across the Mason Dixon Line. Black soldiers were used to root out bands of criminal confederates, and escort certain military and civilian dignitaries.

Moses and I by then had been transferred outside the Maryland area. We had been placed under the direct control of a Major Francis B. Gottenmeyer. This man could back himself into a corner of a circle shaped room. Never understood how he got command. Well, the good major was able to stumble us right into a battle where we were outnumbered around five to one. Needless to say after suffering a substantial number of dead and wounded men, we were captured. The major was one of the lucky ones; he was killed on the field of battle. We were taken prisoner, and shipped down south towards the Libby Prison, Richmond with a few other men. Since the Confederate Army had limited manpower we were placed under little security. Animals received better treatment than we did. White or black it didn't matter we were Union soldiers and that was reason enough to treat us like dirt. The train car was in horrible condition with dirty hay covering the urine and feces laden car. The stench was unbearable. The only plus about the cattle cars was that they had several holes in them so while we were moving the odor carried out. The wounded men that survived the initial battle never made it off that train alive. Complications arising from infected wounds killed off several more men." Corporal Bernard felt a chill race through his body; he took a swig from his cup. "Moses and I, because we were black got the job of disposing of the bodies. The rebels ordered us to throw them off the moving train. One night we tossed off seven corpses."

"I can recall one night in particular I tried to nudge awake a soldier who was almost lying on top of me. Rolling him over we discovered maggots crawling in his open wounds. Scared the hell out of me. We never did get rid of that body until the following morning, tossed him over the side somewhere. Finally after several days aboard the train, they let us out." Removing his pipe, Bernard placed it between his teeth and chomped on it.

"We had stopped some several yards shy of a bridge that spanned a small body of water. The big door slid open, and the rebs yelled for us to get out, striking us with their weapons. We crawled, tumbled and clawed our way off the car and lined with our hands up at the edge of the cliff. The drop was about thirty feet down to the running water below. I had counted around five armed men; three of them were standing on top of the boxcar covering us. We numbered around eight of the original fifteen still alive. What a sight we must have been: six white prisoners and two niggas. Eight broken down battered and bruised soldiers trying to stand at attention. The rebels signaled for Moses and me to clean out the inside of the car as they tossed us some buckets. A small creek ran under an apple tree next to the tracks. The Confederates had a guard covering us as we knelt down beside the water. I've never felt anything so cool and clear as that water as I dipped my face in. Took me back to the days when I swam in the pond back home. We scooped up handfuls and gulped them. We filled up buckets and splashed them over the floor rinsing out the car. Moses was the one that noticed the rebs lining the white soldiers up near the edge of the water. They began pointing to the only officer that we had in the group. We all knew more or less that they would make an example of him, and they did. I recall he was a young 2nd Lieutenant, never knew anything about him, shot in the leg if I remember correctly. If the Confederates didn't get him, that leg wound would have, seriously infected. Our eyes met for a brief moment, but I turned away; I knew what they were about to do. They pushed him up to the edge of the rocks. He was leaning to the side barely able to stand. Next thing I know a Confederate pulls out his pistol and damn if they didn't blast him right in the head. All you saw was the smoke from the barrel and that poor boy sailed over the side. The splash he made when he hit the water was deafening."

"Moses and I both knew that we had to do something quick or it would be curtains. They began babbling over how we were coloreds and they should just shoot us first. One of the men walked up to Moses and placed his pistol right at the base of his chin. I was foolish in thinking that I could stop them. I made a movement in their direction. All I saw was the metal flash of the pistol grip as it slammed against my face. I felt the steel cut right through my face and blood come out, as I tumbled to the ground. They laughed as I was moaning in pain. Moses tried to help me, but all he got was a rifle barrel in the gut. We were rolling around on the ground in pain, when they grabbed another of the white soldiers and marched him to the edge of the cliff." The Corporal's eyes began to well up as he stared into the fire. "That kid couldn't have been more that seventeen years old. He stood there like a scared little child, alone. They stood there laughing and deciding who would shoot him. Finally one Confederate soldier walked over to the kid with his canteen and handed it to him. When the boy turned to drink from it, that rebel shoved his bayonet straight through the boy's back. The kid staggered some five or ten feet and fell down in the high grass, gasping for air. You could make out on his lips, asking the confederate why? The rebel hollered that no Union soldier would ever drink from his canteen. Picking up the canteen, he emptied it over the dying soldier; that was a helluva slap in the face. I guess that's when I really thought that we wouldn't stand a prayer.

Well, God must have been watching over us because a steam fitting burst on the train causing the locomotive to jerk forward. The force threw the men off the car, to the ground. That gave us just the distraction we needed to make a last ditch effort. Moses surprised one of the guards, myself and one of the white soldiers tackled the other man and beat the living daylights out of him. The remaining white soldiers secured the three others; didn't take much effort, one man broke his neck from the fall, and the other two had busted legs. Our soldiers were severely underfed and had very little energy. I glanced over the cliff to see the fallen dead officer. The body was hung up in the rocks some fifty yards downstream. Finally after a battering from the whitewater, the body was freed, and it floated peacefully down stream. Moses held down the rebel that shot the two men. The "gray back" was squirming on the ground, begging for his life. Moses stood him on the edge of the cliff. Pointing the gun at the man, Moses squeezed the trigger. Click, it was empty." Bernard cracked a faint grin. "Moses pushed him over the side. That boy screamed the entire way down until the splash was heard. We stood over the edge and watched as his body shot up, like when you throw a cork in the water. Face down, the body drifted down river and tumbled in the whitewater. Can't say that I was the least bit sorry either."

"We grabbed whatever supplies we could find guns, some canteens, odd ends and a single bar of soap. Moses, uh. Sergeant Trinidad was the one we all followed. Don't know how long we were walking, but it seemed like forever. It was hotter than hell too, sweat pouring down your forehead, stinging your eyes. Dusk began to set in so we picked a spot in a small grassy area to make camp. One of the white soldiers was a good hunter. He laid down some odd-looking things out in the woods, traps of some kind. First we took that single bar of soap and cleaned not only ourselves, our uniforms too, there was a nice shallow area in the water for bathing. One man stood watch on the banks. Another man built a fire to keep warm by at night. That young soldier, the hunter, and well he managed to snag five rabbits. They were skinned and cooked up quicker than you could shake a stick. Some of the men couldn't handle the meat and began to vomit; they were running high fevers and were unable to eat, so we decided to get some much-needed rest. We rose early the following morning and found two more men dead. It wasn't until a week later that we managed to make it to the Union Army train depot where we were given additional medical treatment and shipped back up North." Bernard slugged down the last of his coffee.

"Dang, you and da Sergeant have been through some scrapes together." The soldier shivered as he pulled the blanket up close. "I's gladin yu wit us. Night copol." The boy rolled over on his side and dozed off. Bernard sat by the fire and smiled. The shapes in flames that danced off the crumbling courtyard walls put him in a trance. His mind drifted, no particular thought. Tapping out his pipe on a rock, Bernard let out a silent yawn. The corporal removed his revolver and opened the loading gate, to check his bullets. Holstering the weapon he tipped his hat forward and drifted off.

TEN

Corporal Crawford walked over to the makeshift morgue area. Doc Ames and his assistant were putting the final touches on the men for burial. Crawford couldn't help but stare. He saw the men he once served with lined up in rows, wrapped in white linen.

"Doc," said Crawford. "The caskets are ready whenever you are." The doctor was pulling a sheet over the last body.

"Too many dead," said the doctor, shaking his head as he counted up the number of dead. "No matter how long you do this job it never gets any easier, thirty altogether to bury. My suggestion is one by one we bring in a casket and load up a body. I believe the large wagon's capacity should be about seven coffins per load. That should take about two trips or so per wagon, with three wagons at our disposal." A line of volunteers began forming to help load the dead. Silent inspiration was the only way to describe it. They all died for the same Army.

Over the next few days that little cemetery on the hill was steadily becoming a popular spot, to the dismay of far too many. I guess if you had your choice of places to be buried some might lay in eternal slumber elsewhere. Yet, this cemetery that overlooked the red rock formations had become to some a final stop of a long journey. The coffins were placed beside each grave and a three-man detail would lower the wooden box into the ground. It was hard to understand how these men felt at the sight of so many dead comrades. Some ask, why not them? Others say, better them then us. Their long drawn faces were evidence enough of the day's events. The preacher would say a few words over each grave and the ceremonial gun salute would sound. Then the bugler would play and the graves would then be filled in. There was one more memorial service to attend in town at the railroad station.

The train was taking the sergeant major's casket, along with both officers' bodies, back East. Sergeant Major O'Brien's last request was to be buried with his family in their small plot in Boston. They slid the casket containing the burly Irishman's remains aboard the train. The men stood silently on the platform as the wooden gate slowly closed, engulfing the coffins in darkness. Snapping to attention, they gave an honorary salute.

Meanwhile the sheriff and his men were holding a little meeting at the jailhouse. "I say we grab the rest of the weapons and close up shop," said a deputy cleaning the barrel of his pistol. The man spit his tobacco towards the brass spittoon in the corner. Missing its mark, the dark liquid splashed on the wall. "There's bound to be a lot of heat coming with this last ambush. Let's not be greedy, we made a helluva lot of dough." The sheriff sat behind his desk with his hands in his lap nodding with approval. Another deputy peered out the window at the soldiers on the railway platform.

"They loading the dead soldiers up for the ride back east. Dumb Yankees."

Sheriff Watkins rose from his chair and looked out the window. "Heh, heh, heh," laughed the skinny man. "I agree about the guns. We'll begin to clean out the storage area over the next few days. Johnson, you're in charge. You go with them, make sure they don't screw this one up," said Sheriff Watkins in that southern drawl and waving his hand. "I haven't seen any extra security about, so my guess is that they haven't found our little store. With our good Sergeant Reynolds coming back a might darker than he had anticipated, that just makes one less mouth to feed. If you know what I mean?" The men laughed in delight. "We also got lucky with this ambush occurring. While they're hell bent on finding those Injuns that killed them Yankee soldiers, we slip into the tunnels and grab the remaining weapons. It can't go wrong. Oh, if it comes to the point where we need to run quickly, I have a little surprise in store." Straightening the window curtain, Sheriff Watkins stood there. "The next item of business will be disposing of our good Captain Taylor."

Nighttime had set in over the little military outpost. The customary end of day ceremonies had already occurred, the flag was lowered, folded and stowed for the evening. The men had filed into the mess hall to be fed, and others were going about their personal business. Horses were being watered and fed. Fires were being lit out in front of the barracks like normal. Playing guitars, spoons and any other instruments they could find, the men began a chorus of songs:

> 'Oh the massa he be mad,
> No mor we pick the cotton bales,
> Hab ye heerd de joyful werd?
> We weer da blue suits and hold us a gun,
> Uncle Abe, he free us now,
> Nomore we feel da wips and pain
> Da kingdom come for us taday'

Captain Taylor stood on the front porch of his quarters and listened. Lighting a cigar, he tried to pay close attention to the songs and hear the words. They all told stories, stories of life; the pain and suffering of a people that didn't come here by choice, and had to fight for their freedom. They were now prepared to lay everything on the line for a nation that still thought ill of them. Sitting in the middle of his band of merry men, clapping heartily was Sergeant Nouba. The officer thought to himself, there's so much I have yet to learn from these men. If they were prepared to sacrifice, so will I. The music was pretty. Closing his eyes, he swayed back and forth to the sounds.

"Excuse me, sir," whispered Moses. The young man was a bit startled. "Sorry, sir."

"Not at all Sergeant Trinidad, just enjoying my own personal choir. It's quite lovely."

"Yes sir, I was thinking that we should check up on the situation in the Quarter Master Storehouse," said Sergeant Trinidad. "Just to be on the safe side, and it will give me a chance to bounce some ideas off you." Taylor closed the door to his quarters, and the two men began to cross the compound.

"Good idea sergeant, but first let's grab a bite to eat. I am famished." The two men joined together and headed over to the chow hall. "I hear the cook has made a wonderful stew."

Meanwhile in the barracks a soldier was readying for guard duty. Ezekiel Barnes was a slave's son from Tennessee, no older than twenty years. Staring into the looking glass, he smoothed out his blouse and straightened the cap on his head. Looking down he noticed the shine from his boots; he was proud. Grabbing his side arm and holster he exited the barracks. A stray dog had been hanging around so the boy came to feed it and take care of it.

"Here boy!" The dog ran from the fort and headed for the creek bank. Ezekiel followed him out, without the guard noticing him. "Dog, dog, weya at," whispered the young boy. The moon shone off the water cascading through the creek. The terrain was sloped and had unsure footing; the soldier began wobbling on the hill. Instantly, a pocket of gravel gave way and sent the boy tumbling down the embankment. Head over heels, the young man rolled down the rocky hill, finally coming to rest against a large stump.

"Where in the hell did that greenhorn wander off to," said the guard on his beat. "He's goin' on report as soon as I can write out the paperwork." Doing an about face maneuver, the soldier continued on.

Ezekiel Barnes's head was split open and his vision was blurred. Crawling around the boy tried to get his bearings, while blood ran through his line of sight. He tried to call out, but his lips were swollen and cut. Rising to his feet, Barnes stumbled toward the rushing water. Louder and louder the sounds grew. He noticed the glow from campfires inside the fort. Wobbling forward, Barnes made out the blurred shapes of the sentry on duty. The brush at the bottom of the embankment was thick and covered with twisted tree trunks. Removing his knife from his belt, he began slashing at the vegetation. Catching his hand on a vine, he began tugging furiously. The vine suddenly gave way, hurtling the boy over a small rise. Looking up he had stumbled into the sheriff's men unloading weapons from the tunnel.

"Son of a bitch, a soldier," yelled one of the men. Lying on the ground with one hand holding his bleeding head, Barnes went immediately for his pistol. Before the weapon even came out of the holster, a shovel struck the boy in the head. The force of the blow sent the man reeling into the cold creek water.

"Cut 'em, and keep it quiet." Two men immediately jumped on the boy and held him under water. "Cover us will ya." The other bandit stared nervously at the fort hoping that no one was noticing the scuffle. They weren't! The soldier thrashed desperately for air, but it was no good. One of the bandits removed a knife and shoved it deep into the Buffalo Soldier's chest. Bubbles from the rush of air exiting his lungs, popped in the water. The kicking and thrashing subsided within seconds, as the tired men pulled his body to the muddy shore.

"What the hell do we do with him?" The men bent down in the water and rinsed the blood from their hands. The young man lay face down in the mud, the moonlight shining off his black boots.

"Watch and make sure know one is with 'em." The man they called Johnson stared down at the soldier lying dead in the mud. "Keep loading, we only need to take six crates of guns tonight. We can't leave him here, we have to take him with us." The wagon creaked as the heavy boxes were placed in its bed.

"Hell, just toss him in the water, they'll think the Indians got him," said a man pushing on a case. "His head is busted up anyhow, they'll just think he fell."

Johnson glared at his man. "With a knife wound in his chest, they ain't stupid," whispered the man, running his fingers through his hair. "We leave him here now and this place will be crawling with soldiers by midday tomorrow. We still have two more nights of work ahead. We'll bury him out in the desert somewhere." They began to lift the body.

"Errrrr! Damn this darky sure is heavy." Opening up an empty crate, they tossed in the soldier. Flipping down the lid, it wouldn't shut. "What the hell is the problem?" The boy's foot was hanging over the side of the crate. Johnson kicked at the foot, knocking it in. They covered that particular case with a blanket. Loading up the rest of the treasure, the group crept silently down the creek bed towards town.

"This is a bad sign," said Johnson trotting away. "I don't like the way things are going all of a sudden!" They stared at each other in silence.

* * * * * * *

Deputy Johnson headed over to the sheriff's office and went inside. Through the window shade you could see the figure of Sheriff Watkins, his hands waving around in the air. Johnson stood there while his boss rambled on.

"What the hell do mean, you killed a soldier? Are you plum crazy?" The man threw up his hands in disgust. "I knew, I just knew it, you dumb son of a bitches had to screw this up."

Grabbing the sheriff by his lapel, Johnson pulled him close. "Now listen here, pal, the kid wandered right into the whole group unloading weapons. What the hell would you have wanted us to do? We had to cut him. The body is out back in an empty crate. If we'd have fired off a round it would have alerted the guards and all of us would be hanging from the town square. We killed a soldier, there's no turning back." From behind the curtain to the back room emerged the three Rangers.

"What the hell do we need these guys for," shouted Johnson with a look of disgust.

"Insurance, just in case," nodded the Sheriff trying to straighten out his now wrinkled suit. "Things may get dicey and these men know how to handle those situations. You're not getting cold feet are you?

"Don't be stupid. I'm going over to the bar and grab me a shot of whiskey," said the man pushing his way past the three rangers. "The boys are unloading the stuff now, they're going to be picked up tonight at midnight." The rangers leered at the man as he left the office.

"I'll deal with him," said Armstead with a look of sinister delight. "Let him think everything is all right." Removing a knife from his belt, he began sliding his fingers up and down the blade. McMaster and Collins stood and laughed.

Sheriff Watkins stared in the ranger's direction and nodded. "We move the rest of the weapons tomorrow night, then we close down! If there's any trouble and you have to get out of there fast, about fifty feet from the mouth of the tunnel there's an explosive pack, blow it and run. It will collapse the tunnel structure all the way to the storage area. By the time they're done digging out, we'll be in Mexico."

"Good to know but I doubt there will be any trouble," said McMaster loading his pistol with a smile, while winking at the sheriff.

Reveille sounded and the normal hustle and bustle of cavalry life started over again. Soldiers were moving about and ready the day's assignments. It was a cooler than normal day which was quite nice. Captain Taylor emerged from his quarters and proceeded across the compound straightening his blouse. Sergeant Nouba and Trinidad were emerging from the chow hall and saluted. "Morning, sir."

"Morning men, looks like the beginnings of a relatively smooth day I hope." The officer smiled. "We could use the break."

"Not so quick, sir," said Nouba. Hayes was on horseback moving at a good speed towards the fort. "Looks like something is up."

Hayes rode into the gate and quickly dismounted. "Hayes reporting with a message from Texas Government, sir." The boy handed the folded piece of paper to the officer. Removing his glasses, the man scanned the note quickly.

Urgent message.
Texas Government Affairs, San Antonio, Texas
Commanding Officer, Fort Barre, Texas Territory

Texas dignitaries feared missing, stagecoach overdue. Coach headed into the San Antonio area.

Please dispatch patrol to assist with search for personnel. Your immediate attention is requested.

Thaddeus T. Reynolds
LT. Governor State Of Texas
For Governor N. Q. Rothschild

Rolling his eyes back, the officer passed the note to his sergeants. Reading the note, they both looked at each other.

"Must be urgent, they have bypassed a number of our superiors and sent the note straight to us in the field, not proper protocol. Nouba, you will lead this patrol," said Taylor. "You've just been in this territory, you are the expert." The sergeant stood at attention and listened. "I don't have to tell you what is at stake here. They sucked in the last group of soldiers." The officer whirled around quickly and stared at Nouba. "It will not happen to you, is that understood!"

"Yes, sir!" barked Nouba. Executing a textbook about face the Sergeant stared at a group of soldiers. "Assemble for patrol on the double!" The men raced about and prepared for patrol. "Make sure we have plenty of ammunition, food and water. We don't know how long we'll be gone." The men began to pull horses from the stables and saddle them for the ride.

Moses began to pace back and forth. "I wish that we had the chance to work on our plan first, sir." The captain stood there with his arms crossed. At that moment one of the guards appeared and snapped to attention.

"Sir we have a problem," said the soldier. Returning the salute, Captain Taylor shook his head.

"What is it now?"

"It's Trooper Barnes, sir. He never showed up to assume the watch last evening and he has not been heard from since." Moses tipped his hat back and wiped his brow.

"Sergeant Trinidad," said Captain Taylor. "Make sure that Sergeant Nouba's patrol is in order. I will take five men and begin a search for Barnes." Moses threw a salute and the captain was off.

Sergeant Nouba led his horse to where the men were standing. "Any advice?" he asked with a smile, as he climbed in the saddle.

"Watch the terrain and keep those scouts aware of their surroundings. They'll be watching you, so keep your eyes peeled out for any trouble. If you think that it's time to retreat or regroup, do what you think is right. I'll be awaiting your return," said Moses with a smile and firm handshake.

"Not to worry. Ready forward." The soldiers shot out of the fort and headed into God only knew. On the outskirts of town, three dirty figures also noticed the patrol heading out.

"Well, well, well," snickered Ranger McMaster while lighting his cigar. "Seems our coloreds are heading somewhere in a hurry and a whole bunch of them too." Removing their field glasses, Armstead and Collins watched the line of soldiers flow out of the fort. "Inform our good sheriff we can move those crates tonight with no problem. After that, welcome to Mexico boys." The men all looked at each other and smiled.

* * * * * * *

Corporal Bernard's men began to arise from their night's slumber. Fires now reduced to piles of ash smoldered in the morning breeze. Standing on top of a small rise in the grass on the south side of the ruins, Bernard scanned the horizon; nothing but sky. A small smile creased his face. Turning back he noticed some men beginning to arise from their shelters. They yawned and stretched in the morning sun.

Pike walked over to his corporal. "Morning, any trouble?"

"No, a quiet evening I'm happy to report," said Bernard with a smile. The guards walking their posts reported no activity at all.

The morning scouts, Harrison and Dolan, walked into camp leading their horses by the reins. "Morning, hopin' that coffee is hot," laughed Dolan, waving his hands. "No Injuns at all copol and no tracks either." The men led their animals to the watering hole and sat down on the ground.

Corporal Bernard was carrying his saddle. Tossing it on the beast, he began to tighten the straps. "Fine report Dolan, grab some coffee." Pike walked over to the corporal and began chatting.

"What's the plan, Corporal?"

"Well, Pike, I think we finish our coffee and head about ten miles northeast and circle back to the fort. We'll cover a lot of terrain." After coffee the patrol headed out over the hills.

The day's events went on routinely. Men were still making daily upgrades to the fort and its surrounding areas. Hayes sat behind his desk outside the CO's office. Inside, Captain Taylor and Sergeant Trinidad mapped out plans for dealing with the Comanche problem.

"The point is, Sergeant, how will we find out where they are?"

"We're going to have to send small bands of men out into the well known areas that the Comanche frequent. The simplest answer would be near any watering hole. Do we have a map of this territory, sir?" Taylor walked across his office and pulled down a hanging map from the wall.

"If you'll notice," instructed Taylor. "I have marked out all the watering holes in the territory. Also marked are several spots of strategic importance." Placing his finger on the map, the young officer began to educate the sergeant on any and all significant areas. Showing the surrounding areas and well-known hiding spots of Indian and Mexican outlaws. "My suggestion is that after we deal with our gun smugglers and the problem of these Texas delegates, things should hopefully smooth over then." Trinidad nodded with approval.

"All right sir, when Sergeant Nouba and Corporal Bernard return, we will begin to put this plan into effect. Tonight we will go fishing for some smugglers. My hope is that they saw the large number of men head out this morning, and they may try to make their move."

"I want in on this also, Sergeant. There is no way anyone is keeping me from these people," said the officer with a look of determination.

Moses sat there with a huge smile. "I don't think anyone could stop you, sir." It was late afternoon by the time the plans had been wrapped up.

The sentry watched from his position in the south corner as a patrol approached the backside of the fort. "Patrol coming in."

Corporal Bernard and his men rode quietly into the fort and headed straight for the corral. "Take care of my horse for me will you, Pike?" asked Bernard, tossing him the reins. The Corporal headed over to the CO's office, slapping his hat on his legs to remove the prairie dust. Hayes was still sitting at the desk.

"Welcome back Corporal, how did everything go?"

"Well Hayes, as Moses would say, "all's quiet". Is the Sergeant meeting with Captain Taylor?"

"Yes, just knock before you go in." Bernard rapped on the door and was given the order to enter.

He snapped to attention at the foot of the Captain's desk. "Corporal Bernard returning from patrol. No hostile sightings of any kind, sir."

"Welcome home, Corporal," said the officer, returning the salute. "I didn't notice you come through the front."

"No sir, we went through a pass about five miles away, came out at the rear side of the fort so we just slid in. We covered a lot of terrain."

"Well no news is good news." The Captain clapped his hands together. "Well the men must be exhausted. Let them get cleaned up and enjoy their personal time. However, you will be helping out with our tunnel problem."

Bernard glanced over at Moses. "We had visitors again?"

Moses shook his head back and forth. "Not to our knowledge anyway. We received a distress message from the Texas Government asking for our assistance with some missing dignitaries. We dispatched Sergeant Nouba, along with twenty-five men back in the region first thing this morning. We hoped that whoever was stealing the weapons noticed that your patrol left yesterday and hasn't returned yet, add to that the recent departure of more troops they'll think we're undersized and come looking to finish cleaning out the weapons. We're hoping that it happens tonight. It's our good fortune that you came in from the rear. The element of surprise will be on our side. We'll meet back here in two hours. That will give everyone sufficient time to finish anything they need to do and be ready to go. Sergeant, you and the Corporal can round up the men that we need. Any thoughts?"

Moses sat there tapping his finger on his chin. "There's myself, Bernard and yourself sir. We should take Hayes, Crawford, Oliver, Sullivan, Dobbs and we need one more."

"Pike," said Bernard. "He'll definitely want in on this."

"Pike it is," said Moses slapping his hand on his knee. "Let's get cracking!" The men filed out of Taylor's office. Bernard stopped to fill in Hayes on tonight's plans.

A break in the day's events gave Moses time to write down some thoughts. It had been several days since he last wrote. After going to so many funerals for the men he was weary by day's end. Walking over by the corral he found a quiet spot to sit. He packed the pipe full of tobacco and lit it. The sweet aroma of the tobacco rose in circles above his head. Moses smiled. Removing his pen and journal once again, he began to write.

September 30th 1879

It has been a few days since I have written anything, five days to be exact. This post has been through one

116

trying event to the next. Since the last time I wrote we have had an entire regiment almost wiped out by a large number of superiorly armed Comanche hostiles. We located a hidden tunnel that runs underneath the Quarter Master Storehouse. The captain seems to think that the smuggling has been going on for quite some time. We even believe these weapons were used to kill our own men.

On an even sadder note, we had to lay to rest many fallen comrades. A retiring Sergeant Major, two young officers and over thirty junior enlisted men far too many people.

Sergeant Nouba's patrol performed their duties to the highest of military tradition. The captain expects some citations for Valor for a few of the men, far quicker than normal protocol.

Received distress telegraph from Texas Government requesting detachment of soldiers to assist with locating missing dignitaries. Dispatched Sergeant Nouba and twenty-five men to the same area as the previous day's events, the San Antonio region. Nouba wasn't the least bit apprehensive. Sergeant Nouba wouldn't let the same thing happen to him.

I still haven't had time to look at the town of Flat Fork. I'm going to end this short note now. I'll try to squeeze in some shuteye before tonight's activity. My insides tells me we're going to get into it tonight, don't know how, but I have a feeling I do know where.

Moses closed the book and placed the pen in the sleeve. He was tired today; he seemed to get tired in the late afternoon. "Maybe I'm getting old," he laughed to himself. Tilting his hat over his face he slept right there in the afternoon breeze. There was so much activity going on that no one noticed the sergeant.

Dusk began to set in, and Moses was suddenly jarred from his slumber. Shaking off the sleep, he walked over to the CO's office and knocked on the door.

"Enter! Ah, good evening Sergeant Trinidad, hope your little siesta under the tree was helpful," smiled the young officer. "There's coffee on the table."

"Thank you much, sir," said Moses groggily. Reaching for the pot of coffee he poured himself a cup. "Coffee, sir?"

"Thank you," Taylor said, extending his cup. The smooth black liquid was steaming as it was poured. Placing the cup to his lips the officer slowly sipped the brew. There was a knock at the door; Corporals Bernard and Crawford, along with other men, had assembled in the outer office. The officer motioned them all in. "Please, men come in and grab some coffee."

"All right men let's grab a seat and get down to business. For all of you that are currently unaware, we have a rat problem below the Quarter Masters Storehouse. Tonight we will lie in wait for those who are trying to undermine the efforts of the United States Army, and they will pay. I have been going over these plans in my mind several different ways. This plan I believe to be the most effective." The officer watched the expressions on the faces of his men as he lectured them. They were eager to fight, eager to prove themselves for their leader. "We are ahead of the game seeing as how we have recovered a large portion of the weapons from the field of battle and from the crates located in the tunnel. We will have four men in the tunnel: myself, Sergeant Trinidad, with Hayes and Sullivan. Outside in the high grass and trees by the creek bed, we will have the remaining men and additional soldiers in case of trouble. We should be able to capture them without problem. I would prefer to catch them in the act of stealing the guns. Maybe we could wait until they load the weapons first. Sergeant Trinidad what do you think?"

The officer stood by in anticipation. "First rate plan, sir." The officer smiled with delight. Moses walked over to the window; nighttime had set in over the desert.

"All right you heard the Captain, let's get started," exclaimed Moses. "Bernard take Crawford, Pike, Dobbs and three other men down to the creek bed. It may be some time before our **guests** show up, so be patient. Hunker down and find the best cover you can, you boys may be there a while. Do not shoot until they fire at us first, that is imperative. There is going to be a lot of confusion, so when you fire make sure that you hit the bad guys not us. Last but not least, let's remember that these smugglers very well could have been the men that contributed to the deaths of several of our men, so let's get 'em. All right dismissed!"

The men exited the office in two separate groups. Moses, the captain and their group of men headed over to the tunnel. Bernard's group quietly headed out to their positions.

ELEVEN

The guard snapped to attention when Sergeant Trinidad placed the key in the lock. Moses turned it gently and the group entered the room. "It's going to be cramped down there, so strip off your topcoats. The men immediately removed their gratecoats and had just their trousers and shirts on. "Stay here for a minute, I want to check things out." Lifting the boards that covered the hole, Moses descended first. There was no sound just total darkness. Striking a match he lit a lantern and proceeded down the tunnel with his pistol drawn. Nothing, no one. Returning to the mouth of the tunnel, he called the others to come down. One by one they climbed down into the hole. The group went immediately to the location where the guns were kept to set up positions. Dimming the candle lantern to a small flicker, they settled in.

Meanwhile Corporal Bernard's men crept silently into the creek bed under a full moon. Bernard, Crawford and Pike covered the right flank. Dobbs, Rogers and the others covered the left. Camouflaged in the brush and trees, the men settled down for the night, trying to get comfortable. One thing about staying up on ambush patrols, you never know if and when the bad guys will show up. Several hours passed and it seemed like the night was a bust. Moses glanced over at the men. Captain Taylor made faces as he shifted in the dirt. Hayes and Sullivan stared with excitement.

"Where the hell are they," whispered Pike. "It's been all night." The words had barely left his mouth, when they heard a sound. "Sshhhh!" They all froze at once. The sound of a creaking wagon penetrated the air while it slowly rode over the uneven terrain near the creek. Pike squinted to make out the silhouettes of three figures moving his way.

"Okay boys, let's get these guns out of there," said the voice from the dark. The figure walked over to a thickly covered area of brush. Pulling away a large piece of tree, the men exposed the entry to the tunnel, bathing it in moonlight.

Captain Taylor's men standing guard in the tunnel were beginning to tire. Their muscles were cramping up from crouching behind the crates for so long. Moses tried to stretch his legs so they wouldn't fall asleep. Suddenly muffled voices could be heard, and a match was struck against the tunnel wall.

"Let's start with these here." Walking over to the lantern hanging from the beam a shadowy figure placed the glowing match to the wick. An orange fog illuminated the room slowly and men began to remove boxes of weapons down the tunnel's corridor. Peering out from behind some crates it was Moses who first recognized the men from the sheriff's office. He tapped the Captain on the shoulder and they watched as the men began pulling crates to the tunnel's exit.

"1, 2, 3 crates," counted the man with a smile. "Yes siree, this should net us a tidy some of money from those Injuns and Mexicans. What's the cut on this anyhow?"

"We'll split $700.00 per case. I'll be just as happy when we close down this operation anyway. Besides those rangers give me the creeps," said the man lifting up the crate and backing out. "They just don't sit right with me."

Outside Bernard and his men watched as the group loaded up the weapons. Suddenly, they heard hoof beats. A horse with a faceless rider appeared.

"What the hell is taking so long," said the rider. The man struck a match, pulling it close to light his cigar.

"Put that damn thing out!" A hand flashed by his face slapping the cigar into the creek. "You want that guard to see us?" Armstead shook his head and began walking in the direction of the crouching soldiers. Undoing his trousers he began to urinate, the steam rising in the night air. The men lay still amongst the tangled trees as the yellow liquid splashed on their uniforms.

Bernard bit his lip. "Law men my ass." Armstead climbed into the tunnel followed by McMaster and headed for the storage area.

Moving quickly down the tunnel Armstead spoke. "Damn, how the hell long does it take to load a few boxes of guns anyway?"

"I don't see you lugging nothing so pipe down," said one of the men.

Moses looked over to the Captain. Motioning with his fingers, he was giving all his men to the count of three before they sprung. ONE, TWO, THREE!!!

"All right everyone, hands up, this is the United States Army!"

"Soldiers," cried McMaster. Reaching for his pistol, he fired off several rounds. "Run you dumb son of bitches, move your asses." The men heaved the crates in the soldier's direction. "Shoot the lights." With a quick round from a pistol the lantern was hit, and darkness engulfed the room. The soldiers fired off a quick round of shots in a vain attempt to strike something. The only sound that penetrated the darkness was the scuffling of feet running away.

"Light the lantern quickly," coughed Taylor. Noticing bright flashes flickering inside the tunnel, Collins walked slowly towards the entrance with his revolver drawn. He could make out the muffled sounds of gunshots. Armstead emerged from the tunnel out of breath.

"Damn, they found us. Let's get the hell outta here, we'll take the weapons and head to Mexico." One of Sheriff Watkin's men jumped out of the seat with his shotgun raised.

"Now wait a minute you sneaking dog, don't try double crossing anyone or you may…." Collins whirled around and tossed his hunting knife deep into the man's chest. Staggering backwards, the man collapsed into the rear of the wagon. Collins climbed on and kicked the body into the water.

Kneeling in the brush Bernard whispered, "Damn these are some ruthless bastards." Holding out his hand he gave the signal for all to wait for his command. Placing his lips against his pistol, he gently cocked back the hammer.

"One less mouth to feed." Collins turned toward Armstead. "Let's take the stuff and get the hell outta here." The men began to push the crates further into the wagon. "Where the hell is McMaster anyway?"

"Now," yelled Bernard. "United States Army, you're all under arrest!" The men rose up from their hiding spot, weapons aimed at the ready.

"More soldiers, run for it!" shouted Collins. Removing the pistol from his belt, he fired wildly at the soldiers. Collins was the first casualty of the confrontation. Bullets from the Buffalo Soldier's weapons sliced through his shoulder, vaulting him from the wagon.

The flashes of light and the booms from the gunfire grew closer to the tunnel's exit. "Listen you boys, hold them off, I got something that will really stop them soldiers." The sheriff's men crouched down behind the gun crates and began to open fire on Moses and the men. McMaster ran down the tunnel toward the exit. Estimating fifty feet from the end of the tunnel, he looked down for the fuse. Clearing away some rock and debris he located it. The shots were growing closer. Bullets ricocheted off the tunnel walls showering the man with rocks. "Damn," cried McMaster as a piece of rock sliced into his cheek. "The hell with them!" Grabbing the charge he began running toward the exit leaving behind a trail of wire. As he exited the tunnel, it was showered with a barrage of gunfire. Soldiers from the fort began making their way to the creek bed. Kneeling down in the sand, McMaster began to strike matches, his hands trembling madly.

Ranger Collins began stumbling towards his partner. "Get down," yelled McMaster. "Down!" **BOOM!** A fiery explosion erupted, collapsing several sections of the tunnel. How many, who knew? A huge ball of dirt and debris began traveling down the tunnel's shaft. Collins was hurled backwards over the bank as McMaster dove behind a wall of earth and rock.

Meanwhile back in town, the sheriff who was sitting in his office with his feet kicked up catching forty winks, was sent reeling to the floor. Running out his front door he looked out on the horizon to see a bright white flash.

"My God they blew the tunnel, our gooses are cooked." Scrambling back into his office he ran up the staircase to his room and began gathering his belongings together. After stuffing one bag with clothes, he moved quickly to the closet and pulled out another bag. Checking it quickly, he loaded it with currency and coins. Opening the door he ran down the stairs in a flash and headed to the gun cabinet. He removed a rifle from the stand, then grabbed some extra ammunition and put them in his jacket pocket. Half the shells dropped to the floor in a jingling mess. "Damn, the hell with them!" Taking hold of his bags he left the office heading out back to his horse in the stable. "Just glad I left my nag saddled," mumbled the man securing his bags. Sheriff Watkins removed his revolver quickly to make sure it was loaded, and then mounted up. Turning the horse's head to the right he darted off to the outskirts of town to meet up with the men.

The soldiers in their barracks were jerked awake. What the hell they thought, what was that? Jumping up the men hastily dressed. Eventually one hysterical soldier burst into the barracks and exclaimed. "We're under attack!"

Meanwhile in the tunnel's confined space, the situation was getting hairier. "Get back now," cried Moses as he dove back toward the supply room ladder. **BOOM!** "That's number two, it's a chain reaction," shouted Moses. His massive body seemed to shield the men as they were hurled backwards through tunnel by the explosion's force. **BOOM!** A deafening roar rose up from the earth shaking the fort's very foundation. Massive amounts of dirt and rock caved into their tunnel section. Sullivan struggled to his feet, **BOOM!** The fourth blast sent a huge wooden beam crashing down on Sullivan; it's weight instantly crushing the young man's chest. The sheriff's men inside could only cover their heads and scream as the massive dirt piles caved in on top of them.

"It's coming from the creek bed area," yelled the guard, as he pointed to the dense growth. "The creek bed!"

The explosion sent Armstead reeling into the creek; McMaster was thrown violently to the ground and lay motionless. Splashing in the cold water, Armstead quickly regained his bearings. Ranger Collins, who had regained his composure, knelt down in the water and began to fire on Corporal Bernard's position. "Get him on the horse, I'll cover you guys." Rising from the water, he steadied himself and fired several perfect shots. The bullets struck Shooter Rogers in the chest and throat area, knocking him flat on his back.

"Rogers!" Bernard and Pike raced to their fallen comrade, as Crawford and Hawkins laid down cover fire. Grabbing their man by his blouse they dragged him to safety while bullets whined around them. With all the excitement the soldiers failed to notice Ranger Collins hop onto a horse.

Armstead bent down to pick up McMaster. Holding his bloody head they made for the horses. "Fire," cried Bernard as the men let loose a series of shots that ricocheted off the creek. Collins darted to his friend's position and began firing his weapon.

Armstead pushed McMaster into the saddle while firing his pistol. **BOOM!** Another massive blast shook the ground. The force from the blast sent everyone reeling to the ground. The horse bolted, quickly tossing McMaster off the mount, and ran down the creek bed. Collins held on for dear life as his horse began bucking nervously. Displaying exceptional horseman skills Collins calmed the beast rather quickly and regained control of the animal. Shaking off the cobwebs Armstead jumped on his horse. Pulling the reins to the left, he whirled the beast around and headed for McMaster. Bending down Armstead scooped up the man and they galloped into the dark.

"Shoot them!" Bernard rose to his feet shouting orders. "Keep firing!" Branches and twigs snapped as the shots found no marks. Suddenly a bullet sliced into the back of McMaster, "Unng—gh!" He began sliding from the mount. Armstead used all his strength to hang on to his man. McMaster's legs swung wildly as the horse began to pick up speed.

"Hold on pal, we're on our way." With a grunting heave, Armstead pulled his man up and onto the saddle. Bullets whizzed by as the men galloped through the swelling creek and towards the outskirts of Flat Fork.

Noticing the torches approaching from the fort, Bernard hopped onto a large rock and began shouting. "Men, this is Corporal Bernard, there are soldiers in the creek bed hold your fire!"

Bernard and Pike had their horses tied up over the hill. "Pike we'll follow them. Did you see how many there were on horses?" Tossing the spent shell in the water, Bernard reloaded his weapon on the go.

"I think there was two or maybe three men," said Pike excitedly. Running over the knoll the two men mounted up. Crawford and Oliver had arrived on the seen with more men.

"Crawford, check the men and see if the captain needs help. We're going after them," shouted Bernard, galloping away. "Gather all the bodies up and bring them to the fort hospital, do you understand?"

"You got it, Corporal Bernard," cried Crawford, going from man to man to check everything out.

"Is everyone okay?" Shooter Rogers lay by the creek with a large amount of blood leaking from his neck and upper chest area. Men were frantically holding a piece of cloth over the wound. The blood continued to flow freely no matter what pressure was applied. The man clawed wildly for a breath of air, while his eyes bulged madly. Painfully all the men could do was watch their comrade die. The convulsions stopped after a few minutes and the man lay silently in the grass. Corporal Crawford placed his hand on the dead man's body and bowed his head. Slowly his head rose exposing a look of sheer anger and frustration. The exit to the tunnel was still smoking from the explosion. Cocking back his hammer on the pistol, Corporal Crawford led his men on.

The small band of soldiers moved slowly up the gravel incline toward the mouth of the destroyed tunnel. A huge cloud of dust covered the area. "Cover your faces," said Corporal Crawford as he tied his bandana around his mouth. Walking cautiously, he held up a lantern to get a better view of the tunnel. Dirt, rock and wooden beams were lumped into a massive submerged pile. "My God, let's hope they made it out on the other side. Let's go." More soldiers from the fort began to appear on the scene. "Hold up men, all is secure on this side. Take five men and head back to the tunnel. Leave a small detachment of men to sweep the rest of this area with torches. It's unsure footing and very muddy. Any bodies or weapons that are discovered are to be loaded into the wagon and returned to the fort. We're gonna be here all night if that's what it takes." A fire was lit illuminating a large area. A four-man detail picked up the dead body of Shooter Rogers and carried it back up the incline to the fort.

Inside the tunnel breathing was next to impossible, the air was thick with dirt. All the soldiers were knocked down and covered in layers of dirt and rocks. Moses and the Captain slowly struggled to free themselves. Coughing and hacking they emerged from the debris pile virtually unscathed. Hayes? Sullivan? The Captain's head was bleeding slightly.

"You're bleeding sir," said Moses shaking his head. "You all right?"

The officer dabbed at his head with his hand. "Yes sergeant, I'm fine, just a little scrape." Searching on his hands and knees, the captain came across his pistol lying in the dirt. He picked the weapon up and slid it in his holster. A set of boots sticking out of a pile of dirt was all that could be seen. "Hayes is that you? Hayes? Hayes!" Rushing to their comrade, the men began digging at a hurried pace. Pulling the young man free, the captain started breathing air into his parched lungs. "Cough, cough, cough" hacked the boy. Dirty phlegm and mucus flew from his mouth. He continued hacking for several minutes.

"Captain," said Moses somberly, holding out his hand. Lying in a pile of rubble with a massive beam smashed into his chest was, Sullivan. Taylor bent down and placed his fingers on the boy's neck to check for a pulse; just as he thought. The officer bit his fist and turned away quickly.

Time began to pass; no one was sure how long it was. Suddenly small pockets of light shown through the choking dust. "Anyone still alive in there? Captain Taylor, Sergeant

Trinidad, anyone there?" The sounds of shovels and pick axes broke the silence.

"Yes, we're fine, but we have one soldier that was crushed under a large beam," yelled the sergeant. Walking over to Hayes he quickly checked the boy over. Touching Hayes's arm, the boy winced in pain. "Has that wing been clipped, Hayes?"

"I've had worse bee stings, Sergeant," chuckled Hayes. Moses ripped the bloody shirt to reveal more serious wounds. The sergeant and the soldier stared down at the purple colored bruises. "Hell, it only looks bad," smiled the boy.

"I'll bet you guys could use this." A water pouch was pushed through the small space and tumbled down the dirt pile. Captain Taylor picked up the pouch and walked over to his wounded man.

"Here Hayes drink," said the coughing officer. The boy thanked him and took a swig from the pouch. "I can't stand waiting in here, sergeant. I wonder how the rest of the men fared. What the hell was that anyway, dynamite?"

Moses was on all fours coughing heavily. His throat burned. "That's exactly what it was, sir. Judging by the way it blew, I'd say they set the charges in several different areas, one right after the other. My guess is they were hoping to get out of here, and with the explosions going off they probably could have slipped away undetected." Hayes lay in the dirt leaning against an empty case. The water from the canteen left a dirty ring around his lips.

"We have to get out of here and head into town, Sergeant," said the officer, shaking the dirt from his uniform. "I have a feeling that we could find some answers at the sheriff's office, that's the first stop when we get out of here. There possibly could be an arrest made or at the least an accidental shooting," smiled the officer slyly, while pacing back and forth.

After more than an hour a large portion of the dirt gave way and the opening back to the tunnel was clearing. Captain Taylor and Sergeant Trinidad crawled out and slid down the pile.

"We've got a soldier that was under some dirt for quite a while, so he should need a rest, and we have one dead man, his body is pinned beneath a beam," said the officer on the move. "Remove all remaining weapons from the tunnel. The Sergeant and I are going to take a small group of men into town to find our friends." Climbing the ladder and exiting the shed, Moses and the officer ran to the stables. After saddling up they galloped to the parade area where twelve mounted soldiers were waiting, ready to ride.

"Men, this is a dangerous task, pay attention. First, we plan to follow the creek bed to wherever the hell it leads and for as long as I say, is that clear?" said Moses with a hint of determination.

"Yes, Sergeant!" barked the men.

"Captain Taylor and three men will split off and head for the sheriff's office in town. Remember this is their town and they know their way around, so be careful." Hayes emerged from the office carrying his weapon and heading straight for the stables. Pulling a horse out, the soldier hopped on.

"Well what are we waiting for?" The young man nodded to his superiors. "By your lead sir."

"Good luck sir," said Moses extending his hand. "Come hell or high water, they're going to be caught."

"I know Sergeant, just be careful."

The men spurred their horses and raced out the fort. Their hearts were pounding with excitement as they bounced along in their saddles. The lights of Flat Fork were coming into view on the horizon and soon one could hear the joyous sounds of merriment and fun from the saloon. The group of soldiers trotted silently into the town gathering at the blacksmith's shed.

"All right here is the plan," said Taylor. "Sergeant Trinidad and nine men will proceed down the creek bed and hopefully catch up to our friends. I will lead the remaining three men to the sheriff's office and see what he has to say. Good luck Sergeant." The men split up and headed out in different directions.

Leaving the horses tied up in the rear, Captain Taylor and his men crept silently along the wooden baseboards of the sheriff's office. Sneaking over the railing on the porch they noticed the front door ajar and the lights on. The officer went in first pistol drawn; his eyes scanned over the room slowly. The desk drawers were open and paper was spewed all over it. He noticed the large oak and glass doors of the cabinet were left open. The broken box of ammunition and cartridges littered the floor.

"That's not a good sign," Taylor said, pointing to the floor. Waving his men in slowly, the officer pointed to the staircase.

Corporal Crawford leaned in close to the officer. "I don't think he's here sir. My guess is he heard the commotion and left. Hayes, check it out." The young man slid quietly up the stairs with his pistol drawn. Reaching the top of the stairs he kicked the door open. Nothing! The room was empty other than some clothes left hastily on the floor and a maple wood **rocking chair.** Whoever was here left in a hurry? Retreating back down the stairs in disappointment, the young man entered the rear offices and began to search for anything he could.

"No sign of him, sir."

"Let's check out back and see if there's a barn or something."

"Darnet I forgot I lit a candle. I should run up and blow it out so it doesn't uu..err.. catch on fire, sir," Hayes quickly retreated up the stairs.

"We'll meet you outside," whispered the officer. The two men crept through the rear of the office and out the back door. In the distance they noticed a barn under some trees.

"It's our lucky night, sir," smiled the corporal, pointing to the dilapidated structure that was slowly tilting over. Walking over to the barn the men slid the broken boards open. Hayes emerged from the house, with a lantern to illuminate the area.

"Look at this, sir!" The men noticed several deep grooves in the dirt. "Somebody has been moving some heavy boxes," said Hayes. "Hey what's that?" Pointing the lantern in the corner of the barn, they noticed some large objects under a horse blanket. Pulling back the blanket it revealed two crates.

"See I told you the sheriff was crooked," said the officer with a huge grin on his face.

"Sir, that's not much for evidence against the sheriff," responded Hayes. Reaching down to undo the latch, Hayes noticed a small pool of blood under the corner of the crate. His hand froze. Slowly undoing the latch he flipped up the lid; the smell was bad. Laying face down was the body of Ezekiel Barnes, the soldier who had wandered out after the dog. Taylor and Crawford turned their heads away quickly. "Now that's evidence!"

"Who is that?" The Captain tilted his hat back on his head and shook his head. "Where the hell did he come from?"

"It's Barnes," said Hayes with a note of disgust in his voice. The boy bent down next to the crate. "Crawford, help me move him." The two men slowly turned the young man over on his back. The boy was bound at both wrist and ankles, and had several bruises about his face and head. They had shoved his cap into his mouth to gag him. The officer gently removed the cap from the boy's mouth. "He was beaten up really bad and then stabbed in the chest, here," said Hayes pointing to his face. "Look how the blood stain is bright red and frothy and look at the small rip in his blouse."

There was still the task of the second crate to deal with. "Do we open it sir?"

The men looked over at the captain as he swallowed and nodded his approval. Flipping open the lid they all stood in stunned surprise. Lying inside with multiple bruises and stab marks was Deputy Johnson. This confused everyone.

"What the hell is going on around here," exclaimed Taylor, rising to his feet quickly. "Arrest the sheriff on sight for questioning, is that understood? Pass the word." The group emerged from the building as a small detachment of soldiers was passing by. "Pass the word, arrest the sheriff on sight," said the officer, clinching the cap in his hands.

Nouba's men rode for hours calmly across the desert, swords rattling on their sides. With their military overcoats blowing in the breeze they looked almost like blue angels moving peacefully through the valley. Riding all morning and into the early afternoon, their search was producing little; there was no sign of any Indians. The scouts reported in on a regular basis, so if anything were headed their way they would know about it. Nouba liked to watch the men while they rode, see if they had what it took to be real cavalrymen. The Sergeant began to map different areas for future campaigns, writing them down in his little notebook. Scanning the horizon Nouba noticed a peculiar rock formation that towered above the horizon. The rocks were an orange rusty color. When the sun began to set they turned almost a bloody red. Sitting in the saddle staring at them he was almost hypnotized, they were so beautiful. They had smooth ripples running over them, probably from the sand that has been blowing forever. There were small plateaus that ran along side them, nice spots to sit and watch for soldiers. Jotting down little notes, Nouba placed the small book back in his blouse.

Josey Tiner and Abraham Tote were scouts positioned on a small rise on a rocky cliff area about three hundred yards out when something caught their attention, "Moooo!" "Did you hear something?" "Mooo!" Again the odd sound echoed out. "It's coming from over the edge, cover me," said Tote. Tiner was a young man with chiseled features and one of the better shots in the unit. Raising his carbine he steadied himself against a rock for leverage. His partner Abraham Tote was a carefree giant of a man who loved the army life. Removing his pistol, he moved cautiously to the cliff's edge. Whatever was making the noise was coming closer. Aiming the weapon at the noise, Tote edged closer. Suddenly a young calf bound over the edge and collided with Tote, landing on top of him. The little brown animal rested on the soldier's chest and began licking his face affectionately. Tote began laughing as he stroked the animal gently. Tiner shook his head with a smile.

"What are you doing out here, girl," said the young man. The words barely had left the man's lips when two Indians clawed their way to the top of the ridge. "Tote, get down Indians!" Tiner lifted his weapon and fired two shots knocking the Indians to the ground. Tote cradled the calf and covered up on the ground. Running to check on his partner, Tiner covered the two warriors. "You all right boy, ya didn't get nicked did ya?" The two Indians never had a chance to remove their weapons. Tote sat still on the ground holding the calf.

"No, where did she come from?"

Tiner gazed out at the desert. "I bet I know," he said. "A line of smoke rising about a mile out, look."

Hearing the shots, Nouba whirled around and accompanied by the rest of the patrol raced to the scout's position. As he pulled back on the reins, Nouba's horse came to a halt in a cloud of dust as he dismounted. "What's the situation, men?"

"We got a problem Sergeant, looks like a fire of some kind. We found a stray calf trying to make it up the cliff. These two were right behind him. My guess is they saw it run and thought they could catch her. If it is settlers or homesteaders, they're gonna need help fast." Nouba thought about the situation for a moment as his fingers tapped on his grips.

"Mount up!" shouted Sergeant Nouba as he swung into the saddle. The sounds of carbines being loaded and checked clicked and clacked in the air. "Watch your flanks and keep your eyes peeled out for their scouts. Don't bunch up. Ready forward!" Rearing their horses to the right the patrol headed off toward the smoke. Two scouts bolted ahead of the patrol to keep an eye out. The horses rode neck and neck across the scorched earth. Stopping some five hundred yards away, Tiner dismounted, removing his glasses to have a look. From behind a small grouping of rocks he looked down on small valley and a body of running water. Settlers under siege!

One wagon was tipped over, and one was ablaze. Tiner noticed a woman hunkered down next to a rock with two small children, firing a pistol. A couple of yards away another woman was firing a shotgun from behind a downed tree. Indians rode by on horseback making several passes. The woman continued to fire, hitting one Indian and knocking him off his horse. Arrows pierced the air narrowly missing the settlers. Two men were firing from another position behind some fallen trees. Tiner watched as one of the men was hit by gunfire and fell to the ground. The other man knelt down to check him out when a warrior on a horse leaped off and tackled him to the ground. The man wrestled with the Indian valiantly until another Comanche brave came and sent his tomahawk crashing down several times into the white man's chest. A high-pitched scream was heard as the Indians joyfully scalped their helpless prey. The women began screaming in terror. Tiner's eyes nearly came out of their sockets.

"Hurry it's almost over!" cried Tiner kicking up his horse. "They need our help, com'on!" Spurring their horses on, the two soldiers rode down the gravel incline towards the helpless settlers.

Sensing the situation was in hand; another war party of nine warriors appeared, heading towards the doomed women. The Buffalo Soldier took careful aim at a full gallop knocking the first Indian to the ground. Racing towards the second, he holstered his rifle and removed his saber. With a flawless sweeping motion he decapitated the Indian; the lifeless carcass fell to the ground. Tote thundered toward the woman and children. Removing his knife from the sheath, he leaped from his mount tackling down the advancing Indians. Tote knocked the first Indian down. Turning to run, the second was grabbed by his black hair and dragged down. A flash of his hand and the knife slid across the native's throat, killing him instantly. Tote fired a clean shot in the other brave's chest. Realizing the situation was far from over he ran to the women and waited for the next group to attack. Hearing the bugler's call the Indians turned in surprise.

"Run them down men!" yelled Sergeant Nouba, removing his sword.

From the top of the hill, the bugler sounded, "Char-r-rge!" The earth and heavens opened as the deafening sounds of horses and men of the United States Cavalry thundered into battle. They managed to cross the open incline without causality and ride straight into the war party.

Firing from their horses, the Indians were stunned. They never suspected a patrol would come back to the area so soon. Coming straight towards them was an intimidating group of soldiers. The men were exceptional shots and they tagged several of the Indians from the horses. Killing only one, the additional wounded Indians tried to retrieve their horses but were cut down by the soldiers. The earth began to rumble as the sound of hoof beats came closer. There they are. "Open fire!"

"Cease fire!" The smoke began to lift. Seven warriors and their horses lay in the late day sun under the towering rock formations. The Buffalo Soldiers went from body to body, removing necklaces, knives or any other items they might want.

"We got a live one here." Lying on the ground holding his leg was Screeching Owl at Dawn. The twelve plus Buffalo Soldiers surrounded the man.

Sergeant Nouba came riding in and noticed the commotion. "Put that prisoner in shackles now and make sure someone looks at those wounds. You men get back to your duties now!" Tossing some chains on the ground, Nouba rode back to the civilians.

Tiner and Tote walked slowly up to the woman who had a relieved look in her eyes. The children clung to their mother like scared animals. "You all right, missy," said the man extending his hand. "We won't hurt ya. Tote, check on those fellows over there." The soldier pointed to the bodies lying with the Indians.

"Name is Potter, Lucy Potter," sobbed the woman, as she held her children. A colt pistol dangled from her hand. Covered in prairie dust, she stared sadly at the men, as Tote checked for signs of life; there was none. "That's my sister, Doris May and these are my young ones Max and Sissy." Doris May held the shotgun firm in her hands and watched the soldiers with caution. "Don't look children." Their mother shielded them with her body and walked past.

"Nice to meet you folks, I wish it was under better conditions." Tiner stared at Doris May. "We're not the enemy, you can put the weapon down." She continued staring at the man with suspicious eyes and that shotgun didn't move a hair. "Well, you ain't hurtin me I guess. You a helluva shot anyhow." The soldier brushed past her to check the other Indians lying in the sand.

"Ladies," said Nouba tipping his hat. "Are you all right?"

"Yes, Sergeant, thanks to you and your men," said the woman with tears trickling down her face. "I can't say the same for my husband and brother." Nouba peered over their shoulders and noticed the bodies in the sand.

"I'm sorry for your losses," said Nouba. "We'll set up camp for the night."

Using two horses and some rope, they managed to get the tipped wagon upright again. The soldiers retrieved an additional five horses. They rounded up all the Indian bodies, fifteen in all, and placed them in shallow graves. Mr. Potter's body along with his brother's was wrapped in blankets and placed off to the side. Fires were lit and the sentries posted. The soldiers made a shelter for the women and children. The men cooked some meat on an open fire and fed the civilians first. Screeching Owl at Dawn was treated for his wounds, and then secured to a log for the night. The children seemed to be untouched by the day's events as they laughed with the soldiers for a while until they fell asleep by the campfire. Tote carried them to their sleeping area and tucked them in. Tiner glanced over at Doris May who was lying down, her eyes wide open and her shotgun clutched tight. Eventually that shotgun got too heavy for her to hold, and she conked out. The soldiers sat around the fire and discussed their plans.

"First, you men have performed exceptionally. We still have a mission to finish. Those Texas people are out there and they need some help," said the Nouba, sipping on coffee. "We'll send a four man detail to escort the wagon with the women, children and the bodies back to Flat Fork in the morning. The rest of the group will go on." The men continued eating and drinking their coffee.

TWELVE

Sheriff Watkins sat nervously on top of Chapman's Bluff by the steep gorge looking for any sign of riders approaching. Shivering in the saddle he tried to stay calm. "Where the hell are those idiots," he muttered. "Maybe they're dead? I don't have that kind of luck." A twig snapped suddenly. Aiming his rifle at the tree, the sheriff stayed perfectly still. "Who's there?"

"Well, well, sheriff, you surprised me." Through the brush, walking their horses came Rangers Armstead and Collins. Watkins clutched his chest in relief. A figure lay slumped over the saddle; it was Ranger McMaster, who had been shot in the back. "I figured that you would have left town and headed to Mexico with the money," smiled Armstead, as he lit his cigar. "I see you brought it with you," he said, pointing to the bags slung over the saddle horn.

Watkins patted them with the rifle barrel. "I keep my word, son. Are you sure that you didn't get followed? How's your man?" The sheriff dismounted and walked over to McMaster, looking at his back wound. As he placed his fingers gently on it, the man moaned softly. "He's bad, the blood is getting darker," said Watkins. If we don't get him some help, things could go wrong." Turning towards Collins, he noticed the bloodstains on his shirt. "What about you? You all right?" Collins waved Watkins off.

"What's the worst that could happen, he could die." Armstead and Collins began laughing to each other. They slowly removed McMaster from the horse and set him down on the ground.

"Unnhhggh!" The man wrenched in pain.

"Wrong, he could be paralyzed and still be alive," Watkins said, while staring at the rangers. They looked confused. "That means you idiots, he'll never walk again, ever. So he could talk?" The men slowly stopped laughing and stared at each other. Sheriff Watkins walked over to Armstead. "We have to get him to a doctor soon."

Collins took a swig from his canteen. "There ain't a doctor in this area that can see him." Walking over to Armstead, Collins began asking some questions. "What do we do with him?" Armstead stared at the ground then into the night. He began kicking at the earth. Turning around he walked up to the man. Kneeling down he hugged his comrade and whispered in his ear.

"Sorry old buddy, it's survival of the fittest." Removing his knife from the sheath, he eased it deep into the man's chest.

"Ahhhhh...Ahh." McMaster's whole body tightened up.

Armstead covered McMaster's mouth and pulled the man close to him. "Nice and quiet now," he whispered. McMaster began to shake. Armstead turned the knife with twisted delight as he stared coldly into his comrade's eyes, until man went limp. Laying him back down he began to strip the extra weapons and ammunition from the body. Watkins stood there in shock.

"What's the plan now, sheriff?" asked the Armstead.

"P...l.a.n??? What plan? My god, you men have no morals," Watkins said in total disbelief, as he stared at the body lying on the ground. "Your own man." He covered his mouth in astonishment.

Removing his knife and placing it at the base of the sheriff's throat, Armstead spoke. "That's right, my own man, so rest assured I won't have any problem cutting you if you make me." The blood dripped off the blade as it gleamed in the moonlight. Watkins stood there paralyzed. Collins chuckled softly in the background. "We're not going to be leaving after all. We'll head back into town like there was nothing wrong, I want another crack at those darkies." Armstead wiped the blade of his knife off on the sheriff's jacket.

"Are you crazy or something? If we go back now those soldiers will arrest us as sure as the sun rises."

"My good sheriff, what evidence do they have linking us to the weapons? What evidence do they have saying that we've done anything wrong?" The man smiled as he packed a chew in his mouth. As the juice ran down his chin, Armstead wiped it with his sleeve.

"When they recover the bodies they'll recognize them as deputies from my office; they got us dead to rights." The sheriff placed his hand on his head. "Where did you men put the bodies?" asked Watkins in a scared tone of voice.

"We hid them in the old shack in back of your office. It's not your building right?"

"Correct."

"Well, don't worry about it then," said Armstead climbing into the saddle. "Go back to your office and wait there for us. Oh, by the way, don't open your mouth to anyone about anything. If the soldiers come looking to give you a hard time, just stall them. Say that you don't keep track of your men after hours, it's their responsibility." Watkins stared at the rangers. "Sheriff, remember you still haven't paid us for helping," Armstead seethed. "We'll be at your office after we dispose of the body and change clothes so don't be stupid." Watkins reared his horse's head and galloped west to circle the town.

* * * * * * *

Corporal Bernard and Pike galloped down the creek bank but lost track of the culprits. "Where the hell did they go?" The men stopped and dismounted. The moon was shining brightly, illuminating a large area. They looked in all directions but couldn't see anything. "They were right in front of us, there's no way they could have gotten away."

Bernard tilted back his cap and stared at Pike.

"Sergeant Trinidad won't be happy when we get back," said Bernard, shaking his head. "We let him down on this one, son." Suddenly hoof beats sounded. "What the hell is that? Quick. That grouping of trees." The men pulled their horses behind the brush as a group of riders approached. "Maybe they were meeting up with others?" Drawing their pistols, the soldiers waited in silence. Into the moonlight rode Moses leading a patrol. Bernard and Pike emerged from their hiding spot. "Hey, what happened to you?"

Moses sat in the saddle still covered with the dirt from the tunnel. "Tunnel caved in on us. Did you see where they went?" Moses dismounted and shook hands with his friends.

"We couldn't tell in which direction they went," said Bernard, shaking his head. "Did we get a live one out of the bunch, maybe we could talk to him?"

Moses shook his head. "No, no one! The Captain went into town to try and find the sheriff. Let's try and meet up with them. We can sweep the town. I'll take five men in from the north; you can take the rest in from the south. We meet right in the middle."

As the lights of the town came up over the hill, the men split the column in two and headed off.

Most people had heard the commotion and were crowded into the streets. The soldiers trotted in and tied their horses up to the posts. Dismounting, they began going from door to door and alley to alley in hopes of finding something or someone relating to this evening's horrific events. People began to notice the soldiers walking about town. Captain Taylor along with Corporal Crawford and Hayes had loaded the body of Barnes into a wagon and were pulling him out into the main street. Several soldiers on horseback met them.

"What's in the wagon sir?" asked one trooper.

"Our comrade, young man," was the officer's reply.

"Captain Taylor, over here, sir!" shouted Moses, waving his hands. Walking over to the officer, the sergeant and his men saluted. "No trace of them, sir," said Moses peering into the back of the wagon. He saw the body but said nothing.

Taylor returned the salute. "Nothing at all!" he said, removing his cap and slamming it on the ground.

On the other end of the town, the sheriff rode into the blacksmith's shop. Inside the attendant was banging away at his work. A massive fire was burning as the man stoked it with his irons. "Oh, good evening, Sheriff, what can I do you for?"

The sheriff spoke quickly and not very clear. "I, er, think my horse has thrown a shoe, would you mind giving her a look over? I'll just head back to the office to handle some work." Removing the bag with the money, he discretely opened the lid to a barrel and slid the bag in, closing the cover. "I'll just come back for her in the morning." Waving his hand, Watkins scampered off into the night.

"Whatever you say, Sheriff," called the blacksmith. "Heah, where are you going in a rush? Did you hear all the commotion?"

Soldiers had been ordered to patrol the town in hopes of finding some clues. Peering from behind barrels and fencing, the sheriff moved slowly through town. Tiptoeing across a back porch he inadvertently stepped into a bucket. "Freeze, don't move." Looking up from the ground, the good sheriff was staring straight down the barrels of three Army carbines. "Bring him to the Captain."

Frustrated townspeople were congregating in front of the sheriff's office. There was a commotion moving through the crowd. "I demand that you release me at once. I'm the sheriff of this town. Take your hands off me now you stupid coloreds." Two soldiers had Watkins secured as the third man led the way with his weapon drawn for protection.

The soldier addressed his superiors. "Caught this man sneaking into the town sir."

"Splendid work trooper," said the Captain, returning the salute and smiling.

"He had this on him," said the soldier, holding out a Colt pistol. "It's as cold as a witch's elbow. What will we do with him, sir?" The officer stared angrily at the man.

"You've got some explaining to do, Sheriff. Let's take this into your office and address the situation right now," said the young man holding out his hand. Walking up the stair, the captain was unable to control his anger as he whirled around and grabbed the man by his lapel. "Just where in the hell have you been this evening?" The soldiers stood back as their leader screamed. "Answer me now!"

"I don't have to explain my whereabouts to you or any other person, you hear me boy," said Watkins, pushing the officer away. "You got proof that says I did something wrong son? If you don't, then release me now!" Staring deep into the sheriff's eyes, the captain held the man at arm's length. Rearing back he let loose with a right cross that tagged Watkin's square on the jaw and sent him tumbling down the steps. Leaping on top of the man, Captain Taylor began shouting.

"I can't prove it, but I know that you had something to do with this, you, disgrace!" Moses and Bernard grabbed the officer and pulled him off. "You better pray to God that I find out otherwise," said Taylor dusting off his jacket. Corporal Crawford had made his way through the crowd. Leaning over he whispered something into the officer's ear. Taylor pushed his way back through the crowd and began to make his way up the street towards the saloon. Sheriff Watkins was staring up from the ground.

"All right all you good folks go home now," said Moses waving his hands. "There's nothing left for you to see. Goodnight now!" Slowly the crowds began to file past the soldiers and return to their dwellings. Several of the townspeople smirked and pointed at the sheriff seated in the mud.

"Where did Captain Taylor run off to now?" Moses turned to see the young officer bounding up the street with some other soldiers and head into the saloon. "Aw hell, this can't be good." Moses and Bernard ran after him.

Inside the saloon it was hard to tell there was an altercation going on outside. People went there to drown their sorrows, and tonight was no exception. The girls were looking for a date, and the piano player was hungry for tips. Hayes was at the bar with his back towards the door. Turning around, he motioned with his head to the corner of the room. Tucked away at a small table sat Rangers Armstead and Collins with their stetsons tilted over their eyes. They were playing poker and the size of the pile of chips in front of them showed all who was winning. Several beers and shots of whiskey littered the table. The officer motioned to the men to circle the room and head over to the table. Bernard and Hayes moved unnoticed to the back door area and secured the rear in case they tried to exit. Hayes pointed his carbine through the curtains. Captain Taylor and Moses walked up to the table. Removing the bloody cap from his pocket, Taylor tossed it in the middle of the poker pile.

Armstead tilted his head up slowly. "What the hell is that?" he said. The cap was wrinkled, dirty and soaked with blood. "Well whatever it is, looks like you killed it." The men at the table began to laugh. The officer reached down for the mug of beer sitting on the table. Collins stopped chuckling. The piano stopped playing. Holding the beer up to the light Taylor stared at the golden liquid.

"I can't say that I ever fancied beer at all, not even at the military academy. The men would go out on their passes and drink it by the barrel loads," said the young officer sipping the liquid, he made a sour face. "Well to each his own. There is one thing that disturbs me though."

"Ooh, what is that?" asked Armstead, throwing a chip into the pile, and then saluting sarcastically at the officer. He placed a cigar in his mouth and grinned proudly.

"The fact that you shot my men." Turning quickly, he tossed the beer into Armstead's face.

Armstead leaped up from the table. "What the hell is wrong with you boy?" he yelled. The beer ran down the man's face and all over his clean clothes. Ranger Collins reached for his pistol under the table. Drawing the revolver he pointed it square at the officer's chest. BOOM!

Collins crashed through the glass window and to the ground below. Tables and chairs were flipped upright as customers ran for cover. Armstead stood frozen as Hayes emerged from the curtain with his gun smoking. Captain Taylor and Sergeant Trinidad were both crouched on the ground.

"Put those hands in the air now." Hayes patted both men on the backs and the soldiers stood up cautiously. Walking over to the broken window, Hayes looked out and saw the ranger's corpse lying in a pile of glass.

"You little weasel, I remember your face now," seethed Armstead, his hands raised in the air. "That's the worst and last mistake that you'll ever make." Moses walked up to the man slowly. Reaching down he picked up a glass with whiskey in it. Throwing the shot back quickly he stared at the man. Tossing open Armstead's jacket he reached in and removed his revolver. Armstead leaned over and whispered in the sergeant's ear.

"It ain't over nigga, not by a long shot," he smiled. Moses reared back and smashed the handle of the gun into the man's stomach. Doubling over, Armstead dropped to the floor. Moses lifted his knee and smashed it into the head of the ranger sending him flailing across the table and to the ground. Lying in a puddle of stale beer and whiskey, Armstead was unconscious. Moses reached into Armstead's pocket and removed a bunch of silver dollars. Striding up to the bar, he tossed them on top of the counter. "This should cover the window and any other troubles you may have, barkeep." The bartender tipped his imaginary hat to the sergeant. The soldiers turned around and headed out the door.

The sheriff had regained his wits and was standing in the doorway with two different deputies.

"Nobody strikes the sheriff of Flat Fork and gets away with it! You're all under arrest!" Watkins stood in the doorway with a determined look on his face.

"Not so fast, my good man," called a voice from above. Standing on the second floor landing was Corporal Crawford and small detachment of soldiers, their guns aimed right at the sheriff. "I'd say that you're outgunned, wouldn't you?" The soldiers laughed out loud. "Sir, you and the sergeant can leave whenever you like." The small squad of soldiers walked slowly down the stairs.

"Thank you Corporal, Sergeant, are you ready?" said the captain strolling up to the sheriff. "We've got a lot at home to take care of." The officer stared at the sheriff as he slid his riding gloves on. "Excuse me, please." Taylor flinched quickly, the sheriff damn near jumped clear to the moon.

Laughing loudly, Corporal Crawford and his men eased slowly backwards out of the saloon.

The line of soldiers roared out of the town with a cloud of dust in their wake.

"Excellent job all of you," said Captain Taylor, bouncing over the rocks. "We all did one helluva a job, sergeant." The officer was beaming. This was just the kind of kick in the pants the men needed to boost their morale. "Sergeant, I will need for you to oversee the security aspect of this incident. We may never know who exactly did the robberies unless we can recover some hard evidence."

"Sir, what if we find out that the sheriff's men **were** involved, then what do we do?" Trinidad looked at the officer who was pondering that same question.

"Well, there is still the point of hard evidence, sergeant. If we didn't see the sheriff with our own eyes commit these acts, there is no way I can go to the proper authorities. I will write Regimental Headquarters alerting them to my suspicions in the meantime." The men were just passing over the hill headed towards the fort when they saw the torches burning in the distance. Soldiers were swarming over the creek bed area looking for anything to explain what happened. The men rode into the fort. Hayes grabbed the horses' reins and pulled them into the corral area.

"Sir, why don't you get cleaned up and changed," said Moses, walking over to the office with his commander. "I'll round up all the information there is and make my additional report to you in the morning. There's not much more that we can do tonight." Standing at attention, the group saluted their leader. "Sir, we were proud to have you with us tonight." Grinning, the officer returned the salute and walked into his office.

"Let's get some grub," said Bernard.

"No thanks, I'm going to get cleaned up first." Moses waved to his men, and then headed over to his quarters.

Entering, he lit the candle lamp; a tremendous grin stretched across his face. Walking slowly across the room, Moses ran his hands over it, smooth as silk. It looked comfortable. Grabbing both arms firmly he eased down slowly. A rocking chair! Moses laughed softly as he swayed gently back and forth.

THIRTEEN

The morning started off just like all the other days in the military. Though, there were not many nights like last night. The tunnel complex was caved in, and there was the task of digging out whatever or whoever was underneath all that rock and dirt.

Captain Taylor emerged from his office and headed across the compound. Banging and sawing noises caught his attention. Walking over by the corral he noticed two freshly made coffins leaning against the barn; a third partially assembled was lying on the ground. Taylor hesitated for the moment, and then proceeded out of the fort. Smoke and debris was still rising from the explosion area. Several of the men had been up all night and were now, sleeping by the fires they had been tending. Sergeant Trinidad was down near the tunnel's entrance talking with the men.

"Well, my guess is whoever is in that tunnel is gonna stay in there now," said Moses with a smile. Noticing the Captain coming his way he snapped to attention. "Attention!" The men saluted together.

"At ease and good morning, gentlemen," said Taylor. "Sergeant, your report if you wouldn't mind." The officer sipped on his steaming beverage.

"Well sir, we have three dead men Sullivan, Barnes and Rogers. Sullivan and Rogers we know died in the tunnel conflict. It's Barnes and the deputy's body that gives us the headache. There's an awful lot of dirt in the shaft sir. All of our personnel have been accounted for accurately."

"The deputy was dirty, we can all rest assured on that," said Bernard, poking at the fire. "Agreed?" The men looked at each other and nodded. "Why is he dead though?"

"The best that I can guess," said Moses with his arms crossed over his chest. "Barnes must have stumbled into whatever it was the smugglers were up to, and they killed him."

"To keep him quiet," said the officer with a look of disgust. "Scoundrels, they killed a young man for nothing."

"Looks like that's what happened, sir," said Moses. "That sheriff knows a lot more than what he's telling us. We should watch him. Sir, have you seen Hayes? I was going to need some items, and I know there must be paperwork that goes along with it."

"I believe he's gone into town for the morning correspondence."

"Alone!" The words had barely left his mouth when Corporal Bernard flew into the saddle.

"I'll find him." Off the man galloped.

"What's wrong? They wouldn't try to attack him in broad daylight?" The officer stared at Moses. "Right, Sergeant!"

"Oh, I'm sure that there's nothing to worry about, Hayes is really tough." The two men glanced around at the scene of last night's mayhem. Trees had been blown over and trampled. Shell casings were littered all about. "Secure for now," yelled Sergeant Trinidad, waving his hands "Make sure those fires are completely out before anyone leaves the area." The two soldiers walked back up the incline towards the fort.

Bernard made quick time of the ride to Flat Fork. Dismounting he tied his horse up to the hitching post. Hayes's horse was there, so he was in town. Bernard walked over to the Post & Telegraph operator's office. Entering, he saw a small man with glasses, sitting behind the counter.

"Morning, Corporal," shouted the man.

"Sir, did you see another soldier come in here already?"

"You mean Hayes? Yes, come and gone."

"Did you see which direction he was going?"

"My guess is down towards Missy Blyth's, they have the best penny candy around."

Bernard shook his head. "Thank you, sir."

"Good day Corporal." Bernard walked out of the office. Coming up the street whistling was Hayes.

"Hayes where the hell have you been?" Bernard stood there looking wide-eyed at the boy. "Answer me soldier." Hayes slowed to a stop.

"What's the matter? I checked the morning messages, there was none so I went to get a bag of candy." The boy held out a little paper bag. "Want one?"

"Do you remember what that ranger said to you last night?" asked Bernard looking up and down the streets. "Going anywhere without another person is out of the question until further notice."

"But!"

"No buts soldier, let's go!" Untying the horses the two soldiers climbed into the saddles and headed home.

* * * * * * *

Bacon was sizzling on the grill, its sweet aroma floating on the air. The children and Doris May were still fast asleep. Yesterday's events had worn them down to a frazzle. Lucy

Potter had risen early and was making breakfast for the soldiers. Wrapped in a blanket, she sat by the fire turning the bacon. Screeching Owl at Dawn was tucked next to a fallen tree, the shackles firmly fixed to both his wrists and ankles. Elias was on guard watching in all directions. Nouba nodded at the soldier. Using the butt of his weapon, he popped the Indian in the back of the head to wake him up. Extending his canteen, Elias shook it back and forth.

"Have a drink injun," said the soldier. The Indian gazed at the black man. "Don't you worry none if I wanted you dead, I'd shoot you." Twisting the top back on he tucked it away.

"Good morning ma'am," said Sergeant Nouba in a soft tone of voice. "May I pour you some coffee?" Reaching for the pot on the fire, he extended it to the lady. Glancing over at the Indian, he saw another trooper was positioned behind him; he wasn't going anywhere.

"Why thank you, Sergeant."

"Nouba, Powers Nouba." They shook hands. "Your name is Lucy, correct?"

"Very good memory, Sergeant," said the widow sipping from the tin cup. "My Nicolas had a very good memory too." She covered her mouth and began to weep. "We were going to start a new life out here with the children."

Nouba looked down into his cup. "There now ma'am," said the sergeant, patting her on the knee. "It could have been a whole lot worse. Those two precious children and your sister, well they could have been killed very easily. Count your blessings missy." The big man sat back down and began to fill his pipe. The sweet aroma of tobacco drifted in the morning air.

"You're right of course," she said wiping her eyes. "I shouldn't be so emotional all the time." She laughed calmly.

"Ma'am after what happened yesterday you have the right to feel any way that you like, you earned that. There is one thing that I think we should do before we head out this morning," said Nouba, looking straight at the ground.

"Yes, Sergeant."

"We should bury the two bodies here ma'am." She glanced over in his direction. "We lug those through the sun, that would be a heck of sight."

"Of course." She heard a noise and reached quickly for her pistol. "Someone is coming!" Nouba rose up and withdrew his weapon.

"Hold on now, ma'am." He gazed out across the plains. "Nothing to worry about, ma'am, just the morning scouts coming in." Tiner and Tote galloped over the hills and rode silently into the base camp.

"Morning ya'll," said Tiner with a small wave. "All's secured, Sergeant, no activity." The soldiers dismounted and walked toward the fire. Widow Potter handed each a mug of coffee.

"Thank you kindly, ma'am," said the soldiers, accepting the hot coffee. Tote removed his Bible from his coat and began to mumble some words.

Taking a sip, he spoke softly. "Mighty good coffee ma'am, thank ya." The big man smiled as he read from his book.

"Breakfast will be ready soon," said Lucy, smiling. "Are you men hungry?"

"Yes ma'am," said Tiner polishing the barrel of his carbine. Eyes glued at Abraham Tote, Lucy walked past Nouba over to him and set a plate of bacon, biscuits and sliced apples by them. "Thank ya kindly." Never saying much, Tote smiled while blowing on the tip of each bullet before he loaded it. Nouba chuckled softly to himself.

"This is the least that I could do for your men, Sergeant; after all, they saved mine and my family's lives." Removing another bag of apples she had tucked away in the wagon, she began slicing them up on an old cutting board with a sharp knife. Tote watched her. It reminded him of his mother in the kitchen. Sergeant Nouba shook his head back and forth and reached over to wake up Cole. The camp was beginning to bustle with activity. The children were awakened gently by their mother, and sure as the sun sets in the east, Doris May picked up that shotgun right where she left off the previous day.

The men began to load the wagon with the remainder of the Potter personal items. The furniture and other items were stacked in an orderly manner. Room was made for the children. Tote would drive the wagon with Lucy riding beside him. Doris May could walk or ride; it was her choice. Two graves were dug for the men and their bodies placed gently in the earth. It was a simple and elegant service. Cole fastened a couple of crude crosses and using his shovel, knocked them into the ground. They all stood together, next to the freshly dug graves.

Sergeant Nouba walked up to Tiner. "All right son, this is yours and Tote's patrol now. Take Elias and Cole and escort these civilians and the prisoner back to Flat Fork." Doris May overheard the conversation and began to spout off.

"We don't need **your** kind any more," said the young woman rudely. "We didn't ask for your help."

"Doris May, what has gotten into you?" shouted Lucy, grabbing her sister by the shoulders. "They risked their lives for us, you should be grateful." Tiner had had about as much as he could take. Rising up from the ground, he walked up to the girl. Standing there holding the shotgun she began to shake. A flick of the hand Tiner had disarmed the girl. Lucy turned toward the soldier. "I'm sorry, please don't."

"You'd better shut that mouth, you're bound to catch some flies," said Tiner slyly. Sergeant Nouba and Lucy Potter chuckled lightly. "I don't personally care what you think, little lady. My men and I have been given the task of escorting you safely back to Flat Fork. Seeing as how you don't need our help, you can just go on ahead of us, go on now!" The girl leered at the soldiers and began to well up. "Didn't think so. You'll get this gun back when I'm sure that you won't try and use it on me." Tiner turned toward her sister. "Miss Potter, I apologize for raising my voice at your sister, ma'am." Gathering up his gear, Tiner walked over to his horse and threw on his saddle. Abraham Tote assisted Lucy Potter up into the wagon. She smiled warmly at the man.

"We'll see you in a couple days Sergeant, okay?" said Tiner, high in the saddle. "Good luck!" As he reached his hand down, the sergeant grasped it firmly and pulled him close.

"Be careful with this one." Nouba pointed to the Indian being fastened to the rear of the wagon. "Tell the Captain that we are continuing the search for the others," said Nouba, rolling up his blanket. "No telling where we're going next." Securing it firmly to his saddle, he removed his carbine and checked it out. "Tiner."

"Yes, Sergeant."

"If things get rough, head to the old church. You can hold up there for quite a long time, ya hear?" Tiner nodded.

"Ready forward!" The wheels of the wagon began to turn slowly over the crusted earth. Flanked by a rider on either side, the group began the journey to Flat Fork. Nouba waved to the men as they rode off, the wagon swaying back and forth as it bounded over the rocky terrain.

"Tiner is gonna have his hands full with that gal," laughed Sergeant Nouba, as he finished his coffee. The rest of the men were saddling up the horses and preparing to set out, as a young soldier walked up to the sergeant.

"Patrol is ready, Sergeant." Nouba rose to his feet and dusted off his pants. Reaching up with one hand, Nouba pulled himself into the saddle and looked around in circles. "Ready forward!"

Abraham Tote worked the reins on the wagons as Lucy sat next to him humming softly. The children sat at the back of the wagon with Doris May, playing hand games. Lucy was a stunningly beautiful raven-haired girl of twenty. Her sister Doris May shared most of her features, except kindness.

"How long until we reach the town?" asked Lucy, squinting in the morning sun.

"My guess is dat we should reach the fort by late afternoon tomorrow, dusk at da latest." He glanced at her and smiled. "Abraham is my name. I'm glad that I was given dis task though." Tote smiled sweetly.

"You have a wonderful smile." Lucy Potter had a warm comforting face one you could get easily lost in. "You're very handsome." Tote just smiled and said nothing. "You must think very little of me, with my husband dying yesterday," She hid her face in shame. "We were arranged to be married by my father, it was not a marriage of love. We came out here from Virginia back east. We had a lot back there, but Nicholas wanted to see the frontier. I must admit I was curious myself to see what it was like. My life in Virginia was not very productive. Servants were available to assist with the children, so I never really had the chance to experience life for myself. Everyone did everything for me. But, I did learn to shoot a pistol. I guess I was looking to do something for myself, so frontier life was the plan. I must admit I never thought this would be happening."

"Not at all ma'am, finds you very pretty too." The two giggled at each other like young school children.

"How about an apple?"

"Thanks ma'am"

"Where are you from Abraham?"

"Roun Georgia. My ma and pa was slaves like everyone else. They was shot tryn' to leave the massa's home in da middle of da night. I runs and runs till I can't runs no mo. I joins up and here I am. Nuttin' fancy." The apples were tart and his lips puckered up. "Wooee!"

They laughed, that laugh people make when they find their new loves. Doris May sat frowning the entire way in. Tiner rode past her and she just glanced at him. Tote and Lucy continued chatting along the way for hours. The ruins of the church walls came into view.

"Patrol halt! Circle the area one hundred yards in all directions," ordered Tiner. The soldiers dismounted and pulled out their weapons. Cole and Elias led the horses to water, and the children played in the old church as Doris May stood watch. Tiner scanned the horizon. Tote walked off towards a rock formation; a numerous amount of cactus and other plants sprouted up in these rocky areas. Lucy made a simple lunch of fruit, bread and water. As Tote's eyes scanned the ground, he noticed a beautiful patch of yellow flowers. Gently picking a number of the flowers, the big soldier returned to the group.

He walked up to Lucy Potter and held out the flowers. "These are for you ma'am, they look jus' like a dandelion." The woman stopped and stared misty eyed at the flowers.

"They're lovely Abraham, and yes they are Texas Dande-lions," She took the flowers and gently touched his hand. Her smile beamed from ear to ear. Tiner rolled his eyes back. She laughed because she knew what was happening. In the short day that she had gotten to know the soldier, she was falling in love, and his color didn't matter.

"Momma, come look at these pretty flowers," the children yelled. Tote watched as the children ran in circles and hopped from rock to rock. They laughed and laughed; it was nice to watch children play after these past few days.

"Excuse me, Abraham," Lucy ran to the children and began twirling them around in circles. Tiner walked up to Tote and patted him on the shoulder.

"She's white, soldier, be careful," Tiner stared the soldier in the eye. "I'm happy as hell if you meet someone you like; just remember all folks ain't like us. All right, saddle up and let's head out."

Tote looked at the ground. "Don't care none," said the man smiling. "I could use a little nice." He loaded the children and the woman in the wagon, and then climbed aboard. Turning to Lucy, he gently kissed her hand. "I'd always do right by ya." He slapped the reins, and the horses slowly began to move. Tiner and Cole rode ahead a few yards to scout. Trying to maintain visual contact with the wagon and watch for Indians at times was not easy. The wagon rocked back and forth over the terrain. Some trails had been marked but were not at all maintained. Visibility became more difficult due to overgrown scrubs and weeds. The winds began to howl, rustling the leaves. The children were playing in the wagon and singing songs, as something caught Tote's attention. Turning his head from left to right he slowed the wagon down, then rose to his feet. Something wasn't right.

"Quiet!" There was something on the air, he couldn't quite make out. Holding his breath he stared intensely around. Tote's hand crept slowly to his holster, unbuckling the strap. Elias cautiously removed the carbine from its case and began looking around.

"Injuns!" Their screams penetrated the air like a sharp knife. "Get to da children!" BANG! A single shot penetrated the leg of Cole. "Arrghh!" The man tumbled from his horse onto the prairie floor. Tiner and Elias both turned in their saddles at the same time. Seeing the approaching Indians, they reared their horses around and headed back to the wagon. Ten or eleven mounted warriors stormed down the ridge.

Lucy leaped from the wagon. "Come children, quickly!" Max and Sissy jumped off and scrambled under. Doris May was crouched down behind a wheel.

"If I had my shotgun, we'd be a lot safer," said Doris leering at Lucy.

"If you didn't run your mouth, we'd be a lot safer, too!" Shielding the children with her body, Lucy removed her pistol. Taking careful aim she fired off a shot. BANG! The bullet found its mark, knocking an Indian from his mount. The children began crying and huddled close to their mother. Elias dismounted and took up a position at the rear of the wagon near Lucy May as Tiner rode by on his horse and tossed the shotgun and the box of shells to her.

"Finally coming to your senses, boy!" She looked up smugly at the Buffalo Soldier while she loaded the weapon.

"No, probably losing all track of them ma'am." Snapping the barrel shut, she knelt down. Removing his pistol, Tiner fired two shots and rode off circling around the perimeter. Finding their mark the bullets pierced the midsection of one of the Indians. The impact sent the brave whirling from his mount and crashing to the ground. Staggering to his feet he didn't know left from right. Elias and Lucy May both rose up from their positions and killed the Indian with a single shot each. Abraham Tote stayed close to the family and fired from a prone position. Cole began to crawl towards the wagon's cover. The Comanche riders headed at a fevered pace toward the wounded man.

"On da count of three we alls fire," yelled Tote. "Them injuns reach Cole, they'll trample him. 1, 2,3!" Firing simultaneously the bullets slammed into the riders' backs, hurling them to the ground in a cloud of dust. Slipping through the barrage, the third rider beared down on Cole.

"Noooooo!" The soldier tried to shield his face as the stead trampled over him. "Aiiieee!" The Buffalo Soldier's body tumbled in the brush coming to rest on his stomach.

"Cole!" Tote leaped from behind the wagon, his carbine in one hand, his pistol in the other, and charged. "Yeaaaah!"

Two shots pierced the air, as Tiner's horse began to buck uncontrollably. BANG! Another shot hit the beast causing it to topple over. Tiner was now pinned down by the weight of the horse. He tried to free himself from the animal's body. The soldier's leg was broken; the slightest movement sent shock waves of pain through his body. Using his horse as a barrier, the young man fired from his awkward position. Bullets slammed into the carcass of his horse making horrendous sounds, it still had life. Placing his revolver by the horse's head he pulled the trigger.

Two Indians had broken off from the pack and had snuck up on Tiner's position. Creeping slowly down the incline, they moved with catlike prowess. The Indian fired, striking Tiner in the upper shoulder area, dropping him on his back. Seeing this, Doris May shook her head and crawled over to his position. By this time, both Indians had descended on the soldier and were using the butts of their rifles to beat him. Tiner's face was bloodied and the weight of the horse's dead body restricted his movement.

BOOM! BOOM! The shotgun blasts hurled both Indian's bodies into the low brush. Doris May quickly reloaded and blasted another round into each body. Walking over to the horse, she saw Tiner beneath its body weight. Approaching it slowly, she looked down at the soldier. His face was purple colored and bleeding. Tossing her empty shells on the ground, she bent down near the wounded man and gazed into his eyes.

"I can always count on you to give it to them with both barrels ma'am. Ha. Ha," hacked the man trying to lean up. Again he dropped to the ground.

"Abraham, no!" yelled Lucy Potter covering her eyes. The Buffalo Soldier streaked across the ground yelling at the top of his lungs. Doris May laid down her shotgun and crouched down next to Tiner. BOOM! BOOM! Striking each brave in the head, Tote discarded his revolver. The

Indian rider removed his lance and kicked up his horse. "Woooooooooo!"

The sounds of hoof beats rolling over the earth thundered in the afternoon air. Closer and closer rode the beast. Cocking back his right arm, the Indian was ready to skew the soldier.

At the last possible second, moving sharply to his left, the soldier smashed his carbine into the base of the horse's neck and dove to the side. The animal hit the ground with a thud, shattering the gun in pieces. The force from the fall hurled the rider twenty feet in the air. The native's body came to rest over some rocks. Picking up the lance, Tote raced over to the Indian's position. Placing both hands firmly around the handle, he plunged the sharp metal blade into the warrior's stomach. Tote gazed into the Indian's eyes, and turned the lance slowly. Discarding the weapon, he turned and went to his fallen comrade. Elias leaped up and followed. Slowly turning the shattered body over, they both gazed at the blood streaming from Cole's eye and nose. The man was dead.

Screeching Owl at Dawn huddled close to the ground. He was using a sharp rock to cut away layers of his skin and try to free himself from the chains. Lucy opened up the chamber and removed the spent shells. "Stay down children!" She eased herself around the rear of the wagon and walked over to the Indian's position, reloading her pistol. "Up you son of a ......" Tote watched as his lady friend stood her ground.

Rising to his feet, Screeching Owl at Dawn began his death dance. "Aiiee Oh Ahee Oh Aheiee!" Dancing in circles the chains jingled as the Indian moved about. Lucy's hair blew across her dirty face as she watched the prayer dance. Raising the pistol, she fired three times. BANG! BANG! BANG! Screeching Owl at Dawn dropped to the ground. Emptying the revolver, she dropped the shells on the Indian's chest. "That was for Nicholas." Turning around,

Abraham Tote was the first person she saw. She fell in his arms.

"It's going to be all right darling," said Tote, stroking her hair gently.

"Momma, Momma," yelled the children, leaping into her arms.

Tiner looked up from the ground. One of his eyes was swollen shut; he could barely see Doris May.

"Maybe I was a little harsh with you boys, I'm sorry," said Doris May. Reaching down she slid a rolled up shirt under Tiner's head. "We're going to have to try to move this horse off you. If we don't get that bleeding controlled that leg's a gonner for sure."

Tote and Elias managed to free their man from his dead animal. Doris May and Lucy worked together to control the bleeding and placed a tourniquet on it. Tiner rested next to the body of Cole in the rear of the wagon.

"What should we do with this one," said Elias pointing to Screeching Owl at Dawn's body, still in the shackles.

Abraham Tote undid the latch on the shackles and re-moved them from the body. Gently folding the warrior's arms over his chest, the soldier said some quiet words then stood up.

"Ready forward!" The women guided the wagon as Tote and Elias covered the flanks. Max was given Tiner's weapon to watch for Indians as Sissy, helped tend to the wounded man.

FOURTEEN

It was late afternoon, and the sun was dipping into the valley. Before a crowd of soldiers standing at attention, a young preacher spoke above the winds.

"O'Heavenly Father, we praise you with thy name. Father we offer unto you the souls of our dear departed brothers. Heavenly Father, we ask you to accept them in spite of their faults. Enable us Lord to walk, body and soul in loving obedience of you. Realize we fail in comparison to you O' Lord.

Amen!"

"Honor Guard attention!" The soldiers snapped to attention. "Ready, aim, fire!

The small group from the patrol had just crossed over the large hill not far from the cemetery. "What was that noise?" Max and Sissy Potter looked inquisitively at the soldiers. "More Indians?"

"Shots are too close together. Sounds like an honor guard," said Tiner, removing his pistol from his holster and trying to sit up and see.

"There's only one way to find out," said Elias. "Stay here, I'll be right back. Ya! Ya!" The soldier darted forward toward the ridge. Coming slowly to a stop, he sat there on his horse and listened.

"Present arms!" The bugler played the sad melody of Taps. The men stood quietly at attention. Kaleb Christopher removed his cap and held it over his heart. "Lower caskets." Gently the men lowered their comrades into the ground. "Dismissed!" They slowly began to file out dropping a flower or a bullet in the grave. Captain Taylor and Sergeant Trinidad lingered in the rear.

"All things considered, this was a successful campaign against the gun runners, sir," said Moses, gazing at the soldiers filing out. The officer removed a cigar from his pocket.

"Would you care for one, Sergeant?"

"No thank you sir, I'm a pipe man." Removing the pipe from his pocket he packed it full of some new apple scented tobacco. Both men lit their smokes and leaned up against the fence watching the horizon.

"You know something," said Taylor. "I never fully appreciated a sunset until I was transferred here out West. There is nothing like it in the world, I'm quite certain of that." The red colors seemed to stretch for miles and miles. The streaks of yellow and orange colors burned passionately.

"World's a big place, sir." The sweet smelling tobacco encircled Moses' head like a wreath. The officer gently tapped his ashes on the ground. "Sir, I think that we should consider sending out regular patrols in town. Make our presence felt a little more."

"Sounds like a plan to me, Sergeant Trinidad. I have to write to Regimental Headquarters about our situation with the guns and the deaths of the men. They'll unfortunately care only about the weapons that get recovered. They will say that the men dying is just the price we pay."

"Helluva price," said Moses softly. Suddenly he noticed something moving on the horizon. "What the heck is that?"

"Yooooo!!!" yelled Elias, waving his hat back and forth. Over the hill came the little wagon with its precious cargo of soldiers, women and children. Sergeant Trinidad and Captain Taylor gazed at the figures coming over the hill.

Moses squinted hard to make out who it was. Slowly the visions became clearer. Moses climbed on the picket fence. "Patrol coming in!" Elias rode ahead of the group and galloped towards the cemetery.

"We got wounded, we need help."

"Crawford, Pike," yelled Moses. "Grab the men, we got wounded." Soldiers rushed immediately to the wagon. The men escorted the tired group into the safe haven of the fort. Tiner was carried to the hospital. Cole's body was taken there also. The women and children were taken to the Captain's quarters.

"Report, Tiner," said Moses, standing at his bedside.

"Well, we were on patrol with Sergeant Nouba's group when we came across these civilians getting hit by hostiles. Engaging the enemy, we managed to kill the advancing Indians. Unfortunately, we arrived too late to save the men. Upon securing the area, we buried the bodies and were instructed by Sergeant Nouba to take four men and escort the civilians and a captured native back to Flat Fork. Pushing on for several hours we stopped to take a rest at the church ruins when we were hit for the second time. We lost Cole; my leg got hurt when my horse was shot and fell on me, and the prisoner was shot in shackles by one of the women. We loaded up the wagon and headed back home."

Patting Tiner on the shoulder, Moses smiled warmly. "Get some rest son, you've earned it." He grabbed his hat and headed for the door. "I'll come back later to check on you."

"Thanks, Sergeant Trinidad," smiled the soldier.

Moses walked out into the late evening night and packed his pipe full of tobacco. The lights were on in the Captain's quarters. The young officer agreed to let the women and children occupy the second floor until they found a place to live in town. The skeleton of the new horse corral was almost completely covered. The men had assembled it in astonishingly short time. Moses saw a golden opportunity to get some time to jot a note or two down in his journal. Repairing to his spot behind his barracks, he lit a fire in the pit. The temperatures began to dip and he shivered slightly. Pulling out his chair, Moses sat down by the fire's warm relaxing glow.

September 31st 1879

The command has been hit with a multitude of problems and the men have executed their duties to the highest caliber. We have lost a large number of soldiers. Their deaths, though a tragedy, will serve to remind people of the sacrifices that have to be made to open this vast frontier in the west.

The gun smugglers that we encountered were worthy adversaries. We managed to get a few of the bandits in deadly gunfights in the tunnel complex and the creek bed area. Many of their own men were killed as the tunnel complex was blown up. We managed to re-secure all the weapons that had been stored in the tunnel. They have been moved to the post's powder room. We lost three men of our own. Young men in the prime of their lives, two in combat and one of mysterious circumstances, it breaks my heart.

My duties now include a more supervisory role in the command, which I like. I still do my fair share of patrols, but the Captain feels my skills would be of better use to the command in this capacity.

We think the local sheriff, his deputies, and a rogue band of rangers have been dealing with the local Indians for guns.

The men who were dispatched to find Texas dignitaries assisted in the rescue of some civilians, two women and two children. Their men were scalped. Woman's name is Potter, Lucy Potter. She has a sister, Doris May who loves her shotgun and two young ones named Max and Sissy, Cute kids. We lost another man on the detail that was escorting the civilians to the fort. Young man by the name of Cole. The prisoner who was captured by Sergeant Nouba's men was shot in the exchange of fire; the widow Potter shot him still in his shackles. Tiner was wounded in the leg, credits the sister Doris May with saving his life. Tiner also informed me that he feels his buddy, Abraham Tote has fallen for the widow Potter and she apparently feels the same way.

I feel a headache coming on though. Maybe this will be the start of a nice community of blacks. Once we get established they'll have to accept us. My opinion of the townspeople is most don't care who is who as long as you help a neighbor in a time of need. There'll always be that ignorant individual who will have to raise his voice in protest over a person because he's too narrow minded to understand everyone is different. I suppose that scares most people though. I still can't help but think that they stare at us when we walk by and ask the questions what, who and when? I suppose even I get a swelled head when some people turn in fear from us. I suppose that is just the man in me.

Sometimes I just can't grasp the fact that I am a free man. I never had to suffer the "slings and arrows" like most of my fellows soldiers. The tales of the suffering and pain that they and their families endured makes me proud to lead them.

The men are a wonderful bunch. Many uneducated in a formal setting, as far as skills in the world they are leaps and bounds ahead of most of the white troopers that I have served with in the past. I guess when you're raised to fight for your survival on a daily basis your willingness to win carries over into everything that you do and there are no exceptions.

Moses removed his pipe from his pocket and packed it with tobacco and lit a match. Puffing smoothly, he exhaled a thin grayish stream of smoke. Stretching his back, he yawned and rubbed his eyes; his muscles were sore and tight. The ole body was beginning to shut down for the night. "Can't last like I used to," laughed the soldier.

Tomorrow night I plan on taking a ride into town alone. A little poking around won't hurt anyone. No other word from Nouba's patrol to find Texas dignitaries. The longer it is the greater the risk that we may never find them...

Moses' head tilted down on his shoulder and his body slumped in the chair. The fire crackled softly in the air as the tired man slept. Standing off hidden under the barracks porch, a man struck a match and ignited his cigar. Captain Taylor smiled in the darkness. "That's one hell of a man!"

* * * * * * *

Sergeant Nouba's patrol had not seen a trace of civilians for the entire day. No Indians were spotted as a number of scouts rotated back and forth to scour the area. Nighttime began creeping in, and the men decided to set camp for the night. The terrain was flat and sandy; very little rock formations so visibility was good. The guards were posted, and the campfires were lit. The horses were tied up given water and oats. There was very little vegetation so grass was scarce.

"Make sure the men get fed and rested," said Sergeant Nouba, removing his bedroll. The soldiers began fixing their meals and relaxing for the night. Nouba took off his pistol belt and set it on the ground. Taking a seat on a rock, he slowly removed both of his boots. "Oohh, these pups are sore." Grasping his feet firmly, he massaged them. He pointed them towards the fire, the heat felt nice.

"What's the matter Sergeant, you've been riding all day, how can your feet hurt?" chuckled Jebidiah Mathers. Well built and a joker, the man sat down next to Nouba. "Here maybe this will help?" Removing a small bottle, Mathers took off the cap. "Have a swig." Nouba looked both ways and tilted back. That helped; the brown warm liquid seeped into his blood and brought a smile to his face. "Sergeant, what's are our chances of finding those people?"

"Well, it all depends on whether or not they're still alive. Hopefully tomorrow will bring some better luck," said the man patting the boy on his back. "Get some rest, I have a feeling we are bound to make some contact in the morning."

* * * * * * *

Entering his quarters, Taylor remembered that he was relegated to the first floor. The women and children occupied level two for a few days. Hayes had turned the inside office into a dual purpose quarters for the officer. The captain had been putting off writing to his superiors because he knew it would probably stir up a hornet's nest but it was proper military protocol.

October 1ˢᵗ 1879

Commanding Officer

9ᵗʰ U.S. Cavalry

Washington, D.C.

Follow up report on Indian attacks in the theater of operation. Upon returning from the last patrol we have engaged the Indians on many occasions having much success.

We uncovered a plot to steal rifles from military supply room at the post. Underground tunnel complex discovered and sizeable cash of weapons were recovered in the effort. Plan of action was taken to capture bandits. Explosions and gun fight erupted resulting in the deaths of three Army personnel and an undetermined number of thieves. Many bodies buried in the cave-in.

Received distress telegram from Lt. Governor Reynolds of Texas State, dignitaries have not turned up. I ordered a squad of men to head out in hopes of finding the Texas people.

Captain Hennecker J. Taylor
9th U.S. Cavalry, Fort Barre, Texas

Rising from his chair, Taylor walked over to the burning fire. The winds whipped and howled against the wooden structure. Suddenly a creaking noise was heard. Moving quickly to his chair, he removed his pistol from its holster. "One more move and they'll be cleaning pieces of you out of the walls!" The noise stopped.

"It's Doris May Potter," she called with a crabby sounding voice. "Put your weapon down." She appeared in the orange glow of the firelight. Lowering his weapon, he made a face and tossed it on the chair. Taylor walked over to his cabinet and removed the hidden bottle of whiskey and poured a drink. Doris May was an attractive girl with lovely features and alabaster skin. Unfortunately, her attitude did not match her appearance. "Are you going to offer me a drink?"

"No," said the young man taking a sip and sighing. Sitting down in front of the fireplace he began removing his boots. The girl stood there with her hands crossed.

"No class! I can't even…"

"Lady, don't even start running your mouth or I may have to use this," said the man patting his revolver. "My men died to save your ungrateful life and I have allowed you a place to stay out of the good graces of my heart. I can't even imagine you and your sister being related, you're nothing alike, she's polite!" The man stared deep into the flames.

"Are you forgetting that I saved your man's life," said the woman sitting down. "I didn't have to do that, but I did." Taylor rolled his eyes in her direction and shook his head.

"Bravo, Miss Potter, you're part of the human race. People like you really get under my skin because you think you're above the rest of us. Well, let me tell you that you're far from it." He watched her expression in the firelight and wondered how could anyone, let alone a woman, think that way.

"Why did you choose to lead these men, Captain, or may I call you John?" She walked over to his cabinet and grabbed a glass. Pouring herself some whiskey, she sipped it easily.

"Captain Taylor is fine and **help** yourself," he snapped. Doris May's eyes popped out. "Well, if you must know I think that a Cavalry Unit is a Cavalry Unit white or black.

Most people think the Negroes don't belong in this Army. It was well documented that Colonel Custer was vehemently opposed to blacks. If he had had my Buffalo soldiers with him, they would have never lost. Why do you dislike them so much?" The officer placed another log on the fire.

"Growing up I was taught that they were less then the whites. I never had to depend on them for anything before. I was faced with a situation that I had never encountered in my life," she said, turning away.

"So, the first people you lash out at are the very ones who chose to risk their necks to save you, that's smart. Anyway you should get used to seeing the blacks because it looks like your older sister is growing quite fond of my man Tote," said Taylor smiling. Placing his hand on his chin he proclaimed. "I foresee a wedding."

Rising from her chair, Doris May headed for the stairs. "Don't go pushing your luck, Captain Taylor. Goodnight."

Waving his hand, the officer cleaned up and got ready for bed. Pulling the blanket over his chest, he sank into the mattress with a sigh of relief.

Doris May walked slowly up the stairs and pushed open the door. Her niece and nephew were snoring lovingly in their slumber, and her older sister was curled up in a chair next to the bed. Lucy had made room in the bed for Doris May.

"He's a very handsome man, Doris May," whispered her sister popping one eye open.

"Be quiet, you'll wake the children," she hissed. Turning away she leaned against the window and looked out over the fort. "Me, marry a soldier, surely you must be joking." Doris May had those thoughts and more running through her mind about the young officer. Lucy smiled warmly and fell back to sleep.

* * * * * * *

The men had already broken down the camp when the morning scouts rolled in. There was a single fire burning with a pot of coffee and some dry meat. Horses were saddled up, and the men were readying for action.

Sergeant Nouba emerged from the bushes adjusting his trousers. Tobit Jones and Ezra David were young eager soldiers; both had Seminole blood in them. Experienced riders in the saddle, they trotted into the campsite.

"Morning, Sergeant," waved Jones climbing down from his saddle. "All is quiet; not a single speck on the horizon." David climbed off his horse and gently stroked her mane.

"Can't for the life of me figure this out," said Jones bending down to fill their coffee cups. "Where in the hell did those folks wander off to?"

Nouba looked out across the sand. "Well, there's a whole lot of open space out there; this could take time." The soldiers chewed on the tough dried meat. It wasn't the best of breakfasts, but it filled their stomachs. Sipping on their coffee, the men thought of their next move, as the other soldiers finished their morning routines.

The fire was doused with sand, and the last of the coffee was gone. "Well, let's head over into the western section," said Nouba, pointing to a spot on his map. "Right over here, it links to the Blackbird River just about seven miles here. Maybe the people headed near the water? It would be where I would go." The men were all gathered around in a circle. "Mount up! Scouts ride ahead." Jones and David raced ahead of the pack as normal. The ground was flat and dusty and still no sign of the civilians.

Jones began to scan the surrounding hills for any signs of life. The men sat in the saddle staring out across the desert. Something lying in the sand caught Jones's attention. Straining to look he couldn't make out the object. "What is that?"

"Only one way to find out," replied David. "Ya ya." The men kicked up their horses and pounded over the rock-infested ground. Slowing down to a trot, the men removed their weapons and listened. David eased out of his saddle. "There," he said, pointing to a group of tracks in the dirt. "Someone's been through here with a wagon." Walking another step or two, he noticed a smashed barrel of water, a cowboy hat covered in dirt, and a suitcase. "And judging by this stuff littered around I'd say they were moving fast. Ahh!" Ezra David bent down and picked up an arrow. Holding it over his head so Tobit would see, the soldier walked ahead another few yards. There were more arrows in the sand.

The small strip of sand led to a crest over a hill. Looking over the hill, David saw the remains of a smashed wagon scattered at the bottom with the dead animals still tied, along with two bodies. "Got 'em!" yelled David. Jones pulled out his pistol; raising it above his head he fired. BANG! BANG! BANG! A massive rumbling noise was heard as the soldiers came riding towards the scouts. "We got us a trail."

Nouba dismounted and peered over the hill. "Let's get down there and check this thing out. Have the men secure the entire area." The soldiers split up; half went down the hill and the others secured the sections on the north and south sides. Ezra David was the first man to the bodies. Dressed in suits, the dead men were bruised and had been scalped. Ezra bent down and felt the fabric of the clothes.

"Damn this is real silk, soft as a baby's bottom," he said. Nouba tapped his fingers in the bloodstained sand.

"The blood is still light in color; this happened about an hour ago. We should still be able to track them down." The soldiers searched the bodies checking for anything that could help identify the men.

"Why did they shoot the horses?"

"Well, these are our boys," said Jones, emerging from the wrecked body of the wagon. "There's another man in there; looks to me that he broke his neck." The soldier had found a State courier bag with the Seal of Texas stamped on it. He handed the pouch to his sergeant. Opening the satchel it contained several sealed documents. Nouba closed the bag and tucked it under his arm. Turning, he walked back up to the top of the hill where the tracks were. Nouba noticed there was a gap in the wheel marks; they disappeared after the lip of the hill.

"Well, what can you make of this one?" asked David joining the sergeant on the hill.

Nouba was kneeling down, picking up little pebbles and tossing them to the ground. "They were being chased; my guess is they were coming around the bend from the opposite end of the ridge. They were moving at a good speed too. Did you notice the fresh earth sprayed over the sand at the trail crossing? They made a wide turn quickly. The wheels; they're cracked and splintered. Where the tracks disappear in the sand is where the wagon was actually in the air." Ezra stood back in amazement as the sergeant continued speaking. "It crashed into the ground here at this point." A small shallow hole contained broken wood pieces. "My guess is that both the men were thrown from the wagon."

"How could you tell?"

"There are spent shell casings lying all around. The men returned fire but were overrun. The Indians simply took the weapons. The third man couldn't jump out in time and died on impact. To answer your other question about the horses, they probably had been injured, either broken leg, or the wagon could have hit them, so the Indians shot them. Let's bury the bodies and see if we can pick up their trail." The soldiers dug three shallow graves in the hard earth and placed the remains in each. After covering the bodies with dirt the men stacked rocks on top and used wooden planks as headstones. Mounting up quickly, they rode off after the Indians.

The men had been in the saddle for well over four hours and were growing tired and impatient. Suddenly, Ezra David rode hard to the soldier's position. "We got them Sergeant, Indians about fifteen or so. We found a campsite." Smiling, Nouba left orders for the bulk of the men to hold their position. The soldiers dismounted and walked carefully on foot to a hidden crest overlooking the river. Jones was lying on his stomach, his sites trained in the middle of the camp. Sergeant Nouba crept slowly next to the young man.

"Itching to use that weapon, son," said Nouba with a smile. "Get ready soldier!" Looking over the edge, he noticed several wigwams and teepees pitched on the grassy banks. Several male warriors were tending to the horses penned up near the trees on the bank river. Women were washing clothes and picking vegetables, while the children ran about playfully. Nouba spotted five or so additional men crossing the shallow portion of the river coming in from the back. Jones scanned the rocks and higher elevations for a look out, nothing. "That small crossing in the water is the key; we secure that and they won't stand a chance."

"Sergeant, look!" whispered Jones, pointing to a structure to the far left.

"Noooooo!" A young white girl was pulled from the structure by her hair and tossed to the ground by a muscular looking brave. Although bound by her wrists, she struggled to her feet and tried to swing at her captor. The warrior blocked her attempt and threw her down again. Rising up, she spit in his face. The man's hand crashed into her face hurtling her inside again. Following in behind her, the commotion subsided.

"Get Ruth, pass the word the women and children are not targets, is that understood? We don't kill them unless they're trying to kill a soldier. Go and be quiet!" The man ran back to the horses and passed along the sergeant's orders.

"I don't see a scout or a sentry or anything, do you?"

Jones again scanned the area but saw nothing. "Maybe the tribes not at full strength, they've probably thinned out."

"They still can take a white prisoner though," said Nouba. "All right here it is, we take the men down the smooth section of dirt and head straight into the heart of the camp." Ezra David relayed the orders as instructed.

"You heard the man, load heavy," ordered Ruth. "Leave two men behind to cover us. Remember that Rules of Conduct apply. No innocent people will be touched." Ruth watched the men loading their weapons; they were eager for a fight. Checking his pistol and carbine, the soldier removed his grate coat and tucked it away in his saddlebag.

"Company front," barked Sergeant Nouba. The men lined up in front of their sergeant, cocking back their weapons.

"Char-r-r-ge!" The sea of blue swept over the edge and descended on the camp and its inhabitants. Woman and children ran hysterically about in attempts to flee the camp. Warriors emerged from their dwelling with weapons in hand and were shot down immediately.

"Push them into the center of the village," ordered Sergeant Nouba. Indians were dropping to the ground all over. Nouba was amazed they had no sentries posted; the army was overpowering them with ease. Thunderous noises from the horses created massive confusion in the village.

Rides for the Wind was shaken violently awake. The pain from his bullet wounds made any movement a chore. He was too weak to rise. His mind began racing. Peering through a small hole, the warrior watched as the soldiers rode around. There was nowhere to run and hide; his time on earth was drawing to a close.

The soldiers rode into the village kicking up dust and causing confusion; people were running in every direction. The battle seemed to last forever, but in reality it lasted less than ten minutes.

Suddenly, the covering on Rides for the Wind's dwelling was slashed open violently by several bayonets as the Buffalo Soldiers entered.

"Well, well, well what do we have here?" The Indian stared up at his captors and tilted his head away. Rides for the Wind went slowly for the weapon resting beside him. A soldier's foot came crashing down on his wrist.

The army had swept into the village and rounded up all the inhabitants and herded them to the middle. The men positioned in the high rocky sections were ordered to stand fast and hold the ground.

Sergeant Nouba and Ruth approached the small wigwam where the white woman was seen. Pulling back the animal skin covering, they discovered her huddled in the corner, petrified.

"Ma'am you're all right now, my name is Sergeant Nouba, United States Cavalry. No one is going to hurt you anymore." The woman raised her head slowly. Her face was swollen and her lip was cut. Nouba knelt down and removed his gloves. "It's all right now."

"They tried to have their way with me," she said quietly. "I fought back though, they grew tired of trying I guess. That's when they put me in here. My name is Claudia Rothschild." The woman was clearly traumatized.

"Rothschild, Governor Nigel Q. Rothschild of Texas, you're his daughter," said Sergeant Nouba smiling and slapping Ruth on the back. His look changed from excitement to disappointment quickly. "Ma'am, I'm sorry to have to tell you this but the men in your party were killed."

"Yes, I know," she said, dropping her head. The soldiers stood silently. "Thank you and your men for coming to my rescue, Sergeant."

"You're welcome. I must ask, is this the entire bulk of their tribe, or should we expect company?"

"I'm not sure," she replied. "The group that attacked the wagon was only around seven men. They surprised us, I mean they just came up out of nowhere and shot us for no reason." She began weeping.

"There, there, you're all right now," said the sergeant holding her hand. "The Cavalry is here now, let's get you back to the fort." Taking her by the hand, Nouba led her out of the hut and into the afternoon light. Women, children and old men were huddled in the grass with looks of total wonder and shock in their eyes. Who were these Buffalo Soldiers? How did they find the camp? The soldiers smiled as they walked through the groups of people checking for weapons. The bodies of the dead Indians were placed in rows in the afternoon sun. They numbered fifteen in all. The soldiers found what appeared to be a storage area containing food, blankets, and other items. Grabbing some extra food and provisions, they loaded them on the horses.

Ruth walked over to the sergeant. "All men accounted for and not a single casualty. We have a prisoner."

"A prisoner, where?" Sergeant Nouba turned and looked at the group of civilians. "Take me to him," said Nouba.

The soldiers walked past a couple other huts and came to the dwelling surrounded by four armed men. "He had this in his possession," said a soldier, holding out an U.S. Army regulation carbine.

Sergeant Nouba and Ruth towered over the wounded warrior. Rides for the Wind looked nervously at the men.

"What do we do with him, Sergeant?" asked Ruth.

"The criminal was found with a stolen weapon and more than likely those wounds are from an exchange of gunfire with soldiers. Burn the village and seize their supplies. Take possession of their horses in the name of the United States Army." The men stared at the sergeant. "Do it now!"

"Yes, Sergeant," barked the soldier. "Destroy the village!" Using their neckerchiefs to cover their mouths, the soldiers distributed torches and began to set fire to the dwellings. The villagers screamed and cried as their homes were set ablaze. Two soldiers pulled Rides for the Wind from his hut.

Nouba grabbed the Indian and pushed him to the side. Calmly removing his pistol, the soldier pointed and fired. The body dropped to the ground with a loud thud. The crying grew louder as the sergeant checked his weapon and walked away. The heat from the fires grew more intense and the smoke and flames hindered visibility. "Prepare to mount. Mount up!" Claudia was given a horse, and the soldiers began to file out of the valley. The remaining Indians sat helplessly by as their homes were reduced to nothing. With the yellow hankerchiefs covering their faces, the Indians thought the soldiers were criminals. "Ready, forward!"

Nouba sat atop his horse watching the soldiers leaving. Ruth rode up and stopped. "What happens to the people, Sergeant?"

Nouba looked straight ahead. "That's not my problem, Ruth, nor yours either. These people chose to abduct a civilian, murder others and keep stolen guns. They knew it could come to this. Do you remember your dead comrades that we have recently buried?" Nouba raised his chin and spurred his horse forward up the hill. Ruth looked back and saw the women and children head for the hills with whatever they could carry. The flames rose high as Sergeant Nouba watched on. The soldier turned and galloped ahead with the other soldiers. The mood amongst the men was one of pleasure. Freeing a white civilian from Indian captives could benefit the command. This victory would be shared with all at Fort Barre. The column of soldiers continued to ride for five hours straight. If all went well, the patrol should be back in about two days. Nouba was very proud of the way the men performed. Trotter rode beside the sergeant.

"This is a good one for ya, Sergeant," said the man, bouncing by in the saddle, smiling from ear to ear. Nouba himself couldn't help but grin. This was a rare lopsided victory for the men. The people in Washington would use this campaign as a means to move further west and place additional soldiers along the way. Darkness was looming on the horizon; by the looks of the clouds it was rain. Cold weather and rain were sure signs that flu like symptoms were looming on the horizon. Shaking off a cold in the damp bitter weather could wear down the most hardened soldier. The scouts returned from their ride and reported to the sergeant.

"No sign of Injuns Sergeant," said Jones. "We's gonna be wet soon." Nouba stared at the dark clouds approaching. Ezra David looked around for any area to set up a temporary shelter for the woman. Spotting a small dugout area in the rocks, he trotted over to take a look. The rocks had a cave like structure that went back about ten feet or so, enough room for the woman to sleep and have a fire to keep warm by. "Over here!" The men found some broken trees so he began to gather wood for the fire. The patrol moved over to the area and began to assemble a camp for the evening.

Nouba began motioning the men into different sections from his horse. "Make sure the perimeter is secured." Ezra David walked over to the sergeant.

"We can take the larger pieces of canvas and string them from the top of the cave's mouth and over that tree," said the soldier. "It should be enough for the men to stay relatively dry. We'll take our rope and rig up a crude corral for the horses in groups of five. Let's get it done!" The men had appropriated a few blankets from the villagers and had made a nice bed for Ms. Rothschild to rest. She was still quite exhausted, as she curled up in the bedding and shivered.

"I'm gonna git it warm in no time ma'am." said Jones, as he built a nice fire that warmed the cave. Jones was momentarily lost as he gazed at the shadows dancing off the walls. The men had taken their saddles, haversacks and additional gear from the horses and stowed them in the rear of the cave so they could stay dry. Guards were set in place as the thunder roared, spooking the animals. The rains came and came. The water rushed over the rocks, creating a wall of water in front of the cave. The fire crackled as Sergeant Nouba puffed quietly on his pipe. The men were bedding down and the rain's peaceful sounds made sleeping easier. Hours had past and all was quiet. CRASH! The lightning flashed across the plains. BOOM! The thunder rolled.

"I never got the chance to properly thank you and your men for saving ma life," said Claudia with a Texas twang. She propped herself up on her elbow and stared into the fire. "You and your men were incredible. The way you swept in and surrounded the village."

"Well, I'm just glad we got out with no casualties, that's the big plus." Nouba pulled a piece of thin wood from the fire. Using the glowing tip, he lit his pipe and puffed generously. "It makes all of us feel good to know you held your ground, ma'am." The soldier tapped his palm against the pot of coffee. "Hot!" Wrapping his neckerchief around his hand he lifted the pot. "Coffee, ma'am?"

"Why thank you, Sergeant," said the sleepy eyed girl. "Should warm the insides." Wrapping the blanket tighter around her, she sipped. "This is quite cozy."

Looking around, the sergeant replied. "Yes, it's just like home. All we need is some sweet potato pie with real cream. Yes ma'am that would help this coffee out just enough." She laughed loudly. Nouba looked and smiled as she covered her mouth in embarrassment.

"I'm sorry, Sergeant." She continued giggling.

"Not at all ma'am, laughter is the best medicine. What would you choose to have with your coffee if you were home?"

"Well, my mother makes a very tasty raspberry tart," she said smiling. "Warmed in the oven with a scoop of ice cream, it's decadent." They laughed through the night as they chatted away.

"Sergeant, I must admit that I never.. a…that is…"

"Talked this much with a person of color," he replied, looking into his cup. "It's not something to be ashamed of."

"It makes me feel bad knowing that I never interacted with the coloreds before. We had servants growing up, but I guess I never really sat down and talked to them and heard what they had to say. You must think very little of a person like me," she said, lowering her head.

"Don't you go dropping your head now," smiled Nouba poking at the fire. "We all have lessons in life to learn and you're learning yours now." He winked at the girl. "Get some more rest, we got a long day ahead of us tomorrow." Tossing another log on the fire Nouba leaned back and tilted his hat over his eyes. Claudia stared at the soldier for a moment as he snored.

FIFTEEN

Sheriff Watkins sat behind his desk drinking whiskey. "Aiee!" shouted the man grabbing his lip. "That little twerp, he's gonna get his." Watkins slammed his fist on the desk. "Assaulting me in front of the entire town, he'll get his."

"Will you shut the hell up!" Slowly the curtain was pulled aside and Ranger Armstead appeared. His nose was bandaged, and he had several bruises on his face. Like all men, his pride was wounded the most. Armstead oozed across the room and took a seat. "Well, how about a drink?" Watkins pushed the bottle over to him.

"Glasses are on the shelf, help yourself." Armstead growled, got up, and grabbed a glass. Pouring the whiskey, he splashed some over the desk. "Well what's our next move, genius?" smirked Sheriff Watkins. "Now that you have depleted your entire staff so to speak."

Armstead removed a pistol from his belt and pointed it at the man. "Woooo!" Tipping back in the chair, Watkins crashed to ground.

"Ha Ha!" Armstead howled in delight.

"Teach ya to run that mouth, huh!" Straightening himself and his chair, Watkins sat back at the desk. Armstead holstered his revolver and gulped a quick drink.

"Why don't you just leave," said Watkins, leaning forward. "What the hell are you doing this for?" The Sheriff tilted back the whiskey and wiped his mouth with his shirt.

Armstead refilled both glasses and smiled. "That nigga and me have a score to settle." Whipping his hand back, he gulped the drink and winced.

"That big soldier hell, he'll kill you, you don't stand a prayer. It doesn't matter that his army wiped out both groups of our men." Watkins sat back. Armstead leaped forward grasped the man by his shirt, and hurled him against the wall. Watkins fell to the ground and winced in pain. Armstead poured another shot and tossed it back. Removing the revolver he again aimed it at the sheriff. The man covered his head with his arms. "Wait! Wait!"

CLICK! CLICK! "Ha! Ha!" The drunken man began to stumble with the bottle across the room. "Yes siree, that nigga and his buddies are gonna pay." Armstead tripped forward and crashed over the desk, hitting the ground hard. He was out cold.

Watkins looked over from his desk and poured himself a drink. "My God, what did I get myself into?" Placing the glass to his lips, he drank slowly and coughed. The sheriff walked past the snoring ranger and headed up to his room. The rain continued to come down like cats and dogs. Turning back towards the drunken man on the ground, Watkins sighed. "I guess it's too much to hope you've died."

The streets of Flat Fork were empty because of the weather. One or two lanterns illuminated the occasional building, but it was mostly dark. A lonely rider sloshed through the muddy roads and stopped in front of the General Store. Securing his horse to the post, the imposing figure walked up the wooden steps, while stomping his feet. A small waterfall ran down from the gutters splashing mud against the wooden boards. The sign in the window read "HOT FOOD". Moses Trinidad was hungry!

The black soldier walked in and removed his gratecoat. "Good evening." Shaking off the water, he noticed an empty table.

"Evening, soldier," said the old woman. "Cup of coffee?" Two other women were sitting at a table with one old man who nodded.

"Thank you." Moses pulled out a chair and sat down. He nodded towards the others. "Good evening folks." The old woman returned with the coffee and set it down in front of him.

"Special tonight is beef stew with biscuits," smiled the woman with a brown colored toothy grin. "Sound okay to you?"

"Sounds wonderful to me," he said removing his napkin and placing it across his lap. The food came out steaming hot and was placed in front of the soldier. "Looks great." Moses nodded in approval. The woman smiled with delight. Breaking a flaky biscuit in half he dipped it in the hearty brown gravy and devoured it. The old man in the corner of the room stood up and walked over to his table.

"Evening to ya, Sergeant," said the old man, tipping his hat. "Name is Cyril, Lomas Cyril and that is my wife Mildred. We own the store. I don't mean to interrupt your supper but could I ask you a question?" Moses placed his fork down and wiped his mouth.

"Not at all Mr. Cyril, my name is Moses Trinidad. I'm one of the Senior NCO's at Fort Barre." They shook hands. "What's your question?" Moses blew on the fork full of stew and placed it in his mouth.

"What happened the other night? We in this town have a right to know."

"Well Mr. Cyril seems we have some **people** lurking about that shouldn't be. My job is to see that these certain individuals are taken care of and disposed of as quickly as possible." He held up his cup and motioned to Mildred. "Coffee ma'am if you don't mind." The woman smiled warmly and refilled his cup. "Thank you. That's a lovely gal you have."

"Yes, been with her for 32 years." The old man made a weird face. "You mentioned people? You mean like those spooky men that are always hanging out in the sheriff's office and in the saloon?" Moses' hand stopped, and he gently placed the utensil down on the bowl.

"What men are you talking about sir? What did they look like?"

"Well, I haven't seen all of them together in a couple days." Moses nodded and took another bite. "The tall blond one, he's a mean one that's for sure. Name is Armstead. He's a ranger by law, but he's just a common drinker and gambler." The two men continued to chatter, as Moses finished his dinner.

"How do people feel about having black soldiers at the fort, Lomas?" Mr. Cyril looked over at his wife who turned away. Moses watched his hosts as they tried to avoid the question.

"It's okay, folks, I didn't expect everyone to love us. I wasn't naïve." The raindrops bounced off the wooden roof.

"There are many of us though that are quite pleased about having a stronger garrison at the fort," said Lomas, as he kicked at the ground. "Mildred made some Dutch apple pie. How's about a slice with a fresh cup of coffee."

Moses slapped his knees. "Fantastic!" Mrs. Cyril emerged from the kitchen with a tray containing two huge slabs of Dutch Apple pie and a pot of steaming coffee. The men ate and laughed together, devouring the pie and drinking two pots of coffee. It was early in the morning by the time they stopped chatting. Mrs. Cyril had gone up to bed, and it had stopped raining.

"Lomas," said Moses, extending his hand. "That was one fine evening, what do I owe you?" He reached into his front pocket.

"No, no Moses that's quite all right," said Lomas laughing. "Please come around anytime for a meal, talk or just a quick hello. Watch yourself also." Moses grabbed his grate coat and walked outside. Mounting his horse, he turned and slowly trotted down the puddle-ridden street and headed back to the fort.

As soon as Moses reached the fort, he headed into the barracks section where Corporal Bernard was sleeping.

"Psst! Psst! Hey wake up!" said Moses, poking him gently.

"What the?" Moses covered the man's mouth.

"Sssh! Come in here with me, okay?" Both men walked into the private quarters and shut the door behind them.

"What's going on?" Bernard was still half out of it as he sat down in the rocking chair in front of the fire. Moses fixed some coffee. "Where have you been?"

"I was in town this evening," said Moses, placing the pot on the stove. "I met a Mr. Lomas Cyril, the General Store owner, and his wife. They mentioned that they have seen some unsavory characters lurking about near the sheriff's office. My guess is that it's the rangers. The man described them in pretty good detail."

Bernard yawned. "Well, I think we can pretty much rest assured that the sheriff and his pals are putting their fingers into places they don't belong. We've just about wiped out everyone of his men anyway, what can they do?" Bernard sat there smiling as he looked into the stove.

"It's finding that little bit of evidence that can push this over the edge." Moses handed a steaming mug to his friend.

"I could get the captain to write to the headquarters and get an official arrest warrant. The question that really sticks in my mind is why haven't they left town yet? They have to know that we are aware of the illegal dealings."

"We don't have any hard evidence against them. What everyone else says is just talk," said Bernard, sipping slowly. "The bodies of their men are buried under god only knows how much dirt. The only reason that I would stay around is for revenge!" Moses stared at his friend and sipped his coffee.

"Well, that was my other thought." Moses stood up and walked over to the window and looked out. "It's getting colder and colder out at night. I like coming in here and sitting by the fire or by the fire pit out back. I admit that I find all this activity quite exciting. The shooting, riding and the Indians. Hell, if I'd have stayed in Boston, there is no way I would have ever encountered things like this." Moses was getting excited. Pulling out his pouch, he packed his pipe and struck a match. "We'll brief Nouba in the morning, what do you think?" Whirling around, he saw his good friend was sound asleep. Shaking his head he lay back in his bed and pulled the cover up. The winds whirled and pounded against the structure. Making the sign of the cross, Moses spoke quietly.

"Lord, please help me to realize that these times though trying will make me a better person. I know I feel the weight of all the injustices of the world on my shoulders. Please help me to find a way to deal with those who choose the wrong path over yours Father. Know that in my heart I choose you to follow. I know I come to you infrequently Father, but I do only what I can do. Lord my Father please protect all the men in the United States Army. I pray this in your name. Amen!"

Rolling over, Moses closed his eyes and fell asleep.

Reveille had sounded and the flag was being raised. Strapping on his sidearm Captain Taylor walked out to his porch and breathed the cool morning air. The men were filing in and out of the mess hall, and the work detail for the stables was mustering.

"All right men!" barked Corporal Bernard. "I hope that breakfast stuck to your ribs because I'm gonna work all of you today. This structure will be finished, and horses will be bedded down in here tonight. Is that understood?"

"Yes, Corporal!"

"Dismissed!" The men went to work immediately. In no time at all the sounds of saws and hammers echoed through the fort. Long plank boards were hoisted by rope to the top of the structure. The roof was being finished along with a hayloft to conserve space. Corporal Bernard walked over to the Captain.

"Good morning, sir," The soldier saluted his commander.

"Morning, Corporal," said Taylor, returning the salute. "The men are really putting their backs into it I see. That corral is lovely. Where are Sergeant Trinidad and Hayes, I want a word with them?" The young officer looked back and forth across the compound.

"Sir, Sergeant Trinidad took Hayes and a small detachment of men on the first patrol through the town. They are also trying to find a place to put your guests. There are some homes being built at the south end of town by the blacks and the Chinese. Maybe that can lead to something?" The officer gazed up to the second floor of his quarters. Suddenly the door opened.

"Good morning," said Lucy Potter followed by Doris May and the children. "Once again, thank you for letting us use your quarters, Captain Taylor. I was planning on taking the children into town to wire home what had happened. I should also investigate a place to live. We can't impose any further."

"Well, the good sergeant has already begun the living arrangements investigation, so why don't we wait for him to return. In the meantime, you look as if you could use a hearty breakfast. The mess hall is this way." Lucy Potter looked all around for Abraham Tote, finally looking up to see him high on the cross beams, pounding in nails. He waved; she smiled.

Sergeant Trinidad and his men trotted down mainstreet. The town was bustling, and the morning train was coming into view. The whistle blew, and the stacks were churning out thick black puffs of smoke.

Sheriff Watkins had just stepped out from his door, and froze in his tracks.

"Well, good morning, Sheriff Watkins," said Sergeant Trinidad from his horse. "Out for a morning walk?" Hayes and the other soldiers stared at the sheriff coldly.

"Yes, you could say that," said Watkins. Turning around, he attempted to lock his door, but his hands shook so much he couldn't place the key in the lock. "Come, on damn it!"

"Gee, all that jingling, I thought ole Saint Nicholas was around," laughed Moses. "Don't you worry yourself, Sheriff, you're going to see so many soldiers around, you'll be seeing blue permanently." Turning his beast's head, Moses galloped out of town followed by his men. Watkins opened the door to his office and entered. Walking across the room to his desk he pulled the drawer open and removed the bottle. Splashing a large amount from the bottle, Watkins tossed the shot back quickly.

"Nervous!" From behind the curtain came Ranger Armstead with two different men.

"Damn it," cried Watkins, whirling around. "Must you always do that?" The men laughed and walked into the office. Grabbing the bottle, Armstead took a drink and passed it to his friends. "Go ahead help yourself," said Watkins. The two men weren't white; they had some Mexican and Indian in them. Both large in size, they had black hair and reddish skin color. Each had ammunition slung across their chests and carried Winchester rifles. They said nothing, just drank.

No one noticed the pair of unsuspecting eyes peering from the corner of the side window. Hayes had circled back around and crept behind the sheriff's office. The ranger and his friends continued drinking from the bottle. Backing away slowly the boy crept silently to the rear of the building and hopped on his horse. He galloped to the outskirts of the town where he met up with the rest of his group.

"Well," said Moses. "What did you see?"

"He's got some new blood," said Hayes, slowing down. "They look like they know what they're doing. Two of them Mexican-Indian I think, definitely hired guns."

"All right, let's get back to the fort and brief the captain." The group turned and headed for home.

Captain Taylor was taking a little peek at the horizon. The young officer noticed the riders coming towards the fort. "Here comes the Sergeant now." The soldier galloped into the fort and dismounted.

"Hayes, please take my horse over to the stables, I need to talk to the Captain and the Corporal." Handing the reins to the soldier, Moses saluted the officer.

"Sergeant, your report?"

"The Sheriff and his good friend Ranger Armstead have decided to recruit some new men to help do their dirty work. Hayes reports that they are of Indian-Mexican decent; probably killers, so be on the lookout."

Hayes walked over and saluted.

"Patrol is returning, sir."

"Looks to number a full squad," said Taylor. "They appear to have some new and lovely company." The vision became clearer as the officer focused his sights literally on Claudia Rothschild riding towards him. Moses stood back and watched the young officer.

"Sir, if you try and focus those anymore, they're gonna be inside of your head." The men snickered. Taylor straightened out his blouse. Sergeant Nouba waved his hands as the men approached the entrance, slowing the squad to a halt. Sitting on the porch of the Captain's quarters sat Lucy and Doris May reading to the children.

"Dismount!" The men climbed down from their saddles and began walking slowly into the fort. "Secure the horses." The young woman was helped off her mount by Sergeant Nouba, who took her hand and escorted her to the commanding officer.

Nouba snapped to attention and saluted. "Sergeant Nouba returning from mission." The officer returned the salute. "Sir, may I present Miss Claudia Rothschild." Taking her hand gently, Taylor kissed it. Nouba rolled his eyes.

The young lady blushed "It's a pleasure to make your acquaintance," she replied, as she stared wondrously into the officer's eyes.

"Taylor, Hennecker J. Taylor, Captain, Commanding Officer here." The officer was almost speechless. "Please come into my office." Moses and Nouba stood there as the Captain and Miss Rothschild walked past them all, went into the office, and shut the door.

"Captain Taylor," said Claudia.

"Yes."

"Do you want your men that are standing outside?" Taylor turned around quietly and opened the door.

"Men, I'm err that's to say.. well..." Evidently very embarrassed, the officer couldn't get a word out.

"Sir, why don't you let Miss Rothschild get acquainted with Miss Potter? She can get freshened up so to speak," said Sergeant Trinidad. "That way we could be properly briefed by Sergeant Nouba."

"How rude of me, you are quite right," said the officer, snapping his fingers. "Miss Rothschild, I believe that Miss Potter could assist you in cleaning yourself up first and getting some rest. It will give me time to notify your father," said the officer looking over at her.

"It will be my pleasure, dear." Lucy took her by the arm and led her up to the temporary women's quarters.

"Sergeant, were there any others in the party?"

"Yes sir, but they're are all deceased." The soldiers snapped to attention and saluted.

"Thank you, Sergeant," said the officer saluting. "That will be all for now." The men did an about face and exited the office.

Outside, Abraham Tote had finished his work detail and saw Lucy Potter now sitting on the porch with the children.

"Afternoon ma'am, was wondering if you'd like to take a ride outside da fort after I's cleans up," said the trooper, removing his hat. "Da children are welcome to come." A big smile stretched across Lucy's face.

"Oh Abraham, that sounds wonderful. The children would enjoy that very much." She had a simple beauty in everything she did. The way she walked, the way she dealt with the children. The little things, that's what Tote found most appealing. "I'd rather take the time to get to know you first, alone."

"I's be back soon." The man turned around and walked over to his barracks. Lucy turned and ran upstairs. She came flying into the room with a glorious grin on her face. "Doris May could you see it in your heart to…"

"Yes, I'll watch the children." It wouldn't be a date unless she spent time in front of the mirror and kept him waiting.

Abraham Tote washed up in the basin and shaved. Checking himself in the mirror he was nervous. Nouba noticed his man preparing himself in the mirror.

"Big afternoon planned, soldier?"

"Jus a horse ride, Sergeant, with Lucy," Abraham removed a brand-new yellow neckerchief and tried to tie it correctly around his neck. "Dag!" Nouba walked over to the mirror and correctly tied the knot for him. "I's plan on giving her my yellow neckerchief."

"She's a lucky woman." Nouba liked the idea of preparing one of his men for a date rather than readying them for battle. Made him feel like a parent. "You should take her down by the water, it's very nice and peaceful. Women like that, don't they?" Nouba couldn't remember the last time he had a woman's company, but he didn't mind. He was a widow of the army. Tote thanked the sergeant and headed over to the stables to grab two horses. Nouba headed into his room to get washed up and changed. Lucy Potter was just emerging from her quarters. Kissing both the children, she walked down the steps and saw Abraham pulling around the horses. She thought that he was handsome in his uniform, and the yellow neckerchief was beautiful. The men tried not to be too obvious as they watched their nervous comrade.

"They're lovely animals, Abraham," said Lucy, stroking their manes. Tote smiled every time she called him by his given name. It made him beam. Cupping his hands, Tote lifted Lucy into the saddle.

"You ride before?"

"Yes, many times on my parent's property in Virginia. It has been a while though. Goodbye children, I'll be back by supper. I love you!" The children hung off the porch railing, waving to their mother. "Let's race over to the southern corner of the town by the old mill."

"Ya on!" Slapping their horses, the pair took off across the prairie, kicking up a cloud of dust in their wake.

Moses watched the couple ride off. Mathers walked up to the sergeant. "Sergeant, it's time for the second patrol. Hayes and myself."

"Only two soldiers, that's hardly enough," said Moses, heading over to his barracks. "Corporal Crawford report!"

"Yes, Sergeant Trinidad?"

"Take Mathers and Hayes and do the routine patrol in town. Everyone travels together anywhere they go, don't separate." Moses patted them on the back and headed in to see Sergeant Nouba. "Oh, Hayes, stop by the Captain's office, he has a cable he wants sent."

"Yes, Sergeant."

Captain Taylor sat down at his desk and wrote the message.

URGENT MESSAGE
Commanding Officer
9th U.S. Cavalry
Washington, D.C.

Claudia Rothschild is alive and well in U.S. Army hands at Fort Barre. Individuals traveling with her were killed before soldiers arrived. Numerous hostiles killed, camp found and all supplies and dwellings destroyed.

Await further instructions for the safe return of Ms. Rothschild.

Sincerely
Hennecker J. Taylor, Captain

9th U.S. Cavalry
Fort Barre, Texas

Folding the note he sat back in his chair and thought. Hayes walked into the office and stood at attention. "Hayes reporting as ordered, sir."

"Hayes, take this into town and have the telegraph operator send it out quickly. I'll be in with the sergeants going over their reports." The officer rose from his chair and headed for the door.

"She's one fine looking woman, sir," said Hayes, smiling. "There's no shame in admitting that." The young man walked out the door whistling. Captain Taylor smiled and laughed quietly. The young boy was right, she was a stunner.

* * * * * * *

Moses hadn't visited the Quarter Masters Storehouse since the explosion and a quick check on things would keep the men in line to make sure they were performing their jobs. Walking into the room, he saw Pike and Davis stacking some crates in the corner of the room.

"Afternoon, gentlemen," said the Sergeant running his fingers across the supplies. "How is everything going in here since the excitement?"

"Well, the explosion created a lot of dust and debris. It came down the tunnel and right up the hole. Covered everything in roughly three inches of dust. We just got through straightening up in here only yesterday," said Davis.

Moses noticed Pike limping. "How's that injury of yours, soldier?"

"Just fine, Sergeant, thank you."

"Has anyone gone down the tunnel since then?"

"We haven't been given the orders to proceed, we were told to secure the tunnel until further notice, and we've done just that." The men continued with their tasks. "Besides, there's more dirt and rock blocking the passage way; it will never be dug up." Pike walked across the room and opened the glass windows, letting the clean air filter through.

"Well, there's no problems here, I'll leave now." Moses exited the room and headed across the compound. "A day without problems, what will I do?" Moses enjoyed watching the horses as they grazed. With the additions to the herd, the fort had quite an impressive number. The older nags that the Army had given the soldiers were wearing down, so a herd of young fresh horses was a welcome gift. They were quite spectacular animals to view. Moses wondered how the soldier and his lady friend were enjoying their ride. He looked around and saw the activity around the fort and smiled. He loved the Army life.

SIXTEEN

Abraham and Lucy had decided to walk. Holding hands, they pulled the horses behind them. The hills were covered in wildflowers and trees.

"It's amazing that there can be flowers one second and sand and rock the next. This is a very lovely place, Abraham. Look, you can see the town from here. Do you think that we are rushing this?" The soldier picked a beautiful flower from the ground and handed it to the lady.

"I's happy," said the soldier smiling. "You want to walk by da water?" Tote bent over and gently kissed her soft lips. She thrust her hips against the man and kissed him passionately. Lifting her up, he began twirling her around playfully. She laughed like a giddy schoolgirl.

"A field hand with a white woman," said the raspy voice. "That's just something I can't allow." Armstead and his two new sidekicks peered out from underneath a small grouping of trees. "Can we take them from here?" The half-breeds stared at each other and nodded. "Wait until they're back in the saddle. If the bullets don't get em, the fall from the horses should break their necks." Sitting back down in the grass the men watched and waited.

Abraham held Lucy close to him as they lay beneath the trees. "It will be tough, but we could do it." She squeezed him tighter; the hours passed peacefully.

"I hate to say this but we should probably head back, the children will be wondering where I am." Rising up the couple kissed and embraced. Abraham helped lift Lucy into the saddle, then grabbed his horse and climbed on. Under the tree, the Mexican Indian tapped the sleeping Armstead on the arm.

"W-what?" The man wiped his eyes. "It's about time! Remember, wait until they're at a full gallop, and then we hightail it out of here."

The couple began to streak across the ground, unaware they were heading right into the sight of guns. Rising from the grass, the two assassins aimed their rifles at the riders. As the couple galloped closer, the men could make out the smile on their faces. BOOM! BOOM! The first bullet slammed square into the chest of Lucy Potter, sending her tumbling to the ground. The second bullet found its mark slightly above the right eye of Abraham Tote, killing him instantly. The bandits hopped on their mounts and rode off. The two horses began grazing next to the bodies of their riders. The blood leaked slowly from their wounds, staining the ground red.

* * * * * * *

It was dusk as the patrol from town pulled back into the fort. Corporal Crawford, Hayes and Mathers pulled their horses into the corral and began to remove their saddles. Sergeant Trinidad and Captain Taylor were walking after dinner with Claudia and Doris May. The children were playing games with some of the soldiers. Sergeant Trinidad motioned to Corporal Crawford.

"Everything in town is secure," said Crawford.

Moses placed his arm around Crawford's shoulder and leaned in close. "Have you seen Tote and the Potter lady?"

"No, Sergeant, not since they passed us heading out earlier. Is something wrong?"

"Without making a scene, get some men out there and see if everything is okay, and be quiet about it, we don't want the women and children upset." The corporal walked back to the corral and informed the men of the plans.

"Is everything all right, Sergeant?" asked the officer, escorting the ladies.

"Just an extra security check sir," said Moses grinning. "Nothing to be concerned about." He waved his hand behind his back as the men trotted out of the fort and over the hill.

"Where were they headed, does anybody know?" one of the men asked.

"She likes wildflowers, right," said Crawford. "My guess is they went to the section of land just around the old mill. The flowers grow all over the ground." The group spurred their horses and headed for the old mill. Pounding over the land, they began to slow down. Corporal Crawford peered across the skyline. Suddenly something caught his eye, the figures of two horses grazing in the tall grass.

"Look!" The soldiers trotted slowly up to that area and removed their weapons. Darkness had crept in, and the stars were out. The area was well lit with small pockets of light.

"Let's take a look around." Hayes walked slowly up to the horses and secured them. Looking back and forth he couldn't see anyone.

"Hayes, you got anything?" The boy walked slowly through the grass.

"No, but these are their horses. How's about you, Mathers?"

"Nothing." The metal from their guns gleamed in the starlight. "I can't find a...." There was a small thud as the soldiers tumbled over something. "Damn!" The man got to his feet. "I'm all wet now. This was a dry uniform." Walking over to Mather's position, Hayes struck a match.

"Just as I thought," said soldier, rubbing his fingers together. "It's not water, it's blood." Mathers wiped his hands off on his trousers. Hayes held the match down to the earth; it shone against the dead body of Lucy Potter. There was a huge hole in her chest, and her dress was stained red. "Fan out, Tote's body is around here somewhere." Corporal Crawford walked about two feet before tripping over the body.

"He's over here." The corporal bent down and stared at the soldier lying in the grass. A large section of his head was gone. "Mathers, ride out to the fort and get a wagon and some more men." The soldier whirled his horse around and darted off to the fort.

"Damn, they hit each with one shot," said Hayes kneeling down in the grass. "By the size of the holes, I'd wager on Winchester rifles. They were hiding," said the boy turning and squinting in the night. "From that grove of trees right there. They probably hid in the brush and bang, killed them dead."

About a half an hour had passed, when the men heard a rumbling of horses as the group of soldiers approached in a wagon. Corporal Bernard was seated up front. Stepping off the wagon, the driver handed Bernard a lantern. Bending down to check the bodies, he placed his hand over the wound.

"Winchesters, right Hayes," said the corporal gazing at the boy. Hayes nodded.

"We decided not to disturb the captain or the sergeants. Let's get them loaded up and home." Bernard removed his cap and slapped it in his hand. Hayes and Mathers bent down and hoisted the big man up, placing him in the rear of the wagon. Hayes hopped up and pulled him up to the front.

Corporal Crawford cradled the broken body of Lucy Potter and placed her beside her love. Taking a single blanket, he covered both the bodies. The men followed the wagon slowly back to the fort.

Captain Taylor, Claudia Rothchild and Doris May Potter were just emerging into the crisp night air, as the wagon pulled into camp. Corporal Bernard trotted at the head of the line. Bending down, he whispered in the officer's ear. Taylor's head dropped slightly as he turned towards Doris May.

"No! No!" Doris May ran to the rear of the wagon and looked inside. "Lucy." Her eyes worked their way to the front of the wagon and saw the dead colored man. "Abraham." She fainted away and dropped to the ground. Hearing the cries, Moses and Nouba came running. Captain Taylor lifted her up and inside to his quarters. Carrying the woman upstairs, he laid her down in the bed. Claudia asked the officer to leave the room.

"She needs rest, Hennecker," said Claudia closing the door. The officer walked dejectedly down the stairs and out the front door.

"She going to be okay, sir?" asked Bernard.

"This will take some time. Where are the bodies?"

"We brought them over to the Doc's and Oliver." The men watched as their leader paced back and forth.

"Secure for the evening, gentlemen, we'll deal with this in the morning." Morning came and went as the post held another funeral and burial at the old cemetery on the hill.

* * * * * * *

Doris May decided that frontier life just wasn't the thing for her or the children. She was in charge of raising them now, and they needed a well-structured environment. She decided that she would return back East with the children and her sister's casket. It was rather ironic that it was Tiner who was there to see her off; the rest of the men were on work details and patrols.

"I'm very sorry that I was such a pain to yourself and the men," said Doris May. "I guess this trip taught me something more than just survival skills, it taught me not to judge people."

"I'm glad you learned something," said Tiner. "Too bad you couldn't stay, you're a helluva shot. I'm sorry about your sister. She died with the man she loved, though." The soldier shook her hand.

"All aboard," came the conductor's cry.

"Good luck to you and the children." Grabbing her hand Tiner assisted her aboard the train. The big steel wheels began to slowly turn on the tracks. As smoke poured from the stacks, the massive locomotive steamed down the tracks headed east. Looking down, Tiner began to put his gloves on when he bumped into someone.

"Excuse me." The soldier looked up and saw the two Mexican-Indians standing straight like totem poles. "Sorry fellows, my fault." Patting them on the backs he walked away. They continued to watch the soldier, even after he climbed on his horse. This didn't escape Tiner's sight. The soldier galloped off into the distance. Ranger Armstead popped out from behind the building.

"That's one of the sons a bitches right there," said Armstead, pointing at the soldier riding away. "We gotta get him." The Indians turned toward each other and nodded.

* * * * * * *

The days stretched into weeks as the activities surrounding the fort seemed to calm down. Claudia Rothschild's father, Governor Rothschild cabled and decided to personally come to the fort and retrieve his little girl, or so he thought. Claudia Rothschild had become quite involved with the children of color who lived in the south section of town. The town was looking for schoolteachers for them and she decided this was her calling. She and Captain Taylor grew quite fond of each other. They began a daily ritual of taking strolls around the fort grounds or rides in the country, escorted by a detachment of men. It was also Captain Taylor's idea to have a big dinner party and troop review for Governor Rothschild. A second telegram arrived a day later addressed to the commanding officer of Fort Barre. Upon receiving the note, Taylor raced to find Sergeant Trinidad.

"Sergeant, I need your help look at this note I just received." Handing the note to Moses, the officer paced nervously around in circles. "Who is Brigadier General Gustoff Kerrey?"

"Sir," said Moses, tilting his hat back on his head. "Brigadier General "Gustoff the Great" Kerrey was a hero of the Wilderness Campaign during the Civil War. Are you familiar with the Wilderness Campaign?"

"Very little I'm afraid, could you give me a quick history lesson on the events?" Captain Taylor pulled over a stool and took a seat. "I'm, all ears!"

"Well let's see, the time was around 1864 about a year after we lost Colonel Shaw. I believe the general was a major then, a hot-blooded mixture of Albanian Gypsy and Italian. He was a graduate of the Military Academy, top ten in academics, family was from New York. Anyway, the armies of General Grant and General Lee fought vigorously with massive numbers of wounded, around 29,000 casualties. During the battle, there was a heavy fog that drifted in. Federal troops became confused and fired blindly into the woods, tearing apart soldiers from two Vermont regiments. Then Major Kerrey who was separated from his own unit, assumed command of a group of Vermont soldiers, led them to safety, regrouped, and helped hold the intersection of

Brock and Orange Plank roads from Confederate forces. I believe that act was the prime reason for him receiving the Medal of Honor. He's coming to the end of a hero's career in the army. Must be assigned to Texas Headquarters." The officer sat stunned on the bench.

"He's coming to give citations to some of the men for heroism. I'm sorry to say that neither of us are on the list, Sergeant."

Turning around quietly, Moses continued to gently brush his horse. "Not a problem sir. I didn't join the Army for medals, I know why I'm here."

"Do you wish to see,Sergeant Nouba is on the list," said Taylor. Moses nodded his approval.

The fort was buzzing with activity, preparing for the governor and general's arrival. The men had constructed a new barracks for dignitaries who would come to the fort. They traded in town with Mr. Cyril for furniture that would make the rooms look sharp. Corporal Bernard had read something about dress bands and decided to try it out. Many of the men were very talented musicians; one man was even a chamber organist. Mr. Cyril also helped find instruments to make a band. The time was approaching quickly, so the men were practicing for the big event several times a day. The fort itself looked wonderful. The men had worked nonstop to give the grounds and surrounding areas a complete going over. They had also positioned massive rocks and stones around the base of the fort to shore it up, and completed a set of stone steps leading down to the creek bed area.

It had been another long day. Moses sat and relaxed in his rocking chair. Placing a stick into the stove, he lit his pipe and sucked deeply. He sighed in relief, the reached for his pen.

October 11th 1879

Governor Rothschild and Brigadier General Kerrey are to arrive the day after tomorrow to attend a large celebration on Ms. Rothschild's behalf, and to decorate certain soldiers for bravery on the battlefield. I must admit I was a bit surprised that the Captain had no real idea who Brigadier General "Gustoff the Great" Kerrey was. After he found out, the Captain high tailed it out of here and the wheels were turning in his mind. I informed the men of the guests and all were quite excited, which makes me feel good. Bernard has gone so far as to assemble a band and they're quite good. Some of the men decided they would do something special for the Captain's guests, it's a surprise and they haven't even shared the news with me.

I have plans of discussing the idea with Captain Taylor and Sergeant Nouba of letting the men into town to enjoy the saloon and the girls. I have heard grumblings of why they haven't been allowed there yet. It would be a big boost to the morale and the town hasn't been formally classified as "off limits". We will see what the others think about this, I'm off to check on the men.

Moses walked out of his barracks and into the chilly evening air of Texas. The men were relaxing. Some were playing cards in the mess hall, while others were catching up on chores such as washing and cleaning. Moses caught a glimpse of Bernard and the other men pitching horseshoes near the corral.

"Ahh, Sergeant," said Taylor. The men had assembled to look at the fort's outer appearances. "Just the opinion we needed, the men were trying to figure out a way to dress up the front of the fort to give it a special touch, what do you think?" Moses snapped his fingers. Grabbing Hayes, he whispered in the soldier's ear. Hayes smiled at the sergeant and ran off.

"With your patience sir, I think you'll enjoy this." With the help of Tiner, Mathers and a few others, Trooper Hayes had scrambled up a ladder. The men had taken two cattle head skulls with horns and nailed them over each side of the post's sign. Hayes stuck a torch on either side, above the skulls. The men below cheered with excitement. "Hip hip hooray! Hip hip hooray! Hip hip hooray!"

"I think we're ready, men," said Captain Taylor shaking, Moses' hand. "No, I know we're ready!"

SEVENTEEN

The Captain paced nervously across the floor of his office. Opening the door, he proceeded into the outer office where Hayes was busy doing paperwork. "Are they here yet, Hayes?"

"That's the third time you've asked me that, sir," said Hayes, smiling. "Don't worry, Sergeant Trinidad and Nouba know how much this means to you; they won't let you down, sir." The Captain went back into his office and closed the door. Sergeants Trinidad and Nouba entered the outer office.

"Is the captain in, Hayes?" asked Moses.

"Yes, and he's as nervous as an old lady." The sergeants crossed the room and knocked on the door.

"Enter!" Taylor rose from his desk quickly.

They entered the office and closed the door. "How you holding up, sir?" asked the men, saluting.

"Nervous as hell, Sergeant. This is my first inspection by the Governor and a Brigadier General, no less. Who is meeting them at the train depot, and what time does the train arrive?"

"Both Corporal Bernard and Corporal Crawford are meeting them at the train station with a little surprise for the governor and the general." Both men smiled at each other.

The Captain stood there perspiring profusely. "Do you think that I should have met them at the train. After all, it's the Governor and the General?"

"No, you're the commanding officer of this fort, you don't have time to meet the train. That's a job for the men," said Sergeant Nouba. "Protocol dictates that the enlisted men handle the job of escorting the dignitaries to the fort. Upon their arrival, you will play host for the remainder of their stay, sir." Suddenly, the train's whistle wailed in the distance.

"That's the train whistle." The Captain froze in his tracks and turned as white as a sheet. Moses patted him on the back.

"The cook's prepared a special meal tonight for all your guests. Sergeant Nouba and myself will handle everything else. Why don't you change and get ready."

"Yes, you're quite right men." The young officer ran up to his quarters.

The large black locomotive slowed down as it pulled into the Texas town. The train always drew a large number of people just to watch it come in. Corporal Bernard and Corporal Crawford stood on the train platform and waited for the train to stop. Dressed in their new uniforms, the men looked sharp standing at attention. A young second lieutenant stepped off the train first and looked around. Corporal Bernard approached the young officer.

"Good afternoon, sir," said the corporal saluting. "Corporal Bernard, 9th Cavalry assigned to escort you folks to the fort." The officer stared at Bernard and walked right past him up to Corporal Crawford.

"Well, you look sharp, do you plan on saluting me anytime soon?" Corporal Crawford snapped to attention.

"No I don't!" The man returned to parade rest.

"What?"

"You walked right past Corporal Bernard and didn't say anything or return his salute, I'd say that makes you a first class horse's ass." Bernard covered his mouth so as not to laugh. The young officer turned bright red. Bending over, Corporal Crawford whispered in the man's ear. "Respect all the men on this post or you may not make the trip back in one piece." The officer stood there stunned as Corporal Crawford continued to leer at him.

"Lieutenant Peters!" Brigadier General Gustoff Kerrey stepped off from the passenger car onto the platform and looked around. Corporal Bernard and Crawford snapped to attention. "Where are you, Lieutenant? Slippery little......."

"Welcome to Flat Fork, sir," said Corporal Bernard snapping to attention. "Myself and my men have been ordered to escort the Governor and yourself to the fort." The general walked up to the men and stared deep into their eyes and saluted.

General Kerrey was nearing retirement, and it showed. Fifty-eight years on this earth, a large part of it in the United States Army. The olive skinned man moved a little slower these days but had the respect of every soldier.

"It's a pleasure to be here," said the deep voiced man, shaking their hands. "You men look regulation top to bottom, wonderful. You've met my aide Lieutenant Peters. May I introduce you to the governor of Texas, the honorable Nigel Q. Rothschild." The man was sixty-two years of age and was in decent health. Dark skinned with a medium build, the governor was a scout during his military days. He walked up to both men and shook their hands.

"It's an honor to meet the men who helped save my daughter. I can't thank you enough."

"Begging your pardon sir, we weren't on the patrol with your daughter. You'll get a chance to meet those men tonight sir, during and after dinner. Let me direct you to your coach, sir," said Bernard, holding his hand out. Corporal Crawford drew his hand back and brushed Lieutenant Peters aside.

"Excuse me, sir," said the Corporal smiling.

The people on the platform stepped aside as the horse drawn coach pulled up to the platform. It was a splendid coach with four horses and made from cherry wood. Standing at attention with the American Flag and a guidon stood four black troopers in their dress uniforms. The General and the Governor smiled as they were assisted into the coach. "This is very lovely, men."

"We have some items that we brought along with us," said Lieutenant Peters hesitantly. "They're being taken off the train now." Two conductors carried a large trunk and set it down by the carriage. Corporal Bernard had the men secure it to the rear of the coach. Potter and Pullman were driver and guard. Lieutenant Peters was the last to climb inside. The two corporals climbed on their horses and trotted in front of the coach. "Ready forward!" The small band of soldiers headed out for the fort.

The General stuck his head out from the coach window. "Corporal," he said to Bernard. "Does everyone travel in such style out West?"

"Just the ones that we like, sir." Bernard winked and lurched his horse's head forward. The general laughed.

The ride to the fort was pleasant.

"Ridas approachin, sir," yelled the guard. "With the coch sir."

Captain Taylor squinted at the soldier. Dressed in his regulation uniform his polished sword hanging from his belt and the best shined boots in Texas, he rocked back and forth on the heels of his feet.

"Have you lost your mind man, what the hell did you say?" The men assembled in the compound to line up in perfect rows. Claudia Rothchild stood on the porch of the Captain's quarters. Wearing a new yellow dress and the young officer's yellow ribbon, she waited anxiously. The new company band stood at attention, their polished brass instruments shining in the late day sun.

"Coch, coch." The captain looked around confused.

"He said coach sir," said Sergeant Nouba pointing. "The men thought they'd surprise you, sir." The Captain's jaw nearly hit the floor as the beautifully polished coach pulled into the compound and came to a halt in front of his quarters in a small cloud of dust. Trotter and Pullman jumped down and along with four other men lined up at attention on either side of the door of the coach. The men in the band snapped to attention and played. Pullman reached up and turned the handle. First to exit was Lieutenant Peters. Short in height, he was a well-organized clerk who took his duties with the general seriously. He walked up to Captain Taylor and saluted.

"Welcome to Fort Barre, I'm Captain H. J. Taylor, commanding officer."

"2nd Lieutenant Thomas Jefferson Peters," said the man saluting and shaking Taylor's hand. "May I present Nigel Q. Rothschild, Governor of the State of Texas." The man emerged from the coach and shook the officer's hand.

"Young man, I want to thank you for finding my little girl and watching her until I arrived."

"Not a problem at all, sir," said Taylor.

"Daddy!" Came the cry as Claudia Rothschild holding up her dress scrambled down the steps and into his waiting arms. The embrace lasted forever.

"Captain Taylor, may I present Brigadier General Gustoff Kerrey." The man climbed slowly down from the coach. "Attention!" The men clicked their heels together and snapped to attention.

"Sir, welcome to Fort Barre. We are honored by your presence." The young officer stood straight as an oak tree. The General walked up to the man and got right in his face.

"Damn proud to be here myself, son," said the general, slapping him in the stomach. "I'm not one for formalities, makes it easier for unit cohesiveness." The Captain chuckled. "Son, you and your men have done one hot damn job at cleaning this place up and making it look wonderful." The soldiers smiled happily. The General turned and began to walk through the rows of men. "Yes sir, these men look fine and dandy."

"Sir, shall we repair to my quarters for refreshments, I'll have the men take your bags to your quarters?" Everyone nodded and agreed. "Sergeant Trinidad, please have the General and the Governor's baggage taken to their quarters.

"Yes sir," barked Moses snapping to attention. "Pullman take these bags over." The soldier picked up the luggage and proceeded to the quarters.

"Captain Taylor, the awards are in the trunk, I assume you would want them in your office," implied Lieutenant Peters

"Of course," said the officer as he glanced over at Nouba. "Sergeant, will you see to that for me?" Two soldiers proceeded to the carriage and removed the trunk following Sergeant Nouba inside. Captain Taylor led General Kerrey and Governor Rothschild into the sitting area.

Hayes had decorated the room with stuffed animal's heads such as elk, deer, and several birds. A large decorative rug covered the wooden floor with several couches and large chairs that were placed perfectly about the room. Two young soldiers in dress uniforms stood with trays of drinks handing each guest a glass.

"A toast," said Captain Taylor, raising his glass in the air. "To the safe arrival of our honored guests, to the safe return of Miss Rothschild, and to the Buffalo Soldiers of the 9th Cavalry."

"Here, here," came the cheers of all. Tilting back their beverages, the people beamed with delight. The sergeants set their glasses down and headed for the door.

"Where are you two going?" asked Taylor, smiling.

"Well sir, we figured this was a social event for officers and the dignitaries. We were gonna head back to the barracks," said Sergeant Trinidad.

"Nonsense, if it wasn't for Sergeant Nouba here there would be no reason for celebration." Hearing that Governor Rothschild walked up to the Sergeant.

"Sergeant Nouba is that correct?" Nouba nodded. "Thank you so much for your efforts in freeing my daughter from her captors. I wanted to show you my appreciation."

Shaking his hand, Nouba responded. "That's not necessary sir, the simple fact that the girl is fine is all we need." Nouba sat down in a chair with the others.

"Still I wanted to give this to you, you were in charge, you made the decisions." He snapped his fingers and Lieutenant Peters scurried across the room with a shiny wooden case and handed it to the governor. "Here Sergeant, with all my compliments." The big man looked stunned as he accepted the case. Nouba looked over at Moses and the Captain.

"Well done, Sergeant Nouba," exclaimed Taylor tipping his glass and drinking. General Kerrey clapped with excitement. Moses leaned against the wall and winked.

Nouba sat down on the couch and placed the case on his knees. Gently undoing the brass latch, he raised the lid. The sergeant's eyes bulged out as his breath skipped a few times. Nestling in a crush burgundy velvet cloth was an ivory handle 1860 Remington Army cap & ball type revolver.

"Sir, I...I don't know what to say!" Nouba stared speechless at the weapon.

"Your reaction was thanks enough my good man," said the Governor, slapping him on the shoulder. "How about a cigar?" Reaching into his jacket, Governor Rothschild removed three fat cigars. "General?" He handed one to Sergeant Nouba and one to General Kerrey. Striking a match they lit them and began chatting about the old days.

Sergeant Trinidad's tales at Fort Wagner with the 54th was regaling Captain Taylor, Miss Rothschild, and Lieutenant Peters. The afternoon passed quickly. The Rothschilds went to lie down before dinner, as did the General. Sergeant Nouba and Moses stayed behind with the Captain to go over plans for the evening.

"Who's coming to dinner?" asked Taylor.

"Well sir, we thought it would be good to invite some of the locals to the fort to show the general how we interact with the community. It will bode well for your image." Then Moses smiled. "Miss Rothschild has several lady friends from the school that would love to meet eligible soldiers of the highest morale character. Those ladies and some other couples from the town will be coming to enjoy a meal with the U.S. Army."

"What about all the men, what will they eat? I can't eat a special dinner while they eat the normal food; it wouldn't be right." The sergeants smiled at their commander.

"That's what we thought you would say, sir. So we took the liberty of ordering a few extra special items to make tonight's celebration a little more festive for everyone. The three men walked out of the office and over to the chow hall. Inside the men were being treated to a large meal of sugar-cured ham, turkey, greens, fresh breads and the best milk from the local farms. Off to one side of the room was a table loaded with fresh cakes and pies from the local markets. The men laughed and hollered as they readied themselves to enjoy a wonderful meal.

Moses jumped up on the table and held up his hands. "Men, now hush for a second! How about some cheers for the Captain, and this fine meal you're enjoying?"

"HIP! HIP! HOORAY! HOORAY! HOORAY!" Came the cries from the happy soldiers. The Captain rose up to the table and held up his hands.

"Thank you men, this is all due to the wonderful and professional job that you have done. Enjoy this." He said as he exited the chow hall with his junior men.

"We thought it would be best to serve them a little earlier and that way everyone got a taste of the pie so to speak," said Nouba. "Besides, you don't need the average soldier making an ass out of himself in front of the guests, sir." Taylor smiled. "Dinner is in two hours, sir. We will be back to escort you to the hall, sir." Saluting, both sergeants turned and walked away.

Hayes and Lieutenant Peters were going through the awards and paperwork for the medal ceremony. The officer began removing the small oak case, which held the medal. Hayes stared at the case with an excited look. "Can I see it, sir?"

"I suppose," said the officer, rolling his eyes. "Just don't touch it." Peters unlatched the box and flipped the lid open. Hayes starred wondrously at the shiny medal.

"What's this figure in the middle and those words, what do they mean?" asked the young man. "That ribbon, is it made of silk or something like that?" Peters rubbed his eyes and gazed at the boy in astonishment.

"Don't you know your military history soldier?" The lieutenant removed a cigar and struck a match. Lighting the cigar, he sucked gently. "First of all, this award is the highest military decoration the United States has. It is awarded for conspicuous gallantry and intrepidity at the risk of one's life." The man paused as he sucked on the cigar. "Well, I believe it was the Navy that came up with the original concept of the citation in 1861. It's now called the Army Medal of Honor. The medal is a five-pointed star tipped with trefoils. In the center of each arm is a crown of oak and laurel, representing strength and achievements." Blowing out a stream of smoke, Lieutenant Peters tapped his chin inquisitively. "A circle of thirty-four stars surrounds the center of the star. The stars represent the number of States in the Union as of the outbreak of the War. The Eagle symbolizes the United States of America. It is perched on a cannon and a saber is grasped in its talons. The medal is attached to a blue bar on top with thirteen stripes running vertically. These thirteen stripes represent the original thirteen colonies. White represents purity and innocence, red for hardness, valor and blood, blue signifies vigilance, perseverance and justice. The stripes also represent the rays of the sun." Peters breathed a sigh of relief. "Well young man class is over." The young officer pushed the spent cigar in the ashtray. "Where do we put this for safe keeping?" Hayes removed a key and undid the lock of the heavy cabinet. Placing the box gently inside, he turned the key and locked it back up.

"What if I need to get into there, what do I do?" asked the young Lieutenant.

"Get a hold of me, sir," said Hayes, tossing the key in the air and catching it. "I'll be around tonight for dinner." Hayes grabbed his hat off the rack and walked out whistling. Lieutenant Peters seethed and turned away.

"Every single one of them are wise apples!"

Rising around 1600 hours, the General walked out of his quarters and stood watching the men preparing for the evening's festivities. Several tall torches were used to light up a large area of the parade grounds. The guards were doubled in all spots on the post including some extra roving patrols outside the fort and into the creek bed areas. The general watched with pride; he missed being out with the men. Time and the elements had caught up with him. No longer was he the young and fool hearted officer thirty years ago. Turning he walked back into his quarters and began to dress for the night.

Captain Taylor's nerves had calmed down, so he decided that he would have a little drink before the party. Rocking back and forth, he suddenly felt very much at ease. The men had done a wonderful job. The dinner will go splendidly, he thought. Dressing, he looked out of the window down at the compound. The wagons were pulling in and people were getting off. Soldiers in formal dress uniforms assisted ladies down and escorted them into the hall. Taylor grabbed his hat and walked down the flight of stairs and out the front door. Sergeants Trinidad and Nouba were emerging from their quarters wearing their ceremonial dress uniforms, pistol belts, and swords.

"My God, you men look smashing!" exclaimed Taylor. "This evening is going to be a total success."

"Just want everything to look good, sir," said Moses relaxing. "The General and the Governor should be arriving shortly, so we should head over, sir."

Walking up the stairs to the chow hall, two soldiers saluted and pulled the doors open. It was as if the officer was transported to the fancy halls back East. Captain Taylor's eyes crisscrossed the room several times. Tables covered in white cloths and place settings sparkled under the lights. In the corner of the room was Corporal Bernard's band, dressed in formal uniforms, and were playing selections from classical artists as several couples danced in circles. Several lovely young women sat in groups on fancy chairs and couches gazing at the handsome soldiers as they entered the room.

Lieutenant Peters walked several paces ahead of both General Kerrey and Governor Rothschild, his sword banging against his leg. "Who is planning on making the announcements?" Captain Taylor looked over at Moses.

"I'll make the announcements," said Moses, as he turned toward the general's orderly. "Proper protocol dictates the Captain must accompany the highest ranking member on the base because he is the commanding officer. Please wait here, I'll go inside and make the announcement. That would mean you would be announced first, sir." Lieutenant Peters stood and nodded his head.

Moses entered the hall and raised his hands. "Ladies and gentleman, may I have your attention please?" The band stopped playing, and the people rose to their feet. The soldiers lined up in formation. Moses opened the door and pointed at Peters. "Presenting Lieutenant Peters!" Removing his hat Peters walked in as the group clapped. "All rise, may I present General Gustoff Kerrey, United States Army escorted by Captain Hennecker J. Taylor, Commanding Officer of Fort Barre!" The cheers grew louder as the men strode in and bowed majestically. "Ladies and Gentlemen, would you please remain standing for the Honorable Nigel Q. Rothschild, Governor of the great State of Texas escorting his daughter, Miss Claudia Rothschild!" Several people started hooping and hollering as the politician waved to his constituents, while kissing his daughter's hand.

"Thank you! Thank you!" The governor and his daughter bowed and waved then began going from person to person, shaking hands. "Evening, evening ya'll, evening folks!" The night was off to a rousing success. The group was served refreshments by porters. Several people remarked openly how impressed they were with the post and its soldiers. Sergeant Nouba was busy getting to know a few of the local townswomen by dancing with them. Luck even changed for Corporal Crawford and Oliver as they met two young lovely ladies and attempted to steal a dance or two.

Captain Taylor and Ms. Rothschild stood close to each other the entire evening and that escaped no one's eyes, especially her father's.

"My daughter is quite fond of your commanding officer," said Governor Rothschild to Sergeant Trinidad. "I can see that love has bloomed." Moses smiled.

"They make a lovely couple, sir." Moses turned toward the Governor. "I don't say this about many officers that I have served with, but I would follow that man anywhere."

"That means a lot coming from a soldier such as yourself Sergeant Trinidad. To the Captain and my daughter," said Governor Rothschild, clinking his glass gently with the sergeant. "Here's to your fine soldiers, Sergeant Trinidad, they're one helluva unit, son!" Moses' smile could be seen all the way back to Boston.

"Ladies and gentlemen dinner will now be served!" announced a young black soldier. The people began to take their seats at the tables. Soon silver platters with steaming hot carved meats, vegetables, and breads were placed on the tables. As was the custom, the gentlemen served the ladies first. Laughter rang across the compound as the soldiers and their guests enjoyed their special evening. Time passed quickly as the dishes were cleared away. The guests began to grab their coats and head for their coaches and wagons.

"Captain Taylor, I would like to thank you for a wiz bang evening son," said General Kerrey, slapping the officer on the back. "Yes sir, this was one fine night." Placing a cigar in his mouth he chomped on it for a moment and stared at the sky. Sergeants Trinidad and Nouba stood off to the side. "Sergeant, may I borrow your flame so to speak?"

"Of course, sir," said Moses cupping the match and drawing it toward the general. "Did you enjoy yourself, sir?"

"Did I! Hell this smile is not from being happily married!" The men laughed wildly. Governor Rothschild, Claudia and Captain Taylor strolled across the compound away from the rest of the group. Lieutenant Peters was growing tired. Saluting his superiors, he waddled wearily to his guest quarters to adjourn for the night.

The wagons slowly pulled out from the fort and headed back towards the town. Moses signaled to Corporal Crawford. "Have a four man detachment see these civilians safely back to the town. It's a full moon, so visibility for the ride should be good."

"I'll handle it personally," said Crawford, glancing at the young blonde woman as she waved playfully. Turning towards Moses, he winked. "My pleasure."

"Just be careful, that's all," said Moses as he turned away. Crawford grabbed a mount from the corral.

"Oliver, let's go." The young man grabbed a horse and headed out behind the group.

"Sergeants, we don't have to end this evening do we," said General Kerrey, rubbing his hands together. Moses and Nouba looked at each other.

"No sir!"

"I know it's not typical protocol, but I brought a nice bottle of Kentucky sipping whiskey with me. It will burn the hair in your noses. Ha! Ha! I'll go and get it. Why don't you men make up a nice fire." The General walked off to his quarters.

Moses and Nouba walked slowly across the compound.

"General "Gustoff the Great" Kerrey sharing a bottle of whiskey with two black cavalry sergeants" said Moses, opening the door. Striking a match he lit the two candle lamps and reached up on the shelf for three glasses. Trinidad blew off the dust and set them down on the table. "I must admit Nouba, I'm quite nervous and excited." Nouba smiled as he took a seat and began to remove his boots and then his dress trousers.

"It will definitely be something to remember," said Nouba, placing his dress uniform away in his trunk. "Why don't you change out of your dress uniform and I'll prepare a fire for us and the general." There was a knock on the door. Moses hastily buckled his belt and walked to the door. It suddenly opened. The corner of the door connected with Moses' head and he crashed to the floor.

"Damn, son," yelled the General holding a bottle of whiskey in one hand and a glowing cigar in the other. "You all right?" He placed the bottle gently on the table and bent down to help his man. "Hell son, you're tougher than a pine tree!" Chomping on the cigar, General Kerrey hoisted the big man to his feet and began to wipe the dust off his shirt.

"I'm fine sir, don't trouble yourself." Moses rubbed his head and gazed at Nouba. "As you could see sir, some members of the Cavalry wouldn't assist a fellow soldier."

Nouba sat next to the fire and smiled. "Didn't want to lose my seat." The soldiers laughed joyfully. Turning back towards the fire, Nouba sighed. "Mighty nice fire."

"Enough of this lolly gagging, let's opened this bottle, men." Placing the bottle under his nose, the general sniffed slowly. "A-a-h! Glasses my good men." Moses and Nouba extended their glasses and watched as the smooth brown liquid was poured in each glass. General Kerrey placed the bottle back on the table and gazed at the two soldiers.

"A toast," said the General, stretching his neck. "To the Buffalo Soldiers of Fort Barre and their two fine Sergeants." General Kerrey nodded at both Moses and Nouba. "To the United States of America!"

"To the United States of America!" Raising their glasses in unison, Moses and Nouba clinked glasses and downed the whiskey with excitement. Moses felt the back of his throat burn a little as he squinted his eyes. Nouba stood there smiling as the liquid slid slowly down his throat. Time and most of the whiskey in the bottle passed semi quietly into the early hours of the morning.

EIGHTEEN

The sun had just begun to creep over the horizon, as reveille sounded and the normal rumble of soldiers' feet hitting the ground was heard.

Corporal Bernard knocked quietly on the door of the sergeant's room, as the door creaked open. "Sergeant Trinidad, Sergeant Nouba, is anyone here?" Pushing the door open he saw the three men passed out cold in their respective chairs. The corporal bent down and whispered in Moses' ear.

"Good morning sweet prince," said Bernard, shaking the man gently. "Time to rise and shine." Moses' eyes peeled open slowly as he stared at the shiny white smile of Corporal Bernard. "Coffee?"

"Yes!" Moses turned slowly in the chair while yawning and stretching his back. "Your face is the last thing I need this morning." Rubbing his eyes, Moses made out two forms lying slumped in their chairs. "Where is Captain Taylor?"

"He, Claudia Rothschild and the Governor went out for a morning ride."

"What! You let them?" said Moses, holding his head. "What happens if there's trouble?"

"Not to worry," said Bernard, holding his hand up. "I sent Maxfield and Owens to ride along with them. The Captain has become a good shot and the Governor is a former scout. I'm not worried at all."

"Well, I guess it's okay," said Moses. "I need a bath and a shave."

"Do you want me to wake **them?**" asked Bernard, pointing to Sergeant Nouba and General Kerrey. The General tossed and turned, and Sergeant Nouba rolled back and forth.

"You want to wake **a** General?" smiled Moses.

"No," said Bernard passing him a mug of steam brew.

Moses tried to stand up. "Thanks, oohh my head, you'd better attend to the men and pass the morning orders." Bernard exited the barracks. Stepping into the chilly morning he grabbed Cleetus Ray and instructed him to prepare a bath for Moses.

"Bugler!" shouted Corporal Bernard. "Sound assembly." The sound of the bugle rang across the compound as men scrambled to fill each line. "Attention!" The men snapped to, and not a muscle twitched. "All right men, as you all know at 1400 hours there will be an awards ceremony, so today's work details will be minimal, with the exception of the normal patrols in town and the surrounding areas. The following individuals will report to Corporal Crawford and prepare for morning patrol. Pike! Trotter! Pullman! Cooke! Report to the corral. Work details commence overall clean up of facility, that corral still needs tending to and make sure security is in place, no slacking!"

"Yes, Corporal," shouted the men in unison.

"Dismissed!" Bernard turned and walked towards the corral where Corporal Crawford was adjusting his saddle. "Morning, how ya feeling?"

"That was one helluva night," said Crawford smiling. "I can't remember the last time I had so much fun." He gently patted the horse's head.

"Well, I'm glad that you had a good time, but remember, the captain and his guests are still out there, so let's pay extra close attention," said Bernard, stroking the horse's mane. "You can be darn sure that they'll be watching to see how all of us are doing."

"All right, I'll make sure that everyone stays on the level," said Crawford, pulling his horse out of the corral. Holding a firm grip on the saddle he climbed on. "I know what to do, Corporal Bernard."

"I know, I'll see you men later. Remember be back around 1300 to get ready for formation and review by the General and the Governor."

"No problem, mount up!" There was a loud clap as the men jumped into their saddles and turned their mounts heads towards the fort's entrance. "Forward, hooo!" The soldiers led by Crawford raced out of the fort and bound over the countryside.

At 1300 hours Moses walked slowly across the compound. The men had finished the corral roof with a hayloft and it looked great. Corporal Crawford's morning patrol was just securing their horses.

"Corporal," said Moses. "Any problems with this morning's activities?"

"No, Sergeant," said Crawford, removing the saddle from his horse. "All was quiet, I didn't even see the sheriff about or the rangers."

"Any sign of the captain's party?" asked Moses, biting into an apple.

"We passed them on the bluffs over an hour ago, they should be here at any time."

"Good enough, I'll see you a little later. I'm going to take some time alone." Moses had grabbed his little bag with his notebook and pencil. Looking straight up, he thought the hayloft would be a good place to grab a little quiet time, so up he went.

The party galloped across the plains laughing amongst each other. Governor Rothschild and Claudia rode side by side and slowed to a trot. Captain Taylor was gazing across the horizon as his two scouts were positioned a few hundred yards in the distance.

"I can see that you have a deep affection for the young man," said the governor, while rocking back and forth in the saddle. "Before you go any further, I want you to know that I do approve of your relationship with this young man. He is a very mature officer for a man of his age, and that is something I plan to mention when I return." Claudia turned toward her father and smiled warmly.

"Hennecker is a very respectful, warm person, Father." She straightened herself in the saddle. "I hope that things could move a little faster."

"Has he discussed plans for marriage? I want my daughter to be considered a real lady. I know your mother is smiling down on you right now, honey." Taking hold of his daughter's hand, he kissed it.

Owens scanned the horizon for any sign of trouble, nothing! The man climbed up into the saddle. "It's a lovely day, not a speck in the sky."

"Yes, it appears as if everything is perfect, men." Taylor slowly slid his glasses into the case. "Soldiers ride ahead four hundred yards and then we'll circle around and head home."

"Yes sir," barked the soldiers. Kicking up a cloud of dust and dirt, the troopers sped off into a small area with a clump of tangled trees. Willie Owens and Sandy Maxfield dismounted and tied them off in some branches. Removing the carbines from their saddles, both men disappeared into the brush. Slowly they crept with the barrels pointed in front of them.

"What are we looking for, anyhow?" asked Owens, walking through the heavy brush. The stock on his gun got stuck in the vegetation.

"Nothing," said Maxfield, stopping and looking in all directions. "There's nothing happening, let's turn around and head back." Both soldiers emerged from the brush in time to see the Captain riding furiously in their direction with his pistol drawn.

"Is everything okay men?" asked Taylor pulling the reins on his horse and coming to a halt. "I thought there was trouble." The soldiers stood there standing at attention. "At ease!"

"Everything is fine sir, we thought we saw something," said Owens climbing into the saddle. "It was nothing at all, sir."

Taylor placed the pistol back in its holster. "Well, as long as everything is fine, I'll get back to my guests, thank you men," said the officer tipping his hat and beginning to turn away.

"Why don't you hold on, sir?" Owens glanced over at Governor Rothschild and Claudia. "I think this is the **big** discussion." The soldiers both gazed over at their commander and smiled.

"What are you talking about?" Taylor quizzed.

"My guess," said Owens, leaning on his saddle. "She's already told him how she feels about you." Claudia shot a quick little smile at the officer and waved. Governor Rothschild waved his arm back and forth as they trotted along peacefully. Maxfield sat in the saddle smiling with his carbine across his lap.

The men glanced over at their leader; his face had turned a bright color of red. "Weddings are always good news." The men laughed together.

"Well men, let's get back to our guests and circle around, race ya!" The Captain slapped his horse and darted off. Three young men and their horses streaking across the horizon no barriers. No rivalry, just comrades in arms. What a sight. Governor Rothschild and Claudia, both expert riders, followed quickly, nipping on their heals.

"Race to the tree line," yelled Taylor smiling.

"You'll never beat us Texans," yelled Claudia, bearing down on the soldiers. Owens signaled to both Maxfield and Governor Rothschild to ease off a bit and let the couple race. The lovebirds pounded over the ground and came to a rest by the tree line.

"Looks like we've lost our friends," whispered Taylor. "Perhaps this would be a nice moment to steal a kiss, Miss Rothschild." Nervously the young officer removed his cap and eased in slowly for a soft kiss from his lovely friend. Placing her hands on both sides of his face Claudia kissed the man deeply, passionately.

* * * * * * *

Moses peeked his head over the ladder; the entire loft was filled with bales of hay. A large pulley system and a hatch door had been rigged up to lift the hay to the second story of the barn. Gazing out of the hatch, Moses was treated to a spectacular unobtrusive view of the fort, creek bed and surrounding countryside. Below him the soldiers moved about completing their daily jobs assignments. Positioning a few hay bales, Moses removed his waist belt and began to write down his thoughts over the past days.

October 13th, 1879

These past few days have been ones that will stay in my memory for a lifetime. The party the men held for the Governor and the General was quite impressive if I do say so. Beginning with the men's surprise of a custom carriage ride from the train station to the fort, the impressive musicians and incredible job of turning a frontier fort into the most glorious of ballrooms, it never ended.

Sergeant Nouba received a lovely gift of an antique pistol from Governor Rothschild encased in wood. The Governor wanted to show him his appreciation for saving his daughter and I say it was well deserved.

General Kerrey has turned out to be one helluva an individual. He even brought a special bottle of whiskey with him for Sergeant Nouba and myself. We drank until we couldn't drink any more and woke up this morning with a headache. General Kerrey and Sergeant Nouba were still sleeping when I left. The Captain and his future family were getting to know each other while taking a ride through the countryside, with an armed detail, of course. Captain Taylor needs a good woman in his life and Miss Claudia is the one.

Speaking of women this old dog could use a little feminine affection so this idea of letting the men enjoy the town is looking better and better each day.

Moses put the pen down and laid back on the hay bales, their scent was sweet and fresh. He closed his eyes and was transported back to when he was a corporal posted at Fort Douglas, a small supply post in the state of Delaware. .

Violet was her name, and she could stop a moving train with those lush green eyes and that mocha colored skin. Moses thought to himself she didn't just move, she glided across the room. He remembered the first time he saw her, how she took the breath from his lips and made the Corporal weak in the knees. Moses knew right then and there that she was to be his wife and nothing or no one would stand in his way. This would not be the easiest of tasks because others were vying for the affection of the jade-eyed beauty. The courting of Violet began to cloud the judgment of the soldier and many noticed. Moses thought nothing of this because in the end he had Violet, and as time passed the couple grew closer. Then one day, a quiet storm rode into the post and everything changed.

His name was Watson, Theodore Q., a young first lieutenant and he was white. Moses immediately saw the way that Violet reacted to the sight of the handsome man, and it made him burn with jealousy. Violet was impressed with the way the officer walked, talked and rode. It was very clear to Moses he was losing her little by little. The walks, talks and evenings together slowly came to a halt. Moses felt a piece of his heart break off each time he thought of his beauty, slipping away. Sleep was becoming harder, and small things began to upset the man more easily.

One day, Moses emerged from his quarters to see the officer walking with his lady friend. Something inside snapped and the man bounded over to the officer and confronted him. He shouted and became very aggressive with the officer. Watson said in his defense he wasn't trying to court the woman, just get to know a few people around the area because he himself was new. Violet became embarrassed at the scene that Moses was causing. She finally broke down and admitted to Moses that her feelings for him had changed, and she now loved Watson. Moses hauled off and knocked Watson square in the jaw, sending the man tumbling to the ground. Violet screamed in sheer terror, running to her new love's aid, while Moses escaped off into the night. The following day, Violet came quietly to Moses and revealed that she never wanted to see him again. The soldier felt his entire world crash around him; it felt like someone had kicked him square in the gut. Violet said that an officer would be able to provide more than an enlisted man. Moses felt dejected and walked away quietly. The officer decided that charges against the man would be useless; his heart was destroyed and that was pain enough.

Moses left Delaware, feeling personally disgraced, and was transferred to another fort in the Kansas Territory. Upon arriving at his new assignment, Moses decided he would never let the affections of a woman cloud his judgment. The Army would be his one and only passion.

"Riders approachin'." Moses shook his head and peered out the hatch, Captain Taylor's party was coming back. Brushing the hay off his uniform, Moses grabbed his bag and descended back down the ladder. Strapping on his pistol, he walked over to the Captain and his guest.

"Good afternoon, sir," snapped Sergeant Trinidad.

"Afternoon, Sergeant," replied Taylor. "At ease." The officer held his hand out to assist Miss Rothschild from her horse.

"Afternoon, ma'am," said Moses tipping his hat. "After-noon Governor, did you enjoy your ride?" Moses held the Governor's horse as he dismounted.

"Ah, Sergeant Trinidad," barked the Texan. "Yes I did, this is some beautiful country. The Captain here is a fine guide, and your scouts were very professional." The Governor shook his head and laughed. "Hell, there's nothing you men can't do."

Sergeant Trinidad turned towards Maxfield and Owens. "All right men, secure detail." The soldier saluted, gathered up the horses and headed over to the corral.

Corporal Bernard came walking over to the party in his new uniform and snapped to attention. "Good afternoon sir!"

"Afternoon, Corporal," replied the officer, while glancing up and down at the man. "You look extremely professional I must say." The officer beamed with personal pride.

"Thank you, sir," said Bernard. "May I have a word with the Sergeant sir?"

"Of course." The Captain turned toward his guests as Moses and Bernard stepped aside.

"Everything, okay?" asked Moses putting his arm on Bernard's shoulder.

"Sure everything is perfect. I just wanted you to know that Lieutenant Peters and Hayes are going over the final paperwork and the order in which the citations will be handed out and that sort of thing," said Bernard, wiping his face with his handkerchief. "The men are ready and the guards have been placed in two extra locations to ensure against anything." Moses smiled at his friend. "Don't worry about a thing, nothing could go wrong." Bernard gently knocked on the wooden hitching post and walked away. Moses looked down at the ground for a few seconds.

"Sir, if you would both excuse me, I must prepare myself for this afternoon's affairs." Saluting smartly, Moses executed a textbook about face and walked over to his quarters.

"Well," said Captain Taylor. "Governor, Ms. Rothschild I'm afraid I too must head over to my office to go over details myself. Ms. Rothschild, I'll leave you in good company of course." The officer took her hand and gently kissed it. The Governor smiled approvingly at the couple. Stepping back the Captain threw a quick salute. "Sir." The officer proceeded across the compound and up the steps to his office, disappearing inside.

Governor Rothschild stared and leaned in close to his daughter. "I do like him myself, darling." Claudia gently kissed her father on the cheek.

Mississippi, Georgia, Tennessee, Alabama, Arkansas, Massachusetts, Texas and New York were the states where they came from, some white, some black, but all soldiers. Little shantytowns with dirt floors, plantations where they were whipped and ridiculed, big cities or farms where the day began at dawn and ended at dusk. They all stood proudly in formation, awaiting the arrival of Governor Rothschild and Brigadier General Kerrey. The ceremony was to be held on the parade ground of the fort.

The weather was agreeing with them for the occasion, a hair chilly, but the sky was as blue as the ocean. The men were positioned in three groups and standing at parade rest. A few feet in front of each group stood Sergeant Nouba, Corporal Bernard and Corporal Crawford. The door to the commanding officer quarters opened and Lieutenant Peters followed by Sergeant Trinidad and Hayes. Hayes carried the trunk containing the citations and set them down on a table positioned on the porch. Sergeant Trinidad strode up to the top step landing.

"Attention!" The men snapped to in an instance. "May I present the commanding officer of Fort Barre, Captain H. J. Taylor, the governor of Texas Nigel Q. Rothschild and our most honored guest, Brigadier General Gustoff Kerrey!" Captain Taylor was first to speak.

"Men, there were additional reasons why Governor Rothschild and General Kerrey have graced us with their presence. Since reporting to Fort Barre, you men have been thrust into battle and have made not only myself, but also the entire United States Army proud of your actions. Some of you have answered this above and beyond the call of duty and those individuals' actions have not gone unnoticed," declared the officer smiling. "Governor, if you would please." Governor Rothschild walked over to the Captain and shook his hand firmly.

"Thank you Captain Taylor," said the governor, patting him on the shoulder. "Men, I can't put into words the sheer honor it gives me to present these citations."

"When your name is called, you will proceed up to the top of the steps of the stairs to General Kerrey!" shouted Sergeant Trinidad. "Lucious Potter! Edwin Pullman!" The two stunned men walked to the top of the stairs, where the Governor and the General were waiting.

"Congratulations, soldiers," said the general, as he handed each a letter of commendation and shook their hands. The men proceeded back into formation as Governor Rothschild prepared to speak.

Sergeant Trinidad stepped up front. "Winston Oliver! Paul Crawford!"

"Congratulations men!" said the Governor.

"We seem to have an additional paperwork for some reason, General," said Lieutenant Peters scratching his head and shuffling some papers.

Captain Taylor chimed in quickly. "Unfortunately sir, Sullivan was killed in a skirmish with gun runners." The General bowed his head in a moment of silence.

Governor Rothschild stepped back in front of the men. "There is one last citation to read. For conspicuous gallantry and intrepidity at the risk of his own life above and beyond the call of duty. While in command of a 9th Cavalry patrol, he rallied his men to race quickly to their dying comrades and avoid a total loss of life. His sound and swift decisions and his obvious calm served to stabilize the badly decimated regiment and further motivate the men. His gallant initiative and heroic conduct reflected great credit upon himself and were in keeping with the highest traditions of the United States Army."

Sergeant Trinidad stepped forward and smiled. "Sergeant Nouba front and center!" The clearly shocked man walked slowly up to the porch and stood there. General Kerrey leaned in close and pinned the medal on his chest.

"My sincere congratulations, Sergeant Nouba," said the General, shaking his hand.

"Three cheers for the men. Hip hip hooray, hooray, hooray!"

"Men, we have one further announcement. The town is now open to all military personnel to enjoy on personal time only or on official military business. We plan an informal get-together at the local saloon tonight. Make sure you check your duty assignments. Would all of today's honorees report to the Captain's office before commencing furlough. Dismissed!" The men's cheers could be heard for miles as they hooped and hollered.

The five honorees marched over to the office and stood at attention in front of Captain Taylor's desk, who sat back and smiled.

"Men, let me say that these citations are well deserved. Each and every one of you has made me proud. "Sergeant Nouba, Corporal Crawford, Pullman, Potter and Oliver, enjoy your fun tonight."

"Sir, will you be joining us this evening?" asked Sergeant Trinidad. "I'm sure the men would all be excited if you came."

"Yes, Sergeant, I will be joining you this evening. First, we need to prepare the coach to take the governor, the general and Lieutenant Peters down to the train station." The men snapped to attention and exited the office.

"Hayes," said Sergeant Trinidad. "Have the coach prepared, we need to give our friends a ride to the train depot." Soon the polished wagon was ready to take the dignitaries back in town. General Kerrey, Lieutenant Peters, Governor Rothschild and Claudia all gathered out in front of Captain Taylor's office. The coach and its security detail, led by Taylor himself, headed out of the fort and to town.

Standing on the platform of the train station, Claudia Rothschild hugged her father. "I'm not coming home, Father. I've decided to stay in Flat Fork and start a life for myself," said Claudia smiling.

"All aboard," cried the conductor.

"I was pretty sure that you would say that," said the governor, as he hugged her closely. "I'm very happy for you my dear." The governor turned and faced the Captain. "Welcome to my family, Hennecker." Extending a hand they shook.

"Thank you Governor Rothschild," said the officer smiling.

Moses and Nouba chatted with the General and were laughing up a storm. "All aboard!"

"Damn it, men," said the general preparing to climb on the train. "I've had one helluva time over these days. You ever get to the capital of Texas you come and see the ole General, we'll crack open another bottle of whiskey. Take care now." The governor thanked the men once again and climbed aboard the car."

The train whistle blew as the smoke stacks were getting fired up. "All aboard, final call!" Chugging slowly but surely the train pulled away from the station and out of the town of Flat Fork.

"Well sir, I guess we'll head back to the fort," said Sergeant Trinidad saluting.

"That reminds me, Hennecker," said Claudia smiling. "I've decided to move into Mrs. White's boarding house with some of the young ladies from the school. Classes for the colored children will begin soon, and this puts me closer to town."

"Sounds like a plan to me," said the officer taking her hand. "May I escort you over to the boarding house, then?"

"Why thank you, kind sir," smiled Claudia. The enlisted men saluted and, along with the coach, headed back to town. Moses watched as the young couple strolled along, pulling Taylor's horse by the reins.

"Corporal Crawford," said Moses leaning forward in the saddle. "Take Oliver here and head back to town. Make sure the Captain doesn't have any problems." The men turned their horses' heads to the rear and circled back to town. Moses turned toward his men. "Let's head back and get ready for tonight." The men slapped their horses and took off.

NINETEEN

The soldiers were crowded around shaving basins. Lathered faces smiled happily as they chatted about plans for this evening.

"Man oh man, have I been looking forward to this evening for a long time," said Hayes, tightening the knot in his neckerchief. "I've seen the women at the saloon, they're gorgeous. I have a pocket full of money." Corporal Bernard and Pike were playing cards on the table in the barracks.

"Remember who makes the decisions: Hayes, the big head," said Corporal Bernard laughing. All the soldiers who didn't draw the duty were readying themselves for a night on the town. Moses and Nouba walked into the barracks and stood in front of the men.

"Please do the honors, Sergeant Nouba," said Moses smiling. Nouba grabbed a chair and stood on it.

"Men, I don't have to tell you what tonight means, besides the obvious," boomed Nouba. "You men represent the United States Cavalry and more importantly, Captain Taylor, the commanding officer of this fort. I no doubt anticipate the usual problems, a fight and heavy drinking, that sort of thing. I don't anticipate, and will not tolerate any rude or hostile acts towards the civilians. I do not see myself as a harsh leader; I believe that I am a fair man. Enjoy yourselves tonight men, and don't disappoint me."

Moses who was standing off to the side, chimed in. "Another word boneheads. Respect the civilians and their property, no excuses. You'd better keep your noses clean, or I'll pop a bullet in your hides, understood!"

"Yes, Sergeant!" barked the men.

"Formation, mount up," yelled Sergeant Trinidad. The soldiers climbed onto their steeds and ready to leave. "Remember check your side arms!" The men each removed their guns and checked them over once again. "Ready forward!"

"Weeeehaaaaa!!" The soldiers darted forward at a thunderous rate kicking up clouds of dust and debris. Captain Taylor held his head and closed his eyes. He turned slowly towards his Sergeants. They both shrugged their shoulders.

The ride into town that night was lovely. It was a full moon with a clear sky and the stars simply sparkled in the heavens above them. The men rode joyfully across the hills and countryside singing. The Captain glanced over at his men and nodded his approval.

Sheriff Watkins sat nervously at his desk. He was perspiring heavily. Taking the whiskey bottle from his desk he poured himself half a glass and gulped it. Watkins poured himself another, downed that, and poured one more. The Sheriff felt a calm slowly ease over him. Staring outside the window, he noticed that darkness had set in over the town. The streetlights were being lit by one of his deputies. Watkins watched the little orange glowing light go from post to post illuminating the sidewalks.

"Sheriff," said a voice. "Sheriff, you all right?" Watkins jerked awake and stared wild-eyed into space. Deputy Isaac Flowers was a green deputy sent from Dallas to help control

241

problems in Flat Fork. The boy was oblivious to the goings on with the sheriff and his seedy partners.

"Everything is fine, Flowers," said the Sheriff, smiling and reaching for another glass. "Would you like a drink?" Flowers held up his hand.

"No thanks, not on duty." Watkins poured whiskey into both glasses.

"Hell son, I'm in charge you won't get in any trouble!" Tilting the glass back he drank until the liquid disappeared and smiled. Flowers smiled back uncomfortably.

From behind the curtain emerged Ranger Armstead and his two Indians. The Indians stood straight and silent. Sheriff Watkins turned his chair towards them. Flowers glanced nervously at the Indians.

"Well, Sheriff, are you planning on introducing us?" asked Armstead holding his hand out and looking around the room. "How's about a drink for old friends?"

"Neither of those ideas would have crossed my mind," said Watkins rising from his chair and brushing past the man. Reaching into the top shelf of a cabinet, he pulled out another bottle of whiskey. "Well, since you came, this is one of the new deputies, Flowers is his name." Flowers extended his hand to Armstead who smiled eerily.

"Welcome to the wonderful world of law enforcing." Grabbing the young deputy's hand, Armstead shook it firmly.

"Flowers," said the Sheriff, sitting back down in his chair. "Why don't you head out on a little patrol of the town? Meet up with the other fellows and make sure everything is all right?"

"Sure thing, Sheriff." The boy headed over to the door and turned around. "Nice to meet you, ranger."

"Same here, son," said Armstead, picking up a chair and placing it backwards between his legs. Flowers opened the door and exited into the night. "Don't be a stranger," called the ranger.

Sheriff Watkins pulled a box of cigars out from his desk and removed one. Extending the box to Armstead, he also took one. Armstead struck a match and lit his cigar. Watkins struck his own as he watched the Ranger chuckle happily.

"We're going to have to kill that young man quickly and quietly," said Watkins easing back in his chair.

Armstead laughed loudly. "What? My good Sheriff, I don't participate in those sorts of things. I also think you have had too much whiskey. You're starting to act like me." Armstead went to grab the bottle and heard a click! From under the desk, Watkins slowly pulled out a pistol and aimed it square between Armstead's eyes.

"You didn't ask me!" Sheriff Watkins eyes never moved from Armstead's. For the first time the ranger thought that the sheriff was going to double cross him. Armstead thought it over and shook his head. Leaning in close, he rested his forehead on the barrel of the pistol and smiled. Glancing over at the Indians, Armstead laughed. Watkins eased slowly up on the hammer and set the gun down on his desk. He poured himself another glass.

Suddenly, two more of the sheriff's men barged into the office. "Sheriff, you better come outside and take a look at this." The men quickly rose from their seats and headed out the door. It sounded like a mountain crumbling to the earth, as the massive wave of soldiers rode into the town.

"Well, well, well," smiled Ranger Armstead picking his teeth. "It's our friends, the black sojas." The men watched as the riders dismounted in front of the bar. A single rider broke off from the pack and proceeded through town and past the sheriff's office. It was Captain Taylor.

Watkins retreated angrily back into the office. "I saw that little weasel. Captain Tatum or Taylor or whatever the hell!" Grabbing the bottle he took a long hard slug. "Damn it, damn it! That little son of a bitch, that stankin' rat." The Sheriff was getting all excited and throwing his fists in the air. Armstead sat back and watched the man ramble on. Suddenly the sheriff's eyes rolled to the back of his head as he fell backwards into his seat and then onto the floor.

Armstead shook his head in disgust. "It's a wonder he lasted this long. Well, we're gonna be a lot better off without him tonight." Passing the bottle to his men, he took small sips from his glass and stared out of the window. "Slaves in uniforms," he whispered. "Get ready to lose a man tonight sojas. Let's go!" The men blew out the lamps and exited the office, leaving Sheriff Watkins lying passed out drunk on the floor.

The saloon was jumping with activity as the soldiers entered the smoke filled room. Piano music was playing, girls were making the rounds, and the whiskey flowed like water. Most people only gave the black soldiers a passing glance; they were too busy having a good time.

"Where did the captain go?" asked Corporal Bernard. Noticing an empty table by the back wall, the soldiers went over and grabbed a seat.

"He went to see his lady friend at the boarding house," replied Moses, waving over a barmaid. "He'll be here later." Moses shifted around in his seat for a minute. He gazed over the room to get a feel of the atmosphere. "Speaking of girls, look over there." Leaning up against the wall were five lovely women who waved playfully at the soldiers. Moses beckened them over as Hayes' eyes nearly bulged out of their sockets. Nouba watched as the girls glided over to their table and took a seat in each soldier's lap. The barmaid set a large tray of drinks in the middle of the table.

"This night is off to a very good start," said Moses, raising his mug. "To the Cavalry!"

"The Cavalry!" The men clinked their glasses together.

Corporal Crawford had made his way over to the poker table with Oliver to take a look at the competition. Walking near the head of the table, he grinned widely. "Mind if I sit in, gentlemen?"

"Always room in my pockets for a gringo soldier's dollar," smiled a Mexican man with a sly, greasy little smile. His name was Renaldo Q. Morales, a small time gambler. The reason he was small time was because he was a lousy gambler, and when he drank he got even worse.

Oliver leaned in close to Crawford. "I'm going to the bar, whattaya want?" The soldier leered at the Mexican, who shifted oddly in his chair.

"Beer and a shot, thanks!" Crawford removed a small wad of money and placed in on the table. Oliver patted him on the shoulder and headed over to the bar.

"Well, Corporal," smiled Morales. "Shall we dance?" Crawford loosened his collar and took a seat.

After much pushing and shoving, Oliver managed to make his way up to the bar. He called to the bartender.

"Two beer and two shots," hollered the boy. Grabbing the drinks, he thanked the man and headed back over to the card table. Behind a massive mound of cash, coins, and other expensive objects, including a pearl handled pistol, sat Corporal Crawford with a huge grin.

"Full house!" he said, placing his cards down on the table. The other gamblers threw down their cards in disgust. Mr. Morales was perspiring heavily, and it was soaking through his garments. Crawford tossed a clean cloth to the man. "Here, before you float away!" Reaching forward, Crawford pulled the prize towards himself, smiling delightfully. Oliver placed the drinks down beside his friend. The Mexican gambler tilted back in his chair holding his head.

Meanwhile Hayes had found some female companionship with a young red haired beauty by the name of Mary Lou.

Joined by the lips in the corner, the young man held tight to his new prize surfacing only to swallow a mouthful of beer.

"Looks like Hayes is doing fine for himself huh?" said Elias. Moses looked over and saw the young lady lean in close and then point to the rooms on the second floor. Hayes' eyes bugged out as the lady led him to the staircase.

"Do it for the Cavalry, Hayes! That a boy, Vermont!" The men continued to cheer as the couple climbed the stairs and shut the door behind them.

"A dollar says Hayes makes a bold statement," said Moses, tossing a couple of coins in the middle of the table.

"You're on," said Nouba finishing his beer.

"Whoaaaiiieee!" came the cry from the second floor.

"Damn," said Nouba, tossing his money at Moses. The big sergeant laughed as he placed the money in his pocket.

Deputy Flowers walked across the wooden porches of the local shops peering into each window and checking each door lock. Sheriff Watkins had found two additional deputies from his days in the Confederate Army. Their names were Winchester and Hollis, former die-hard rebels with an axe to grind against the new Union. They especially hated the blacks, which they blamed for their problems. Hearing the noise from the saloon, the deputies headed over. As they pushed open the shutter doors, their tin stars gleamed in the chandelier light as they scanned the room.

Moses nudged Nouba in the ribs and kicked Bernard under the table. "Front door, three of them with badges." Bernard watched coldly as they made their way up to the bar and called for a drink. The young deputy waved his off.

"Not drinking I notice," said Nouba, lighting his pipe and puffing. "Looks green to me!" Moses watched with curious eyes.

"The two following him are scum," frowned Bernard. "You're right though, the kid is still wet behind the ears." Moses stood up and headed over to the deputies.

Deputy Winchester slapped his partner on the shoulder. "Look what's comin' towards us."

"Evening, Deputy," said the massive soldier, holding out his hand. "Name's Trinidad, Sergeant Moses Trinidad 9th Cavalry."

Flowers shook Moses' hand. "Nice to meet you, Sergeant, I'm Deputy Flowers. This is Winchester and Hollins." The two men nodded slyly and turned around. "Are your men having a good time?" asked the boy.

"By the looks of it, I'd say yes!" Moses downed the last of his beer and turned towards the bartender. "Barkeep, how about a refill! Can I buy you a beer, deputy?"

"No thanks, not while on duty," said the man, holding up his hand. "Perhaps some other time though, I have to get back to my job." Deputy Flowers shook Moses' hand and turned to leave the bar. The fact that the other two deputies continually stared at the Buffalo Soldiers didn't escape Moses' eyes either.

Nouba watched the deputies leave the building. "There's one thing that bothers me though. How long will it be before that Flowers kid has an accident like the Johnson boy?" The soldiers looked at each other and continued drinking.

Ten minutes later, Hayes came down the stairs straightening his suspenders with a grin the size of the Texas plains.

"Well soldier," said Moses, raising his mug. "Are you planning on marrying her?" The men began to laugh hysterically.

Hayes banged his fists on the table and tossed back a quick shot of whiskey. Wincing hard, the boy wiped his face with his shirtsleeve. "That woman was incredible Sergeant." Hayes leaned on Moses and almost fell in his lap.

"Steady son, steady!" Moses grabbed Hayes by the shoulders and placed him in a chair.

* * * * * * *

Across town, Captain Taylor and Claudia Rothschild sat comfortably, hand in hand, on the porch swing. Yawning and stretching his arm, Taylor curled it gently around Claudia's shoulder. She adjusted her positioned and relaxed in her man's arms. The couple had just returned from a nice stroll along the banks of a small creek.

"It's a very lovely evening," said Taylor, squeezing Claudia gently. The chair creaked easily as it swayed in the evening breeze. "The men will be expecting me soon my darling, so I have to get going."

"Oh, Hennecker, a few moments longer won't stop the Army from moving will it?" Claudia leaned in close and softly kissed his lips. Taylor eased back in the chair and closed his eyes.

"My dear, I must," said the officer rising from his seat. "This is something that I promised the men. I wouldn't want to disappoint them." He took her hand, and the young couple walked down the steps towards the officer's horse.

Standing in the moonlight, Taylor noticed the expression on Claudia's face. "What's wrong?"

"I love you, Hennecker, I'm sure of it," said the girl, tilting her head down. Taking her chin in his hand gently, he lifted her head up.

"Never lower your head my dear, it's too beautiful," said Taylor, taking her in his arms and hugging her closely. "I love you too, my darling." He kissed her passionately. "I must go now, though." Climbing on his horse he smiled warmly. "Good nigh,t my love!" The officer bolted off into the night. While riding towards the town the man thought, she loves me, damn!

Ranger Armstead and his Indians friends moved quietly through the dark sections between the buildings around towards the back of the saloon. Peering through the window, Armstead watched as the Buffalo Soldiers were enjoying their evening.

"Look at those sons a bitches," spouted Armstead, showering the window with saliva. "Those blacks and their Yankee buddies are drinkin' up a storm." The two big Indians stared inside and said nothing. "We gotta figure a way to snag one of them without causin' a ruckus." Armstead looked around and saw the two outhouses tucked under some trees. The glow from the lantern hanging on the back porch gave off a weak light and made visibility very poor.

"There," said Armstead, pointing to the dark section under the trees. "That's where we'll hide and wait for one of them to use the crapper. When they come out, it's curtains!" A small crooked smile quickly passed over both the Indian's faces.

Inside the saloon, the atmosphere was jumping as more people began to file into the watering hole. Moses' table was packed with empty glasses and most of his men were in the bag. Nouba was tipped up on the back legs of his chair with his hat covering his face. Anderson, Combs and Maxfield watched as Nouba's chest went up and down as he snored; it was hysterical. Sandy Maxfield squinted for a moment and rubbed his eyes. Combs looked over at his buddy and made a weird face.

"What's wrong?"

"Are my eyes deceiving me or did the Captain just walk in?" Moses rose slowly up from his chair and gazed across the room.

"Captain!" yelled Moses waving his hands. "Over here sir." Taylor tried to make his way through the crowd of drunken men; he accidentally bumped a man and spilled his drink. The man whirled around quickly and stared the young officer in the face. Moses went to rise but Nouba grabbed his arm. Nouba flicked his head towards the men.

"I'm terribly sorry," said the officer, handing the man a towel. "Let me buy you another drink." The man snatched the cloth from Taylor's hand and wiped the beer from his face.

"Whatcha say, boy?"

"I said I was sorry and offered to refresh your beverage," said the Captain standing straight in the man's face.

"Dang right ya will," snarled the man with a dirty grin. He looked to be a former Confederate soldier by his tattered blouse. Taylor couldn't make out the unit, because it was worn out. Looking over his shoulder, Taylor noticed the group of drunken rebels behind him egging the man on. "I outta make ya buy for all of the boys and me," laughed the man while grabbing the officer's arm. "Come on son, give up some of them Yankee greenbacks." The man pulled the officer close while picking his teeth with a piece of hay.

"I advise you to remove your hand." Captain Taylor's eyes eased their way slowly up to the rebel's face. The man turned to look at his friends and smiled.

Laughing a large belly laugh, the man grabbed Taylor by his shirt collar. "Ya gonna make me Yankee? You and what army!" CLICK! CLICK! CLICK! CLICK! The words had barely left the man's mouth when four U.S. Army pistols came to rest simultaneously next to the man's temples. Maxfield, Anderson, Combs and Dobbs leered deep into the man's eyes, while their hands tightened around the handles.

"My army," smiled the officer, while winking. "Meet my **Buffalo Soldiers**." The officer glanced around the room as the music came to a sudden stop. The patrons in the saloon stared with their mouths wide open at the colored soldiers and their white leader. The piece of straw dropped from the Confederate man's mouth, and there was a faint noise and odor in the air. Perspiration wasn't the only bodily fluid that was cascading from the man.

"Jus' foolin' around there, general," said the man, standing in a puddle of his own urine. Smiling four pearly white grins the soldiers lowered their pistols and laughed. The now cowardly man breathed a large sigh of relief.

"Barkeep," said the officer smiling. "I believe this man needs another towel. Now if you'll excuse me, my table is waiting." The officer brushed by the man and patted him on the back. "Another round for all of my men!"

The men cheered their leader as he came to the table. The piano player jumped right back into mood with a rousing rendition of "My Darling Clementine." People made fun of the rebel as he stormed out of the bar swearing and spitting.

"Well, men," said Taylor, taking a seat. "What are we drinking tonight?" The men grinned at their leader as he looked around the table and smiled a young man's grin. Moses pushed a shot of whiskey towards the officer. The Captain made a weird smile as he took the shot and glanced at the men. Nodding in their direction, he placed the glass to his lips and tilted it back easily. The men watched as the boy made several small convulsions and turned a bright pink. He coughed loudly, as the men began patting him on the back.

"Hang in there sir! Take it for the Cavalry, soldier!"

Nouba handed the officer a beer and smiled. "That made a good impression with the men, sir!" Winking quickly the big sergeant patted him behind the neck and massaged it for a moment.

Hayes was feeling on the top of the world, so he thought another round with a lady would be in order. After he was done, he sat fixing his trousers. Hayes turned to gaze at the half naked red haired beauty lying in the sheets. "You're very beautiful. I know I'm not supposed to say that to you."

"I always take compliments from handsome young men. How old are you, anyway boy?" The woman rolled over on her side and held her hand out. Reaching into his pocket, Hayes pulled out a few coins and placed it in her palm.

"Don't worry how old I am, my money is in your hands now anyway." Straightening out his neckerchief, Hayes stood up and headed for the door. "Goodnight ma'am!" He danced down the stairs with a huge grin. Maxfield tapped Combs on the chest and pointed.

"Take a look at this one!" Hayes jumped off the last two steps and headed over to the men. Pushing Maxfield and Combs up to the counter, Hayes slammed his fists on the bar top.

"Barkeep," yelled the young soldier. "Three shots of whiskey and three beers." Grabbing the shots, he passed each one a glass. "All right, we drink at once. Ready, one, two, three drink!" Snapping their heads back, the men slammed each glass on the bar. "Wooo! Alrighty guys I gotta use the outhouse." Hayes looked around the room. Seeing the way to the back door, he slowly shuffled from side to side as he crossed the room and headed out back. Three additional pairs of eyes watched the boy.

Staring out into the dark, he could barely make out the roofs of the outhouses. "Walk way out there to take a ....," said the boy, looking ahead. Turning to his sharp left, he noticed a little section of earth between the saloon and the hotel. Undoing his trousers he began conducting business off the corner of the porch. "Ahhh!" Steam rose from the puddle on the earth.

Ranger Armstead and one of the Indians had crawled silently through the brush to the front of the outhouses. Crouched down low to the ground Armstead whispered in his partner's ear. "All right we get near the front door. On the count of three, we swing the doors open and whoever is nearest stabs the son of a bitch to death. Cover his mouth, we don't want to take any chances." The Indian crossed in front of Armstead to the structure on the left and removed his long hunting knife. Armstead heard a twig snap and whirled his knife to his right. Staring nervously out into the night he waited for a moment. Then slowly reached up and grabbed the handle on the door. Armstead looked over to the Indian and mouthed one, two three! Swinging the doors open quickly, they crashed into each other and made a loud noise. Empty! Armstead turned toward the Indian who looked totally confused.

"Where the hell is he?" Armstead burned with rage. "I can't believe this, we missed him." Turning around, they headed back to the rear of the saloon. Hayes was still fiddling with his trousers. Looking down, the soldier noticed he had stained them with urine.

"Damn! The Captain won't like this." The boy tried to wipe the stain clean and began walking out from the shadows. Turning the sharp corner, he walked right into the two men, sending them backpedaling off the porch.

"Watch it, you idiot," yelled Armstead.

"Open your eyes, you fool," responded the drunken soldier. Hayes stood straight up and stared them both in the face.

"It's him!" The ranger was momentarily stunned.

Snapping out of his whiskey haze, the boy let loose a massive kick, landing in Armstead's midsection. In a flash, Hayes removed his knife and tossed it at the second man, sending it deep into his stomach. Armstead watched as the big Indian dropped to the ground and groaned in pain. Hayes instinctively went for his pistol.

The Indian's twin brother had eased up behind the soldier. Seeing his brother laying on the ground, the big man removed his own blade and thrust it deep into Hayes's back. The force from the blow lifted him up in the air, pinning the soldier against the wall. Hayes clawed desperately at the night air.

"Heh, heh, heh," cackled the ranger jumping up and down in place. "Snap that boy's neck!" With a quick jerk, crack!

The Indian let Hayes' limp broken body, drop to the ground. Stepping over it, he walked to his brother. Armstead watched as the big Indian dragged the corpse under some brush and walked back to his horse.

"We gotta take the soldier with us," said Armstead, climbing on his horse. The Indian removed his lasso and tossed it over Hayes' body. Tying the rope off to his saddle, he kicked his horse and trotted off, pulling the body behind him. Armstead watched as it was dragged through the mud and rocks. He smiled a sick smile. "One down...."

TWENTY

Inside the saloon things were still jumping, as the soldiers were hooping and hollering up a storm. Maxfield, Combs and Anderson all had too much to drink and were preparing to leave.

"Captain Taylor sir," said Maxfield, slurring his words. "We's gunna head out."

"Well lads, have a safe ride home," said the drunken officer, raising his glass. Moses rolled his eyes and stood up. Nouba rested comfortably in the corner.

"Just be careful," said Moses, placing his hand on Maxfield's shoulder. "Watch for the bad guys okay!" The men saluted and headed out of the bar.

Several of the local workers had assembled to smoke and drink in the streets, they didn't like the blacks. Inside, the bar catered to everyone; in the streets it was every man for himself. Combs watched carefully as the white workers moaned, groaned. Maxfield was wobbling from side to side calling for his horse.

"Mable, where you at girl." Combs held his friend up as he continued to call for his horse. "Mable!" The soldier looked around in all directions.

"Nigga can't find his horse," laughed a drunken lumber worker. "Ain't that a sorry sight boys?" Maxfield turned toward the man and responded.

"Can't be any sorrier then your tail," laughed Maxfield. Anderson stood back against the building and laughed, the white workers were not amused.

"Think you're funny, huh," said the man, pushing the soldier back a few steps. Maxfield smiled at his comrades, and then violently shoved the man backwards, slamming him into a hitching post. "You're gonna regret that nigga."

The man removed a knife and lunged at the soldier. Stepping to his left, Maxfield blocked the man's arm and disarmed him in two fluent motions, sending him tumbling into the street. Combs removed his revolver and aimed it at the group of men. Maxfield dropped the knife down by his side and climbed on the first horse he saw.

"Don't move!" shouted the soldier, cocking back the hammer. "The first man that moves one step will see the almighty quicker than they ever expected."

"Horse thief!" yelled a man. "That nigga has stolen my horse." The man removed his pistol and aimed it at the rider. As Combs turned to look at his comrade riding off, the men tackled both him and Anderson.

"No!" yelled Combs from under the weight of the white workers. "He's drunk, he's drunk!" BOOM! BOOM! The bullets slammed into the black soldier's lower back throwing him from the horse. Wrestling free, Combs and Anderson ran to their comrade lying in the dirt and mud. Blood was trickling from his lower back he was still alive. Combs held the man in his arms as the life drained slowly from his body.

The patrons in the bar heard the shots and came running from saloon. Several of the soldiers, including Moses, Nouba and the Captain, emerged into the streets with their weapons drawn.

"Damn!" yelled Moses as he saw Maxfield's body lying crumbled in Combs' arms. "What happened?" Taylor noticed the civilian standing there with his pistol still smoking.

"What in the hell did you do?" asked the officer. The man sneered at the soldiers and holstered his weapon. "What in the hell did you do?"

"Nigga stole my horse, lucky he didn't get lynched." The man began to walk away. Moses turned toward his commander and shook his head back and forth.

"You son of a bitch!" Moses grabbed the man from behind and punched him in the back of the head.

"Sergeant Trinidad," hollered Captain Taylor.

Several of the workers jumped on the big sergeant and tackled him. Taylor and Nouba leaped immediately to their sergeant's aid. Moses removed the man's pistol from his holster and began beating the man about the face with the handle. Anderson and Combs rearmed themselves and covered the other soldiers as the fistfight raged in the street. Nouba was gaining the upper hand with his opponent as the Captain Taylor and his foe tumbled around in the dirt. Moses picked his man up and carried him towards the window of the bar, throwing him through. The glass shattered as the man's body coming to rest on the bar floor. The men wrestling around in the street stopped and stared.

The music came to an abrupt halt; the bartender jumped back in awe. Customers cleared out of the way as the black sergeant climbed through the broken window and stood in front of everyone. Removing his revolver, Moses held it over his head and fired.

Moses leered at the bar patrons. "You people, you people are pathetic!" The crowd stood stunned and silent. "They killed one of my men for climbing on the wrong horse, the wrong horse!" Holding his head, Moses felt the room spinning. "You people better pray that you never need our help!"

"We never asked for you colored boys to come here," shouted a white man from the bar. Moses slowly lifted his pistol and began walking towards the man. Grabbing the man by his collar Moses heaved him against the wall and put his pistol under the man's chin. The man's eyes began to bulge as he wriggled and squirmed trying to escape the soldier's firm grasp. CLICK! The man jumped. CLICK! CLICK! Moses began deriving pleasure in watching the man cower. CLICK! CLICK! CLICK!

"Stop it! Stop it," yelled the man, frantically trying to get away. "I'm sorry, I'm sorry!"

Suddenly a hand reached forward, and gently took hold of Moses' arm and revolver. "Take it easy, Sergeant Trinidad," said Captain Taylor. The two men turned and walked towards the door. "Bartender, send the bill for the new window to the fort, I will see to it personally." The bartender nodded and the two soldiers walked out of the building. Deputy Flowers had appeared on the scene and was beginning to question people.

The evening patrol was just riding into town, when the lead rider saw the disturbance by the saloon. Dobbs and four others headed over in search of other soldiers.

"Captain," waved Dobbs. "What's the commotion here?" Gazing down in the street, the soldiers noticed the dead man's body.

"Secure the area," called Captain Taylor. "Dobbs, send one of the men to find a wagon to bring this man back to the fort. If anyone gives you any problem, arrest them on the spot." The officer walked in circles, while running his hands through his hair. The soldiers dismounted and secured the perimeter quickly.

One of the local women, Mrs. Cyril, was up later than normal finishing up her cleaning duties in the restaurant; she was walking outside to dump a bucket of water. "Aiieeeee!"

Sergeant Trinidad turned quickly in her direction. "What now! Dobbs and Pike secure the area with the others."

"Quickly men," said the officer.

"Help! Help please!" Moses and the others ran quickly in her direction. "Aiieee!" Deputy Flowers and Deputy Hollins ran behind. Mrs. Cyril was on her hands and knees covering her mouth pointing up. Coming to a quick stop, Moses skidded across the dirt. Hanging from the hayloft rigging rope swaying back and forth in the night air was Hayes. Moses' heart nearly dropped. Taylor and Nouba, who were a few steps behind, trotted slowly and came to a stop.

Deputy Flowers spoke softly. "My God!" The body was bound with rope around the feet and his hands were tied behind his back. A small puddle of blood had formed on the ground.

Corporal Bernard who had stepped outside to relieve himself came running from behind the group and collapsed to his knees. "Hayes! Oh no!" Bernard had become quite fond of the young man and was considerably shaken at the sight. Moses placed his hand on his friend's shoulder.

"Search the area!" hollered Captain Taylor. Armed soldiers with torches began searching the barn and surrounding areas. "Find that ranger character and his buddies, arrest them for questioning." Three soldiers on horse back galloped back towards the saloon. "Go from building to building if you have to Corporal Bernard," cried the officer.

"Let's get him down," said Moses with a sigh. "Anderson, Combs get up there!" The somber faced soldiers walked into the barn and climbed up to the hayloft. Undoing the rope, they carefully lowered the boy's body down to the waiting arms of his comrades. Moses watched as the rope jerked and wobbled bringing the body closer. Corporal Bernard cradled

Hayes' body in his arms like a newborn, whispering to him. Moses and Nouba looked up and down the street. The remaining soldiers crowded around the body. Captain Taylor bent down and gently removed the bloody ropes from Haye's hands and feet. Nouba grabbed a bedroll from one of the horses and spread it out on the ground. The men picked the boy up and placed him gently down on the blanket. Deputy Flowers and the sheriff's men were holding back the civilians as they began crowding around the area.

Moses was standing off to the side by himself, looking down the street towards the sheriff's office. He noticed there were no lights on. Leaning in close to Nouba, he whispered. "Keep the deputy and his men occupied for a while, I have an idea." Nouba nodded as Moses, Bernard, Oliver and Crawford all disappeared. Nouba walked slowly over to the Captain and whispered in his ear.

Pike and a few other men returned from a small security check of the surrounding area. "Nothing at all sir, and no sign of the ranger. If someone was here they are long gone by now." The officer rolled his eyes in frustration.

Moses and the men had made their way quietly over to the sheriff's office via the back streets and dark alleys. Creeping up to the back door, Bernard tried the handle. It's locked." Moses shook his head back and forth.

"Find me a way in," he whispered. "Now!" Bernard saw a landing of stairs and proceeded up with caution. Reaching to the top step, he slowly tried the doorknob, locked! Crawford stepped back and noticed a window that was opened slightly.

He drew his revolver and climbed in. There was a little click and the rear door flung open.

"Spread out, if anyone is here, they're ours," said Moses in an angry tone. Crawford and Bernard went upstairs to check out the rooms. "Oliver will cover the main office and the cells."

"What are we looking for, Sergeant Trinidad?" The young man moved cautiously through the dark room.

"We'll know when we find it," replied Moses heading towards the backroom. Walking a few steps Oliver tripped.

"I found someone, Sergeant," yelled Oliver. Moses darted through the building where the soldier was sitting on the ground. Striking a match, Moses lit a candle.

"Close the curtains, hurry!" Lying on his back and snoring like buzzard was Sheriff Watkins. Moses leaned in and took a whiff.

"Dang," said the sergeant, waving his hands. "Drunk as a skunk." Lying next to Watkins was the broken bottle. "Watch him while I get back to the rear rooms." Oliver nodded as Moses went out back.

Upstairs, Crawford and Bernard were quickly searching through the rooms.

"Sergeant Trinidad," called Oliver nervously. "He's waking up!" Moses walked quickly back into the office area and stood over the Sheriff's body. As Watkin's eyes started to crack open, Moses popped the man in the face, knocking him out cold again.

"That should buy us some more time." Moses smiled and went back to work.

On the second floor, Crawford was tipping over every piece of furniture checking for any form of evidence. "There has to be something here to help us." Bernard walked into the parlor.

"Nothing in the bedroom, did you check this closet yet?" Crawford shook his head no. Opening the door, Bernard stepped in and stared at a large collection of suits hanging up.

"Damn this man has some good taste in suits," said the corporal feeling the fine silk materials. Reaching up onto the back shelf, Bernard felt a box and pulled it out. "Sergeant." Bernard walked across the room and set the box on the table.

"What's that?" said Crawford.

Removing his knife, Bernard pride open the metal box. "Money, I knew this guy was dirty!" Bernard called quietly. "Moses get up here now!" Moses heard the shout and ran up the stairs.

"What's going on Bernard?" Holding up the box, Bernard winked at Moses.

"Money, I knew he was dirty!" Moses walked across the room and patted his men on the backs. Pulling out the bills, Bernard began to count. "20, 40, 60, 80 …100 that's it!" The soldiers stared at each other in confusion. Crawford noticed something gleaming in the moonlight and walked back towards the closet. Bending over, he picked up a few clumps of dirt from the floor.

"Sergeant Trinidad, take a look at this," said Crawford, waving him over. "What do you see here in my hand?" The corporal stood next to him and starred.

"Dirt," said Moses looking crazily at the man. "Corporal we're wasting time." Crawford rolled the piece of earth between his fingers and licked them. "Boy, you lost your mind, you're eating dirt now?" said Moses.

"That's not dirt, it's clay. Look. The dirt on our boots is brown and this is…"

"Red," replied Moses grinning. "Like creek mud!" The sergeant's eyes widened. "Bernard, check the back of the closet again, this time on the floor." The soldier reached in and felt something wet and cold. He pulled out a muddy boot.

"Sergeant Trinidad," said Crawford. "I would bet a whole month's pay that the mud on those boots matches the mud down by the creek near the fort." Moses looked down at the boots again.

"Sergeant," shouted Oliver from downstairs. "Deputies are coming, we gotta run!"

The soldiers put the boots back and scampered down the stairs. "Out, everyone, out!" Moses stood near the back door and watched the deputies climb the stairs. Bernard pulled him by the arm and they took off into the shadows.

Captain Taylor was standing in the street talking with Nouba when Moses and the others returned. Moses noticed the men's bodies had been loaded in the rear of the wagon and were ready to head back to the fort.

"Is everything all right Sergeant?" asked the officer, climbing into the saddle. Moses held up his hand and climbed on his horse.

"New details sir," said Moses. "We'll get into it further when we get back." The officer nodded his head.

"Men," shouted Taylor. "Move out!" The soldiers and their precious cargo left the town of Flat Fork feeling the painful sting of death. The men had sent a rider ahead. Doc Ames who was awoken from his slumber, watched as the wagon pitched back and forth over the uneven terrain and rode quietly into the fort. Climbing into the back of the wagon, he peeled back the bloodstained blankets from each man.

"Bring them inside men," said the doctor wiping off his spectacles. Combs and Anderson carried Hayes, followed by Oliver and Dobbs with Maxfield. Captain Taylor and the others headed into his office.

"Sergeants," said the officer in a sobering tone. "I'm not feeling so well. Can we do this in the morning?"

"Of course sir," smiled Moses and Nouba, as they saluted. Captain Taylor could at best muster a lack luster salute, and with good cause.

"Go on ahead I'll see you in a few minutes," said Moses. Nouba waved and headed back to quarters. The Sergeant sat down in Hayes' old chair and opened the top drawer. Running his hand through, he knocked into a package wrapped in paper. Undoing the paper, Moses dropped his head; inside was the secret stash of penny candy. A single tear rolled down the sergeant's face.

Reveille sounded the next day and life in the Army was beginning again, and once again the sound of shovels and picket axes were tearing into the Texas dirt. Only this time a layer of snow covered the area. Nouba and Crawford had passed on the daily duties, while Captain Taylor and Sergeant Trinidad walked quietly.

Captain Taylor broke the silence. "Sergeant, you must be used to snow, being from New England."

"Yes sir," said Moses with a blank expression on his face.

There was a long moment of silence. "I couldn't even sleep last night," said the officer. "I started drinking after you left and continued until I passed out." The officer lowered his head in disgrace. "They had no classes at the Military Academy on what leaders do in the event their men are murdered in cold blood. My emotions were all jumbled up when I saw Hayes hanging like that." The officer shook nervously.

"Hell, I think a few honest feelings and emotions are healthy sir," said Moses, looking straight ahead. I knew what I was getting into when I was given this post, Captain. I never thought I would end up seeing my men murdered in cold blood, either. I must have stayed up poking that fire a thousand times last night." Moses raised his head. "Sir, when we disappeared last night, we broke into the sheriff's office and looked around a little." The officer's mouthed dropped. "We found a pair of boots coated in red clay mud; the sheriff was down by the creek near the fort. There's not a doubt in my mind," Moses shot the officer a quick look. "Sergeant Nouba is heading to the creek with Bernard to check it out. One more thing sir, the grave is being dug as we speak." The Captain turned and looked at Moses.

"Grave," said Taylor oddly. "Only one?"

"Hayes left some papers saying he wanted to be buried at home in Vermont on his folk's land. We've made arrangements to ship him on the train back east." Moses stared blankly ahead. "Maxfield will rest on the hill with the others."

"I almost forgot to tell you, Sergeant," said Taylor. "I have to inform headquarters of the murders, I have no choice in the matter."

"The patrol is scheduled to depart around 1300 hours," said Moses. The officer stopped walking. "There is no doubt in my mind that Sheriff Watkins and Ranger Armstead were involved in this. I think a few days in the saddle will help me to think of how we can get these guys. It also gives them time to think we're being **extra** cautious. They may relax, get careless."

Moses stared over the bluffs. "When we see them the next time, it's going to get dirty. They'll both be dead after we're through." Moses looked his commander square in the eye. "Permission to lead the patrol, sir?"

"Granted!" The men turned around and headed back towards the parade ground.

The men gathered at the cemetery on the hill. Moses gazed up into the sky and spoke as the wind blew across the plains. A dark gray cloud quickly engulfed the sky.

"Oh Lord, hear us this sad day. God please take the soul of our brother and seat him at your right hand Father. He wore the blue uniform and crossed sabers of the United States Cavalry. We do not understand why he was murdered and we only hope he went quickly dear Father. God Bless and forgive us for what we do. Amen!"

"Ready!" The hammers clicked. "Aim!" The weapons were hoisted to the heavens. "Fire!" Sandy Maxfield was laid to rest. The remaining soldiers were dismissed and headed back to the fort.

Captain Taylor turned and began walking towards the exit alone. Moses turned towards Nouba, and the two soldiers started walking and talking. "I asked the captain for permission to lead this patrol," exclaimed Moses.

"Sounds like it will be good for you to be in the saddle again," said Nouba, gazing at the soldiers walking by.

Moses smiled. "They're in the Army and that means sleeping in all different and interesting places." Moses liked being out on patrol. Sometimes the politics of Army life wore on him; getting back to the basics was going to be somewhat therapeutic. "I'd like to take Corporal Bernard and about six men with me. We'll do a complete sweep of the area in a twenty-five mile radius. One more thing, I think we should find a replacement for Hayes as soon as possible. Could I trouble you to handle that?"

Nouba nodded his head in approval. "No problem, Sergeant Trinidad, I'll handle everything in your absence."

Captain Taylor leaned on the cemetery gate, watching the grave being filled in. He still couldn't get over it, murder! Throwing a quick salute, he turned around and walked away.

The officer could not bring himself to accompany Hayes' body to the train depot and Moses knew why. The soldiers stood quietly on the platform as the whistle blew and the train left town carrying the remains of their friend home. Simultaneously, the Buffalo Soldiers saluted the train and headed out.

Moses emerged from his quarters with his carbine and a heavy pack. The men were assembled around the corral, saddling up their mounts.

"All right men, the weather is bad, so you'd better make sure you bring your gratecoats and blankets," ordered Corporal Bernard. "Grab extra ammunition and prepare for departure."

Nouba walked over to the other soldiers and began going over all the details. "Ahh Sergeant," said Taylor, extending

266

his hand. "Ready for patrol I see." The two soldiers shook hands. "Sergeant Nouba has been going over the duty rosters and other important aspects to help out."

"Nouba is a very good soldier sir, you could learn a lot from him and his experiences." Moses removed his revolver, and checked the bullets in the chamber. Reaching toward his back he pulled out the second pistol he kept hidden in case of an emergency. The Captain's eyes raised a hair.

"Are you expecting problems on the patrol?" asked the officer, looking over the men.

"Well, trouble is what we've had since the day we arrived here. I'm not planning on losing one man on this patrol. Don't you worry, sir, I'll bring you back a nice memento. Mount up!" Grabbing hold of his saddle, Moses climbed on. Saluting smartly, he turned towards his men. "Ready forward!" The men headed out of the fort and over the hills.

Taylor pulled a cigar out from his pocket. He placed it in his mouth and stared at the soldiers riding over the hills.

"Can I offer you a match, sir," said Nouba, packing his pipe in his tobacco pouch. "Don't worry about them, they're professional soldiers."

"Sergeant Trinidad has changed Nouba, since he saw Hayes. I hope he knows how to separate his emotions from his duties; it's not an easy job." The officer patted Nouba on the back and walked back over to his office.

Moses sat high in the saddle smiling. He was at his best out on the open plains where everything you learned in the Army was put to use on a daily basis. The temperature was now dropping. Moses watched the expressions on each man's face. As he pulled his coat close around his neck, the cold reminded him of his childhood in New England and the many winter days he spent with the one person he could trust, his father, Obediah. Moses thought often of him and the hard times he had experienced. Having to be a servant to others and listening to their gripes and groans about superficial things made him angry at times. If those people were to put themselves in the shoes of a black man, they probably wouldn't be able to handle it. Moses only wished he could meet the people who were disrespectful to his father, they'd think twice about mouthing off to a Cavalry Sergeant of his size. That made him smile. The memories of the times he spent with his father helped Moses through many a rough time in his life, like now. Even though he was with the other soldiers and his best friend, Moses couldn't get rid of the feeling that he was totally alone in his quest for equality. Not just from the Army, but from everyone who had a problem with blacks.

Hours passed by as the soldiers continued moving across the plains. The men had come to a large rocky area about three miles west of the church ruins. It was there they decided to take a rest from the riding and give the horses time to regain their strength. Combs and Anderson were placed on guard duty as they others undid packets and relaxed on the ground. Bernard took a seat on a rock and began chewing on some hardtac. "Hungry?"

"No thanks," replied Moses. "I don't have much of an appetite today." The big sergeant was picking up small rocks and tossing them in the air. "I can't get the image of Hayes hanging there out of my head. I've seen men die before, why is this man's death so different? Can you tell me that?" Bernard stared straight ahead.

"I know what you mean." The soldier stood up and took a seat next to his friend. "I liked the kid too. What do you think really happened?"

Moses Trinidad looked out across the open desert. "My guess is when he went to take a piss they were waiting for him. Damn! I should have watched the door more carefully."

"Moses, you can't go blaming yourself for this death or Maxfield's either." The Sergeant removed his knife from its holder and began to shave a stick he found on the ground. One of the men named Riley appeared from no where.

"Sergeant," said the man anxiously. "We's got company!" The soldiers leaped up and grabbed their weapons.

"Pull the horses around the back side of these rocks near the trees and keep them still," said Moses. The others formed defensive line and prepared to fight.

"Indians!" The men removed extra rounds from their packs and placed them nearby. Anderson's hands shook nervously on the trigger of his weapon. Riley reached over and took his hand and smiled. Around thirteen Comanche were loaded with weapons and wearing war paint.

"All right men," whispered Moses pulling out his revolver. "This is our time, let's show these Indians what being a cavalry soldier is all about." Moses looked at the Indians riding quietly back and forth over the terrain. He stared deep into their eyes, maybe even into their souls as they rode closer and closer. Their lack of attention surprised Moses, as they seemed to be in a fog or a daze. Holding his fingers out, Moses began the count down. One, two three! Instantly, the soldiers rose from their hiding spots and with a fusillade of bullets knocked seven of the Indians down.

"The horses shoot the horses!" The Indians scattered in groups and began to return fire. Two more Indians were hurled to the ground hard. Anderson and Combs aimed for the horses and fired. The ponies slammed into the ground with a loud thud.

Moses was on one knee firing his pistol. "Don't let them get away!" Holstering his pistol, he picked up his carbine, took careful aim, and knocked an Indian off his mount. Bernard smiled as he aimed, fired and dropped another one to the ground in a cloud of dirt. In an instant it was over. "Cease firing!" Moses held up his hand; the soldiers climbed over the rocks. "Watch them!" The men poked at the bodies, as steam rose from the open wounds.

"Well, let's get to it," said Bernard. Removing his knife he bent down and cut open the brave's cloths searching for trinkets. The other men swarmed over the bodies. Moses stood back and watched as they pulled the clothing from the dead braves bodies.

"Damn," said the soldier, trying to remove a beaded coat. "It's stuck on his arm." Combs walked over to the man and tugged on the coat. "Don't rip it, it won't be worth nothing!"

Moses bent down and noticed the red, brown and white colors on the Indian's face. Removing his pipe, Moses dipped it his pouch and placed it between his teeth.

"Pipe in the afternoon," questioned Bernard, walking over to another body. "Are you feeling better now?"

"Yes," smiled Moses. "In fact, we'll camp here tonight. By the looks of those clouds bad weather is coming this way. This will give us plenty of cover and stop anyone from moving in our direction."

"Wull, wull," said Riley, standing over an Indian. The brave's arm was mangled, and there were numerous bullets holes leaking blood in his chest and side. "Sergeant, he's alive!" Moses removed his pipe and placed it back in his pouch. Walking towards the warrior, he slowly removed his gun. Moses grabbed Riley from behind and moved him out of the way. Aiming the pistol at the wounded man Moses waited. The soldier watched as the life drained slowly from the Comanche's body, and his head slumped to the earth. Holstering his weapon the sergeant turned and walked back to his horse.

"Set fires and make camp for the night," ordered Moses. Corporal Bernard stared at Moses and went back to his business. The men found some dead trees that were relatively dry and made small fires. The horses were fed and tied off to a small crop of trees. The coffee was brewing. Laying a buffalo hide beneath a crude blanket tent, Moses began to write in his journal by the crackling light of the fire.

October 16th, 1879

Back on patrol and I'm happy as hell! This week has been an emotional one for me personally. A ranger named Armstead murdered Hayes and as of yet I can't prove it. They beat the boy, stabbed him and hung him in the town square. The civilians turned out in large numbers to see the soldier hanging, damn near made me throw up. The Captain was a mess and with just cause, Hayes was there from the start and looked up to the Captain. Another soldier was shot, by the white workers for climbing on the wrong horse while drunk. Maxfield was his name and his death is one that makes me burn inside because to the workers he was nothing more than a worthless animal, not a soldier.

My reasons for leading the patrol were selfish to say the least but it was something that I needed to do. I've been letting my emotions get the better of me again and this angry feeling is beginning to overtake my outlook on the Indians as well as the criminals. Today we ran across an Indian war party that never saw us coming. I ordered the men to attack them, I can't remember such a one sided victory in my entire career. One of the Indians was still alive when one of my men found him. My insides were boiling over. I thought of killing him, but my mind knew better. After he died, I walked away without looking at anyone. Am I becoming cold and heartless? I wonder did I lose the respect of my men?

The men were able to rig up a few crude but effective tents with our blankets and some rope. The fires are continuing to give off enough heat as well as light to write by. Someone is coming............. That was Corporal Bernard informing me that everything was secure for the

271

night and the guards are in place. He also gave me a hot cup of coffee, which always hits the spot.

Sergeant Nouba and the Captain stayed behind at the fort to keep things under control. I didn't get the chance to talk to the men before I left. I'm sure that they have many questions concerning their fellow soldiers' deaths. What do I say? How do I rationalize the concept of murder to them, when I still don't understand it myself? Why do we have to endure these angry feelings from people? This is the cross we black men must endure, God help us!

Moses placed his journal and pen in the pouch. Pulling the buffalo skin blanket up over his shoulder, he laid down.

Bernard walked up Moses and whispered to him. "Hey, are you asleep?"

"No, what's on your mind?" Moses leaned up on his elbow.

"Have you thought about a way to get the Ranger and the Sheriff?" Bernard grabbed a stick and poked at the fire, sending the thin stream of ambers into the sky.

"I have and when we get back in a few days, we're **gonna** set a trap and snag some criminals." Moses leaned back against the rocks and sighed. "Yes, they're in for a royal surprise." Taking his hat, Moses tilted it down over his eyes.

"Moses?"

"Yes, Corporal?"

"It's **going to** set a trap, **not gonna!**"

From under his hat, Moses spoke. "Good night, Corporal Bernard!"

TWENTY-ONE

Taylor sat across the table from Claudia with a blank look on his face, picking at the food on his plate with a fork. "The meal is wonderful, dear."

"How would you know Captain Taylor, you haven't touched a single bite." The officer looked stunned by the comment.

"Why so formal?" he replied in stunned tone. "What's the problem with you this evening?" The officer slammed his napkin on the table.

"Me?" she replied. "Why did you bother coming over here this evening, if you are going to sit there with a scowl on your face." Claudia rose from her seat and walked around the table. "What's the matter Hennecker?" asked Claudia, placing her hands gently on his face. "You haven't even said I look pretty!"

"My men were murdered last night, darling. How do you expect me to act?" The look on the young officer's face was one of sadness and pain. "I have to write a letter to the boy's parents in Vermont. What do I say? I've never had to write a letter like this before. To have to tell some poor parents their son, who joined the army to fight for those who can't fight, was murdered by common hoodlums. Tell them I had to have him lowered to the ground and remove bloody ropes from his hands and feet." Claudia covered her mouth. "My hands were literally frozen solid and covered with his blood, a boy's blood. I'm sorry dear, my appetite seems to have left me suddenly." Taylor pushed away from the table and stood up. "I've been avoiding going to the office because I have to pass his desk." Opening the door, he walked out into the crisp night air. Leaning against the porch railing he gazed at the stars. Claudia watched through the window as Taylor struggled with his demons. Exhaling, he sighed in frustration.

"Hennecker," said Claudia, emerging from the house. "You're becoming more and more distant." Taylor turned and looked at Claudia with a weird expression on his face. "What's that look for?" she asked.

"Didn't you hear me?" he screamed. "Murdered, my men were murdered!" Taylor turned his head quickly back and forth. "Sergeant Trinidad never has moments like these I bet, he's always in control."

"Don't raise your voice to me!" she hollered. Grabbing him by the arms, she began to shake him. "I know how fond you were of that young man, but it was not your fault. I love you, I'm here for you!" Taylor began to step backwards and stumbled over. His hands were shaking uncontrollably as he sat on the ground, covering his face. Claudia cradled him in her arms, as he began to sob.

"I'm, I'm not cut out for this role as a leader. I didn't think I would feel this way."

"Hennecker," she smiled. "You're a natural leader. Many people, including your Sergeant Trinidad, admire you very much." Claudia looked deep into his red swollen eyes and stroked his face lovingly. She pressed it against her bosom.

"Go home, Hennecker," she said, patting his shoulders. "You need time to be by yourself, time to think about what you'll say in those letters." She helped him to his feet.

"I can't believe that I broke down like some first year cadet," said Taylor wiping the tears from his face. "I'd hoped my skin would be a little thicker!" He chuckled. Claudia walked across the room and grabbed a basket from the cabinet. Scooping some more helpings of food from his plate, she wrapped it with a cloth and placed it in. "I'm packing your supper, you'll be hungry later. Don't worry I gave you plenty of my biscuits and two pieces of my apple pie." She smiled with delight.

"Thank you." Claudia grabbed a wrap and escorted the officer outside to the stables. Strapping the basket on the saddle, he stopped. "I was an incredible ass tonight," he said staring at the saddle. Claudia turned him around and placed her fingers over his lips.

"Sssh, there'll be no more of that talk." Taking her in his arms, he kissed her long and hard.

Climbing up in the saddle, Taylor reached down for her hand.

"You'd better go in now dear, you'll catch your death out here."

Claudia looked out into the dark night. "Do you have your pistol?" The officer smiled and patted his side. "I wish some of the men could go with you."

"Claudia, I'm an officer in the Army." She smiled and patted his leg.

"I love you!" The officer spurred his horse gently and galloped off toward the center of town; it was lit with a few street lanterns but relatively quiet. Pulling his overcoat tighter to cut down the chilly wind, the rider trotted through the streets of Flat Fork. Taylor watched both sides of the street and pulled his coat away from his holster. If he needed to draw, he wasn't going to have time to move it. The

Captain was beginning to feel like someone was watching him, and he was probably right. The wind began to pick up and howl, banging the signs and shutters on the buildings. Taylor's arm moved slowly to his holster undoing the leather flap. Horses were coming and by the sounds, it was several riders. The Captain's hand moved down a little further.

"Hooo! Captain Taylor!" The officer breathed a sigh of relief. Riding towards him was the evening patrol led by Corporal Crawford. The soldier threw a crisp salute.

"Evening sir, what are doing out this late, alone?" The officer returned the salute and smiled.

"I was having dinner with Miss Rothschild," said the Captain. "I'm on my way back to the fort." Crawford turned in the saddle.

"Mathers, front and center!" The soldier trotted slowly up on his horse.

"Yes, Corporal Crawford!"

"Escort the Captain back to the fort, understood!"

The officer held up his hand in protest. "Corporal, I'm more than capable…"

"Sir, let me stop you right there," proclaimed the soldier, holding up his hand. "These are orders from Sergeant Nouba and Sergeant Trinidad. Until this mess with the criminals is cleaned up, you're to be escorted by a man at all times". Sergeant Crawford placed his hand on Mathers' shoulder. "Remember, shoot first and ask questions second, that's a direct order!" The soldier nodded. "Sir, have a pleasant evening. Men let's go!" The detail mounted up and trotted up the street. The officer looked at his escort and smiled.

"Let's go home now, son." The officer and the Negro turned and rode out of town. The torches from the fort were glowing in the distance of the night. Captain Taylor and Mathers dismounted and walked their horses in.

"Identify yourselves," challenged the guard.

"It's Mathers," called the soldier. "Escorting the Captain in from town."

Two guards emerged with weapons and snapped to attention. "Evening sir, can I take your mount?" The Captain handed his reins to the man and saluted.

"Thank you," said the officer, removing his package from the saddle.

Mathers smiled an ebony white grin. "My pleasure sir, have a good evening." Saluting the soldier did an about face, and walked to the corral. Taylor turned and headed over to his quarters. Walking past the desk he tried not to look and proceeded into his office. The warmth of the fire enveloped his face. "Sergeant Nouba must have made a fire, very nice."

"Not the sergeant," said a young man's voice. The officer whirled around. From the rear entrance came a young ebony skinned soldier carrying logs. The boy placed them down on the ground and snapped to attention. "I did sir. I'm Jupiter Pivens sir, your new clerk." The officer stood back in silence.

"Welcome to the job, Pivens," said Taylor staring blankly ahead. The young boy extended his hand and shook the officer's firmly. "Thank you for making the fire, son." The officer reached up to the cabinet and removed a glass

"Where are you from?" asked the officer pouring himself a glass.

"Delaware, sir!" The boy smiled while stoking the fire. "I've been in the Army about a year; this is my first Cavalry Unit." Placing the iron back in its holder, the soldier wiped his hands off and stood up. "Well sir, I'm sure you are tired; I'll see you bright and early in the morning." Taylor stood in silence as the soldier saluted quickly and exited the office. The echo from the door seemed to last for days. Taylor gulped his drink and refilled the glass. Taking a seat behind his desk he removed a piece of paper from his top drawer.

October 17th 1879
Commanding Officer
9th U.S. Cavalry
Washington, D. C.

Dear Sir,

I am writing to tell of the murder of two cavalrymen stationed at Fort Barre in Texas in or around the town of Flat Fork.

One soldier, his name was M. W. Hayes of Vermont. The second, a soldier by the name of Sandy Maxfield from parts unknown. Maxfield was shot by white civilians in the back while riding off on another man's horse while drunk. The civilians claim the man was trying to steal the horse. Sheriff's deputies came but no arrests were made and I'll be very surprised if the authorities prove to be any help. Hayes is the real odd case. The boy was found bound and gagged hanging in the town square. The body had multiple bruises and knife wounds. We believe that his murder was a form of retaliation for an incident, which took place a few days back in a saloon while confronting some "bad characters".

Sergeant Trinidad thinks the Sheriff and his men may be party to the rash of thefts and trouble that have been plaguing the area. We have tried to keep tabs on them as much as possible. Patrols have been lengthened in town to show soldier's presence and to try to keep them bottled up. The supposed ringleader's name is Armstead an unscrupulous ranger who travels with one or more large Indian companions.

I will keep headquarters alerted to any and all circumstances or situations that arise.

Captain H. J. Taylor
Commanding Officer Fort Barre
9th U.S. Cavalry

Taylor's hand began to shake slowly as he reached for another piece of paper from his desk. This was the letter he was dreading to write. Grabbing the whiskey, he drank straight from the bottle as the liquid trickled down his shirt.

Dear Mr. and Mrs. Hayes,

My name is Captain Hennecker J. Taylor, Commanding Officer of Fort Barre. It is with a heavy heart that I inform you of the tragic death of your son, Morse.

Though junior in rank he was Instrumental in keeping the daily operations of the entire outfit in check. While trying to apprehend a band of criminals and murderers, he was ambushed. Though outnumbered, he fought gallantly until he was overpowered and eventually succumbed to his wounds.

Nothing I say can bring him back to you, but you should take pride in the fact he was mature, responsible and well liked by his fellow soldiers. Many of the men spoke highly of your son and I can say from my own personal experiences, Morse was a fine man and a credit to the Cavalry.

Respectfully yours,
Hennecker J. Taylor
Captain United States Army

Taylor pushed the papers away and held his head while sighing. Rising from his desk he walked across the room and took a seat by the fire. Gazing into the orange glowing flames, he drifted off momentarily to another place and another time. No matter how hard he tried, he couldn't shake the image of Hayes' body tangling from the rope and the drops of blood hitting the ground. Taylor felt low and helpless; his body began to tremble lightly. Walking to the window the soldier gazed out into the night. He said to himself, "I can't wait for the Sergeant Trinidad to return. I have to do something myself." Opening the door to his office, Taylor went to the outer area and opened the door. "You there, soldier," called the officer. "Fetch me a horse from the corral on the double." The guard ran over to the corral and readied a mount. Turning quickly, the officer grabbed his holster and headed out the door.

Inside the enlisted men's barracks the men were enjoying their off-duty time. Some were playing cards, shining boots and mending their uniforms. Corporal Crawford had returned from patrol and was walking around, while Nouba rested on his rack. Crawford wandered over to the window just as the Captain Taylor was walking down the steps from his quarters.

"What's the Captain up to now?" Nouba turned and rose from his rack. Looking out the window he made a weird face.

"I have no earthly idea, Crawford," said Nouba, walking back over to his rack and laying down. "Why don't you find out?"

Crawford turned toward Nouba. "I'm going for a ride, Sergeant!" Nouba nodded in agreement. Crawford walked out into the soldier's barracks and headed over to Trooper Oliver's cot. The boy was curled up peacefully. "Olie! Oliver get up!" Crawford shook the boy awake.

"What?" Oliver rolled around in his blankets.

"We got a mission, com'on!" Crawford turned as the boy leaped from his bed in an instant, grabbing his boots, jacket and weapons. The men walked into the sergeant's room. Crawford looked out the window.

The sentry, Eugene Cross, walked slowly back and forth. "Evenun sir!"

"Evening, Cross," waved the officer from his horse. "I'm going to town." The officer slapped his horse and galloped out. Crawford and Oliver had snuck over to the corral and were saddling their mounts.

"Corporal Crawford, you going after the Captain?"

"Yes Cross, where is he headed to?" Crawford steadied his horse and climbed on.

"Town!" Cross smiled and held open the door. The two soldiers proceeded out after their leader.

Taylor dismounted and tied his horse to a tree behind the saloon. "All right I think that the sheriff's office is the building through those bushes." Taylor removed his pistol and moved through the high grass and trees. The stars gave off just enough light to see by.

"Damn, this brush is thick!" Tree trunks and vines made it hard to pass. Pushing down on a branch Taylor lost his footing and was thrown to the ground as the branch sprang back. As he rolled around amongst the roots and vines, the officer felt something. Clearing away some debris, Taylor found the body of one of ranger's Indian companions and flinched back with fright. Climbing out of the brush, he saw the lights from the office. Captain Taylor snuck up close to the window and peered in.

Inside the sheriff and his deputies were laughing it up with the ranger and his men. "I gotta get closer so I can hear what they're saying," whispered the officer. Looking up, he noticed a set of stairs rising up to a landing. "Sergeant Trinidad mentioned a second floor, and I bet it's up there." The officer removed his cap and moved up the stairs towards the door. Reaching the top he grabbed the doorknob and turned it slowly, it opened! Moving across the room Taylor eased up to the bedroom door and cracked it open.

"Well, I'll tell you one thing," said Armstead, kicking his feet up on the desk. "Those blacks are going to be feeling a different kind of pain after we get done robbing that

Paymaster's Coach next week. Pain in their pockets! Ha! Ha! Ha!" They all laughed.

"How much money will we net from this little robbery?" asked the Sheriff lighting a cigar.

"Two thousand to twenty two hundred easy," smiled Armstead, patting his Indian friend on the back. Pulling out a knife he began tossing it playfully in the air. "Should give you enough to slide on out of this two bit little town and head back to Georgia a rich man, Sheriff". The Captain gazed over the railing at the criminals and clinched his fists. "But before this ranger clears out he's gonna personally slice that big black sergeant's throat."

Closing the door, Taylor backed slowly out of the room towards the landing. Suddenly a hand clasped over his mouth; he was thrown down and pinned on the bed. Flipping over, he stared into the eyes of Corporal Crawford.

"What are doing, sir?" whispered the man, climbing off. "Are you out of your mind coming here without any help? You could have been overpowered easy." Oliver covered the door as Crawford and Taylor talked quietly.

"Who sent you, anyway," said the officer straightening his blouse.

"Sergeant Nouba," said Crawford, moving the officer towards the backdoor. "Let's go now, Oliver cover us!" The men crept back down the stairs and over towards their horses.

"Corporal, you're not going to believe what I found," said the officer all excited. "I found the body of one of criminals hidden in the thick brush." The soldiers climbed on the horses and headed for the outskirts of town.

"That's great news sir," smiled Oliver.

"That's not all," said Taylor, bouncing in the saddle. "They're planning on going after the Paymaster's cashbox when they come in for the company's monthly issue." The men all stared at each other. "Let's tell Sergeant Trinidad about the new news, it will sure make him happy." The men's horses' puffed and snorted across the ground until the fort's lights came into view.

Galloping over to the enlisted men's barracks they hopped off and burst into the Nouba's quarters.

"Nouba, Nouba wake up!" yelled the officer. The sergeant squinted and shook his head. "We've had a great discovery tonight." Nouba sat up in bed and looked around the room at the others.

"Well, as long as the gang's all here," he said rising to his feet. "Let's put on some coffee!" Nouba walked across the room to the stove. Opening the door he placed a log in and stoked it. The flames rose up from the embers and warmed the room immediately. "Sir, have a seat, Crawford have Oliver put on some coffee." The Captain sat down across from Nouba, as the men gathered around him.

"I rode into town hoping to find some information on the sheriff and his men, so I headed for his office," said Taylor removing his gratecoat. "While sneaking through the underbrush I tripped over something lying in the brush, a body." Nouba sat up straight and leaned in closer. "One of the big Indians, it was one of the big Indians! He had a knife wound right in the middle of his chest."

The men watched as Nouba rose to his feet and began to pace back and forth. "Very interesting!"

"My guess is Hayes probably got the man before they killed him," exclaimed Taylor. "There would be no way one of those Indians would double-cross the other, they'd sooner kill the ranger." The officer could barely contain himself.

"Thatta a boy Hayes," whispered Nouba.

"Why would they just toss his body in the bushes like that?" asked Crawford.

"**Time**," said Nouba taking a seat again. "They were pressed for **time** and he was already dead. They weren't about to take him with them, it would be too much weight to carry."

"The body was white and very stiff, and there were no weapons on him," said Taylor standing close to the fire. "He was under there at least twenty-four hours if not more!"

"They're hoping for a big payday," declared Nouba shifting in his chair.

"The Paymaster's coach," said the Captain smiling. Nouba's eyes lit up as he sipped his coffee quietly. "I was on the second floor landing spying on them when they said it, Sergeant. They're gonna make a run at the Paymaster's coach and walk off with our payroll." The men began to grumble. "I'm sure that I speak for everyone when I say I like my pay."

"Are you sure they said the Paymaster's coach," said Nouba. "They'd have to know that it's guarded."

"With only two men," said Crawford. "With the way those guys shoot they could knock them off at a hundred meters easy!" Nouba placed his hand on his chin and began to think.

"Well," said Nouba slapping his knees with his hands. "When Sergeant Trinidad returns, we'll begin to put a plan together to knock these people out for good! Meantime, business as usual; nothing so they suspect we're on to them."

"Why don't we adjourn for the evening, men," said the officer drinking the last of his coffee. "We could all use a good night's rest." Before leaving, Captain Taylor walked over to Nouba.

"Sergeant?"

"Yes, sir?"

"I feel it in my bones that we have them, I won't let them get away this time. They'll pay for what they did to Hayes,

Maxfield and the man that died in the tunnel and in the explosion." Placing the mug down on the nightstand he headed for the door and turned around. "They will pay!" Nouba saluted.

* * * * * *

Back at the sheriff's office the men had all left except Armstead. Sheriff Watkins was pulling the shades down and closing the curtains as Armstead walked around the sheriff's desk and opened his drawer.

"How about a drink?" Watkins turned and nodded in approval. Armstead took out two glasses and poured them full of whiskey. "How much do you have saved, Sheriff?"

"None of your concern," Watkins said, picking up his glass. He took a sip and licked his lips. "Most of it has been sent back East to a bank in Atlanta, where it will be waiting when I arrive next month." Looking over at Ranger Armstead he drank easily. "What about you? Blow yours all on booze and women?" The Sheriff snickered and sat down in his chair.

"Na, bought land in California and Nevada!" Watkins looked in surprise at the man.

"Real estate," said Watkins laughing. "To be quite frank, I thought you were too **dumb** to invest properly." Armstead swallowed the last of his drink and grabbed the bottle.

"You know something, you're not a half bad partner to have. It's just when you say **stupid** things, that really steams me!" Armstead smiled that sick twisted smile of his. "I have enough to keep me in high cotton, so to speak."

"Well, ranger," said Watkins standing up and heading across the room. "In a few more weeks we'll probably never see each other again." Turning the key he locked the door and blew out the candle on his desk. "But we'll both have quite a bit of money because of our brief friendship, so it

285

hasn't been all bad." Walking past the man, Watkins grabbed a lantern and headed up the stairs. "There's a spare room with a bunk in the back feel free to relax and sleep." Armstead removed his gun belt and placed it on a hook on the wall. Taking a seat on the bunk he removed his boots and laid back. He rolled over on his side and quickly fell asleep.

TWENTY-TWO

SNAP! CRACK! Moses shook awake. Crawling out from underneath his makeshift tent, he saw Bernard making a morning fire. The big man stretched his back and yawned. "Everything okay?"

"Yep," said Bernard, sparking the fire and lighting the leaves and branches. "Guards reported no movement. Coffee will be ready in little bit and bacon. There is a small pool of water about fifteen yards to the north and it wasn't on our map, so let's make a note of that."

"Looks like the sun is breaking through." The smell of coffee and floated on the chilly air.

"What's the plan for those bodies?" inquired Bernard pouring a cup and handing it to Moses.

"Nothing," said Moses, sipping the black liquid. He turned and looked at Bernard. "We don't have the time to bury them." Bernard stared into the small fire.

"How long are we going to stay out here on this little personal getaway of yours," said Bernard. "The men we have to get are back there, and we are out here?" Moses sat next to Bernard.

"Are you mad that I had us leave the post?" Moses asked, in a surprised tone of voice. Bernard said nothing. "This idea of ours should be planned out; we can't afford to have another patrol wiped out. I thought getting away would give us a clearer perspective." Moses took a drink. "Every day, I look at Oliver, Crawford and the other white troopers and think, my God, they're all that's left! I see those graves being filled, I hear that bugle playing and I see that train with the coffins on it in my dreams. It scares the living daylights out of me. Failing scares me worse, though." Moses stared ahead at the sky.

"We're all in on this together, Moses, don't forget that," Bernard looked him in the eyes. "You can't make this a personal war, because it's not." Moses nodded at his friend.

"We'll do a ten mile circle, then head back in." Moses rose to his feet. Looking out over the horizon, there was nothing but a clear morning. "After the men have had their coffee and wake up, we'll dig shallow graves for the bodies of the Indians, and we'll be on our way." Bernard smiled at Moses and slapped at him playfully.

"Riley, Anderson, Combs, burial detail!" The soldiers went to work digging and burying the Indian corpses. Mounting up, they shoved off to complete the final circle of the patrol and head back to the fort.

Back at Fort Barre, morning duties were being attended to as the soldiers hustled around the fort. Sergeant Crawford was passing on orders to a group of men by the south perimeter.

"Sergeant Nouba!" hollered Pivens. "CO wants to see you on the double!" Placing the glasses down on the counter Nouba ordered the men to keep a look out. Crossing the compound, he noticed Oliver saddling a patrol.

"Where you going, Oliver?" shouted Nouba.

"Two man patrol with Corporal Crawford about a half mile around the perimeter." Oliver removed his carbine and checked it.

"Make it three men. Take the greenhorn here, Pivens." The young soldier froze in his tracks. Oliver smiled as he slid the carbine back in its case.

"Go grab your gear, soldier," called Oliver. Pivens did an about face and went over to the office to retrieve his gear. Emerging from the office with his gun, coat and gun belt all jumbled together he headed for the corral next. As the man fumbled about trying to saddle his horse, Oliver laughed. After a few minutes, Pivens pulled out his horse ready to go.

"Sorry, Oliver," he said climbing on. "It's been a while since I've ridden a horse."

"How long?"

"About a year or two." Oliver rolled his eyes. Corporal Crawford walked over and prepared his horse.

"Ah, Pivens nice to see you," said the corporal climbing on and extending his hand. "We can always use another shot in case of an attack." Pivens swallowed hard and held on. Oliver patted him on the shoulder.

Fixing his gloves, Crawford called. "Patrol forward!" The men rode out of the fort and headed slowly down towards the creek bed area near the old tunnel entrance.

A few minutes passed in the saddle as the men rocked slowly back and forth. "So Pivens, what do you think of your new assignment?" asked Crawford glancing in his direction.

"Well, the Captain seems like he's pleasant. What happened to the last clerk?" Riding in silence for a few seconds, Oliver finally spoke up.

"He was murdered a few days back." Pivens stopped his horse and stared at the two soldiers.

"Murdered, what do you mean murdered? Was he the man I heard they found hanging in the town square?" Crawford nodded his head. Pivens sat on his horse and stared straight ahead wide eyed. "I'm sorry about your friend."

Oliver rode ahead a few hundred yards and scanned the terrain. Corporal Crawford and Pivens rode along slowly. "Well as soon as Sergeant Trinidad returns, those guys are going to be sorry they ever messed with the U.S. Cavalry." The men trotted along easily in the morning sun. Suddenly, Oliver rode up to the corporal.

"We got company," he said, removing his carbine. "Five Indians on foot about fifty yards to the west." The men dismounted quickly and tied their horses off to the tree.

"Pivens, stay here," said Crawford, taking out his weapon. "Get behind those rocks and take out your pistol, set it down on top of the rock. Keep your weapon pointed straight ahead. As soon as you hear any shots, don't get excited; watch for other soldiers that come from the fort, and they will."

"Where are you going?" asked Pivens nervously. "You're not leaving me are you?"

"Don't worry," said Crawford, cocking back the hammer on his gun. "Stay down and just watch who you're shooting at." Ducking down behind the rocks, Pivens stared nervously at the tree line.

Oliver and Crawford cut through the trees and came up on the other side of the hill: five warriors completely painted up and carrying weapons.

"What are they doing this close to the fort?" asked Oliver, easing against the rocky terrain. "They can't be lost." Crawford raised his head slowly and watched them as they fiddled around.

"I'd be just as happy if they keep going right on by us," said Oliver looking around in both directions. "What are the chances they will go by?" Crawford looked at his friend,

Oliver sighed. Unbeknownst to both soldiers, someone had noticed them crouched down low behind the hill and that someone just eased his weapon between the bushes behind them. BOOM! The bullet slammed into the man's back tearing and ripping the flesh open. The body flew out of the bushes, landing down on the ground between Crawford and Oliver. The warrior's face was smashed against a rock and blood trickled from his wounds. Crawford was momentarily stunned as Pivens emerged from the growth with his weapon smoking.

"Here they come," yelled Pivens, letting loose a barrage of gunfire at the group of hostiles, knocking one brave down. Oliver rose from behind his dirt barricade and fired two precision shots sending two Indians to their deaths. Crawford fired his pistol, hitting two ponies. The Indians returned fire, pinning the men down as four more braves circled the soldiers and launched an attack from the rear. An arrow came flying threw the air and landed square in Oliver's leg.

"Ahhh!" Oliver fell against the dirt barrier and slid down to the ground. Turning over on his side, he fired his pistol, hitting a warrior square in the chest. "They're coming from the rear!" The other brave jumped on Crawford's back and wrestled him to the ground. Pivens took the butt of his carbine and bashed the Indian into the back of the neck, knocking him out cold. Corporal Crawford rose to his feet and fired two shots in the warrior's back. The Indians were coming straight on, firing at the soldiers and pinning them in a small section of the terrain. Two more braves penetrated the soldiers' cover and were firing at will, striking Crawford in the leg and shoulder. Pivens removed his knife and tackled an Indian, sending the blade through his midsection. Reaching around, Oliver grabbed the second warrior in an attempt to disarm him. Pivens whirled to his left and using his gun, pistol-whipped the Indian to the ground. The remaining Indians were still charging head on towards him.

"My god!" exclaimed the soldier. From out of nowhere, a barrage of gunfire ripped through the air. Pivens covered his head as the charging Indians disappeared in a hail of smoke and lead. A terrible quiet loomed across the smoke clouded area.

"Cavalry, come out with your hands up," echoed a commanding voice.

"It's Pivens!" he yelled, huddled close to the dirt wall. "I'm coming out, don't shoot." Climbing out of the ditch, the soldier saw the patrol, led by Moses move slowly among the dead bodies. "Sergeant Trinidad. Crawford and Oliver are hit bad."

Moses turned in the saddle. "Bernard, send someone back to the fort, we need a hospital wagon." Dismounting, Moses ran to the wounded men's position and climbed into the ditch. Pivens was bent down applying pressure to Crawford's leg wound. Anderson went to Oliver and turned him over slowly.

"Easy, easy," said Oliver wincing. "The arrow is stuck in there pretty good." The remaining soldiers secured the area.

"Crawford," said Moses, turning the man on his back. "How are you doing soldier?"

"No problem, Sergeant Trinidad," said Crawford lifting his head up off the ground. "Is everyone safe...?" Crawford's head hit hard on the ground.

"He's out cold," said Moses waving his hand. "How's Oliver doing?" Anderson had removed some clean bandages from his bag. Pivens held Oliver still as Anderson began cutting away his trousers.

"Ooohhh!" Pivens patted Oliver's shoulder.

"Don't pull that arrow out," called Moses, cradling Crawford in his arms. "I wouldn't even break it off, Bernard, just place him in the wagon carefully; he'll be fine."

"Sergeant Trinidad," said Oliver easily. "Pivens did one helluva a job, credit to the Cavalry." Anderson began wrapping a bandage softly around the arrow and the wound, as Pivens smiled. Bernard walked over to the Indian bodies and kicked one. The other soldiers grabbed what they could, including some weapons, and began moving the bodies together. Shovels and pick axes were broken out and started crushing the earth. The wagon pulled into the small gully area driven by Nouba and with Captain Taylor riding shotgun.

"How's everything, Sergeant Trinidad?" yelled Taylor, leaping from the wagon. "How are you feeling, Oliver?" Glancing down on the ground he saw Crawford's body. "Oh my God, he's dead?"

"It's all right sir," said Moses, motioning to the soldiers. "Lift him up slowly, the wounds are tender." The men hoisted Crawford up, placing him gingerly into the rear open section of the wagon, and covered him with a blanket.

"Watch that arrow, men," said Moses, helping place Oliver face down in the wagon. Riley held the leg steady to prevent unwanted movement.

"Moses, come take a look at this," called Bernard, kneeling down in the snow. Taking hold of the Indian's face, Bernard turned it. "Look at these markings. Red, brown and white, who the hell are these guys?" Moses clinched his fist. "They sure were loaded down with the right guns," said Bernard, holding up a carbine. Nouba walked over to another body.

"Same here," sighed Nouba.

"Captain Taylor, over here!" The officer patted Oliver gently on the shoulder and trotted over to the sergeant.

"What's going on, Sergeant?"

"By the looks of the weapons, they hooked up with our gun smugglers," said Moses. "Looks like we have a whole new group of rogue Indians and that means trouble!" Nouba tilted his hat back on his head and sighed.

Captain Taylor got up and began walking amongst the bodies. "Sergeant Nouba we need to pick three men to finish the patrol into town, understood?"

"Yes sir," barked Nouba. "Combs, take the wagon. Riley and Anderson you're going with me." The men saluted and rode off in the direction of town.

Walking through the grass, Captain Taylor kicked something. He pushed aside a bloody corpse and clumps of stiff dirt. Lying in the soil was the small mud covered silver flask. Taylor's heart began to beat fast. It was Sergeant Major O'Brien's gift. He calmly placed it in his pocket.

"Sir, we're ready to go." The men hopped in their saddles and, along with the wagon holding Crawford and Oliver, headed back to the fort. Captain Taylor sat on his mount staring over the hills. Bernard motioned to Moses who trotted over to the officer.

"Is everything all right, sir?" asked Moses, coming to a halt. The officer stared straight ahead as the cold breeze blew across his face.

"They're getting closer to the fort." Captain Taylor looked Moses straight in the eyes. "I won't let them get any closer."

"By the way sir, I forgot to give you this sir." Moses removed a bone handle Indian hunting knife.

The officer's eyes lit up. "Thank you, Sergeant Trinidad!"

"That's all right sir. It's like that old Indian saying, all brave warriors carry good knives!" The officer smiled.

Back in town at the saloon, Armstead sat with his back towards the door as he tossed some poker chips in a pile. "Deuce's wild, ha ha!" The man smiled as he pulled the pile of chips towards him. Deputy Winchester walked into the bar and made his way over to the ranger. Leaning in close, he whispered into Armstead's ear.

"Our **red** friends just became acquainted with the black soldiers!"

"Why thank you for that little bit of information deputy, have yourself a drink on me." Armstead motioned to the barkeeper as Winchester headed over to the bar. Placing a cigar in his mouth, the man smiled. "This must be my lucky day!"

* * * * * * *

Doc Ames emerged from the hospital with Tiner walking slowly with a cane. He saw the wagon pulling into the compound quickly.

"We got wounded!" yelled Dobbs, yanking on the reins to a halt. "Men, we need help over here." Several soldiers, who had congregated near the corral, ran to assist. Doc Ames emerged with a stretcher. The men lifted Oliver gently and took him straight into the hospital. Crawford who was still passed out was next. Combs and Cooke lifted him up and placed him on a stretcher. "Easy now men, he's bad." He was taken quickly inside and the door was closed.

Captain Taylor, along with Moses, Nouba and Bernard, went straight back to the office to plot the counterattack. They stayed in there most of the afternoon and into the night. It wasn't until well after dark that the men emerged from the office. Taylor shook each man's hand as they left. Nouba and Bernard repaired to their quarters, as Moses headed to the hospital to check on the men.

Entering quietly, Moses stood back in the shadows. Doc Ames was changing the bandages on Crawford as the fire crackled and popped in the corner. Tiner limped across the room with a basin of hot water.

"Doc, how's it going," whispered Moses quietly.

"Ahh," said the doctor. "Sergeant Trinidad, your men are resting comfortably." Doc Ames motioned Moses into the side room. "Oliver will be up and going in a week or so. Corporal Crawford's wounds will take a little longer to heal, but he will be okay."

"Thanks, doc," said Moses, shaking his hand. The stars were twinkling against the black night as the sergeant walked across the compound.

"Evening, Sergeant Trinidad." The man slung his carbine over his shoulder and leaned against the wooden fence. "Another active day here, huh?"

"Yes, it was Ruth, and it's getting ready to come to a halt," said Moses sighing.

"We're ready, Sergeant. Ready to follow you and the captain wherever you need us." Moses turned towards the young man and smiled.

Reveille sounded as the men watched the flag being raised. Captain Taylor saluted smartly and stepped down the stairs from his quarters. Nouba, Moses and Bernard were readying horses near the corral.

"Morning, sir," said Moses saluting. "Patrol is ready to go." Taylor was putting his gloves on.

"Good morning, Sergeant Trinidad."

"Morning, sir," said Bernard holding his mount. Captain Taylor nodded. Pivens emerged from the office carrying his carbine.

"Sir, can I go?"

"Do you have ammunition," said Taylor. The boy nodded. "Let's go, grab a horse." Pivens trotted over to the corral and saddled up a mount.

"Sir, we are going to scout the area we think they plan to make their attack at. The terrain is quite even for the most part, a lot of desolate flat spots. There are two areas where we think they could launch a well hidden attack," said

Nouba. Moses removed the map from his pouch and laid it out on the ground.

"This spot here is Giant Yankee Cross a large area of rock formations that winds along with the main road about ten miles east of here. The next area is about another eight or so miles further. It's Pala Grande Banks a large tree covered area near the river, the water flows right through the middle of it. That would be my spot," said Moses, Nouba nodded his approval.

"Why?" queried Captain Taylor, holding his chin.

"The water running through it will muffle gunshots, and it's a good haul from the fort and a lot of rocky areas to hide and use for cover. Reinforcements would take some time to get to the position if they were alerted at all." The men all agreed and mounted up.

"All right," said Moses. "Let's get to Giant Yankee Cross first and get a few ideas." The men galloped out of the fort and headed east, with Pivens coming up from behind.

The men made sure to keep off the main trails, trying not to kick up any large pockets of dust. The soldiers dismounted and crawled silently up to the top section of the rock formation and scouted the area. The Captain peered through his glasses at the formations.

"That pack of rocks in the south corner, Sergeant Trinidad, offers easy access to fire at an oncoming coach and for a man to jump onto the coach itself," pointed Taylor passing the glasses.

"Outstanding idea, sir," said Moses, handing the glasses to Bernard. "Right down near the pocket, there." Bernard looked and nodded his approval.

"Moses, we could take a small detail of men around the side onto the rise about ten yards behind it, up near the bushes growing on the incline. Anyone hunkered down would be easy pickins' from above; we'd have them surrounded easy. Have another detail of men take cover behind that crop *corpse* of trees and old trunks over there." Bernard rose up on his knees and moved his hand to the right. Nouba and Taylor moved three hundred yards further down the rocky area and scouted some additional hiding spots.

"Sergeant, those are the spots we need to cover," said the officer staring over the edge of the rocky cliff. Moses was observing the rest of the terrain to make sure the soldiers were alone. He then signaled to the men to retreat back to the horses.

"Everythings okay," said Pivens. Moses slapped his shoulder and nodded.

"All right men, if we need to do this, we have plenty of cover to box them into the ravine, and the steep incline will work to our advantage," declared Sergeant Trinidad. "They'll have to fight uphill and that always hampers any soldier or fighter. Let's go to Pala Grande Banks and look it over." Mounting their horses, the troopers headed (headed) further north.

Pala Grande Banks was a very beautiful spot. Lush with snow covered trees and vegetation; a crystal clean river ran through it with muddy steep banks on either side. The vines from the trees hung low to the water's surface. About five feet deep and fifteen feet wide, it was another well-known watering hole for the Indians, military and civilians alike.

"This is my plan if you have no objections, sir," said Moses. "You, Bernard and myself will head down a little closer to get a better idea of the terrain. Sergeant, I need your weapon for cover from this position. Pivens, you'll secure the horses to the trees and move about ten yards over there to provide additional cover fire only if it is needed." Moses looked at the captain for approval. He nodded. Removing their caps the men slid slowly down the slick inclines and came up quietly through the twisted and contorted vegetation and growth.

"There's the road," whispered Taylor as Bernard and Moses covered the flanks. Suddenly from over the hill, a large cloud of dust appeared. Pivens called softly to Nouba.

"Rider coming!" Sergeant Nouba waved his hand and crouched low, while Pivens flattened on the ground. Two riders came to a gradual halt and dismounted. It was Sheriff Watkins and Ranger Armstead.

"This is the place," said Armstead, placing a cigar in his mouth and lighting it. "The wagon will have to come through this narrow stretch, near the water. As they slow to cross the river, we wait until they're in the middle and bang, the money is all ours." Watkins looked around in circles.

"It does have sufficient cover," said Watkins, stepping close to the water's edge. "When we kill the rider and guard, we can hide the bodies under the banks in those tangled vines. They won't come loose for a good while. Are you positive we took a way in here where know one would see us?"

"I'm sure," said Armstead staring off down the river. "After I take the slaves' pay, their leader is dead!" Removing the cigar from his mouth, Armstead tossed it into the brush. It landed a foot from the Captain's Taylor's nose. As the tip of the cigar glowed, Taylor watched the men mount up and ride off. The soldiers popped up from their hiding spots.

"Let's head back up to the others," said Captain Taylor, turning around. The soldiers climbed up the embankment and met up with Nouba and Pivens. "Did you see our friends?"

Nouba nodded satisfactorily. "Scouting the terrain for an attack." Taking hold of his saddle, Nouba climbed on.

"Let's get back to the fort and begin to put together our plan, "said Moses, turning his horse's head. Waving his hand forward, Captain Taylor led the way as the soldiers crept out of the valley and back to the fort.

TWENTY-THREE

Five days had passed at Fort Barre. Pivens was saddling up a horse for the morning ride into town, when Corporal Bernard happened by.

"What are you doing?" The soldier whirled around in a state of surprise.

"Morning, Corporal Bernard. Just saddling up a horse for the ride into town. I'm gonna grab the Captain's telegraphs from headquarters."

"Where's your escort, son?" asked Bernard with his hands on his hips. Pivens patted his holster and winked.

"The standing order is all soldiers leaving the post are to be riding in pairs of two or more. You're replacing a man who was killed because he had no reinforcements!" Pivens' hands slid slowly down the side of his horse and saddle. Dolan and Harrison were tending to the stables. "Dolan, Harrison, report!" The two men dropped the shovel and pitchfork and walked over to the men.

"Yes, Corporal Bernard."

"Saddle two horses and escort Pivens to the town's telegraph office to retrieve official correspondence. You men go there and back, that's it, no side trips and no excuses, is that understood?" The men hurried as they saddled two horses. Pivens climbed on and the three men trotted past the guards.

Upon entering town and tying off the horses, Pivens walked into the telegraph office. The area was small with two desks on opposite sides of the rooms. There was one teller, and Deputy Winchester was sitting down with a deck of cards, playing by himself.

"Morning sir, good morning deputy," said the boy, tipping his hat, Winchester didn't respond.

"Morning Pivens," said the clerk. "Message for your captain. Heard you boys got into a little scrap with some Injuns. How are your comrades?"

"Yes," said Pivens, tucking the envelope in his blouse. "We got em good and they got the sergeant and one other man. Have a good day, sir." Walking past the deputy, Pivens tipped his hat. Dolan and Harrison were chatting on the porch watching the people going by.

"Ready," said Dolan, walking down the steps. The men climbed on their horses and rode back out of town.

Meanwhile, back at the telegraph office, Deputy Winchester had eased his way up to the clerk and began talking to him.

"What's the word, Earle," said the deputy, leaning on the counter. "Any big military secrets headed our way?" Winchester and the clerk began laughing.

"Na, nothing like that," said the man, separating the different messages. "They just were wiring the post that the Paymaster's Coach is on time and will be here two days from now." The deputy smiled.

"Well listen, Earle, I gotta get back to work, I'll see you later." The clerk waved as Deputy Winchester exited the building and headed back over to the office.

Sheriff Watkins was just descending the stairs from his second floor living quarters. "Well good morning, Winchester, how's your day going?"

"Not as good as yours will be now. I just came from the telegraph office. The Army Pay Wagon is on schedule to arrive two days from today." The sheriff began laughing to himself.

* * * * * * *

The men rode swiftly to the fort and dismounted in front of the CO's office. Pivens walked up the stairs and went inside.

The Captain was sitting down with, Moses and Bernard discussing strategies. "Pivens what can we do for you?"

"Message from headquarters, sir," as he handed over the telegram.

October 18th 1879

Regimental Payroll Department
Washington, D.C.

Commanding Officer
Fort Barre, Texas

Paymaster's Coach will be arriving on the 20th of October 1879 to deliver payroll for troops. Route running on time, no reason for delay.

Respectfully,
Whittaker K. Sarsfield
2nd Lieutenant Payroll Division

"The payroll is on its way men." The officer's insides began to tingle, he felt excited.

"Ooh, so that's why he was there," said Pivens nodding and smiling. The men turned and gazed at the young soldier.

"What are you talking about, Pivens?" asked Moses. Corporal Bernard sat with his hand on his chin listening attentively.

"The sheriff's deputy, was hanging around the telegraph office while I was waiting for the message." Captain Taylor rolled his eyes, as Moses rose from his desk slowly.

"That's it! That's how they've been keeping tabs on us, through the telegraph office!" yelled Moses pounding his fist in his hand.

"Let's arrest the telegraph clerk," said Captain Taylor.

"Well, let's think about this, sir," said Nouba rising from his seat. "Chances are that the telegraph clerk has been just chatting with the sheriff's men casually. I've seen those folks, they're hardly criminal material." Taylor tilted back in his chair and gazed at the ceiling as Moses nodded in agreement.

"Sergeant," said Taylor. "I believe we should adjourn this meeting now. I have a good many things to accomplish today."

"Yes sir!" The men stood up, saluted and exited the room.

"Are you thinking what I'm thinking Nouba?" The sergeants walked over to the barracks.

"We should give that Pala Grande Banks another looking at," said Nouba grinning. Moses smiled as he grabbed two carbines from the rack. Nouba loaded his weapon and removed his revolver to check the chamber. Moses rolled his revolver over his sleeve and then slid fresh rounds into his carbine. Exiting the barracks they proceeded over to the corral and saddled two horses. Corporal Bernard approached the two sergeants.

"What's going on?" Moses turned and looked at his friend.

"I need you to do me a favor," said Moses, climbing into the saddle. "We'll be back in a couple hours, keep everything in check. Remember, I'm counting on you." The corporal waved as the two sergeants rode out of the fort.

"We'll map out the area as best as possible," said Nouba, trotting along in the saddle. "Remember to jot down as many of the rock formations and trees that we can use for cover." After a while the men dismounted and tied off their horses. Removing their weapons, the soldiers started climbing up the incline. They lay down on their stomachs and crawled to the edge of the cliff, overlooking the banks. Nouba gazed over the barrel of his gun and kept watch. Moses pulled out a pencil and paper and started to sketch the landscape as quick and as accurately as possible.

"There's quite a bit of cover on both sides of the banks," said Moses. "My guess is that's where they'll be attacking first." Moses' hands flew back and forth over the paper. Nouba looked at the page and pointed.

"There should be trees right there," said Nouba. Moses turned and looked at Nouba. "Sorry." Moses smiled and patted his leg.

"All right," said Moses, stowing his paper and pencil. "We've got all we need, let's not overstay our welcome." Easing back the men saddled up and headed for home. Darkness was beginning to set in.

In their quarter, the fire popped and roared in the stove. Moses leaned in and poked at the log.

"This battle is going to be costly," said Nouba, easing back in his chair and sipping gently on his coffee.

"They're all costly. Where was the first place you fired a shot at another man, Nouba?" Moses asked while pouring another mug.

"The first Battle of Bull Run. The Union Army had twenty nine hundred dead, wounded or missing. We got our tails handed to us on a silver platter by the rebs. Watched my friend's head splatter all over my shoulder and the side of my face." Moses grabbed the coffeepot and refilled Nouba's mug. "Thanks, how about you?"

"You're gonna laugh," smiled Moses. "I can't remember when." Moses stared ahead. "It seems after that I had a gun in my hands all the time."

Nouba's smile turned to a stern face, as the laughter subsided. "I remember all those bodies laying twisted and contorted on the field of battle, or the ones lying in the ditches and roads." Nouba gulped the last of his coffee. "**Our** boys are tougher!"

"I've never been on a mission quite like this before, where we know the enemy is coming." Moses grabbed another log and tossed it in the fireplace. "**Well, I guess to save a race of men, all victories will be hard fought!**"

"Very poignant, just remember we've got two days to make sure they are in the best possible fighting mode," said Nouba, removing his boots and trousers. Nouba crawled into his rack. "Don't worry, goodnight."

"Good night, Nouba." Moses was too tired to write, he felt his eyes getting heavy. Dropping his head to his shoulder, he fell asleep.

* * * * * * *

The moment was almost at hand. It was after dark on the night of the 19th and the men were mustered in the compound as the wind blew over the plains. Captain Taylor emerged from his quarters with Sergeant Trinidad, while Moses began to speak.

"Men, good evening, tonight we are headed out on an important mission, one that is near and dearest to us all," said Moses. "The same criminals, who robbed our supply room of weapons and killed our fellow soldiers, are right now plotting to rob the Paymaster's Coach. That's right the

Paymaster's Coach, your pay, our pay!" The men began grumbling and moaning in the ranks. "We have learned through certain intelligence that these criminals plan on hitting the coach at Pala Grande Banks. We are going after them, and they will feel the wrath of the United States Army. Captain Taylor and I will take a group with thirty men, and position ourselves by the rock formations that are raised about one hundred yards above the spots we suspect they will use for cover. Sergeant Nouba, Corporal Bernard and twenty men will be down river. They will act as a net to snag anyone who tries to flee."

"Do they have boats for the water?" hollered a man in ranks. Moses paced back and forth.

"I don't know the answer to that question, so don't take any chances. We are dealing with dangerous, unscrupulous characters here. They will go to any lengths, including killing their own men to escape and cover their tracks." The Captain rocked back and forth on his heels, listening attentively. "The area we will be in is small and dense so the fighting will be close, very close, so be careful. We will be leaving under the cover of darkness tonight. There's a full moon so we should have little or no problem getting into position. Men, I say this with a sound mind and a stern fist, these men will not leave that area alive!"

The men roared. "Hooray! Hooray! Hooray!" Moses turned to look at the Captain who was smiling in approval.

"All right, all right settle down," said Moses, waving his hands. "Listen up! Every man will make sure they have a side arm and a carbine with as much ammunition as he can carry. We don't want to be caught with our pants down. The fort will be left with a garrison to handle all daily operations. Get some rest, we will begin to saddle horses and do a weapons check in three hours. Attention!" Snapping to attention the men saluted. "Cavalry," cried Moses.

"Cavalry," shouted the men in unison, and then went their separate ways.

Moses was excited inside; he knew sleep would not be found this night. The rest of the men, including Nouba and Bernard, had drifted off quickly. Moses grabbed his writing pouch and sat down in front of the fire.

October 19th 1879

As I write this entry in my journal my fellow soldiers are snoring loudly. I'm too excited to sleep, my stomach is in circles. Tonight, the bulk load of the men will set out on a mission to capture or kill a band of criminals responsible for the rash of thefts and possibly the murder of a soldier. The Captain discovered evidence that the Sheriff, Ranger Armstead and some of the deputies have indeed been plotting to rob a U.S. Army Pay coach.

The spot of their planned robbery is called Pala Grande Banks about ten miles north of us, the Pinto River runs through it. Nouba and I scouted around and have jotted down all the areas of cover we could use to our advantage. We are taking a large force of men, which will be broken into two groups. The men are eager and ready for a fight.

I only wonder if I can handle this situation? Leading my own army. It's funny though I spend most of my time reassuring my young soldiers of their abilities, yet I constantly question my own. If all goes well, my next entry will be late tomorrow night. I'm scared, pray for me Father.

Closing the book, Moses stood up walked over to his rack and lay down.

"Moses, Moses wake up!" Wiping his eyes, the big sergeant cracked them opened. Standing over his rack was Sergeant Nouba in his overcoat and cap. "Time for us to get going!" He handed Moses a cup of coffee.

"Thanks," yawned Moses, taking the mug. "What time is it?"

"0200 hours!" Moses leaped up, but Nouba placed his hand on the man's shoulder. "Easy now! The Captain ok'd everything. The men needed more rest. I won't tolerate heads bobbing up and down before a fight." Moses dressed quickly and exited the barracks into the crisp early morning air.

The men had saddled their mounts and were lined up beside them at parade rest. "Attention!" barked Nouba. Captain Taylor emerged from his quarters with Pivens following behind. Throwing his men a quick salute, he spoke.

"Evening or morning men," said the officer smiling. "Are we ready to go?"

"Yes sir, ready on your command," said Nouba. Moses and Bernard stood at attention. Captain Taylor raised his hand.

"Prepare to mount. Mount up!" All at once the men climbed into the saddle. "Ready forward!" Trotting out of the fort, the soldiers headed north. Their destination, Pala Grande Banks!

The full moon made visibility perfect as the soldiers kept a watchful eye out for anyone.

"How much further is this place?" asked Mathers turning around in the saddle, looking at his comrades. "Jones, do you know where we're going?"

"No, but we's gonna find out!" Corporal Bernard trotted up next to the column.

"No talking in ranks!" Bernard gazed coldly at the men and moved past them further up the line. The men tilted their heads down and moved on, as they continued to push north. Trotter and Hawkins, the forward scouts appeared.

"The spot is right up here, sir," said Trotter, pointing towards the tree line. Captain Taylor waved his men forward as they rode up to secure the area. It was a gully around five feet deep, sunken into the earth. A large crop of trees on either side cut the moon's light almost completely out. The scouts dismounted and with weapons drawn checked out the area from end to end.

"All secure, sir," said Trotter. "We can fit a large number of the horses under the trees with the banks acting as a corral." The men dismounted and began securing the first group of horses under the trees.

"We'll leave five men here to guard the horses," said Moses sliding his carbine from his saddle. "Harrison, Dolan, Potter, Hawkins and Danzig you're on guard duty, don't disappoint us." Moses turned toward Nouba and Bernard and he shook their hands. "We'll see you when it's over, be careful." Captain Taylor waved his hand, then maneuvered his horse slowly under the tree and disappeared. Nouba tipped his hat and rode by with a group of men. Bernard sat on his horse and stared into his old friend's eyes and winked. Spurring his horse, he and the rest of the soldiers headed down the river. Moses watched as the men disappeared into the night.

"Well, looks like we wait again, Sergeant," said the officer. Taylor patted Moses on the shoulder and walked back under the trees. Moses' hand began to twitch, the sun would be rising soon and the coach should be arriving at Pala Grande Banks, around first light.

Down river, Sergeant Nouba's men had begun setting up their position. Horses were tied off, and the men were broken into groups of four.

Nouba walked over to Bernard's position. "Make sure these boys stay awake!" He then moved cautiously from place to place making sure no one was dozing. Ruth's head was leaning against a tree when Nouba passed by. Rearing back, he slugged the groggy soldier in the shoulder and cupped his mouth. The soldier fell to his knees in pain. Nouba pulled him close. "Fall asleep, again and I won't be as nice!" Pushing the soldier away, the big man walked back to his position. Bernard followed him over.

"A little hard," said Bernard. Nouba turned toward his comrade.

"This is war, Corporal, and I intend to go home tomorrow afternoon!" Bernard nodded his head and returned to his position, hunkering down for the long haul. "Make sure they keep their weapons low," said Nouba. We don't need the rising sun to shine off those barrels."

Daylight began to splash over the rock formations, casting golden circles on the water. Moses and his men had lined up along the higher rock levels looking down into the valley. Captain Taylor was crouched low to the ground.

"Sergeant," whispered Taylor. "When do we think they'll …" Hoof beats echoed off the rocks and the Captain froze. Moses looked over the ridge at the oncoming riders.

"All right, boys," said Armstead in his loud voice. "This is the place." There were about seven riders, including the sheriff and the big Indian. Watkins trotted to the edge of the water as it rushed by.

"Well, again, I must give you credit, this is one hell of a spot. With the water rushing by, no one will hear the shooting, and we could wash the bodies right down river." Turning towards his partner in crime, Watkins tipped his hat as Armstead nodded in reply.

"There looks to be about seven, sir," whispered Moses, scanning down the slope. The officer was flat on the earth. From out of the north came four more riders. "We got more company!" Moses' hand tightened firmly on the grip of his pistol.

"It's coming, Armstead," shouted a man riding near. "About a half-mile out and headed this way." Armstead smiled as he jumped down from his horse and removed his rifle.

"Take the horses into the group of trees. After we grab the cash we'll follow the river south and go right to Mexico."

"Georgia for me," said Watkins dismounting. "But a little trip to Mexico could be nice." The man laughed.

"All right, this is the plan. We shoot the guard first, then the driver, then simply hop on the coach, pull it into the woods and grab the cash box." The men all signaled their approval.

Unbeknownst to both the criminals and the soldiers, another group had picked up both their trails. It was a party of fifty or so heavily armed Indian warriors coming up the rear. They had war amulets in their black hair and odd-looking medicine cords around their necks. Some were dressed in animal skin pants, while others had tucked breechclouts up for battle. Heavily armed with bows and rifles, they moved with stealth like precision up the rise. Splitting in two groups, the Comanche began sneaking up behind Danzig's troops guarding the horses and Ranger Armstead's men hidden down by the banks although, they were unaware of Nouba's men down river. The sun was rising steadily. From behind Danzig and his men, there was some rustling in the trees. Suddenly the ground began to shake and everyone froze; the stagecoach was coming.

"Get down," yelled Armstead waving his gun. "Take cover in the tall grass." Sheriff Watkins and the others crouched low and covered their faces with bandanas.

The Indians continued to sneak closer, their movement concealed by the thunderous roars of the coach. About ten yards from the spot where the men had their horses, a soldier noticed a tree limb move.

"Someone's coming," said Danzig. "Right over there!" Dolan squinted over the barrel of his gun. The trees were now silent, yet something was on the air. Removing his pistol, Danzig crept ahead a few yards and flattened against the side of a tree. Ever so slowly the soldier moved his head an inch or two from the bark, an Indian! What was he doing out here alone? Danzig's hand tightened around the handle, as the lone warrior crept toward the unsuspecting soldiers. Young in age, the warrior looked nervous as he moved slowly through the trees. Danzig knew that a single shot would warn the robbers and possibly send them fleeing to safety. Holstering his side arm, he slid his knife easily from its sheath. He also knew if there was one Indian, there was bound to be more. Planting his feet firmly Danzig bent down at the knees and positioned himself to leap. Vaulting in the air, the soldier tackled the Indian quickly, subduing him with little trouble and shoving his knife straight into the warrior's chest. The Indian flailed and clawed as the soldier pushed his opponents face in the dirt. Lifting the body, Danzig dragged it near a ditch and rolled it in. Picking up his weapon, the soldier ran back to his position to warn his friends.

Dolan heard the approaching noise and raised his weapon.

"Hold your fire, it's me Danzig." The soldier leaped into the small earthen area. "Get ready, we got Indians coming up from behind us!" The men stood up and stared at Danzig. "I just killed a scout," said the soldier wiping his hands on his trousers. "If we don't hold them back, Captain Taylor and Sergeant Trinidad will be in deep trouble. We need to rig up a small barrier, quickly." Hawkins, and Harrison disappeared into the trees and emerged with extra ammunition. The other soldiers made a hastily built wall of saddles.

The coach had reached the mouth of Pala Grande Banks headed for the crossing at Pinto River. The driver pulled back on the reins to slow down, as the coach began to creep into the water. The guard watched in all directions, scouting for trouble, the sun gleaming off the barrel of his shotgun. Moses watched from over the rocks and waited nervously.

"Can you see where they're hiding, Sergeant, so we can direct fire on those positions?" asked the officer still on the ground. Moses looked again, but the reflections off the water blocked his line of sight.

"My guess is the tall reeds and grass by the banks sir," whispered Moses checking out his pistol. "But they haven't fired any shots yet, the wagon's almost in the middle of the crossing."

Intense gunfire erupted from the valley below. The bullets tore through the flesh and bones of both the driver and the guard, sending them crashing into the waters.

Armstead stood up from the brush with his rifle smoking. The rest of his men emerged from their hiding spots, as Sheriff Watkins cowered behind a tree. Two more insurance shots in each man's body and the robbers swarmed over the coach. Moses eased up over the edge and signaled to the Captain that things were ready, now!

"United States Army!" The soldiers rose up from behind the barriers with their weapons drawn. Captain Taylor stood on top of the barrier with his pistol pointed at the criminals. "Drop your weapons on the count of three or you're all dead!" Armstead and his men stared at each other. "One! Two! Thr..." A hail of bullets smashed into the rocks behind the soldiers.

"Indians, Indians coming up from the rear!" The men ducked low to the ground trying to avoid the barrage of gunfire. It was just the distraction Armstead needed. Swinging his rifle up, he fired twice. Captain Taylor who had turned away from the robbers was hit in the shoulder and upper chest.

The officer fell to the ground and landed in the grass. Pivens ran to his commander, as the soldiers opened fire at the banks. Ranger Armstead's men dove for cover. Sergeant Nouba, who was waiting down river, heard the gunfire and shot a quick concerned look at Corporal Bernard.

"Wooooo! Weee! Wooo!" The second grouping of Indians swung out from their hiding spots and fired on

Armstead's left flank. Deputy Winchester and Hollins dug in for a fight. The big Indian raised his rifle and dropped two oncoming braves.

"Captain Taylor," cried Moses, running over and kneeling beside him. "Cover the right and left flanks. The captain is down, secure the area!" Four soldiers hopped into the trench creating a defensive perimeter around the fallen officer. Behind him Moses heard the cries and gunfire of more Indians.

Both Pivens and Davis swung their guns on the flanks and laid down cover fire. Trotter climbed down into the trench and looked over the officer's wounds. Undoing Captain Taylor's blouse he saw the man had small holes in his upper shoulder and chest. Gently lifting him up, Trotter felt the officer's back.

"Are you all right sir?" asked Moses, easing the captain forward. "Hurts doesn't it?"

"Damn," exclaimed the officer. "Early going into the battle and I'm hit."

"Well, the bullets went right through, that's good," said Trotter, taking some fresh bandages from his bag. The soldier applied pressure to the wounds and tied them off. "He's going to be all right, let's tuck him over here."

"Nonsense," winced Taylor. "Sergeant.. ungh...send more men back to Danzig's position and reinforce it, now!" Moses waved his hand and the men ran back down the trail towards the others. "Pivens, grab my belt, I'll use it as a sling."

"Sir, permission to take men and head down into the valley floor," asked Moses. Taylor signaled his approval as Moses called to five men. Checking over their weapons the soldiers slid over the edge and moved closer to the fight.

From where he was hiding Sheriff Watkins could see the paymaster's box lying near the water's edge. The top was broken off and the bags of money were in full view.

Armstead's back was to the sheriff as he was firing at the oncoming Indians. Watkins crawled through the gunfire and managed to snatch two bags of money. Crawling back to his cover he tucked them in his pouch.

"Well, well," said a crackling voice. Watkins looked up to see Armstead standing over him with his pistol drawn. "Puttin it in a safe place?"

"Rr..rr.rr....ight," said Watkins, shaking uneasily. Armstead shook his head back and forth.

"I was gonna kill you sooner or later..." BOOM! The Sheriff covered his head and ducked as a bullet shattered Armstead's leg, sending him tumbling backwards down the bank. Watkins stared straight ahead at Sergeant Moses Trinidad and his smoking carbine. Moses dove down for cover as the Indians redirected their fire.

Sheriff Watkins ran to his horse and climbed on. He noticed a small narrow strip of land leading to the southern exit of the banks. Slapping his horse, Watkins darted in its direction. From his position, Armstead tried to fire his pistol with accuracy, but the shots found no target. Deputy Hollins stood up and fired at Armstead lying in the grass. BANG! A single shot from the big Indian slammed into the deputy's chest, dropping him instantly. Reaching for his rifle Armstead waited until the right moment. BANG! The lone bullet found its mark. The sheriff grunted in pain but continued to hang on. The big Indian lifted Armstead up, and they moved back into the wooded section by their horses.

"Son of a bitch double crossed me." The Indian ripped open the ranger's shirt. "I think I got him though," winced Armstead as his comrade dressed the wound quickly. "He'd better pray I never see him again. Oohh!" Climbing on their horses the criminals turned to ride south down the river. Straight into the oncoming soldiers.

TWENTY-FOUR

Meanwhile back in the town of Flat Fork, Claudia Roths-child was emerging from her house to fetch some wood for the stove. It was then that the morning patrol was trotting by. "Morning, Miss Claudia," called Cleetus Ray dismount-ing and walking slowly to the edge of the porch steps. "Message fu ya ma'am." Handing her the note, Ray tipped his hat and walked back to his horse and climbed on.

"Thank you," she said. "Would you and your men like some breakfast?"

"No dank ya ma'am, mitey nice of ya." The soldiers waved and rode off back towards town. Walking back into the house, Claudia had forgotten all about the wood still on the porch. Removing her wrap she sat down in front of the fireplace and undid the message.

Dearest Love,

I am writing you this note to tell you how much I love you and hope that you think of me often. The men and I have gone on a mission to capture the criminals that killed Hayes and have been dealing guns to the Indians in the area. I won't lie to you and tell you this will be safe. I

316

only know that if we don't try and get these men for what they did, I will fail this command in more ways than one.

Keep safe my love and know that you're in my thoughts.

Hennecker

Claudia's hands began to tremble as she covered her face with her hands. "I love you always, Hennecker."

* * * * * * *

The reinforcements just reached Danzig's position, as the Indians breeched the line. Swarming over the lip of the gully, they met stern opposition from the soldiers.

"Fire at will men!" yelled Ruth, waving the men forward. Blackened smoke from gunfire engulfed the two groups of men.

Danzig fired from an unprotected area and was shot between the eyes, tossing him to the ground with a thud. Harrison bent over to check him and quickly scrambled for cover; it was mayhem.

Hawkins smashed the butt of his carbine into one warrior's chest knocking him to the cold earth. Removing his pistol the soldier fired from a kneeling position and struck two Indians, killing them instantly. One soldier was lying on the ground with his leg twitching feverishly. A single Indian approached the soldier and mercilessly shot the boy.

"Retreat, head for the rise, we'll have an elevated position to hit them...," hollered Hawkins. SPLAT! The bullet passed right through Hawkins's cheek and the man's body slowly crumbled to the ground. There seemed to be no end to the wave of Indians. Harrison and Potter were in a well-barricaded area, taking out targets at will.

Suddenly, a cavalry bugle cry broke through the gunfire; more reinforcements would soon be arriving. Potter saw a warrior wave his hands, and the others fell back down the trail. Firing two quick shots at the retreating Indians, Anderson rose up cautiously from his barrier. Looking around the soldier saw the bodies of several warriors and his comrades lying over the rocky terrain. Grabbing whatever weapons they could find, the remaining soldiers backed up to the top of the lip of the gully and prepared to dig in.

"They've scrammed," said Potter, wiping the sweat and dirt from his brow. Opening the chamber, the soldier began to reload his gun.

"Fine by me," replied another soldier hidden behind half of a bullet ridden tree. "I wouldn't care if they never come back."

Back down in the trenches, Captain Taylor fired his pistol, while leaning up against a rock wall, as Trotter and several others fired at the sheriff's men, keeping them pinned down. "Watch your flanks, men!" yelled the officer.

Down river, Nouba was getting worried. "Corporal, assemble the men." Bernard waved his hand and the soldiers mounted up. "Ready forward!" Retreating south, Ranger Armstead and his companion were rounding the bend of the river when they rode smack dab into the soldiers. The two riders froze as the soldiers came to a halt. Nouba and Bernard stared straight at them.

"Bugler sound the charge," said Nouba. Looking past the two criminals the soldiers noticed the warriors attacking. Nouba removed his sword. "Fire at will!" The soldiers swarmed forward, Armstead's big Indian was struck in the arm, chest and leg, tossing him from his mount and killing him instantly. Glancing down at his partner in crime lying on the ground Armstead turned and tried to ride off.

Sergeant Trinidad, who was crouching down low on a small rise, burst through the trees, tackling Armstead from his mount. The men slid down the banks, coming to a rest on a flat piece of ground. Nouba, Bernard and the others rode past the scuffling men and towards the advancing Indians.

Moses' big fist smashed into Armstead's face, tossing him further towards the roaring waters. Rising slowly to his feet, Armstead smiled an evil grin with blood dripping from his lips. Removing a large knife, he moved slowly in a circle. Moses stood still, staring Armstead straight in his eye, his heart pounding through his uniform.

"I'm gonna enjoy cutting you open," said Armstead, walking tenderly on his leg as Moses grinned. The ranger made several quick striking motions, as the soldier jumped back, missing his midsection by inches. Moses slid in the mud and dropped hard to his knee. Armstead leaped forward slicing open a section of Moses' arm. The proud ranger stood over his prey and nodded in approval. Moses went quickly for his pistol.

"Not so fast," said Armstead, throwing a punch, landing square on the soldier's chin. Moses landed face down, hurtling his side arm into the water. Climbing on his back Armstead began landing several punches in Moses' lower back and kidney area. "I! Hate! Coloreds!" Standing up, he kicked the soldier several times in the mid section. Armstead continued to taunt Moses. "Yer kind will always be nothin', boy!"

Grabbing Armstead's foot, Moses removed his knife. "My name is Moses Trinidad, a Sergeant in the United States Cavalry!" The blade came down with such force in Armstead's good leg it lodged deep in the bone.

"Aaiiieee!" Armstead's eyes bulged as he dropped to his knees. Reaching forward with an adrenaline charged punch, he connected on the sergeant's face. Moses tumbled to the ground. Armstead turned and tried to crawl away toward his horse. Shaking off the effects of the punch, Moses lunged at Armstead pulling him back down the bank and towards the water. Trying to kick free, the pain shot through Armstead's entire body.

"Do you feel helpless?" asked Moses, pulling him closer to the water. Armstead tried feverishly to kick himself free. "I bet that's how my friend Hayes felt when you and your pals were beating him to death!" Armstead had a frightened look on his face, as Moses continued to pummel him. Armstead rose slowly to his feet.

"You stinkin' slave," he yelled, spitting blood and saliva. "Yeahhh!" Armstead vaulted at Moses and swung wildly. Moses ducked under Armstead's arm and stuck the ranger in the side with his knife.

Removing the blade from the Ranger's body, Moses fell over onto his side. Ranger Armstead stutter stepped three paces and fell down. Moses rose slowly to his feet exhausted and still bleeding heavily.

"Help, help me," whimpered Armstead trying desperately to stop the bleeding with one hand, while the other reached out. Moses walked slowly to the man and knelt by his side. "Don't leave me for the injuns, soldier." The steam from Armstead's lips clouded his beaten face.

Moses stared long and hard into the man's eyes. He had won! Moses could have smashed the man's face, but he didn't have to, because this time he had won. "I'll help you if you tell me where your friend the good sheriff went. You see, it's him we really want, not you." Armstead's eyes crisscrossed back and forth in all directions.

"Ssssure," said the man as blood trickled down his chin. "He went into town to collect his things, the coward." Armstead continued hacking and coughing. Using his good arm, Moses reached down and pulled the ranger to his feet. "It's a dang shame," said Armstead smiling and spitting out blood. "I never did get to cut your heart out. Ha! Ha! Ha! You have to take me in now!" Moses felt his insides begin to rumble and a weird feeling take over his body.

"Well that's just **not** going to happen!" In that instant Moses whirled the man around and tossed him over the bank.

"Wait......" Tumbling over, Ranger Armstead crashed into an old tree holding on for dear life. "You double crosser," he shouted. The tree shifted in the dirt and Armstead slid further down the trunk. "You ain't nuthin!"

Slowly it began to crack. Cautiously, Armstead began trying to inch his way back to the banks, but the branch began to fracture. "Come on soldier man, help me. I can't swim!" CRACK! The branch dropped closer to the water. "Nooo!" Without skipping a beat Moses thrust his foot into the branch.

"Noooooooo!" The tree gave way and Armstead dropped into the water. The man tried desperately to grab anything, but there was nothing around. Moses stood on the shore watching as the ranger flailed about helplessly. "Hhheelpp meee!" The weight of his wet cloths was beginning to take its toll on the man. Growing weary of trying to stay afloat, Armstead's limbs tired out and his body slid under slowly. Moses dropped to his knees in total exhaustion.

Bernard rode over to his friend. "Moses, Moses you all right?" Dismounting Bernard removed a cloth from his bag and wrapped up his wound. Waving his arms, the corporal watched as additional troopers secured the area.

"**Are you** all right, and yes, I am. How's the Captain? Are the men all right?" Moses turned his head in all directions. "Cover the left side!" Two soldiers redirected fire as instructed.

"Everyone has their hands full," groaned Bernard, lifting his friend up off the ground. "Captain Taylor and his men have the high ground under control. David, over here!"

"The Sheriff was headed back to town, we need to get to him and arrest him." Moses pulled himself into the saddle. "You and some men are going to have to get him, Bernard."

"All right, this is the plan David, you'll stay with the Moses and wait for Sergeant Nouba and his men, you others are coming with me," said Corporal Bernard. Climbing onto their mounts, the men headed off in the direction of Flat Fork.

Up on top of the ridge, the soldiers held their positions as an overwhelming number of Indians reemerged and descended on them. Harrison was barely alive as his comrade Potter lay on the ground with half his head missing. Dolan slid fresh rounds in the carbine, took aim, and fired. BOOM! Gradually, more men fortified the position and began providing cover fire as the wounded were tended to. The Indians saw the soldiers now stiffening up the lines and decided to retreat.

"Counterattack, get to the horses!" hollered Taylor being helped to his feet. "Drive them men, drive them to their deaths!" The men urged their steeds forward.

"Combs, help me with the Captain!" yelled Pivens grabbing the reins to a horse. Combs pushed the officer into the saddle. Taking another mount, Combs hopped up and followed after the officer. Pivens fired his weapon from the saddle and dropped an oncoming brave. The detail of soldiers with Sergeant Nouba in command managed to find the open cash box and secure the remaining funds.

"Looks like someone already got their hands on a few bags," proclaimed Nouba. "Place the money in my saddle bags and let's see who's still alive." Snapping off a few rounds from his pistol, BANG! BANG! Nouba looked around, and noticed a young soldier named David waving his hands.

"Yo, over here!" Nouba climbed on his horse and rode swiftly to their position. Sergeant Trinidad was on the ground again his arm wrapped in bloody bandages. He looked drained and in need of proper medical attention.

"Moses, you all right?" Nouba dismounted and knelt down.

"I'm fine, how is everything?"

"The valley is secured, some of the men are pushing back the Comanche to the river's edge. It appears we've recovered a large portion of the money I'm pleased to say. I can't give you a casualty count though."

"Get me a horse, we need to rally with Captain Taylor." Assisting him to his feet, the men hoisted Moses on to a horse and the small band of soldiers galloped off. "I ordered Corporal Bernard and some men to head after Watkins, he's on his way to collect his things in town and hightail it out of here," said Moses, struggling to hold his reins.

"Who told you that?" said Nouba, bounding in the saddle.

"Ranger Armstead did, right before he went for a **dip**," winked Moses. Nouba smiled as the soldiers headed out of the southern exit and up the elevation. Gunfire filled the air as men on horseback smashed through the underbrush pursuing the hostiles.

Moses reached for his pistol; it was gone. "I need a weapon!" Elias turned to hand his pistol to Moses when he was shot through the stomach and neck area. Moses looked down and saw the man was dead. He aimed the pistol and fired two quick shots.

The Indians retreated back down the inclines and bluffs unaware the soldiers, who were joined by ten more men on foot, were heading their way.

"Aim low," bellowed Nouba. The soldiers knelt down and took careful aim. Instantly, the Comanche emerged in the open. "Fire, fire, fire!"

"Charge!" The soldiers moved in and engaged the enemy in hand-to-hand combat. Moses removed his saber and with his one good hand began slicing a trail through the Indians for his men to follow. Captain Taylor's men bound over the ravine and joined the fight. Anderson was wrestling with one Indian, when Riley shot the warrior in the head at point blank range. Extending his hand, Riley assisted his comrade back to his feet and they rejoined the battle. The cavalry had turned the tide and had the Indians on the run again.

Corporal Bernard and his men raced back across the plains to the town of Flat Fork, and soon found themselves in front of the sheriff's office. Noticing the commotion, Deputy Flowers scurried across the street.

"What are you men doing?" asked Flowers. Corporal Bernard drew his revolver. "I said what's going on here?" asked the deputy.

"Where is the Sheriff?" Bernard whirled around and stood right in the boy's face. "You're either with us or against us."

"He's inside!" Flowers stepped aside and the group moved forward. Bernard pointed at the steps. Walking cautiously, the men noticed the narrow trail of blood leading up to the front door, which was open. The group moved in, following the blood trail, which continued across the floor and towards the stairs.

"This can't be good," said Bernard, pointing his weapon forward. The soldiers covered the second floor landing as they pressed on. Inching slowly up the stairs Bernard stopped suddenly. He saw a pair of boots on the floor. "It's all over for him." The men walked up and into the bedroom. Lying in the middle of the floor in a pile of bloodstained money was Sheriff Watkins, his luggage bags lying right by his hands.

"**Almost** never counts," snickered Bernard, holstering his gun. "Okay boys, let's gather up this money and bring it on home!"

* * * * * * *

Down the street at the blacksmith's shop, two workers were piling wood in a hole to burn. "Zeek go on and fetch that ole barrel from the porch!" The boy reached down and hoisted the barrel up.

"Somethins in it!" The blacksmith shook his head back and forth and grumbled.

"It's just scrap wood boy, now come on!" Carrying the barrel with the hidden bag of money in it, the young man tossed it on. Dowsing the wood with coal oil, they ignited it. WHOOSH! The flames rose high.

TWENTY-FIVE

November 5th 1879

It has been several weeks since I've written but I am still recovering from my arm wound. I never did fill you in on what occurred. We managed to capture both Armstead and his companions, but in the middle of the battle they were killed. The money, I'm happy to say was recovered in full. It looks like the good Sheriff got what was coming to him. Bernard informed me that he was found shot in the back, dead in his room. Both of his deputies and the hired henchmen were killed in the riverbed. I understand the young deputy named, Flowers will be placed in command. I think the townspeople have made a wise choice.

Captain Taylor is recovering nicely under the close personal supervision of Claudia Rothschild. There is even a rumor they will be married before the end of the month.

We lost a total of seven men, two of whom were on the coach, and only five wounded which is amazing, considering the fact we were ambushed by a large number of hostiles.

The unit presented the Captain with a unique flag. The flag has the American eagle in the center and the crossed sabers of the 9th Cavalry with a scrolled message under the eagle's claws, which reads, "To save a race of men, all battles are hard fought." A profound and deep message in its own right.

I'm of course happy with the way it turned out for us and myself. I faced my fear and when it came time to act I did it. Killing Armstead was something I hoped I'd never have to do. I've shot men before, but this was something different. I've been on light duty, which I must admit is nice. Nouba says I'm milking it a little too much, maybe I am.

As for the rest of the Buffalo Soldiers, they became a legend of sorts around these parts because of their bravery and toughness. I even think the people in town have respect for these soldiers and they should.

Thank you, Father, for watching over me.

Moses set his pen down on his book and stepped outside. With his arm still in a sling he walked out into the bright clear morning and noticed the captain sitting on his porch. Moses decided to go over and have a visit. "Good morning, sir." Captain Taylor smiled and held out his hand.

"Gentle Sergeant," he said smiling. "Congratulations on this victory! I've decided to put you in for the Army Medal of Honor." Moses turned toward his commander.

"That's all right, sir," said Moses, noticing the pot of coffee. He poured a cup for the captain and himself. "I'm not here for the medals!" The two men clinked mugs and smiled. The winds and dust kicked up across the Texas plains as the American Flag snapped smartly on the air.

THE END

Come follow Sergeant Moses Trinidad and the men of the 9th Cavalry on their next thrilling adventure in,
Moses Trinidad:
The Siege at Cripple Banks Crossing